FALLING LEAVES & VILE DEEDS

A SOUTHERN PARANORMAL COZY MYSTERY

A DARKLY SOUTHERN MYSTERY
BOOK TWO

TAM LUMIÈRE

A NOTE FROM TAM

If you would like a free novella to this series, you can sign up for my newsletter and receive a copy of **Conch & Circumstance**, the one where Win and her friends visit the merpeople living at the bottom of the ocean off the coast of Cradlerock.

Free Book Here 👉 https://tamlumiere.com/bonus-book-1

CHAPTER 1

*T*he moment I focused, it snapped into view.

A glistening ethereal barrier arched high above Oakspider Park, curving into a dome that shimmered like light trapped in water. An oakspider acorn dropped from the sky, struck the obstacle with a sharp ping, and bounced harmlessly to the grass.

I tapped the dome, and it rippled beneath my touch, undisturbed by the whirlwind of chaos surrounding it.

Festival workers hammered at half-constructed booths, people rushed about with popcorn and cotton candy carts, and somewhere in the fray—

"Why are you putting that THERE?! Must I do EVERYTHING?!"

I flinched, tugged my oversized cardigan tighter, and ducked my head.

Borda Wrathfell, the organizer of Gumbo Fest and a weather demon, stormed past. Lightning crackled around the gray-streaked frizz of her hair, her fiery fury fully engaged.

"Quick, Pyewacket! Before Borda sees us!" I hissed, gesturing to the constantly shifting symbols swirling over the dome's surface. "What's the password Chase gave us?"

1

Pyewacket's head popped out of my bag, his ears twitching. My black cat familiar had only one golden eye but that didn't stop him from glaring at me with the intensity of two.

I hadn't had time to decorate the Magically Enchanted Travel shop (or MET as it was known) for Darkly's annual fall Gumbo Festival. No pumpkins, no gourds, not even a lonely chrysanthemum in a planter by the door.

I admit I probably shouldn't have been taking a break. However, in my defense, I'd been working almost 24/7 preparing all the portals for the arrivals and departures of festivalgoers.

After all, I'm sure Borda would agree that MET travel was the most efficient way for paranormals like me—those tragically cursed with neither wings nor veilshifting abilities—to get around. Which meant keeping the portals running smoothly was basically my sacred duty.

Besides, Shadow Pumpkin Farm was already penciled in for this afternoon's adventure, so really, I was just being responsible. Until then though? Operation Avoid Borda Wrathfell was my top priority.

And yet, here I was. Right in the middle of enemy territory.

"Fine. Don't help." I was used to my temperamental familiar's hissy fits. This one was brisket-related, specifically, his lack of access to any.

I gazed at the symbols spinning by—pink hearts, yellow moons, orange stars, green clovers, violet eyes...

Violet eyes!

I reached out and plucked a twirling, vibrant eye from the swirl of symbols.

And in a blink, the entire park transformed.

The festival vanished. Gone were the booths, the throngs of people, and Borda's festival-induced rage.

Instead, we stood under a perfect sunlit sky on a lush green field, cleared for Hexbee, a favorite sport of the Charming Isles. A sparkling golden border ringed the circular field. Small bleachers stood off to the side and I climbed to the second row and sat.

Pyewacket hopped out of my bag and scowled. "Not even a vending machine in sight."

I scratched his cranky little head. "Tragedy of the highest order."

Magic was real, and even now I was still trying to wrap my head around that fact. A few months ago, I'd never heard of Hexbee, let alone believed in wands, witches, or warlocks. Back then, I was a professor and conservator at a university in New York, until my fiancé-slash-boss denied me tenure and handed my office to his newest infatuation. So yes, when I got word that my grandmother had left me our ancestral home and the MET, I was more than ready for a fresh start.

I looked around the stands and a few familiar faces stood out. Clobber Mudkipp, bartender at my favorite restaurant The Green Gator Tavern and a tall and rather handsome goblin, gave me a wave before stepping onto the field.

Zelda Merryman—as sweet as sun tea but cursed with questionable taste in friends—patted my shoulder gently before sliding onto the seat beside me. How Borda had become BFFs with my scheming half-sister Elspeth—you know, the one who crashed my grand opening with a surprise "we're related!" announcement—and Solara Nova, Darkly's resident mean girl who'd declared war on me the moment her ex, Keir Bane, started flirting, was honestly beyond me.

Everyone knew Zelda was too good for them. It's a shame *she* didn't know it.

The rest of the spectators were undoubtedly wolf shifters, their sharp eyes watching the game with relaxed amusement.

A familiar blur of red ponytail streaked toward me as Jessamin Wilde, close friend and hearth fairy, hopped onto the bench beside me, still slightly out of breath from the game.

"Hi y'all," she said, tugging her water bottle from beneath the bench. "Did you have any trouble getting onto the plane, Win?"

Pye sidestepped me and curled up in her lap with a huff.

"Hey, Jess. Nope. None at all." I smiled, searching for Keir, alpha of the Silverfangs, the local wolf shifter clan, and my...well, I wasn't actually sure what he was.

Then my brain caught up to her wording. "Wait. I stepped onto another *plane*?"

Zelda nodded, eyes bright. "Sorcerers can manipulate elements and time. They can literally tear open the fabric of reality and create a new space. This one is just an empty version of Oakspider Park."

I let that sink in for a moment. "That's...a rather powerful ability."

Jess nodded. "Chase is a rather powerful sorcerer."

Zelda nodded. "It's a good thing he's full of heart."

I snorted. "He's full of something, but I wouldn't call it heart."

We shared a good laugh before I turned my attention back to the playing field, scanning for Keir—

—and found him instantly.

On the far edges of the circle, Keir stood in shorts and a tank top, his ridiculously fine muscles and the dark intricate ink winding over them on full display. I tore my gaze away and tried to make sense of the bedlam taking place before me.

Four large spectral hoops spun lazily in the air—two red, two blue—positioned at equal intervals around the playing circle. Every so often, the hexdisc—glimmering like a shard of enchanted light—streaked across the sky, only to vanish behind another player.

I frowned. "Okay, can someone please explain this game to me?"

A voice leaned in close from behind us. "Sure."

I turned to find a ruggedly handsome man with long blond hair and deep green eyes leaning between Jess and me, flashing an easy-going grin.

"Talmadge Prescott. But everyone calls me Tal."

With a dramatic flourish, he tossed his hair over one shoulder, tucked a stray lock behind his ear, and pointed.

"See the four hoops? Red is Chase's team, blue is the winners —I'm sorry, the shifters."

I laughed and my eyes followed his gesture, taking in the field before giving a quiet nod.

"The goal," he said, "is to get the hexdisc through your team's hoops. Bonus points if you can score successively between the two goals in a row. Sounds easy, right?" He grinned. "But—"

"Let me guess. Magic," I said, watching the field as Chase clapped his hands together and the blue hoops began spinning at warp speed.

Tal snapped his fingers. "Exactly! Every player can use their magical abilities to block, pass, or score. That's what makes it fun."

He turned to Jess and smiled.

I looked back at the playing field. Keir stood in the middle of the circle. The golden glow of afternoon light caught the edge of his roguish smile as he pointed a thumb to his chest and then made a fist.

I laughed. "Shifters are winning, I take it."

Jess stretched out her legs with a groan. "Every time. They're just too fast and too strong."

A sharp whistle blast echoed across the field and the shifters groaned.

I looked around for a referee but saw no one.

Jess nudged me. "It's magically refereed. No bias. No cheating —" she hesitated "—mostly."

Tal's deep voice rumbled behind us again. "Guarantees fair play, but it doesn't stop the whining."

We watched the play in companionable silence for a few more minutes. I still couldn't make sense of the rules though. I was just about to give up and face the wrath of Borda when Tal cocked his head and smiled. "So, you're Keir's girlfriend," he said. "Was beginning to think you didn't exist."

Wait.

What?

5

Did he just—?

"It's nice to finally meet you, Win." He winked. "Tell Keir to bring you to the Cairns sometime."

I muttered something vaguely polite in return, but my brain was short-circuiting over one very, very important word.

Girlfriend.

The bleachers suddenly exploded with sound as the shifters pounded the wooden boards and whooped their approval. Apparently, the wolves had scored again.

Jess groaned.

"Watch Keir." Tal gestured toward the game. "He leaps easily twenty feet into the air. And he's so fast, half the time the other team can't even track him."

Right on cue, one of the shifters launched the hexdisc high into the air. It arced toward the goal, but veered slightly off-course—

And then, in the span of a heartbeat, Keir sprang upward, twisting mid-air like a wolf in flight, catching the disc with one powerful hand before redirecting it through the hoop. The entire move lasted seconds—a perfect, fluid motion, raw power and grace combined.

The crowd roared.

I stared, awestruck. "He's amazing," I murmured.

As if he could sense my gaze, Keir turned his head. His brown eyes locked onto mine.

The noise of the crowd faded. For a long moment, he just looked at me, the corner of his mouth curving into the faintest smile. Something inside me tightened, then softened.

Before I could spiral any further, the whistle shrieked again, announcing the end of the round—or quarter—or whatever Hexbee used for timekeeping.

Keir jogged toward the bleachers, grabbed a towel and a bottle of water, and then—without hesitation—hopped up beside me.

"I'm glad you came." His voice was low, warm. He pressed a quick kiss to my lips before pulling back. "Sorry for the sweat."

Even after running around the field, he still smelled amazing

—fresh pine and warm spices, like nutmeg and cinnamon—like Keir.

Tzazi Strangeland, close friend, lawyer, and badass vampire, plopped onto the bench below me, guzzling water. "We would've had that round if Chase hadn't fallen on his arse during the last play."

Chase Abernathy-Wyatt strolled over with his partner Lorenzo de Zavala trailing behind—Ren to those of us who didn't have time for fancy first names—still gleaming with post-match sweat.

Chase cut quite the figure even in defeat. He was the first soul I'd encountered when I'd stepped off that rickety airboat onto Darkly's weathered dock, all designer luggage and wounded pride. Tall and golden-bronzed, this sorcerer never met a crisp linen suit he couldn't make look effortless, though I'd heard whispers that his magic packed considerably more punch than his laid-back bourbon-and-Sazerac aesthetic suggested.

Ren, trailing a step behind, couldn't have been more different if he'd tried. Where Chase was all pressed cotton and smooth charm, Ren kept things simple—faded jeans, soft tees, and that sweep of sleek black hair that always seemed to catch the light just right. Quiet where Chase was bold, Ren possessed the kind of gentle, intuitive nature that made him our group's emotional anchor, reading between the lines when the rest of us were too stubborn or too proud to say what we really meant.

Chase waggled a finger at Tzazi. "If the Silverfangs hadn't cheated, we would've had that one."

Quinn Ainsley, Keir's beta, a tall, dark-skinned woman, chuckled, her voluminous afro softly bouncing with her mirth. "If you call 'playing better than you' cheating, Chase," she teased, "then, yeah, we cheated."

Ren chuckled, slinging a towel over his shoulders. "Hard to argue with facts."

"Whatever," Chase harrumphed and sat down on the bottom bench. "Everyone knows I'm right."

He grabbed Tzazi's water bottle and took a large gulp.

She grabbed it back and slung an arm around his shoulder. "The terror that is your ego."

He tossed her arm off, cocked his head, and grinned. "Ah, but darling, my ego isn't a terror. It's a well-earned legend."

His smirk faded slightly, a flicker of unease passing over his face. "Speaking of terror... Last night, as I was leaving the salon, a swamp phantasm appeared clear out of nowhere. Scared the sin right outta me."

The warm buzz of friendly banter dimmed as a hush settled over the group, Chase's uncharacteristic seriousness drawing everyone's attention.

Even Pye's head popped up and he moved over to my lap and sat, posture rigid.

A chill traveled up my spine. "What's a swamp phantasm?"

Jaime Mayór, tall, lanky, with a mop of ginger hair and a scatter of freckles, spoke up. His voice was even, but there was a weight to it. "They're shadowy creatures that live in swamps and bayous. They usually keep to the deep, uninhabited places, but if one showed itself in town..." He let out a slow breath, clearly unsettled. "Was it inside the shop?"

"Good lord, no," Chase said. "Just outside clinging to the shadows next to the window. One second, I was locking up, the next, there it was." He shook his head. "Didn't move. Just stood there looking at me." He drummed his fingers on his knee, a nervous habit of his, before adding, "I reached my hand back inside and flipped on every light. I'll be keeping them all on from now on."

Tal, lounging next to Jess, frowned. "We've seen a few near the Cairns lately. Which is strange, of course, since we're nowhere near the swamps."

Pye tapped me with a paw. "How often? Where exactly?"

"Pye wants to know where and when," I said to Tal.

Tal shrugged. "A handful of times in the past month. Usually lurking just outside the perimeter, near the treeline."

Quinn blew out a breath, rubbing the back of her neck. "Imps too."

The wind shifted, rustling the trees lining the field, a whisper of movement that felt heavier than the usual autumn breeze. A few of the shifters glanced at each other, their casual posture tightening just a fraction.

Keir draped an arm over my shoulders, his Scottish lilt a warm, steady reassurance. "Whatever's stirrin', love, we'll handle it."

His casual confidence didn't quite erase the unease creeping along my skin, but I leaned into him anyway, letting the steady thrum of his presence chase away the shadows clinging to my thoughts.

A harsh whistle sounded, and the players jumped up from the stands. Keir's hand lingered on my leg for a second before he flashed a smile and joined his team.

Tzazi set her water bottle down next to me, fished out a set of keys from her windbreaker pocket and handed them to me. "The Jeep's parked in front of the law firm when you're ready to head to Patch's farm."

"Perfect. Thanks, Tzazi."

My only ride since moving to Darkly Island was a mint-condition Schwinn I'd found in my grandmother's shed. Beautiful, yes. Practical for hauling a load of pumpkins? Not so much.

"His name is Patch Priddyholm," Tzazi continued. "Maman says he's expecting you."

"You sittin' out, sugah?" Chase asked me as Tzazi and the other players thundered onto the field.

"I think it's best I just watch today," I said. "Maybe I'll try it next time."

Chase nodded and shouted as he ran out onto the playing field. "I'm coming for you, Bane."

Keir cupped a hand to his ear, grinning. "What's that now? Speak up, lad, I cannae hear yeh."

"I said I'm coming for you!" Chase yelled.

Keir smirked. "Ach, sorry, still nothing. Must be the sound of the scoreboard ticking up our points."

Chase shot the finger at him as a disc suddenly appeared in the air before him. He grabbed it, mumbled a few words, and with a flick of his wrist, released it into the air.

"Goodness, they're silly." I laughed at their taunting.

"I know, right? Men and sports," Jess replied as her eyes swept to somewhere over my shoulder probably in the direction of a shifter with blond hair.

After the game (shifters won), Keir walked me to the MET, his hand warm against mine. He turned me toward him, his fingers grazing my chin.

"I better get going," I said, though I didn't especially want to. "I have an afternoon date with a very successful pumpkin farmer."

Keir kissed me, slow and deep, before pulling back. "Aye? So that's what impresses yeh? Successful pumpkin farmers? I'll need to file that away for later." He took a few steps and then turned. "See yeh the night, then?"

"Definitely." I made a mental note to stop at Bosada's Grocery on the way home and grab some wine.

I tossed Tzazi's keys into the air and caught them. Time to see a man about a pumpkin!

CHAPTER 2

*a*igrette Road peeled away from downtown Darkly just past The Magic Cup coffee shop. It curved into the Darkly swamp, threading carefully between bald cypress knees and alligator nests, before emerging into golden sunlight and marshes where dragonflies danced and the occasional pelican glided by.

I couldn't remember the last time I'd driven anywhere; cars were a useless luxury in New York, of course. I was eager to travel out into the Darkly countryside on my own. Well, almost...

"Cool. Have you seen enough? How 'bout if we have GourdDash deliver the pumpkins to the MET," Pye grumbled. "I'll even pay for it."

"With what? Last I heard they weren't accepting annoying sidekicks."

I sighed deeply and he settled into his seat, hopefully finally realizing he was going to a pumpkin farm whether he liked it or not.

We had only driven about five miles beyond the town when the scenery outside the passenger window abruptly changed. A thick gray fog rolled along the ground, enveloping the Jeep and concealing the whispering cattails and soft rushes that I knew should be there. I slowed the car to a stop and gazed into the swirling miasma.

Pye cleared his throat. "This isn't a good place to sightsee, Win."

I looked down at him and was surprised to see him hunched in his seat, gripping the straps of the seatbelt he had insisted I belt him into when we left.

It took a lot to unnerve Pyewacket.

A crumbling pair of stone pillars rose up outside his window. That eerie, dark mist twisted and pulsed between the columns. The flicker of gas lamps was barely visible beyond the entrance.

The fog suddenly parted. Not randomly but purposefully, like we'd caught the attention of whatever lurked behind it.

"What in the world is this?"

Pye looked steadily ahead.

"Pye. I hate it when you do that."

"It's called The Graves. Now please drive."

"The Graves? Has it always been there?"

"No. It was miraculously conceived overnight, along with all the beings who live within, just to surprise Windsor Ebonwood on her way to waste my day at a dreary pumpkin farm." He sighed. "Yes, it's always been there."

"Well, you never know around here." I turned to face him. "Why have I never heard of it?"

"It's not a place most people visit." Pye wrapped both paws around the seatbelt again. "Its official name is the Gaslight District." He turned to me. "If there's ever bad business going on in Darkly, it usually originates in The Graves. Now. Please. Drive."

I shook off the foreboding chill and pressed the accelerator, understanding Pye's wish to leave that imposing entrance behind us.

The fog quickly dissipated as we drove further down Aigrette Road. The highway twisted through the swampland and soon we were passing long clusters of adorable row houses in rich pastels of lavender, mustard, and rose. The homes dotted both sides of the roadway, appearing suddenly, and then gradually disappearing as the cattail stands and bald cypress groves gave way to flat marshland. The late afternoon sun shone lazily through the ripples.

After a sharp turn, the turquoise sea stretched out before us and rising next to it, a towering gothic mansion with windows as dark as pitch and iron cresting running along the roof edges. It perched on the rocky cliff, like some ghoulish Colossus of Rhodes.

There was no mistaking it. This had to be Sângele, the home of Veronique della Morte. Once a silent film star, Veronique spent most of her time here at Sângele, with the infrequent visit to Darkly in search of the perfect martini. I'd found her wildly captivating and more than a little frightening. She had that cinematic, old-Hollywood *vampire* allure—the kind people picture the moment they hear the word.

I slowed to a stop in front of the dilapidated mansion and rolled down the window. A soft, chilly breeze tumbled in and around the car. The sound of the waves crashing on the rocks below was almost feral in its fury but also somehow calming at the same time.

Pye curled up into a ball and covered his head. "I'll catch my death of cold! Close that window!"

"Oh, stop being silly. It's beautiful out here!"

Pye glared at me. Then promptly began licking his nether regions.

"Are you going to be like this all day?"

"No. Only until you buy me brisket. Lots and lots of juicy brisket."

I ignored him and gazed at the crumbling grandeur before me. Dark spires rose high in the sky cloaked by low hanging, dark, ominous clouds. Blood-red roses spilled across the mansion's facade, twisting and coiling round black iron railings, eventually surging onto the ground.

I stepped out of the car and cautiously climbed the cracked, uneven stairs winding up the cliffside. The view was breathtaking, but the crumbling path beneath my feet kept me wary. A few loose pebbles skittered away, tumbling out of sight. I took another step, then lurched to a stop, heart pounding.

The ground beneath my toes had suddenly dropped away!

Steadying myself, I stepped back and glanced up at the roof's jagged peaks, where a committee of vultures hunched, their beady eyes fixed on me, staring, most definitely mocking.

"Yeah, thanks for the warning," I yelled up to them.

Carefully peering over the edge, I saw the violent waves below, rolling in between the cliff I stood on and the one where the brooding mansion loomed.

How interesting. The only way to reach the mansion was by veilshifting—a form of teleportation—or by flying. Could it be some type of vampire protection tactic?

Hurrying back to the Jeep, my eyes turned back once more to the ghostly mansion. I did a doubletake. Dark headstones rose up amidst the twisting vines and spiky thorns. Was that a cemetery laid out on the grounds of the mansion? Could one of those mark Veronique's resting place? I shivered, hopped in the car, and pressed the accelerator.

After only a few more miles, the road curved once more against the sea and a large wooden sign fastened to a fence popped into view. *Shadow Pumpkin Farm* was burnt into the wood in large block letters.

"Oh, Pye! Look!" I popped him on the rump to draw his attention to the rolling knolls covered in patches of color that rose next to us. "Pye! Oh my gosh! Those are pumpkins!"

The hills were covered in gourds of various sizes, shapes, and colors including pink and purple, alongside more traditional hues of orange, white, green, and yellow.

A smaller sign hung over the entrance and we turned onto a dirt lane. We parked next to a wooden cottage covered in winding pumpkin vines. A soft breeze ruffled my hair and some bamboo windchimes clonked on the porch. Otherwise, the farm was eerily silent.

"Much quieter than I was expecting," Pye said, as we both exited the car.

I pushed open a wooden gate. Its screech caused us both to flinch and then chuckle at our nervousness.

A heart-shaped gourd hung next to the front door, and I ran a hand over its smooth surface. I felt waves of magic coursing through its very core. I jerked my hand back when the gourd gave a quiet sigh and nestled further into its bed of leaves.

The large wooden door was cocked open a few inches and when I stepped forward, it creaked open a few more.

Pye wrapped his paws around my ankle. "I've seen this movie. It never ends well for the cat. Let's go home."

He wasn't wrong. A sharp, electric jolt of warning shot through me, a relentless pounding like sirens blaring through the night. An ominous weight pressed down on the farm. Even the breeze and the wooden wind chimes had stilled.

I stuck my head in the door. "Patch?"

No answer.

Just as I leaned further into the house, Pye leaped into my arms, scaring the bejezus out of me, and I stumbled against the door facing. I froze, silent and listening, Pye clutched tightly against my chest.

After a moment, I took another step forward. The only sound was my heart thumping out a staccato SOS. Something was *wrong* here.

Stepping fully into the room, I found a small, yet clean and welcoming space. Two overstuffed skirted chairs in pink floral fabric faced an ancient television covered in dainty figurines, doilies, and teacups. Between them, a small wooden table stood, two half-finished glasses of whiskey and a stack of papers littering its top. I would bet the cottage and farm had been in Patch's family for generations.

As we passed behind the chairs, I bumped into the small table in-between, knocking the papers and one of the glasses to the hardwood floor. The glass rolled out of sight under an ornate chifferobe pressed against the wall. Pye hissed his disapproval when I stooped to pick up the papers. Reaching under the armoire, my hand brushed against a soft, whispery something… moving! I screamed and yanked my hand back.

Pye crouched to peer under the cabinet and sniggered. "Ooh, Win's afraid of a fetish."

"A what?"

I reached back underneath and pulled out the "fetish," the tumbler, and the remaining pages I'd knocked to the ground. I glanced at the top sheet: *Last Will & Testament of Phineas Jack Priddyholm*. Curious.

I quickly set the pages down next to the whiskey tumbler and examined the small item I'd found. It appeared to be a carved human image, made of bone perhaps, with a hook at one end and a bright pink feather at the other.

A sudden chill ran down my spine, warning me we were being watched. I jammed the carving into my pocket, tucked Pye back into my shoulder bag, and instinctively raised my hands, magic pulsing to my fingertips.

"We're not the only ones here," Pye whispered, confirming my suspicions.

My eyes shuttered closed as I tried to pinpoint the cause of my unease, but I couldn't pick up on one point of reference.

The feeling of being watched suddenly eased. I relaxed my arms, but not my caution, and opened my eyes. Pye jumped to the floor and padded into the kitchen at the back of the cottage. Through a sliding glass door, acres upon acres of brightly colored pumpkins came into view, along with a large red barn smack dab in the middle, its barn doors gaping wide. Pumpkin-head scarecrows in overalls and checkered shirts hung from wooden stands spaced throughout the fields.

I breathed a sigh of relief. "Patch'll be in the barn, Pye. C'mon. But let's avoid those scarecrows. They're terrifying."

"Win, we should leave. Let's go get Keir."

"What if Patch is hurt or ill? We can't just leave without making sure he's okay."

Behind Patch's house, seemingly random paths ran through the fields sometimes circling back onto themselves and then shooting off in a different direction. I chose a path that appeared to be the shortest one to the barn, and Pye fell in step beside me.

The pumpkin patch was just as eerie and silent as Patch's home. It was as if a bubble of silence had been cast onto the whole property.

I passed close by a scarecrow. Its silent, staring eyes seemed to follow us as we walked past. Three large crows sat on the nearest pumpkinheads staring at us with interest.

I laughed nervously and pointed. "Great job."

"Actually," Pye said, "those aren't scarecrows. They're Patch's farm workers."

"What?" My screech startled the crows into flight. Their wings rustled through the crisp autumn air like the shuffle of dry leaves.

"If that's your reaction, you better hope they don't come down and start harvesting the pumpkins while we're here."

I shuddered.

Despite the pumpkinheads, I was struck again by the beauty and tranquility of Shadow Pumpkin Farm. A calmness not even creepy pumpkinheads and a sense of foreboding could completely curtail.

"Pick me," a soft high-pitched voice said.

At my feet lay a small orange pumpkin with bright white polka dots. I squatted next to it. "Did you say something?"

"Uh-huh. Pick me."

"Oh my gosh. They're enchanted! Just like the one on the front of the house!"

"Yeah, yeah. Cute. Let's get this done and get home. It's time for tea."

Pumpkins continued to call to us as we moved along the path. When we drew close to the barn, the adorable pleading faded, replaced by a low sobbing. The wails grew louder with each step.

Pye halted, the shiny black hairs along his spine standing straight up. "Bloody 'ell."

I followed his gaze to find a shattered scarecrow lying in the path, mounds of pumpkin pulp and seeds littering the ground around it. Orange plaid sleeves poked from faded green overalls.

A sharp jolt ran through me. I didn't want it to be... It couldn't be...

My eyes scanned the fields hopefully. "Patch!" I yelled. "It's Windsor Ebonwood."

I turned toward the barn again. He had to be out here somewhere. I took a few hesitant steps forward.

Pye dashed ahead of me and tugged off a gardening glove at the end of an outstretched arm.

A human hand flopped to the ground.

I hurried to Pye's side and dropped to my knees as the cursed bells of Darkly began to toll.

We were too late.

IN MOST TOWNS, the tolling of bells announced life's most joyous moments—weddings, births, Christmas Eve. But Darkly's cursed bells? They only rang for the dead.

As the final bell tolled, its last note lingering unnervingly in the heavy silence, I knelt beside the body sprawled across the path. The man lay face down, arms outstretched, the pulpy remains of a massive pumpkin splattered across the back of his head.

Carefully, I turned him over. Then sucked in a sharp breath. His head wasn't just covered in pumpkin. It *was* a pumpkin. Literally.

A perfectly round, vine-entwined, harvest-orange gourd replaced his head entirely.

The wrongness of it sent a shudder through me. My fingers, trembling, reached for his neck to search for a pulse I already knew wouldn't be there. Before I could make contact, an unnatural chill stole the air from my lungs and tightened around my ribs like a vice.

Bodderick Grim had arrived.

A twisting coil of black smoke slithered into existence beside the barn, curling into the tall, skeletal figure of Darkly's resident coroner, a former grim reaper. His deep red eyes locked onto mine, glinting like embers in the dim light. A gust of frigid wind swept through as he strode forward, his long black cape billowing behind him. Skeletal hands slipped from its folds, reaching toward Patch's body with deliberate, bone-white intent.

Boddy's unearthly cold crept into the air and I stepped back, arms wrapping around myself before I even realized I'd moved. Nearby, the vines recoiled, frost glistening along the edges of their leaves. The enchanted pumpkins shuddered. One let out a high-pitched whimper. Another sobbed into the dirt.

"Boddy, I—"

"Tell it to your boyfriend." His voice rasped like wind through dead leaves. He crouched beside the corpse, dismissing me with a flick of his hollow-eyed gaze.

"Well, I wouldn't call him my boyfriend," I muttered. "We're—"

Boddy silenced me with a glare.

"Right. Wrong time, wrong place. Got it."

I wasn't ashamed to admit Boddy Grim terrified me. He had once been Death's minion, after all. And ever since my arrival in Darkly, he had regarded me with deep suspicion, particularly after I stumbled across the body of Dorian Wilde, the town's corrupt alderman, dangling from a grave marker not long after I arrived. It hadn't helped that he outright accused me of Dorian's murder either. He'd been wrong, of course, but Boddy Grim was not a man who easily let go of a hunch.

The wailing pumpkins suddenly crescendoed into full-blown

hysteria, and then—a shadow, massive and swift, tore across the field.

A wolf.

No. Keir.

The beast was the size of a pony, his dark brown fur gleaming in the sunlight. Keir thundered across the pumpkin patch, massive paws leaving deep impressions in the dirt. When he skidded to a stop, the enchanted pumpkins nearest him trembled so violently that, in any other moment, it might have been comical.

Keir lifted his muzzle to the air and inhaled deeply. Then his chocolate-brown eyes locked onto mine.

In the space of a heartbeat, the shift overtook him. One moment, he was a towering beast of muscle and fur. The next, he stood human amongst the vines, unashamedly bare, dark hair tousled from the wind, silver necklaces tangled at his throat, tattoos scrolling down his muscular arms and across his stomach, down to…

Heat surged to my face, my gaze flicking skyward as I scrambled to focus on literally anything else. By the time I dared look again, Keir was clothed and striding toward me. He gave me a tense wink before turning his attention to Boddy.

"Och, Patch," Keir murmured and shook the coroner's outstretched hand. His gaze flicked back to the body. "Cause of death?"

"Not yet determined." Boddy's bony fingers hovered over the pumpkinhead. "But I suspect asphyxiation. I was unable to remove the pumpkin."

Keir crouched, studying the gourd as his fingers ghosted over its surface. "I've never seen anythin' like this."

I pulled my cardigan tighter, my breath misting in the cold. "Could magic have been involved?"

Boddy's red eyes flicked to me. "A magical pumpkin patch sees many visitors. The spectral lines are muddled. Difficult to discern."

Keir frowned and put his hands on his hips. "Aye. Same here. I've picked up scents of near everyone in Darkly."

Across the patch, the scarecrows loomed, unnervingly still, their straw-filled heads tilted at odd angles.

Pye padded up to my side and flicked his tail. "You notice something strange?"

"They're motionless," I murmured. "They should be working, shouldn't they?"

Keir turned to me. "What's that now?"

I relayed Pye's words and let my eyes roam across the pumpkin patch at the motionless figures on their pedestals. My eyes settled on the one closest to Patch, the one whose eyes appeared to follow us when Pye and I moved up the path toward the barn. Even now, its eyes glistened strangely, a bright contrast to the others. "It's pumpkin season but they look like they've been switched off."

"'Tis odd." Keir gazed around the pumpkin field. "Any spells cast o'er Patch's land lately? Aside from his own, o' course."

"Indeed, it does appear that a witch cast a spellveil over his land within the past hour." Boddy sharp red eyes stared into mine. "Can it be a coincidence that I personally observed Windsor Ebonwood standing over the body when I arrived?"

I stiffened. "I—"

"Yeh okay?" Keir asked softly, pointedly ignoring Boddy and running his hands up and down my arms, soothing the goosebumps that Boddy's not-so-subtle insinuation had brought on. "Did yeh see anything?"

I shook my head and described our drive to Shadow Pumpkin Farm, entering Patch's house, and finding the body in the pumpkin patch.

"Are you sure it's Patch?" I asked hopefully. "I thought it was one of his scarecrows at first."

"No doubt," Keir said, his grip on my arms tightening. "It's him, right enough."

Before I could respond, a small bat flitted between us, its

wings brushing against my cheek. I gasped, stumbling back. Keir's arm curled around my waist, steadying me.

"Wo there, hen," he murmured softly.

The bat shimmered for a moment, a fevered red haze outlining its body, then melted into the shape of Tzazi.

I barely had a moment to feel the sting of disappointment when Keir let go, and Tzazi was there, gripping my hands, her dark eyes sharp with concern.

"You're okay. That's good." Tzazi exhaled in relief, then looked around. "What's happened?"

I pointed to Patch's body on the ground.

Tzazi turned to Keir. "Accidental, natural, or murder?" she asked, inherently switching into attorney-mode.

"Still investigating," Boddy growled, his unearthly voice hinting at his former job.

As if on cue, a loud clap split the air.

The pumpkin cracked into two halves and slid off Patch's face.

A sudden breeze blew in, sweeping a swirl of fallen leaves down the paths.

The scarecrows lurched to life.

One by one, they hopped down from their posts, returning to their duties as though nothing had happened. Overhead, the birds resumed their songs. The entire farm shifted from eerie paralysis to unsettling normalcy in an instant. It was as if someone had pressed *Play* on a paused movie.

And yet—

The scarecrow with the gleaming amber eyes turned its head.

Not toward the field.

Not toward the barn.

Toward me.

I stiffened as he ambled over to Patch's body, crouched silently, respectfully, for a moment before rising and striding into the barn.

I clutched Tzazi's arm and swallowed hard. "It's like watching zombie clowns reanimate."

Tzazi tugged on my arm. "Mind if I get her home?"

I didn't argue.

Keir gave Tzazi a grateful pat on the shoulder. "I'd be much obliged. Thank yeh, Tzaz."

He turned to me. "I'm sorry, Win. Looks like I'll be here most o' the evening. Our new detective inspector's meant to arrive sometime today, and I'll need to get him up to speed. Mind if we raincheck tonight?"

He pulled me close and nuzzled into my hair, breathing in my scent.

"I promise I'll make it up to yeh." he whispered, finally pulling away but still holding my hand.

Tzazi tugged on my arm, and we wound our way through the pumpkin patch to the front of the property. The news of Patch's death had obviously spread throughout the fields and every pumpkin now sobbed and wailed, their mourning a macabre and disquieting sound.

Pye trotted along beside us, unusually silent, stopping periodically to examine one of the enchanted pumpkins.

I tossed Tzazi her keys and climbed into the passenger seat. Pyewacket jumped in after me and made himself at home in my lap. A sudden thought hit me.

"Tzazi," I said, putting a hand up to stop her from shifting the Jeep into gear and driving off. "Boddy said a spellveil was used over the farm."

"Interesting. And?"

"So then why were the pumpkins still crying while the spellveil was in effect?"

We both turned and looked out over the farm, the mournful wailing stabbing at my heart, enchantment or not.

CHAPTER 3

"*W*indsor Ebonwood! What'd I tell you 'bout gettin' tangled up in another one o' them murders?"

Hildegarde Orso's voice rolled through the room like distant thunder, low and dangerous. She filled the doorway between the sitting room and the hallway to the kitchen, arms crossed, her dark eyes flashing with something between exasperation and concern.

She jabbed a thick finger at Pyewacket, who had the audacity to stretch luxuriously on the sofa's back. "And *you*, of all creatures, oughta know better."

"What'd I do?" Pyewacket protested, his golden eye gleaming with feigned innocence. "I told her not to go in there."

I narrowed my eyes at the little traitor.

Hilde, a bear shifter of formidable size and even greater presence, had been the steadfast guardian of Fernwood and the Ebonwood family for longer than I'd been alive. The weight of history clung to her like the scent of cinnamon and oak in an old apothecary.

"Ain't no good ever come from meddlin' in things like this," she warned. "Need me to remind you what happened last time?"

She didn't. Last time a murderer set their sights on me, I barely lived to tell the tale.

I absently picked at a fraying seam on my favorite OMD sweatshirt, the once-thick fabric worn soft and threadbare with time. I brought my steaming mug to my lips, inhaling the warm bite of cloves and cinnamon before taking a cautious sip.

"Oh wow! What is this?" I asked, swirling the deep red liquid. "Reminds me of sangria...but different."

"*Swedish* sangria," Hilde said, setting the infamous never-ending pitcher on the coffee table. "Glögg. Perfect for cold nights." She settled into her favorite chair near the fire, the flames casting flickering shadows against the walls.

Tzazi sprawled languidly at the other end of the sofa, one of Hilde's fuzzy blankets pulled up to her neck. Through the windows behind her, the murky waters of the swamp lagoon caught the last slivers of sunlight, flickering between the gnarled cypress trees.

The Ebonwood ancestral home Fernwood sat on the edge of both Darkly Swamp and Darkly Forest, just half a mile outside town but so secluded it might as well have been at the end of the world. Just the way I liked it.

The house was built in the old Southern style where one room bled into the next, meaning you had to pass through the library to get to the guest rooms and the music room doubled as a corridor to my office. It was a strange, winding labyrinth, very different from my New York apartment, but just four short months after arriving here, it felt like home.

Tzazi lifted her mug and frowned at the bits bobbing on the surface. "Certainly has a kick. What's in it?"

"Cinnamon, orange peel, cloves, and cardamom," Hilde said, ticking each off on her fingers. "Then you're gonna need port wine, a splash of rum, and enough whiskey to wake it up. Raisins, candied lichen if you've got it, and a good handful of almonds."

"That'd be the kick, then." Tzazi tipped back half the mug in one go.

I eyed my own cup warily. "Did you say candied lichen?"

Tzazi merely nodded in approval, tipping her mug toward Hilde. "Now *that's* how you beat back a bone-deep chill."

Let's hope so. Because the cold creeping into my skin had little to do with the weather.

A sharp rap at the back door sent Hilde bustling toward the kitchen. "Sounds like the rest of your lot's showin' up."

Seconds later, a faint hum of magic filled the house, and Jess flew into the room. Her marmalade-colored wings fluttered behind her, shimmering with golden-peachy veins. She dropped a large bag next to the sofa as her feet grazed the floor, then rushed to my side. I stood so she could wrap me in a hug that smelled of honey and wood smoke.

As a hearth fairy, Jess practically radiated warmth—literal and emotional. Cozy and comforting, she had an uncanny way of making everything feel just a little less awful, which explained why she owned the most popular tavern in town, The Green Gator.

"Oh, you poor dears," she cooed before scratching Pyewacket's stomach. He responded with an undignified flop, purring like a rusty engine.

Tzazi chuckled.

"You hush," Jess scolded, wagging a finger at the vampire before pulling her into a hug as well. "I've been worried ever since you left the Gator."

Despite her teasing, she settled into one of the overstuffed chairs with a relieved sigh. Hilde handed her a steaming mug of glögg.

She tucked her legs up into the chair, fingers wrapped around her mug. "How are you two holding up?"

"We're fine," I said, though the tremor in my voice gave me away. "But I can't stop thinking about Patch."

A heavy silence settled over us. I plucked a swollen raisin from my drink, rolling it between my fingers before popping it into my mouth.

"He was a good man," Jess said softly. "I don't know anyone who didn't love him."

Hilde sighed, setting aside her knitting and standing. A ball of green yarn tumbled across the floor, and Pyewacket perked up, tracking it with lazy interest.

"Always was generous with his pumpkins, bless him," Hilde murmured, tucking the blanket around me with surprising gentleness before moving to do the same for Tzazi and Jess. Her way of comforting. Fussing, mothering—whether we admitted we needed it or not.

"And poor Dixie-Deen," I added, thinking of Patch's longtime girlfriend. "I can't imagine how she's holding up."

"Not well, I'd bet," Jess said with a sigh. "They'd been together forever. I'm sure Mathilda's looking after her."

Dixie-Deen Poplar ran Lila & the Piggles, the local paranormal animal sanctuary known for taking in everything from flying griffins to fiery phoenixes. Her best friend Mathilda Broomthistle owned the broom shop next to the MET, Besoms & Britches, a respected establishment known for its expertly made flying gear and some of the finest brooms on the island.

"Oh! I almost forgot!" Jess set her mug down and plucked the gift bag from the floor, thrusting it toward me. Bold, bright letters across the front read Happy 75th Birthday!

I lifted a brow.

She shrugged. "It's all I had."

With a mix of amusement and curiosity, I reached inside. The first thing I pulled out was a plastic container of cat treats.

"Yum!" Pyewacket yowled, launching himself at the bag like he hadn't been fed in days.

I held it out of reach. "Manners, mister. There's more in here." Setting the treats on the table, I reached in again and withdrew a perfectly wrapped chess pie.

The scent of butter and sugar hit me like a warm embrace. I moaned. Chess pie, I'd learned since moving to Darkly was comfort in its purest form. Life unraveling? Chess pie.

Existential crisis? Chess pie. Murder in the pumpkin patch? Chess pie.

"I'll do the honors," Tzazi announced, snatching up the bag and striding toward the kitchen.

I blinked. Tzazi…serving pie?

Now, don't get me wrong. Tzazi was a fierce friend. Witty, loyal, always ready to throw down in a fight. But domestic? Not in her repertoire.

Suspicious, I pushed the blanket aside. "I'm gonna see if she needs help. Be right back."

Hilde gave me a knowing nod and turned to ask Jess about her family in the Charming Isles.

I stepped into the kitchen and found Tzazi leaning against the counter, staring out the window into the lagoon beyond. The swamp stretched like an ink spill beneath the moonlight, tangled cypress trees casting long, gnarled shadows across the still water, a gentle breeze rustling the treetops. And out there, bobbing like a ghostly lantern, was the mysterious light that had been appearing since my first night in Darkly.

"Does it ever come closer?" Tzazi asked, not taking her eyes off it.

"I can't tell."

She finally turned to me, her sharp gaze assessing. "We need to get out there and find out what it is. It's not *feu follet*."

The light dimmed for a breath, then flared brighter, sending a ripple of silver across the swamp.

"*Feu follet*?" I asked.

"Swamp sprites," she said. "Tricky little things, but that"—she gestured at the light—"is too big. Too steady. Good chance whatever's out there is leaving footprints."

My skin tingled with foreboding. I'd never considered the light might be something alive, walking on two feet through the swamp, not floating like a will-o'-wisp. Ren had once sworn up and down that the light was a sign of the swamp hag, a legendary witch that supposedly prowled these waters.

"Who would be wandering the swamp in the dead of night?" I asked, my voice quieter than I meant it to be.

Tzazi's expression darkened. "No idea. But I can tell you this much. There's been enough weirdness around here lately."

My ears perked up. "Like the sightings?"

She turned away from the window and grabbed a knife from the rack, slicing straight through the center of the pie. "The rougarous are the ones that worry me."

I frowned. "They flat-out unnerve me."

Tzazi didn't look up as she continued cutting. "They should. They're werewolves. Not shifters, like Keir and the Silverfang Clan. Rougarous are the werewolves depicted in human horror movies. They have no control. Full moons force the change, sure. But stress, fear? That'll do it too. And when they turn, they don't just run through the woods." She flicked me a look. "They hunt humans."

My gut twisted into knots. "Have there been reports of anyone being hurt?"

"Not yet. But there's been damage. Gardens, homes."

For a long moment, we stood in silence. The fire in the other room crackled, Hilde's voice a low murmur as she and Jess talked, but here in the kitchen, the air was thick with unspoken words.

Tzazi finally turned back to the window, her shoulders tense. "Do you ever feel in danger from the light?"

I hesitated, then shook my head. "The exact opposite. It makes me feel safe."

Tzazi's brow wrinkled, rolling that over in her mind. "Does Keir know about the light?"

"I might've mentioned it."

"And?"

"He told me to stay out of the swamp. Especially after dark."

"Smart man."

Her voice trailed off, but her gaze remained fixed on the lagoon, and I had the distinct impression she wasn't thinking about the light anymore.

I stepped closer, sliding the knife from her grip before she could cut straight through the counter. "Tzaz," I said carefully. "You okay? You've been off lately."

She exhaled sharply, then shook her head, gold hoop earrings swinging. "I'm fine."

I leveled her with a look.

She sighed. "I am fine. Honestly? The trial can't come soon enough. I'm ready to wipe the floor with that little scumbag."

I arched a brow. "Which one?"

She pulled plates from the cabinet. "Does it matter? I'll wipe the floor with both of those little scumbags."

Remember the nasty half-sister I mentioned? She and her lawyer—Mason Beckworth, who also happened to be Tzazi's ex—were suing Jess to claw back the inheritance she rightfully received after Dorian, Elspeth's father, died. To make matters even messier, Dorian wasn't just Elspeth's father—he was Jess's brother-in-law too. Starting to sound more like Peyton Place than Darkly Island, isn't it?

I still wasn't satisfied with Tzazi's explanation. "You know I'm here for you if you need me, right?"

"I do, Win. And I appreciate it."

And just like that, the sharp edge of tension dulled. For now.

But outside, the light still flickered, steady as a heartbeat.

TZAZI and I carried the chess pie, plates, and silverware into the sitting room, the scent of warm butter and sugar wrapping around us. Cozy, familiar, and just the kind of comfort we all needed.

"I'll take that, hun," Hilde said, setting down her knitting with a soft thunk and sliding the pie effortlessly from Tzazi's hands. "You two get comfortable."

She didn't have to tell me twice. I curled up on the velvet sofa, tucked my legs, and pulled a thick blanket over me. Pyewacket stretched himself over my lap, his soft purring settled the restlessness humming in my bones.

I stroked his sleek fur. "Thanks, Pye," I murmured.

He cocked his head, his eye gleaming, then let out a deep, grumbling purr louder than before. Feelings of security and contentment flowed through me.

Smug little thing. As much as he loved to test my patience, life without him would be far less interesting.

Hilde handed me a plate, and I wasted no time taking a generous bite. The creamy, custardy filling melted on my tongue, buttery and sweet, with just the right hint of nutmeg.

Another series of knocks echoed from the kitchen.

"That'll be the boys." Hilde stomped back toward the kitchen.

A few seconds later, Chase swooped into the room in a blur of warm cologne and expensive linen, pulling me into a hug, and nearly crushing Pyewacket in the process.

"You," he announced dramatically, releasing me only to scratch under Pye's chin, "are going to be the death of me." He ran a hand down the cat's back. "If I were you, Pye, I'd be down to my last life." Then his gaze landed on my plate. His eyes widened. "Ooooh, is that chess pie?"

Before I could blink, he whisked it from my hands, fork and all.

"Oh, no, you don't." Hilde, quick as a viper, intercepted the plate midair, handed it back to me, and swatted Chase's hand away before he could try again.

Chase pouted, rubbing his knuckles.

"Would you like some too, honey?" Hilde asked Ren, who lingered just inside the doorway.

He hesitated, always careful not to impose. "If it's not too much trouble, Hilde."

"Of course not, dear. I'll be right back with more plates and mugs."

As Hilde disappeared into the kitchen, Chase plopped down

on the plush loveseat, plumped up the pillows around himself and gave Ren an affectionate nudge when he sat.

Then, with a dramatic sigh, "What a horrible accident!"

I blinked. "Accident?"

"The salon's been abuzz all afternoon." Chase accepted a plate from Hilde with a grateful nod.

Ren leaned forward, brows furrowing. "Win, are you saying it wasn't an accident? We heard he tripped over his pumpkins and fell. Hit his head."

I considered that for a moment. Could it have been a freak accident?

I shook my head slowly. "No. There were no rocks. Nothing he could've hit his head on. And the pumpkin was—" I hesitated, searching for the right words. "It was attached to his head. Not under it, like he fell on it."

Jess paled. "Like his pumpkin-head workers?"

I nodded. "Exactly. At first, I mistook him for one of the workers. From the moment we arrived, the whole farm felt off. All those scarecrows standing there. It's like they were watching us." I took another sip of glögg, letting the heat burn away the lingering unease.

Chase reached for his own mug, raising it in a small toast to Hilde before leaning back, crossing one long leg over the other. "Well, that *is* interesting," he mused. "You say none of Patch's scarecrows were working?"

Chase, like Patch, was a sorcerer. If anyone could shed light on what had happened, it was him.

"I'm sure Patch's enchantments were mostly aesthetic," he explained. "Little incantations to make the pumpkins cuter, more personable. So they could, you know, sell themselves." He shrugged. "Maybe a preservation charm here and there. But it's strange that none of his helpers were active. I'm sure they're enchanted to automatically do their jobs each day. It is high season after all."

"Boddy said a spellveil was cast just before Patch's death," I added.

Chase took a slow sip, considering. "That would explain it. Did you notice it being unusually quiet when you found him?"

"Yes!" I sat up straighter. "Everything was just stopped. No birds. No wind. No chimes. No sound at all. Well, except for the pumpkins."

"The pumpkins?" Jess asked.

"They were talking to us. At first, begging us to pick them. Then the closer we got to the body, they started sobbing and wailing," I said. "It was awful."

Chase raised a brow. "If they weren't silenced by the spellveil, then they weren't enchanted by Patch." He took a generous bite of pie and closed his eyes with a groan of approval.

Now, that was odd. No, not the groan. That was quite predictable. But the pumpkins not being enchanted by Patch? That was unexpected.

Pyewacket flicked his tail to get my attention. "And there was someone else at the farm when we arrived."

I nodded. "Pye and I both sensed someone else there when we were in the house."

"And you stayed?" Jess looked horrified.

"I didn't know we were walking into a crime scene!" Geez, I do have *some* common sense. "Besides, whoever it was disappeared right after we felt them."

"I doubt Patch saw a reason to use anything more than a light incantation on his workers," Chase continued, tapping his fork thoughtfully against his plate. "If that's true, then anyone with basic magic knowledge could've suppressed his enchantments. Not permanently, but certainly for a moment or two."

"Like me?" I asked.

Chase hesitated. "Well, no, probably not."

Pyewacket sniggered. I yanked the blanket over his head.

"So, someone with more than my level of magic, but still only basic knowledge, could've re-enchanted the pumpkin to—what? Attack him?"

Chase frowned. "I was thinking more along the lines of putting the scarecrows to sleep. But sure, maybe that too."

Jess frowned. "But you didn't see or hear any evidence of who might have been there? No car, no broom, no voices?"

"Nothing," I admitted. "Which is why it was so weird. Pye and I even checked inside the house. But—" I paused, remembering. "I do think he had company before he died. There were two half-filled whiskey glasses and his will out on the table."

Tzazi leaned back into the cushions, narrowing her eyes. "His will?"

"Mm-hmm."

"Did you read it?"

I gaped at her. "No!"

"I would've." She shrugged, wholly unrepentant.

Jess gasped. "No, you wouldn't have!"

Tzazi just took another bite of pie. "Well, if she had, we might know who killed him."

I had no argument for that.

Chase reached for the glögg pitcher. "You know, there is another pumpkin farmer. Gordon Mulch."

Tzazi nodded. "Runs a smaller farm halfway to Nocturnelle."

"Nocturnelle?" What an intriguing name.

"The vampire area," Ren said quietly. "Where it's always night."

On second thought, not all that intriguing.

"I know Mulch used to complain about Patch using enchantments on his pumpkins, which isn't illegal," Chase drawled, swirling his glögg. "Other than that, they seemed to get along fine."

"Not surprising," Jess said. "Patch was always such a happy-go-lucky guy."

We tossed around theories for another hour, but nothing stuck.

And as much as I hated to admit it, I was starting to regret not reading Patch's will.

Then—*rap-rap-rap*—a sharp knock at the front door shattered the quiet. A pulse of magic trembled through the room. Everyone stiffened, staring at each other.

"Who is it this time? The whole dang Silverfang Clan?" Hilde muttered, tossing her knitting aside with a sigh.

"Maybe it's Keir," I said hopefully, rising from my seat. "I'll get it."

But as I neared the door, my easy smile faltered. The silhouette on the other side of the stained glass was all wrong—short and oddly rounded, like a hobbit who'd let himself go.

I cracked the door open, and before I could say a word, an exuberant voice rang out like a bell at a revival meeting.

"Well, bless your heart and pickle me gin!"

CHAPTER 4

$\mathscr{A}$ short, elderly woman stood on Fernwood's porch, her wild silver hair gently tousled by the breeze puffed out in every direction. A grin tugged at her face—wide, mischievous, and capable of charming moss off a cypress knee. Her outfit was an absolute riot of color—patchwork trousers in clashing turquoise, violet, and yellow, topped with a long velvet coat that somehow managed to be louder than the pants. Between the velvet duster, feathered earring, and sequined top, the woman looked like a fortune teller who'd just stepped off a stage.

She reached out, gripping my hand with neon-pink lacquered fingers that squeezed with unsettling strength.

"Excuse me?" I managed, stepping back, but her grip only tightened.

"Honey, you look just like your mother. Now, come give me some sugah!"

Then she yanked me into a hug. A forceful one. A possibly rib-cracking one. "Hilde!" I squawked, flailing.

The door wrenched wider and Hilde appeared, her expression sliding from irritation to something I'd never seen before. Shock. Pure, unfiltered, slack-jawed shock.

Hilde stared at the woman. The woman stared at me. I looked

back and forth at the two feeling like I was front row at a ping pong match.

"Sibella?" Hilde finally whispered. "Is that really you?"

The old woman threw up her hands. "Do you think anyone else would want this face? Get over here!"

Hilde let out a choked laugh, then barreled forward, wrapping the woman in a bone-crushing hug. I'd seen Hilde happy before, but never like this. Not even the time she changed into her bear form and knocked Mason Beckworth flat on his butt. Ah, good times.

Sibella patted Hilde's back, then marched into the house. Her stilettos clicked out a fine, high-pitched tick on the hardwood floors.

"Good ol' Fernwood," she mused, surveying the foyer with a misty-eyed grin. She plopped a massive leather bag on the floor, its contents clanking ominously, before sauntering into the sitting room.

By then, the whole gang was on their feet, watching her like she might pull a rabbit—or possibly a mathom or two—out of her handbag. She stuck a pipe between her teeth and puffed at it, despite it being unlit.

I had officially reached my limit. "Will someone please tell me what in the stars is going on?" I demanded, throwing my arms up.

"Windsor, hun," Hilde drawled, still looking dangerously close to giddy. "Meet your great aunt, Sibella Ebonwood."

Great. Aunt. Sibella.

"Back from the dead," Tzazi deadpanned.

I took a step back. *Zombie?* Because, in Darkly, that was a valid concern.

"Everyone thought you were dead, Miss Sibby!" Chase finally blurted, uncharacteristically breathless as he launched himself forward and wrapped Sibella in a hug. Chase didn't run. Chase ambled, maybe sashayed. Crawled even, depending on how many mint juleps he'd drank. Never ever ran. The fact that he was moving at full speed only made this situation more surreal.

Sibella cackled, holding him tight. "Me? Dead?" she scoffed. "It'd take more than a skulk of undead polecats to take me out, Sugarbritches!"

Sugarbritches?

Chase looked like someone had just dumped sweet tea in his designer shoes.

She released him and plopped onto the sofa with a dramatic sigh. "Now, tell me, is there any of that glögg left?"

Chase poured her a mugful, and Sibella took a long, approving sip, then fixed me with a stare so intense I felt like I was under a microscope. She finally turned toward Tzazi. "How are Azalea and Lazarus?"

Tzazi huffed. "Haven't seen Lazarus in years. But Maman..." She softened. "She's wonderful. You should visit her at The Magic Cup."

"Still running that coffee joint, huh? Well, I'll be." Sibella grinned, sinking into the cushions and hugging her mug to her ample chest. "Good ol' Darkly."

A lull fell over the room. The fire crackled in the hearth, casting flickering shadows on the walls.

Sibella suddenly snapped her fingers. "Jessamin Wilde!"

Jess jerked, spilling glögg down her blouse.

"I hear you own the Green Gator now. Fabulous!"

"I do," Jess said, dabbing at the stain. "You should stop in."

"Oh, you know I will."

Sibella took another gulp of glögg, then tilted her head at Ren, who had been quiet as a church mouse. She squinted, then turned to me. "And who does this tasty morsel belong to?"

Poor Ren's face turned scarlet.

I choked. "That's Ren de Zavala. Chase's better half."

Sibella nodded sagely, then elbowed Chase. "Good job, Sugarbritches." She kicked her feet up onto the coffee table and I gasped. Louboutins. And not just any Louboutins. The shoes squeezed onto her tiny little feet were $4,500, limited-edition, Louboutin stilettos. Blood-red soles flashed like a crime scene.

Chase groaned. "I let you get away with that once, Miss Sibby. No need to resurrect old nicknames."

She waved her hand in his face, as if shooing away a troublesome fly. "Hush now."

Then she turned back to me, her bright green eyes pinning me in place. "And you, of course, must be Windsor, our Genevieve's daughter."

It wasn't a question. It was a statement.

Tzazi cleared her throat. "But where have you been, Sibby? We heard you were captured and killed."

"Tzazi!" Jessamin hissed. "Not *killed*. Missing."

Tzazi shrugged. "That's what I heard."

Jess shot her a glare. "Fine. But do you have to say it out loud?"

Sibella just chuckled, watching them bicker like they were kids again. "Some things never change."

I swallowed. "Do you know about Grandmother?"

Sibella's smile faltered; a shadow crossed her face.

"Dropped my trowel and got here as soon as I heard," she said quietly. "What happened?"

"Illness," Hilde said, voice thick. "It came on fast, but she was ready."

"That was Minta," Sibella murmured, wiping her sleeve across her nose. "Always prepared for whatever came."

Then she turned to me, her eyes warm. "And now you're here, little Winny. And I'm pleased as rum punch."

She drained the last of her glögg and stretched out her arm for more. "Speaking of…"

Chase filled her mug and then patted his partner's knee. "And on that note, Ren and I should probably head out."

Ren nodded and drained his mug.

"Miss Sibby, once you're settled, we must catch up." Chase said. "Perhaps an evening of pickleball and piña coladas?"

Sibella barked out a laugh. "Pickleball? Sounds absurd. Count me in!"

Jess yawned. "Time for me to head out too."

Tzazi murmured her agreement, already gathering her things.

After a round of hugs, I walked them to the door.

The chill that hung in the air didn't bother the bullfrogs who called from the lagoon, their rhythmic croaking no match for the chirping of the crickets in the grass, steady, unbothered by our presence.

After the taillights vanished into the darkness, I shut the door, sealing out the cold and retreated to the fire's golden warmth. Sibella stretched with a satisfied groan.

"Do you have a place to stay?" I asked, my voice careful as I settled back onto the sofa, pulling Pyewacket onto my lap.

She waved a hand. "I was hoping to stay here for a bit, if you don't mind. But only if I'm not any trouble."

"You're welcome for as long as you need," I assured her.

"Only for a bit," she echoed, though her tone made me wonder. "Got my own place in town. I imagine it's lookin' a bit worse for wear after all these years."

I frowned. "How long were you gone?"

"Let's see," Sibby said, mumbling and calculating on her fingers.

Hilde cut in before she could answer. "Forty-seven years."

The number landed like a thunderclap in my chest.

Forty-seven years!

I sucked in a breath, my gaze flicking to the woman now lounging on my sofa like she'd never left.

Time worked differently for paranormals. They lived much longer lives than humans. (Jess and Tzazi were both over one hundred years old and they were considered young.) But forty-seven years was still an awful long time to be gone without a word.

And why *had* she been gone so long? And why now, on the very day of a murder, had she returned?

Sibella Ebonwood was a mystery, wrapped in silk and Louboutins.

And I intended to unravel every inch of her.

AFTER SIBBY RETIRED to one of the guest rooms, I plucked *Wuthering Heights* from the library shelf and curled up on the velvet chaise. The scent of aged paper and woodsmoke curled through the air, mingling with the melancholic strains of Edith Piaf drifting from the ancient turntable. Outside, the swamp hummed its soothing nocturnal lullaby, a symphony of rustling reeds, distant croaks, and the occasional splash of alligator gar beneath the water's surface.

But no matter how much I tried to lose myself in the doomed romance and brooding landscapes, my mind wouldn't settle. Thoughts of the day's events gnawed at the edges of my concentration, circling like restless spirits.

Magic had to be involved. It wasn't possible for a man to simply trip and end up with an overgrown pumpkin affixed to his head, enchanted or not. Or was it? This was Darkly, after all. The rules of nature bent differently here, and I wasn't exactly an expert in supernatural horticulture. Could one of Patch's own spells have gone awry?

I sighed, set the book aside, and reached down to scratch Pyewacket's soft belly. He sprawled beside me like royalty, his golden eye slitted open.

"What do you make of all this?" I asked.

"Another normal day in Darkly?"

"Certainly seems like it. And you were unusually quiet tonight. Any thoughts on Great Aunt Sibella's miraculous return?"

"Are you being snooty?" he said, narrowing his eye at me.

"No. Well, maybe a little. But I'm also being serious. Assumed dead. Returns after forty-seven years. It *is* quite miraculous."

Pye yawned, stretched, then settled back onto my lap, tail swaying lazily. "I'm as surprised as you, but I'm glad she's back. How do I put this..." He smacked his lips and pointed imperiously at the open bag of treats he'd insisted I bring with us into the library.

With a sigh, I plucked one out of the bag and popped it into his mouth.

"Sibella brews to the heat of her own cauldron, if you know what I mean." He chewed thoughtfully, then continued. "Where Minta was refined and elegant, Sibella was rough around the edges, always stirring up trouble. But both had good hearts and gave me plenty of treats." He smacked his lips again and pointed.

I tossed another treat his way.

The warmth of the fire, the lingering taste of glögg on my tongue, and the sheer exhaustion of the day pulled at me. My limbs sank deeper into the cushions. My eyelids were growing heavy when the door to the library creaked open.

Hilde stepped into the room. "Alright then, honey, if you're squared away, I'm goin' on up to bed."

"We're fine," I assured her.

She gave a nod, moving off to check the front door and bolt the locks with a firm clunk.

"You gonna be okay, hun?" She stood in the doorway once more, hands on her hips. "I'd say today was quite a day."

I stood and wrapped my arms around her in a hug. "Quit worrying. We're heading to bed too. I'm wiped out."

I grinned up at Hilde who stood a good foot above me. She reminded me of an Amazon warrior. Even in human form, she was quite formidable.

"If I quit worryin' about you, I wouldn't know what to do with myself." She kissed the top of my head, then strode off toward the back of the house.

"Hilde?" I called after her.

She turned, one brow lifting. "Yeah, honey?"

"What do you think about Sibby just appearing out of

nowhere?" I glanced around as if expecting her to materialize from the shadows. "It feels off."

Hilde's expression turned thoughtful. "I get what you're sayin'. But truth be told, I always figured she was out there somewhere. I knew she'd make her way back when the time was right."

"But why is this the right time? Showing up after Minta's gone? And she dodged every question about where she's been."

"She'll talk when she's good and ready." Hilde's lips quirked. "One thing's for sure. It's gonna get interesting around here with her back." She nodded at the library fireplace. "And don't forget to put out that flame. I'll take care of the sitting room. Night, honey."

As I watched her disappear up the stairs, I prodded Pye with a finger. "C'mon, let's go to bed."

"But I'm still hungry," he grumbled.

"You just had two treats. Can't you wait until breakfast?"

I picked him up off the chaise, then froze.

A low rumbling, deep as distant thunder, vibrated through the floorboards.

I held my breath. "Did you hear that?"

"My stomach growling? Yes, I did. Let's fix that pronto."

I flicked a finger at the turntable, lifting the needle. The house fell into a hush, save for the crackle of the dying fire.

Then—

Thump!

"Did you hear that, cat?"

Pye's body tensed, his fur bristling. "Cat heard that."

The sound had come from the dock area behind the house.

Pye leaped from my arms. I dashed into the kitchen and grabbed a flashlight from the kitchen drawer. As I turned, a flicker of movement outside the window caught my eye.

A grotesque face—skin mottled green and warty, eyes sunken and glistening like wet marbles—leered at me through the glass.

Its mouth twisted into a jagged grin. Rows of spiky teeth glinted in the moonlight.

I screamed, stumbling back. The face vanished just as a heavy thump rocked the side of the house.

Before I could react, Hilde thundered down the stairs, shifting mid-stride into a massive brown bear. Sibby barreled in from the hall, a swirling orb of fire hovering between her palms. I rushed behind them into the backyard.

The night trembled. A guttural growl, low and vibrating, rose from the swamp like some monstrous engine revving to life. Then —splash. Something massive hit the water, sending a spray of swamp droplets onto the pier.

I swept the flashlight beam across the yard. A low fog clung to the swamp's edge, blurring the light and swallowing the distance. But nothing moved. Nothing stirred.

Hilde sniffed around the dock, prowling toward the window. I followed, then stopped in my tracks. Something had carved deep gashes into the wooden sill.

"What was that thing?" I whispered.

Pye leaped into my arms, his nose twitching as he inspected the grooves. "Swamp imp."

"Swamp imp," I echoed.

Hilde, still in bear form, gave a solemn nod.

Sibella swiped a finger through the gashes, lifting a string of slimy green goop. She grimaced and held it out.

I recoiled. "Oh, yuck."

From the edge of the dock, Greta Garbo's hulking form surfaced, water dripping from her armored back.

Hilde shifted back to her human form. "Let's get inside." She glanced at Greta. "Extra snacks for you tomorrow. Good gator."

Sibby ushered me toward the house.

Once I entered the kitchen, I spun around. "Tell me what just happened. Are we in danger?"

"Not at the moment," Pye said darkly, slipping through the door just as Hilde threw the locks.

I frowned. "But the claw marks—"

"Greta's," Hilde interrupted.

My insides coiled. "Why would she attack the house?"

"She wasn't attacking." Sibby flicked her wand, sending a golden spark fizzing into the fireplace, setting it ablaze. "She was trying to protect it."

I swallowed hard. "From the imp?"

Sibby dropped onto a stool with a sigh. "Well, if ever there was a night that called for another tankard of glögg, this is it. Everybody in?"

"Absolutely," Pye declared, his tail flicking.

I arched a brow at him.

He scoffed. "What? You think I haven't indulged in a tankard or two in my time?"

Shaking my head, I sank onto the chair across from Sibby. "I don't know about a *tankard* but, yeah, pour me a double."

"IMP," I repeated. The word sat heavy on my tongue. I downed a generous gulp of Swedish sangria. The tart sweetness did nothing to wash away the unease twisting in my stomach. "I heard they've been spotted in town and in the Cairns."

Hilde nodded, patient as ever, despite this being the third—no, fourth—time she'd explained it. "I've heard that too. But don't you go worrying," she said. "Imps are nosy, but they ain't usually mean."

Sibby wrinkled her nose. "Curious and ugly. Like umpires."

I blinked. I'd never thought of umpires as particularly ugly. Or curious. But I let it slide.

"Imps love shiny things," Hilde continued, her voice steady. "They'll snatch up anything that sparkles. Jewelry, buttons, even your granny's good teacups if you ain't watchin'. Swamps 'round here been crawlin' with 'em since before I was born."

"So it could have just been curious," I said, grasping at hope. "Not actually trying to get inside the house?"

"It could have," Hilde admitted, though her expression darkened with thought. She perched on the edge of her recliner, fingers drumming against her knee.

"They usually stick to things left outside," Pye added from his perch on the mantle. "Not peeking in windows or rattling doorknobs."

"Unless..." Hilde's voice dropped and the candlelight flickered as if leaning in to listen. "Unless something—or someone — was pullin' its strings."

A hush settled over the room.

Sibby muttered something into her glögg.

Hilde frowned. "What's now?"

Sibby exhaled, her breath ghosting over the rim of her glass. "Just sayin', could be feeling the pull of the hag's power."

Imps. Phantasms. Creatures that thrived in the unseen corners of the swamps, slipping through shadows and stories more than through the town itself. So why now? Why were they stirring?

And perhaps more importantly—what did any of it have to do with Patch's murder?

I pulled the blanket tighter around my shoulders, my fingers pressing into the fabric as if I could hold onto something solid, something normal, something that wouldn't shift underfoot like everything else in Darkly seemed to be doing. But nothing happening in Darkly right now was normal—even by Darkly standards.

CHAPTER 5

*M*orning sunlight burned through the clinging fog, leaving the courtyard dappled in shifting gold. A floating fireball hovered just above the table, radiating enough heat to make the whole space feel downright tropical.

I unfolded *The Daily Shade*, letting my gaze drift over the top of the pages to my Great Aunt Sibella.

She was sprawled across one of the loungers, a silk sleep mask embroidered with two enormous, unblinking eyes covering her face. Her chest rose and fell with the soft rhythm of sleep. She looked as peaceful as a cat in a sunbeam—utterly unbothered by the fact that she'd just waltzed back into Darkly after forty-seven years of being "lost" in a jungle. Supposedly held captive. Supposedly escaping just in time for my grandmother's death.

Yeah, right. And I was the Queen of Mardi Gras.

I straightened, my fingers tightening on the paper. Was it possible she returned to claim Fernwood and the MET, knowing I was still finding my footing as a witch? The thought prickled. I shot her one last look, but she remained oblivious, snoring lightly beneath the unsettling stare of her embroidered mask.

I took a sip of chai, letting the spiced warmth settle in my chest before turning back to the newspaper. Patch Priddyholm's murder dominated the front page, bold ink stark against the thin, crinkling paper. I scanned the article quickly, searching for my own name—no mention, thank the spirits—before I went back to the top and read the entire article.

Stunned, I tossed the paper onto the metal table, the sound sharp against the hush of morning. "He did *not* trip and hit his head!" I shoved the offending article toward Hilde. "This reporter —Beatrice Snarkle—I can't believe she wrote that."

Hilde, ever unfazed, leaned over the water's edge and lobbed another thick slice of raw bacon to Greta Garbo. The massive alligator let out a pleased rumble, her scaly tail flicking as she swallowed the treat whole.

"Maybe that's what the new inspector told the reporter," Hilde mused, scratching the underside of Greta's jaw with surprising tenderness. "Tryin' to throw the murderer off their guard, y'know?"

"Hmm. Maybe." I flicked open the paper again, determined to ignore its nonsense.

From the lounger, Sibby stretched with a lazy sigh. "What's this now?"

Oh, and did I mention she was wearing a ridiculous Harry Styles flannel onesie? Because she absolutely was.

"A man was murdered yesterday," I said.

Sibby bolted upright, yanking the mask off her face. "Great jumping mudbugs! Here in Darkly?" Her sharp gaze landed on me. "Anyone I know?"

Hilde's eyes darted to mine for a second as if trying to convey a message I had no way of interpreting.

I exhaled. "The farmer who owned the local pumpkin farm."

Three things happened at once: Sibby shot to her feet, Hilde reached for her hand, and all three of us said in unison, "Patch Priddyholm."

"I'm sorry, Sibs," Hilde murmured. "I was gon' tell you after your mornin' nap."

I narrowed my eyes at her.

"Let me see that," Sibby said, snatching the paper from my hands with a speed that suggested a long-lost career in competitive snatching.

Her eyes darted across the page, her lips moving soundlessly. Then, with a small, strangled noise, she shook her head. "No, no, no. That can't be right. I just saw… This isn't true. It can't be."

"'Fraid it is," Hilde said, her usual gruff voice softened. "Windsor's the one found him."

Sibby turned to me, eyes searching. "You say he didn't trip. What happened?"

I hesitated at the intensity of her gaze, then told her about the drive to the pumpkin patch, how I'd first mistaken the shape on the ground for one of Patch's pumpkin-head workers—until I got closer.

"I don't know what killed him," I admitted, the memory curdling my stomach. "But it was like the pumpkin attached itself to his body. Over his head."

Sibby pressed a hand to her mouth, shaking her head. "I never thought—" Her voice drifted to a whisper.

Her reaction was strange, to say the least.

I studied her, suspicion curling in my gut. "I'm confused. You've been gone nearly fifty years. What relationship could you possibly still have with Patch Priddyholm?"

Sibby exhaled and dropped back onto the lounger, pulling the peculiar eye mask into place once more.

"We were engaged when I left for the Nymara Ormani Jungle," she murmured. "Planned to marry when I returned."

My thoughts scrambled. I stared at her, trying to reconcile what I knew about Patch Priddyholm, the jungle, and the woman now hiding under a pink silk mask embroidered with unsettlingly large eyes.

"Well, bless your heart and pickle me gin," I breathed, stunned.

~

"Can you slow down?" Pye grumbled, sinking deeper into the wicker basket attached to the front of my mint-green, vintage Schwinn. His golden eye peered up at me, glinting with pure feline exasperation. "I wish you'd never found this bloody contraption."

I grinned and pedaled faster. The wind rushed past, cool and crisp, carrying with it the faintest scent of woodsmoke and something sweet. Perhaps the promise of pumpkin spice yet to come.

"The fresh air is invigorating," I declared, lifting my face to the brilliant blue sky. "It's finally starting to feel like fall."

"The only fall I'm anticipating is mine—right out of this basket if you don't slow down!"

I relented, easing my pace. Pye had a flair for dramatics, but even he couldn't ruin the perfection of this morning. The sky was a rare, unmarred blue, so blue it looked conjured, not natural. It was the kind of day that made you grateful to be alive.

And just like that a shadow slid over my heart.

Patch.

Excitement over the change of season soured into something heavier, something tinged with loss. I swallowed against the sudden lump in my throat and rolled up to the entrance of the MET.

I opened the door with a flick of my wrist. The spell woven into the frame recognized me instantly. I wheeled the bike inside and ran a soothing hand over Pye's sleek black fur. He stretched and shook himself out of the basket.

"Fantastic job, Win. Not a single bump missed," he sniffed, his whiskers twitching.

"Oh, stop it."

"I mean it. One more minute, and I'd have redecorated that charming little basket with the remains of my breakfast." He made a gagging motion for good measure.

I ignored him and propped the bike against the front window.

"I'm heading to The Magic Cup for another chai," I announced, slinging my bag over my shoulder. "Wanna come?"

"Naturally," he purred, and I spread my bag wide so he could leap inside, curling up like the tiny, judgmental prince he was.

The streets of Darkly bustled with the usual motley assortment of citizens—witches in high-heeled boots, a shifter or two in half-human, half-animal form, and the occasional spectral figure flickering in and out of sight. The town pulsed with life, a swirl of magic and mischief under the dappled morning light.

The crowd carried me forward and spit me out in front of The Magic Cup's front door. The scent of roasted coffee and spiced tea enveloped me, rich and comforting. Tzazi's mom Azalea's brews were more than just delicious; they were imbued with enchantments, subtle and lingering. Even the air inside the café seemed to hum with warmth and well-being.

"Morning, hun!" came a familiar, bubbly voice from behind me.

I turned to find Jess, bright-eyed and effervescent as ever, a pink crocheted cardigan draped over a floral sundress. Practically bouncing on her toes, she threw her arms around me in a hug.

Beside her, Jaime lingered, all tousled red hair and easy charm. I managed a tight smile in his direction, still harboring resentment over his past allegiance to Solara Nova, Keir's insufferable ex. Did I want to hold a grudge? Not really. But was I capable? Absolutely.

"I love fall weather," Jess chirped, clutching her cardigan and shivering theatrically.

Jaime pulled her close, tucking her against his side with a protective arm. Perhaps I couldn't hate him entirely.

"It's a welcome break from the heat," I agreed. The transition from New York to Darkly's stifling humidity had been jarring. I'd long since learned to embrace the constant sheen of perspiration and stick to light cottons and linen like everyone else did.

Except for Solara. Of course, she remained flawless no matter the temperature. Her mother's goddess genes likely shielded her from such mundane inconveniences as heat and humidity.

A soft voice interrupted my thoughts. "Well, hello there, dear."

I turned to find Maybelle Hathaway ensconced at a table, her prim frame nestled into a velvet-cushioned wheelchair. Beside her sat her ever-dapper husband, Dewey, their longtime friend Conny Verity, and an unfamiliar dark-haired witch with a regal air. Dewey partnered with Tzazi at Hathaway & Strangeland, Esq., Darkly's one and only law firm.

Maybelle, Dewey, and Conny—white-haired, sharp-eyed, and infinitely nosy—were fixtures in Darkly, their presence as woven into the town's fabric as its moss-draped oaks.

"How are y'all?" I smiled, leaning down to hug Maybelle.

"Good, good, sugar," she chirped, her soft Southern drawl smooth as sweet tea on a sweltering afternoon. "Windsor, let me introduce you to one of Minta's dearest friends—Zephyra Nightshade. Zephy, I believe you know who this is."

"My, my," Zephy said, her voice rich and commanding, like a bass string plucked just right. "It is with great pleasure I make your acquaintance, Windsor."

"Likewise," I said, shaking her hand with a polite smile.

"Conny's been telling me how well you're fitting in," she said, lifting her mug with elegant fingers stacked in glittering rings, each one catching the light with every slight movement. "And rumor has it a certain well-regarded gentleman has taken quite the liking to you."

My brows shot up. "Conny!"

Conny laughed and flapped a hand. "Oh, honey. You know how things work around here. Everyone notices everything."

Ain't that the truth.

Zephy took a sip from her mug and smiled. "I'm rarely in town these days. Just here to finally collect my broom from Besoms & Britches. Mathilda makes a fine flyer, no doubt, but once she takes it in for a tune-up, you'd best find alternate transportation for at least a fortnight."

"Oh, don't I know it," Conny groaned and leaned back in her seat. "Mathilda's a perfectionist—bless her heart—but her idea of 'quick' is sometime next season. Had my broom in her shop for weeks last fall, and all it needed was one snapped twig replaced."

"You timed it right though, Zee," Maybelle added. "With the Eldritch Council on break right now."

"True," Zephy agreed. "And it gave me time to tend my garden instead of gallivanting around the island smoothing over some magical mishap after another."

The mental image of this stately woman gallivanting made me grin.

"Well, I won't keep you any longer, dear," Zephy said with a smile. She reached into a large, floral embroidered bag at her side, and a small furry head popped out, blinking up at me with comically large eyes.

"Is that a lemur?"

"Why, yes. This is Mouse. My familiar."

I stared. Mouse was, without question, the cutest little thing I'd ever seen.

Zephy pulled out a card and offered it to me. "Since I'm rarely in town, I hoped we might meet. I'm so delighted we did." Her eyes dipped briefly to the card. "I live in the hills above Strawbridge. If you're ever nearby, stop in. I'd love to visit with you."

A sharp EEP! sounded from the bag.

"Mouse concurs."

I glanced down at the card. Swirling, nonsensical script covered the surface. Just looking at it made my eyes blur.

Dewey leaned in, chuckling. "It's a magical calling card. When you're ready to visit Zephy, the script'll shift into a spell. Just say it aloud and it'll take you straight to Zephy's home."

Of course, it will.

I slipped the card into my bag and looked back at Zephy. "Same here."

"Before you go, Win..." Conny leaned forward, her blue eyes

twinkling with mischief. "Tell me, dear, is it true Sibella Ebonwood is back in town?"

The café fell into an abrupt, unnatural hush.

I glanced around. Every ear was tilted in my direction.

Jess, ever unfiltered, blurted out, "It is! Can you believe it?"

I nodded, my stomach twisting. "She showed up at Fernwood last night."

"Well, I'll be," Dewey murmured, his cane tapping rhythmically against the floor. "Ladies, I believe we should call on Miss Sibby this afternoon."

"Yes, yes, definitely," Conny agreed. "Thank you for confirming, dear. That is very good news."

From the reactions around me, Sibella Ebonwood was well-loved, almost revered. But I couldn't shake the feeling that something about her didn't sit right. She was hiding something. Of that, I was certain.

Azalea's rich, silken voice brought me back to the present.

"Jess. Win. Jaime. How are you?"

Her gaze flicked briefly between Jess and Jaime, sharp and assessing. A skill I'd seen Tzazi use often. Today Azalea wore her bronze braids pulled back from her face and a short-sleeved caftan that flowed and fluttered around her.

"The usuals for all?" she asked.

Pye's head popped up from my bag. "One sprinkle today," he declared. "I feel like being adventurous."

I shook my head at my spoiled and demanding cat and placed our orders.

But Patch's death kept pressing at the back of my mind. I couldn't shake the image of him lying in the pumpkin field. Then there was the imp in the window last night. That gruesome grin was going to haunt me for a while.

A soft paw smacked my wrist, yanking me from my thoughts. Pye stared up at me, full of judgment and thirst, like I'd made him wait an eternity.

Azalea slid our drinks across the counter.

"Have a nice day, sugar," she said, already turning to the next customer.

I murmured my thanks, but my mind was elsewhere.

I kept thinking about Chase and the phantasm outside his salon. Could there be a connection between the swamp creatures drifting into town and Patch's death?

Because if there was one thing I had learned since arriving in Darkly, it was that nothing—absolutely nothing—was ever as it seemed.

CHAPTER 6

The Magic Cup's outdoor courtyard was a pocket of old-world charm, tucked away from the bustle of Tataille Street by an ironwork fence draped in bougainvillea. Cool air, touched by the fading fog and the faint crispness of fall, carried the scent of roasted chicory. It mingled with the clink of porcelain, the occasional trill of wind chimes, and the soft bubbling of the courtyard's central fountain.

Jess, Jaime, and I threaded our way through the courtyard until we reached our usual spot—three wrought-iron tables shoved together in a haphazard but familiar way. Tzazi, Chase, and Ren were already there lounging languidly in their seats, their conversation punctuated by the occasional sip of coffee and amused glances. After pressing quick kisses to Chase and Ren's cheeks, I slid into my seat across from Tzazi. Pyewacket hopped onto the table with slow, deliberate grace. His eye fixed on me expectantly.

I set his tiny cat-cup of steamed almond milk in front of him. He lapped at it with the air of a nobleman sampling the finest vintage.

Tzazi leaned forward, resting her chin in her hand. "Any updates on Patch's murder?"

"Nothing but the usual drivel from that hack reporter at *The Shade*, Beatrice Snarkle," I said, exhaling a sharp breath. "Hilde thinks the authorities might be leaking misinformation to the media in hopes of throwing the killer off balance."

Jess nodded. "Could be."

"I'd really like to find out who was there with him that morning. Patch felt comfortable enough with them to bring out his best whiskey." I relaxed into my chair and took a sip of my chai latte, breathing in the comforting scents of cloves, vanilla, and that special something Azalea served up in her brews.

Tzazi's cup hit the table with a clatter. "I can help you there. Dewey was the person drinking with Patch that morning."

I blinked. "Mr. Hathaway?"

Chase let out a soft, incredulous laugh. "Honey, don't even go there. Dewey Hathaway wouldn't kill a man unless there was a breach of contract involved. And even then, he'd do it through a very thorough and legally airtight loophole."

"No, no. Of course not," Tzazi said, waving a hand as if to brush away the absurdity of it all. "He was there to drop off a copy of Patch's new will. Shared a bourbon while he was there." She thought for moment. "Dewey's rattled but trying not to show it."

Ren tapped his fingers against his cup, his voice thoughtful but even. "A changed will could give someone a motive if they were left out."

"Or left in," Chase said, raising an eyebrow.

Ren nodded. "Fair point. Either way, we'll have our very own royal inspector soon. Maybe they can make sense of it."

"Speaking of. Ran into Delilah Rageheart this morning," Chase drawled, lounging back with the ease of a man born to sip expensive whiskey on wraparound porches. "She was downright swooning over Darkly's new royal inspector sent over by the MEA. Said he had 'quite the presence.' She's beside herself with admiration, bless her heart."

"You remember Delilah, right, Win?" Tzazi asked.

How could I forget? "The woman who worked for Boddy in the Sheriff's Department."

"That's the one."

Ren drummed his fingers against his coffee cup. "So, does that mean the Sheriff's Department is now the Royal Inspector's Department?"

I lifted a hand. "Hold up. Y'all forget I'm new to this world. What exactly is the MEA, and why does a 'royal inspector' sound like something out of a Regency novel?"

Chase grinned. "First of all, congratulations on properly using *y'all*. That's a big step." He high-fived me before continuing. "MEA—Magical Enforcement Agency. Think of it as the supernatural FBI. And royal inspectors are their elite detectives. Best of the best."

I frowned. "And one of them just happened to be assigned to Darkly? Seems like overkill for a small island town." Of course, considering the body count since I'd moved here, maybe I shouldn't have said that out loud.

Ren shifted uncomfortably. "Might have something to do with the trial tomorrow." His voice was quieter now, and he reached over to squeeze Jess's hand.

Silence settled over us like a town in the eye of a hurricane.

"Now, that's a good point," I said, also turning to Jess. "With a bit of luck, maybe this inspector will grab up what's-her-name and her shyster lawyer and drag them back to the Isles."

"Now that would be nice, wouldn't it?" Jess smiled tightly, obviously worried about the outcome of the trial.

"You ready for tomorrow, hun? You know we'll all be there for you," Chase said, patting Jess's hand.

Tzazi smacked the table. "Damn right, she's ready. If there's one thing I enjoy, it's putting a sleazy lawyer in his place. Well, that and getting justice, of course."

Jess let out a tight smile. "I just want it over with. I dread my life with Brychen being laid bare for everyone to turn into town gossip. It's tough enough being a widow without this uncertainty hanging over my head."

Chase sighed, shaking his head. "You know how Darkly is, *chère*. Folks here don't just love gossip, they thrive on it. And if they don't know the truth, well, they'd sooner spin a scandal than let a story go untold. At least this way, you get to set the record straight."

"Exactly," Tzazi agreed. "Now, as I was—"

Her eyes flicked over my shoulder, and she went very still. For a second, I thought she was ill, but then a slow, mischievous grin curled her lips.

Oh, no. I did *not* like that look.

A warm presence hovered just behind me, close enough that I felt the heat of it against my shoulder. I turned to find Keir standing there, his dark hair falling into his eyes, that wolfish grin of his firmly in place.

"Morning, love." His voice was low, the Scottish lilt rich and lulling. "What's this about a scandal then?"

"We were telling Jess we'd all be there for her tomorrow. For the trial," I said, determined to ignore the way my pulse had kicked up.

"Aye. As will I." His gaze flickered toward Jess, a shadow passing through his eyes. Guilt. I knew he still blamed himself, even if none of this was his fault. "It'll turn out in your favor, Jess. Yeh've got the best attorney on the island."

Tzazi beamed. "Not exactly a secret, but thanks for the endorsement."

Chase rolled his eyes, and we all groaned.

I took a sip of my latte. "Listen, Keir, I wanted to talk to you about Patch—"

Before I could finish, Keir cleared his throat and stepped aside. Only then did I notice Quinn, his beta, at his side along with a man in a blue pin-striped suit standing directly behind him.

"I want to introduce yeh to our new inspector sent over from the Isles," Keir said, his tone neutral.

The stranger stepped forward, and the sight of him nearly made me choke on my drink.

"Windsor Ebonwood," he said, his voice warm and familiar. "As soon as I heard I was transferring to Darkly Island, I looked forward to seeing you again."

Keir stiffened beside me, and I swore the air around us dropped a few degrees.

I blinked. "Ransom?"

His smile widened as he extended a hand to me. But I slid mine away when the inspector bent to kiss it. A little jealousy was one thing, but I didn't need Keir thinking there was anything between us.

I glanced at Tzazi who was giving a winning impression of the cat that got the cream.

"It's good to see you," I finally stuttered.

Tzazi, Jess, and I met Ransom Belleclaire and a friend of his on a weekend shopping trip to Cradlerock a few weeks ago. Turned out, he and his family were good friends with Tzazi's family members in New Orleans.

Ransom straightened and waved to Jess and Tzazi. "Hi, Jess. Tzazi."

Keir, clearly flustered, composed himself. "Well, for anyone who *doesn't* know the inspector, this is Ransom Belleclaire, the royal inspector assigned to Darkly Island."

Chase leaned back in his seat, a casual hand stirring the tea before him. "I'm sure we can round up some chairs, if y'all'd like to take a seat."

"Thanks, Chase, but we're heading out to the pumpkin farm so Belleclaire can see the scene of the murder."

Ransom turned to me. "I understand you found the body. I'll need to talk to you later."

"Of course. I'll be at the MET the rest of the day."

Keir squeezed my shoulder, giving me a questioning look, and the men left the courtyard, passing Solara and Elspeth who hovered near the exit. Solara took a step toward Keir but he ignored her as the men strode out to Keir's Land Rover waiting at the curb.

Tzazi laughed. "Well, that was awkward."

"Tzazi! Only because you didn't warn me."

"I did warn you," Tzazi said. "I smirked."

"A smirk is not a warning!"

Tzazi shrugged and took a big gulp of her coffee, still grinning.

Chase, ever the dramatist, sucked in a breath. "Win, you scoundrel. You never told us you had a history with the new inspector. I am miffed. No. More than miffed. I am devastated. I can't believe you kept this to yourself!"

I groaned. "I didn't know! And just to set things straight, we don't have a history."

Jess laughed. "Well, he *was* interested. You just didn't notice."

Chase wagged a finger at me. "How could you have not noticed that man?"

I scowled and swatted his finger away. "Ransom and I are just friends. We talked to him for all of two minutes."

Tzazi snorted into her coffee. "Try two hours at The Drunken Gull. We had quite a few eelgrass elixirs that day."

Ren leaned in, amused. "You have to admit, it's rather interesting that he's suddenly transferred to Darkly."

I ignored their friendly jabs, but they did have a point. Was it coincidence Ransom had transferred to Darkly?

CHAPTER 7

*W*hen Pyewacket and I returned to the MET, we found the storefront transformed into a celebration of autumn. Two grand urns flanked the weathered wooden entrance, spilling over with gold and rust-colored chrysanthemums, their spicy scent wafting through the crisp air.

I pushed open the door and let out an unabashed squeal of delight. Everywhere, small tables held artful displays of gourds, squash, and Indian corn, their jewel-toned colors deepening the cozy charm of the shop. Twinkle lights draped the stained-glass windows. A bouquet of chrysanthemums, lush and radiant, sat on the front counter in a misted gold vase. Above it, the antique, gilt-edged mirror hung heavy on the wall, catching the blooms' golden light and scattering it in delicate prisms across the room.

With the burst of autumn hues and the peppery sweetness in the air, the MET was perfectly fall-ish.

"But how?"

I picked up a card propped up on the counter.

Win,

You said you were fine.

But just in case—

– K

A tight ache rose in my chest, the kind that made breathing feel like work, and tears sprang to my eyes. No one had ever done something so thoughtful…so meaningful for me before.

I stood there a moment, letting the familiar scent of parchment and musty books, mingling with the spicy scent of the mums, settle me. Then I tossed my bag onto the shelf behind the counter, rolled up my sleeves, and got to work straightening books, dusting shelves, and absorbing the peaceful lull before the inevitable arrival of travelers.

Pyewacket grunted and vanished into the stacks.

I never knew when a traveler would arrive in Darkly, or how. Some materialized as though stepping from the folds of a story, fully formed. Others wavered on the edges of existence until, bit by bit, they became whole.

Mizizi, Tzazi's grandfather and a renowned voodoo priest, created and maintained the protective wards around Darkly, including the MET. I'd learned to watch for his shadowmen. Their frantic, fluttering chaos always signaled an impending arrival. The first time it happened, I nearly jumped out of my skin. Thankfully, the traveler had been a kindly old woman, a friend of Conny and Maybelle. Otherwise, I might have karate chopped her straight into next week.

Not all visitors set foot in the MET at all, though. Some simply blinked into existence elsewhere on the island, drawn to whatever place had summoned them through their book.

And yet, for all my encounters with book portals, I had never used one myself. Not because I was afraid. Okay, fine, that might have been a lie. The idea of an enchanted book unraveling me into a thousand wisps of magic and flinging me across reality made my skin crawl. But lately, the itch to try had been creeping up my spine, whispering to me.

Maybe soon.

I hopped onto the stool behind the counter, cradling the note card in my hand. Pyewacket, emerging from his nap, stretched luxuriously before giving me a pointed stare with his bright, unblinking eye. "I suppose it's time to visit the cemetery?"

I nodded. "You don't have to come if you'd rather not."

He yawned, slow and deliberate. "Of course, I'm coming. But I do require a moment to fully wake, if you don't mind."

Every month, I made a quiet pilgrimage to the Ebonwood mausoleum, carrying flowers for my mother and grandmother. It was a way to feel close to them, these women who had shaped my fate yet remained strangers to me.

Pyewacket stretched again, a long, dramatic extension of tiny limbs. He lifted each leg one by one, then yawned a second time for good measure.

I examined the imaginary wristwatch on my arm.

"Don't rush perfection, love," he murmured, extending a final, theatrical stretch.

"Pye."

"All right, all right." With a flick of his tail, he leaped into my bag and I slung it over my shoulder.

I bid farewell to the shadowmen (I never knew if they could hear or even understand what I said to them, but it felt rude not to do so) and twirled my wrist, sending a ripple through the wards to signal my departure before closing the MET's door behind me.

The Darkly cemetery loomed across the cobbled street, its iron gates wrapped in fragrant star jasmine and its ancient oaks draped in the silvered lace of Spanish moss. A stone and wrought iron fence encircled the graveyard where, at its heart, the cursed bell tower stood rigid and solemn. Its slate roof rose above the foliage of the giant magnolia and the twisted oak like a watchful sentinel.

I stepped into Oopsy Daisies, greeted by the soft chime of bells and the heady scent of blooming magic. The tiny shop brimmed with color—blush roses, golden marigolds, deep indigo violets—all humming with the faintest pulse of enchantment. At the counter, Dianthe Petalsigh, the ever-bubbly sprite, perched on a stool, her gossamer wings fluttering as she arranged a handful of fire lilies.

"I was just thinking about you, Windsor," she said, flashing a smile.

She slid two massive bouquets of forget-me-nots from a rack on the wall, their tiny blue blossoms glowing faintly, like they'd caught the memory of starlight. A delicate fragrance rose from them wistful and sweet and I drew in a big whiff. Each bundle was wrapped in a pale ribbon as soft and sheer as spun moonlight.

With my flowers in hand and Dianthe's magic lingering in the air, I stepped back into the cobbled streets of Darkly and walked towards the hushed, timeworn cemetery looming ahead. The wrought iron gate was cool beneath my fingertips when I pushed it open.

Stepping into Darkly Cemetery always felt like slipping between worlds. Light filtered through the dense canopy of gold and red and cast flickering patterns across the tombstones. The enchanted angel statue twirled among the graves, pausing only long enough to offer a cheerful wave before pirouetting into the trees.

Since my last visit, the cemetery had grown wilder. Vines curled hungrily; flowers bloomed in unexpected places; nature reclaimed what was hers. I loved it. It made the place feel more alive.

Pye and I wound our way toward my family's mausoleum, passing the tower's weathered stone. No one I'd asked remembered the origins of its curse, though many had tried to remove it, even my grandmother Minta. None had succeeded.

Passing the tower entrance, I meandered back to the far side of the cemetery nestled against the Darkly swamps where the Ebonwood family mausoleum stood. I pushed open the metal doors. Their groan echoed in the cool chamber. Inside, tree branches arched overhead, forming a living ceiling. The tombs of my ancestors rested on raised platforms on both sides, white columns separating the lower vestibule from their eternal slumber. The two newest sat at the back, each at the end of a row of tombs.

I placed one bouquet on my mother's tomb, then crossed to my grandmother's, placing the other atop the smooth granite. My fingers traced the carved edges of the marble statue standing in between the two tombs—a witch holding a book with sprouting wings.

I then settled onto the cold stone bench below. Pyewacket curled in my lap with a low purr.

Then—movement. A flicker of something just out of sight.

Before I could react, something small and sharp struck my cheek.

I turned, arms raised to protect my face.

Another hit my arm, bouncing onto the floor with a soft clatter.

Pebbles.

Someone was throwing pebbles at me.

I shot to my feet. "Who's doing that?"

A figure emerged—or rather, floated—before me.

A young man in a black shirt and green cargo pants, red curls haloing his head, hovered just above the ground. His Doc Martens didn't so much as stir the dust.

I folded my arms. "Who are you, and what are you doing in my family's mausoleum?"

He cocked his head. "You're an Ebonwood?"

I gave him an exasperated look. "Obviously. Why else would I be in here?"

He grinned. "I'm not an Ebonwood, and yet, here I am."

Pyewacket snickered. "I like this guy."

I sighed.

After Pye and the young man got over their team laughing fit, the man floated closer to me and stuck out a hand. As he drew nearer, I saw he couldn't have been much out of his teen years.

"Twitch Houlihan, at your service. And, to answer your

question, I'm here because your mausoleum is the nicest in the cemetery." He wrinkled his nose. "Ours is a little crowded."

I shook his hand, eyeing him warily. "Lovely to meet you, Mr. Houlihan, truly, but this is a private moment, so why don't you just...skedaddle?" I shooed him with my hand.

Pye gasped. "Oh, now you've done it. Never, ever antagonize a poltergeist," he hissed.

I went still. "He's a poltergeist?"

Twitch grinned wider. "Oh, this is going to be fun."

Before I could fully process the gravity of my mistake, Twitch spun into a blur, whirling through the mausoleum in a streak of color and mischief. A sudden gust of spectral wind tousled my hair before he stopped inches from my face, jabbing a translucent finger at my chest.

"I was here first, so why don't *you* just skedaddle! And take that little mutant cat with you!"

Pye's fur bristled. "Hey, mate! What did I ever do to you?" He rose up on his hind legs, claws extended, swiping at the ghost as Twitch darted effortlessly out of range.

I sighed, rubbing my temples. "You know what? Stay. Go. Rattle some chains. Stack some chairs. I really don't care."

Twitch grinned. "Great! I'm glad we came to an agreement." With a theatrical bow, he vanished through the mausoleum doors, narrowly avoiding another swipe from Pyewacket.

I flopped back onto the cold stone bench, dropping my head into my hands. "Can this day get any weirder?"

Pyewacket stiffened. "Don't say that!" he screeched. "Don't ever, ever say that!"

I ran a soothing hand down his soft fur, feeling his tiny body vibrate with nerves. My gaze drifted back to my grandmother's tomb, unease coiling in my stomach. She left me with so many questions, questions I should have asked when I had the chance. The night she visited me as an apparition, I had been too overwhelmed to think straight. Now, all I had were mysteries and a silence that stretched on for eternity.

From my pocket, I pulled out the key, scratched, tarnished and heavy with questions. "Why did you give me this, Grandmother?" I whispered again, just as I had a dozen times already. And, once again, no answer came.

At my mother's crypt, I pressed my palm to the cold stone. The surface was smooth, unyielding. For a long moment, I stood still, willing some kind of connection. A sign that this legacy didn't begin and end with me.

Pyewacket wove himself around my ankles.

I scooped him up, nuzzling my face into his warm fur. "You do have a way of making me feel better."

"Naturally," he said, his voice softened slightly.

"But I could do without the ego."

"As if you could separate one from the other," he sniffed, leaping gracefully from my arms.

With a final glance at my mother's crypt, we stepped out of the mausoleum. We strolled slowly toward the entrance. The weight of unanswered questions pressed on my shoulders.

Then, just as we passed the bell tower, I heard it. The distant, rhythmic cadence of children's voices—singing. Laughter, high and sweet, punctuated the strange melody.

I stopped. "Do you hear that?"

Pyewacket's ears twitched. "This way." He took a sharp right, disappearing into a part of the cemetery I'd never explored.

Carefully pushing aside the sprawling, thorny branches of a bougainvillea vine, I found them.

Three little girls. A jump rope swinging in hypnotic arcs.

The one in the center looked vaguely familiar.

I listened, frowning. "What in the world are they singing?"

Pyewacket sat beside me, tail flicking. "The Ballad of Killer Katey."

I gave him a flat look. "You say that like it's normal."

"It *is* normal," he said. "Jump rope songs are everywhere."

"Not ones about a 'vile and vicious foe.' That seems too intense for children."

Pye shrugged and pounced on a swirling leaf as it floated to the ground. "You don't think the Lizzie Borden rhyme is a bit intense?"

"Touché."

The jumping girl suddenly caught sight of me, her bright face lighting up.

"Miss Windsor!" she cried, abandoning the rope and dashing toward me.

Recognition clicked into place. Bettina Starles. She'd brought me a welcome gift when I first moved to Darkly. Granted, it was a mud pie, but it's the thought that counts, right?

I stepped forward. "Hi, Bettina. How are you?"

"I'm wonderful, Miss Windsor!"

"And your mother?"

Her smile faltered. "Um. She's okay."

Bettina inhaled deeply, then forced brightness back into her voice. "Did you come to watch me jump rope?" She giggled, pushing a stray bow out of her face.

I hadn't meant to upset her. "You bet. That was some fancy footwork you were showing off."

"Oh, good! Come meet my friends."

Before I could protest, she grabbed my hand and dragged me toward the other girls.

"Miss Windsor, this is Takota and Cherish. This is Miss Windsor." Then, in a stage whisper, she added, "Miss Minta was her grandmother. But don't say anything, so she's not sad."

The two girls nodded solemnly.

Bettina clapped her hands. "Ready to hear our jump rope song?"

"Of course. Right, Pyewacket?" I said sitting on a concrete bench under a magnolia.

"I'd rather be at the dentist getting my teeth cleaned," Pyewacket groused.

"He says he'd like nothing better."

The girls proudly moved into their positions, as if on a stage rather than in an overgrown cemetery. As Bettina hopped into the swinging jump rope, the girls began to chant:

> *"One, two, Katey flew.*
> *With her broomstick, evil grew.*
> *Three, four, higher they soared,*
> *Nanny's pleas and screams ignored.*
> *Five, six, darkness surrounds,*
> *Katey's cackle, haunting sounds.*
> *Seven, eight, a lug she'll yank,*
> *Nanny's end, so vile and rank."*

The sing-song voices sent a shiver down my spine as I watched the girls jump rope to the tale of Killer Katey.

> *"Nine, ten, a vicious foe,*
> *A chilling fiend, a tale of woe.*
> *Katey, with your deathly skill,*
> *How many nannies did you kill?"*

"Witchfire whip! Witchfire whip!" the girls shouted in unison, and the rope snapped into a faster tempo, humming with each turn.

The jump rope kept flying as the girls counted, higher and higher, until Bettina stumbled against the rope and leaped out of its way, sending a flurry of brown leaves spinning into the air.

Cherish and Takota yelled, "Katey got you!"

Then came the laughter, high, breathless, and wild.

I swallowed. "Who is Killer Katey?"

"You don't know about Killer Katey?" The girls looked at me as if I'd suddenly grown a third arm.

I almost laughed at their shocked responses. "Not until today."

Bettina turned to the tallest of the three, a pretty girl with red ringlets surrounding her head. "You tell it, Takota. You're the oldest."

"Well," the girl began, tossing back a curl, obviously enjoying the attention. "Katey was a little girl who lived in the Charming Isles. Her parents divorced and she lived with her father in a castle. She was very spoiled."

"That's not how it goes," Cherish frowned. "Her daddy ran away. That's why she was angry and sad all the time. And poor. She didn't have a nanny, just a babysitter."

"Not everyone would be sad if their dad ran away," Bettina whispered. I noted her sad face. She looked up at me and her face lit up in a smile when she caught me watching her. It broke my heart that Bettina, at her young age, seemed to have already learned to cover her feelings.

"No. I know she was rich because she had a nanny," Takota insisted, feeling she had gotten the upper hand with that bit of analysis.

"Why don't we agree that she was spoiled and leave it at that?" I said. "Does that work for both of you?"

"Fine," both girls agreed.

Takota straightened her back once more. "As I was saying before I was so rudely interrupted..."

Cherish rolled her eyes.

"...Not only was Katey spoiled, but she was also a really good flyer."

Takota put her hands on her hips and turned to Cherish. "Do you have anything to add?"

"No, you've got that part right. Katey could do ten loop-de-loops in the air, one after the other."

Bettina laughed as Cherish turned to me. "Katey competed in the Hexathlon Games."

I cocked my eye at Pye, not wanting to interrupt the girls.

"Like your Olympics, but on brooms," he whispered.

"One day, her *father*," Takota continued, emphasizing the word for Cherish's benefit," left her with a *nanny*—"

"Babysitter," Cherish uttered under her breath.

"Katey wanted candy, but it was too close to dinner and the *nanny* said no," Takota continued. "Katey got mad, grabbed the nanny, and took her high in the sky on her broom."

I leaned toward Pyewacket. "Is this real?"

His whiskers twitched. "Oh, it's real."

"What happened next?" I asked Takota.

"Katey pushed her off the broom!"

CHAPTER 8

I stepped out of the cool hush of the cemetery and onto Tataille Street headed for the MET. Pyewacket trotted at my heels, his tail flicking in time with my steps. "Bettina's jump rope rhyme has me thinking, Pye," I mused.

His ears twitched. "What? You want to drop me off the roof of the MET? I protest! I despair! I shall flee with all the chess pie!"

"Oh my gosh, so dramatic! No, silly. I just think it would be nice to be able to fly. Everyone else does. Tzazi. Jess."

"Oh, yes. That's everyone."

"Besides, can I really call myself a witch if I don't have a flying broom?"

"Just because you own a tennis ball doesn't mean you're Serena Williams."

I squinted at him. "What are you trying to say?"

"Nothing at all. Oi, heads up. Beefcake incoming at three o'clock."

I hadn't even begun to make sense of that before a deep, unmistakable voice called my name.

"Win!"

I turned to find Ransom Belleclaire striding toward me, looking as if he'd stepped straight out of a tailor's dream. His blue three-piece suit hugged him in all the right places, and his sandy blond hair gleamed in the afternoon sun.

"Hi, Ransom." I put my hands on my hips. "What can I do for you?"

"Glad I caught you," he said, the easy smile not quite reaching his sharp detective eyes. "Do you have a few minutes?"

"Of course," I said, opening the MET's front door with a flick of my wrist. "I take it this isn't a neighborly visit?"

He sighed. "I wish it were."

Inside, I waved him toward the cushy chairs by the fireplace. "Tea?"

"Please."

A gentle puff of steam curled upward as two cups of tea materialized on the table, their floral scent mingling with the crisp air.

Pyewacket made himself comfortable in Ransom's lap, purring shamelessly while getting his ears scratched. Sometimes Pye was utterly brazen.

"Smart, demanding, and always in charge. What's not to admire?" Ransom chuckled.

"I told you this man had excellent taste," Pye purred, throwing me a self-assured glance, which I ignored.

I handed Ransom a cup of my special Earl Grey blend before curling up in the chair across from him. I swirled my finger over my tea, stirring the sugar cubes in with a whisper of magic.

"So," I said, taking a sip. "What's on your mind?"

Ransom's expression turned serious. He set Pye on the floor and pulled out a leather notepad. "Can you walk me through what you saw from the moment you arrived at Shadow Pumpkin Farm until you found Mr. Priddyholm's body?"

I nodded and recounted everything. My drive along Coastal Road, the odd silence when I arrived, the way the farmhouse felt not right.

"And you didn't see anyone? Not even on the road?"

I watched fascinated while his notepad automatically filled

with words. "Not a soul," I said, then glanced at Pye. "What about you?"

Pyewacket stretched, then flicked his tail. "Didn't see anyone. But we *were* being watched while we were in the cottage."

"Oh, right." I turned to Ransom. "We both got the sense someone else was there when we first entered Patch's home."

Ransom looked up. "But you saw no one."

I shook my head. "No one."

Ransom's examined his notes. "And inside it looked like he'd been meeting with someone?"

"Dewey Hathaway. He had a drink with Patch that morning when he dropped off Patch's new will."

Ransom's eyebrows lifted slightly, but he didn't comment.

"And did you notice—" I continued "—how Patch's head was *inside* the pumpkin? He didn't just fall onto it. It was stuck. Like the heads of those creepy scarecrow workers."

Ransom's lips tightened, but he said nothing, just took a slow sip of tea, weighing my words, clearly unconvinced.

"Win, I observed no such thing," he finally said with a weary sigh. "The body I saw had no pumpkin attached to it. Which is why I'm inclined to believe this was an unfortunate magical accident."

I snapped my head toward him. "But—"

Ransom lifted a finger. "Patch was using magic to move his prize pumpkins, wasn't he? Boddy said the entire farm was thick with enchantments. If his magic faltered, a giant pumpkin could have fallen onto his head and, due to whatever spell he'd cast, temporarily…adhered."

I chewed my lip, mulling it over. "I suppose that's…maybe… sort of…plausible."

Ransom set his notepad aside with a measured nod. "It's tragic, yes. But at this point, all signs point to an accident."

He took another sip. "This is delicious. Your blend?"

I nodded, still distracted by his conclusion. "Um. It's a special Earl Gray blend Azalea makes for me."

Ransom stood. "I appreciate you making time."

"Of course."

I wanted to believe Ransom, that Patch's death was simply a horrible accident. But as he smiled and made his way to the door, I couldn't shake the feeling that someone in Darkly was getting away with murder.

Ransom paused, running a hand through his hair. "One thing. You and Bane. Are you…together?"

Pye's ears perked. "Ooooh, I *knew* it."

I attempted to nudge him with my foot, but he nimbly sidestepped.

"Yes," I said, folding my arms. "For a few months now."

Ransom nodded. "Bane's a good man." He opened the door and then lingered for a beat. "Well then. I'll let you know if I have any more questions."

With a quick wave, he crossed Tataille and disappeared behind the cemetery's wrought-iron gates.

Pye peered up at me. "Wow. So much to unpack. First—do you believe Patch managed to gourd his own noggin?"

"Nope," I said. "Not at all."

"Second—I'm telling Keir," he said in a sing-song voice, bobbing his head from side-to-side.

"Oh, that's real mature. Hungry?"

"Starving."

"C'mon. My treat."

"Naturally."

AFTER STUFFING ourselves at the Gator, Pye and I meandered back toward the MET, the warmth of the afternoon sun lifting the chill still sifting through the air. I raised my hand to unlace the major wards when—

"WIN! WINDSOR EBONWOOD!"

A voice, deep and gravelly like a five-pack-a-day smoker, stopped me in my tracks.

Next door, Mathilda Broomthistle flapped her arms wildly in front of Besoms & Britches, reminding me of a crow flying through a storm.

"You deaf, girl? I'm talkin' to you!" she squawked, a gleam of mischief in her dark eyes.

Behind her, a display of brooms swayed in the faint breeze, each one adorned with elements of nature—twining ivy, dangling shells, humming cicadas, and in her hands, a broom spilling over with crimson flowers.

"Those are gorgeous," I said, gazing at the display and inhaling the soft, sweet scent curling through the air.

"Bougainvillea. Plumeria. Oleander," Mathilda replied, lifting the red star-shaped cluster of blooms into the air. "Hardy, fragrant. Some of the most beloved flowers on the island."

She adjusted the blooms a bit more, then nestled the broom back among its enchanted kin, its ruby-red petals blending seamlessly into the vibrant, untamed display.

"Now tell me, when were you planning to come see me?" Her dark eyes twinkled. "You don't have a besom yet, do you?"

I blinked at the brooms in the display. "One of these? They're much too pretty for sweeping."

Mathilda barked out a laugh, deep and delighted. "Oh, honey, these aren't for cleaning floors. These are for flyin'."

She leaned in, her scent a curious mix of wet leaves, fresh air, and a tart sweetness, like gooseberries. "My besoms are the best in the Isles. Strongest. Fastest. Prettiest. And perfectly suited to their witch."

I shot Pye a glance. "I was just saying this morning it was time I got a flying broom."

Mathilda nodded sagely. "I had a feelin'."

She leaned even closer, lowering her voice. "And they're called besoms, sugar. Brooms are for mortals. Besoms are for witches."

"What do you think?" I asked my snarky familiar as he gazed longingly at a besom covered in tiny hummingbirds.

He sighed. "Can it be any worse than riding that bicycle with you every morning? Wait—don't answer that."

Mathilda tugged on her ear and gestured to the shop. "Why don't you come take a gander?"

We followed Mathilda inside and my jaw dropped. Besoms hung or lay on every available space. Each one unique and utterly gorgeous. Flows of magic pulsated through the room in rhythmic beats. Only a few months ago, I would never have noticed. Now it called to me like a siren's song.

I stepped toward a besom with golden apricots sprouting from its leafy wooden shaft. Honeybees buzzed lazily in the light pink blossoms twining in and out of the bristles poking out at the end of the shaft.

I cupped one of the fruits in my hand. "Are these real?"

"Of course," Mathilda said. "And watch out for those bees. Their stingers are quite real too."

Removing my hand, I gazed around. Besoms with shells, roses, live animals, sea coral, and dozens of other objects covered the walls and shelves. A counter ran along the back of the shop beyond where a young woman stood behind a wooden table, a bare besom before her, its knotty shaft twisted and gnarled.

I looked around in awe. "I've never seen anything like this. These brooms—"

"Besoms," Mathilda corrected me sternly.

I nodded. "—besoms are beautiful. But what are the britches for?"

"Why, flying pants, of course."

"Ah. Of course."

Mathilda gave me a gentle push. "Just remember. A besom chooses its witch. Not the other way around. Walk around. See what happens. I'll be back in the workshop, if you need me."

Mathilda vanished and reappeared next to the girl behind the counter.

"This is my assistant, Fara Boughweaver." The girl smiled and waved. "She can assist you if I'm not around."

I waved back and then wandered through the maze of besoms, running my hands along any besom that drew my interest. I saw besoms decorated with twirling ivy and blooming flowers. Others with strings of shells draping from the handle. Tiny red and black ladybugs flew in circles around another.

Then—a tug. A pull deep in my chest, demanding my attention.

My heartbeat raced and I felt a surge of excitement as I reached into the dark recesses of a lower shelf and carefully slid out the green handle of a besom.

A quiet "Oh" escaped my lips.

Mathilda materialized at my side. "I thought you'd like that one."

The besom lifted slightly, hovering like an obedient dog.

"And, apparently, it likes you too."

I'd never seen a more exquisite work of art. I ran my hand along its braided shaft and tiny ferns burst forth at my touch, unfurling in greeting. Orchids cascaded down the bristles in delicate sweeps of white and magenta. Gold and silver charms jingled softly beneath the bristles, and at its tip, a vibrant blue dragonfly perched like a living hood ornament.

"What beautiful orchids!"

"Recruited from the Darkly Swamp behind your house," Mathilda murmured. "Do you not recognize them?"

What a strange question. "Should I?"

"Never mind, dear," she said, a flicker of surprise passing across her face. "Every witch has a very special relationship with their besom. Your besom is your closest companion, next to your familiar, of course." She gave Pyewacket a scratch under his chin. "Wanna take her for a spin?"

I backed up like she'd suggested jumping into an active volcano. "Oh, no. No, no."

Mathilda clicked her tongue. "Well, why else would you get a besom if not to ride? Don't worry. You'll be fine."

She turned to Fara, her assistant. "I'll be right back, dear. Say, when do you think you'll have Antigone's besom ready?"

The girl shrugged. "Before the end of the day. The starfish keep arguing over placement. We're negotiating."

Mathilda laughed. "Yes, they are impossibly competitive." She turned to me. "Living beings are only enchanted with their agreement, but that doesn't promise they'll be easy to work with."

She led Pye and me outside to a hidden courtyard, surrounded by thick bushes bursting with bright red blooms. The besom hovered expectantly.

I backed up to sling my leg over the handle.

Mathilda rolled her eyes. "Oh, for heaven's sake. Sidesaddle, like a proper lady. She'll compensate for your weight and movement."

My face flushed as red as the blooms bursting through the green foliage.

I settled onto the braided staff of the besom, half expecting it to feel like a high school bleacher—hard, unforgiving, and not made for comfort. Instead, it was like sitting in one of the cozy plush chairs at Fernwood.

My delight must have shown on my face.

Mathilda smiled and turned to Pyewacket. "Now, you jump on up onto the back sprigs."

Pye furrowed his brow. "I'm not comfortable with this. Have you ever ridden on a bicycle with her? And the bike doesn't even leave the ground. Well, it's not supposed to, anyway."

"I take it you don't like the idea of riding on a besom. Tell you what. I'll bespell the besom to hold you in place. It's important that we see how you and Marais get along," Mathilda said.

I snorted. "The broom has a name?"

"How else would you call your *besom* to you?" Mathilda asked.

She carefully picked up Pye and placed him on the sprigs of

the besom. She whispered a few words and Pye plopped his rear down on an orchid. He let out a long-suffering sigh and settled himself between the bristles and spiraling vines. "If I die, I'm haunting you both."

"Duly noted," I said, gripping the handle.

Mathilda gave me a wicked grin. "Lean forward and pull up. Just a little."

I did.

The besom lifted gently off the ground, swaying like a boat on calm water.

"Very good. Now push down slightly, and it'll lower. For the most part, a besom will protect its witch from ever hitting the ground. However, it *is* taking its flight instructions from you—your movements, your thoughts. So know this. Wherever you tell it to go, it will go. At the beginning of the relationship, there can be miscommunication, if you're not careful and precise with your instructions."

Mathilda swept her arm toward the rolling hills with a wide grin.

"Well, don't just sit there like a bump on a log. Go! Take her for a spin. Feel the wind in your hair. And maybe don't crash." She winked and leaned in closer. "Take your time, dear. Have fun."

I swallowed hard, then leaned forward again. The besom responded instantly, gliding up and forward out over the rolling hills. The fresh air blew through my hair, and I cautiously increased our speed. I glanced back at Pye, who sat on his haunches, the wind rippling his fur and a look of happiness on his face.

Well, that was unexpected.

The blue dragonfly still sat on the tip, slowly flexing her wings, completely oblivious to the winds rushing at her. As if she heard my thoughts, the dragonfly suddenly fluttered into the air and landed on my shoulder.

Everything about this broom felt right.

I laughed, adjusting our course. Coastal Road snaked beneath us. The gothic silhouette of Veronique's mansion loomed ahead, the sky above it dark with rolling thunderclouds.

We traveled further along the coastline until we arrived at Shadow Pumpkin Farm. We coasted over the farmhouse, the crime tape still up cordoning off the farm to visitors.

Then—movement. A shadow at the back of Patch's cottage.

My stomach flipped. "Pye," I hissed. "Someone's at Patch's house."

He stretched onto his belly, peering down. "Probably Ransom. He—"

We both gasped.

Emerging from the back door and heading toward the barn— my Great Aunt Sibella. Her silhouette cut through the fading light as she moved toward the barn, purposeful, unhurried.

My breath hitched. I had suspected she was keeping secrets, but *this*? Patch's house, the crime scene, the unanswered questions hanging heavy in the air? I hadn't wanted her tangled up in whatever had happened to Patch. I hadn't let myself *really* believe she might be involved.

"Oh, Pye," I whispered, my voice thin, unsteady.

"I know, *ma chère*," he murmured, the weight of what might be, pressing into those four simple words.

My throat tightened and I yanked the besom around, making a beeline back toward Darkly. My heart pounded a rhythm of doubt and dread.

By the time we hovered above the courtyard with its welcoming shrubs and ruby red blooms, my heartbeat had ceased its murderous thumping. One thing was clear. I needed to talk to Sibby about Patch's murder.

Mathilda stepped out of her shop, arms crossed, as if she'd been standing in the doorway, anticipating our return. "Well?"

I landed—barely. The besom wobbled beneath me before settling in the courtyard, and Pye tumbled off with an *oof*.

I felt unsteady too. My pulse still pounded in my ears, but not from the ride. Sibella. At Patch's house.

I swallowed hard and shoved the image of her into a dark corner of my mind. Focus. Broom ride. Safe ground. Mathilda.

"That," I gasped, forcing a laugh that came out shaky, "was amazing."

Mathilda smirked, her sharp eyes flicking between us, catching the strain beneath my words. "Told ya."

Pye wobbled to his feet, shaking himself out like he could rid himself of our mutual feelings of dread. "Got any with cushions?"

I blinked, grateful for the distraction. "Pye wants to know if you can add a soft seat for him on the back."

Mathilda chuckled. "As a matter of fact, I can. It's a highly requested upgrade."

I nodded absently, running my fingers over the besom's jingling charms.

"What are these?" I asked, my voice a fraction too quiet.

"Talismans," Mathilda said, studying me now. "For safety. Good health. Whatever you need."

Safety. Good health. A knot twisted tight in my stomach.

I exhaled. "That sounds great." More than great. Necessary.

Pye cleared his throat. "Can you double up on those?" He turned to me, nose in the air and cocked his head. "She's never ridden with you."

I mustered a small smile. "Mathilda, can you take some of those charms off the back sprigs?" I shot Pye a look. "Pye says he's ready to live on the wild side."

Mathilda cackled, just like a witch, as a matter of fact. "Sure. One bumpy ride on the back coming up."

Pye gulped. "Thanks a lot, witch." he snarled.

"Anytime, cat," I murmured, before turning to Mathilda and extending my hand. "I'll take it."

She clasped my hand in hers. "Great! I'll make your changes, shine it up, and deliver it to Fernwood later today." Her grin was easy, but her gaze lingered. "You won't be sorry."

I already was.

But not about the besom.

CHAPTER 9

I stormed into Fernwood like a hurricane on a bender, my boots clicking sharply against the polished floors. The aroma of pork chops and cheese grits floated through the air. Pye slunk in behind me, tail pinging in agitation.

Sibby sprawled on her usual plush chair in the sitting room, what looked like an apple core in one hand and a whiskey glass in the other. She sipped from the glass, set it down on the table, and picked up the small chisel lying next to it.

I eyed her warily.

Hilde sat in her rocker by the fireplace knitting a cat sweater of bold zigzag stripes in maroon and burnt orange. Her expression was one of complete serenity, as if she and Sibby were merely two old hens gossiping over a porch railing.

"I'm makin' your favorites tonight. I figured—" Hilde looked up at me and her eyes widened in surprise. "Honey, you all right?"

I took a deep breath and steeled myself.

"Sibby, we need to talk," I huffed, willing myself to continue.

"Whatever about, Peanut?"

Peanut? Why—? Never mind.

I stopped short, eyes narrowing as I caught sight of Sibby's lone, pink-feathered earring swaying with her every move. The carved bone twirling above the feathers as she peered at her apple. Something in my brain clicked into place. I checked the other ear. Nothing.

I *knew* that "fetish" looked familiar. I hurried back to my bedroom and snatched it off the dresser.

Seconds later, I was back, the fetish clutched in my hand. I wiggled it in Pye's direction, but didn't slow as I crossed the room, stopping only when I was directly in front of Sibby. "You want to explain why this"—I thrust the object under Sibby's nose—"looks an awful lot like your earring?"

Pyewacket gasped and jumped up on the table to get a better look at the earring hanging from Sibby's ear. "Mm-hmm. Same."

Hilde set down her knitting, her brows knitted in confusion. "Windsor, baby, what in the world is goin' on?"

Sibby thrust out a hand, her mouth quirked in a nervous smile. "My applehead earring! I've been looking everywhere for that thing. Where'd you find it?"

I examined it closer. Yep, what I thought was a bone was actually an apple core carved into the shape of a man.

"Patch's house."

Sibby froze and her hand fell to her lap. The apple core in her hand rolled to the floor with a soft thud. For the first time since arriving in Darkly, she looked genuinely startled.

"It's not what you think," she said.

"How do you know what I think?"

She bit her lip. "You think I killed Patch."

"Do I? Now why would I think you killed Patch?"

"Because I'm the spurned lover," she said snarkily.

"Also because I saw you at Patch's cottage today."

The room was silent. The only sounds, the crackling of the fire and the soft creaking as Hilde nervously resumed her rocking.

"You saw me," she finally murmured, more to herself than

anyone else. She, surprisingly, didn't ask me where I was when I saw her. Sibby's fingers curled around the whiskey glass, nails tapping against the crystal. "I thought I was careful."

I folded my arms. "Not careful enough."

Hilde stared at Aunt Sibby. "Sibby. I need you to be straight with us."

Sibby sighed, set down her glass, and leaned back into the chair. "Well, hell. Guess the jig is up."

Oh goddess! She did kill him!

She let out a long breath, staring at the ceiling as if debating where to start. Then, her shoulders slumped, and she looked at me, her expression softer than usual. "Fine. You want the truth? Here it is."

I stayed silent, my heart pounding.

Sibby took a sip of her whiskey before she spoke. "When I got back to Darkly, the first thing I did was go see Patch. I had something for him. A magic pumpkin seed." She gave a half-smile. "A rare one. I knew he'd like it."

The knot in my stomach unraveled a tad. "You had a gift for him?"

Sibby nodded. "Forty-seven years, sugar. Forty-seven. I figured a man that handsome had surely moved on. But stars help me, I still needed to lay eyes on him."

She took another sip, and I noticed her hands were shaking.

"He was the same Patch. Sweet, kind, polite. Told me he was with Dixie-Deen Poplar now."

She sighed heavily, her shoulders folding in slightly at the thought.

Pye, ever the tactful one, gave a small, understanding nod. "Dixie-Deen's a good woman."

Sibby let out a soft chuckle, but there was something wistful in her expression. "That she is. And I'm sure they are good together. He was happy. That's all that mattered."

I tried to picture it. Patch, standing in his cozy cottage, telling

Sibby he'd moved on. It was hard to imagine. Especially knowing that hours later, he'd be dead.

I took a breath. "So why go back to the farm today?"

Sibby's grin faded. "After you'd told me Patch...died, I knew how it'd look. Me showing up after all these years. Patch dying soon after." She began the nervous tapping of her glass again. "Even if I knew I didn't have anything to do with it, suspicion has a way of creeping up on people."

She picked up her grisly looking applehead from the floor and began carving again. I got a good look at its face and noticed it suspiciously looked like me.

My fingers tightened around the earring. "And you thought taking back the seed would help?"

Sibby rubbed her temples. "I didn't want anything that day tying me to him. But I did *not* kill him."

I exhaled, feeling the weight of it settle over me. Sibby wasn't the enemy. She'd been trying to protect herself. But more importantly, she'd cared about Patch.

I studied her, her wild silver hair and neon nails, her ridiculous clashing outfits. There was something in Sibby's eyes that wasn't there before.

Regret.

And grief.

"All right," I said finally. "But if you keep anything else from me, I will throw you out the window and let Greta Garbo have you."

Sibby grinned. "Fair enough."

Pye sighed dramatically and hopped into Hilde's lap. "Well, I for one am ecstatic that Sibby isn't the killer."

Hilde patted his head and then turned to me. "Told you things'd liven up with Sibby home."

I nodded and turned to my great aunt. "I'm sorry, Sibby. I really am. I saw you coming out of the cottage and...well, I'm sorry."

"Aw, no skin off my butt, Peanut. I understand." She took a

long sip of whiskey before continuing. "I've asked Conny and Maybelle who in Darkly they thought would have had it in for Patch. They couldn't name a single person."

Sibby turned her applehead carving over in her hands and began digging into the side of it with her chisel. "But obviously, someone did."

CHAPTER 10

I placed the freshly repaired copy of *'Twas the Night Before Christmas* on the counter, giving it a little pat for good measure. The book quivered, then spun into the air like a leaf caught in an updraft, whisking itself up the staircase to its proper spot.

The front bells jingled merrily as the heavy oak door swung open, ushering in a gust of chilly wind and Jess. She stumbled inside shivering and slammed the door shut behind her.

"Brrr! There's already a real nip in the air," she announced, rubbing her arms. "The Blue Elves seem to come earlier every year." She wriggled out of her coat, flung it onto the rack, and followed me toward the fireplace seating area.

"Who are the Blue Elves?" I asked, dropping into my favorite plush armchair.

Jess unwrapped a light cashmere scarf from around her neck and draped it over the back of an old, tufted chair facing mine. "They bring winter to Darkly," she said, as she settled into the seat. "Otherwise, we'd never get any snow down here, much less a white Christmas."

I took a sip from my own mug, steam rising toward the ceiling as Jess's favorite beverage appeared on the table between us. "Think we could ask them to do something about the humidity?"

Jess chuckled, her smile curling at the edges. "Wouldn't that be nice?"

Pyewacket hopped onto my lap, never one to miss out on any possible gossip.

I was about to mention the strange day I'd had when a thick book materialized in front of us, fanned its pages dramatically in the glow of the fire, and then shot up to the gallery. My gaze flicked back to Jess. The amusement had faded from her eyes, replaced by something far more serious.

I sensed a sadness in her. My strange experiences today could wait.

"What brings you to me and my not-so-humble assistant here?" I took a sip of my latte and ran a hand down Pye's soft fur.

"Two things," she said. "First, I wanted to check on you. Finding Patch like that couldn't have been easy."

A knot formed in my chest. "It wasn't." The memory rose, cold and unwanted. "But I'm fine."

She gave me a skeptical tilt of her head.

I forced a small smile. "Really."

Jess hesitated, then nodded, red curls bouncing around her face. "And second…Dixie-Deen. I want to check on her."

"I've been thinking about her too." I absently stroked Pyewacket's sleek back. Then, more decisively, "You don't think she had anything to do with his murder, do you?"

Jess's freckled face crumpled. "Dixie-Deen? Noooo. Never." Then, in a quieter voice, "Well…I don't think so."

I set my drink down with a sigh. "In the morning, let's go see what we can find out."

Jess perked up. "I'll take her some cozy croissants. That always cheers her up."

"How about some truthful treacle?" I suggested, only half-joking. "Might be more useful."

Jess wagged a finger at me. "Win, you must learn to have faith in your fellow man...or woman."

If life had taught me anything, it was quite the opposite.

After Jess left, Pye and I headed back to the workroom. I hadn't even made it to my stool when I heard a faint rattle from the front of the shop.

I stilled, listening for the chime of the bell above the door.

Nothing.

I poked my head out from the lab.

"Jess?" I called out.

Silence.

Then came a slow creak, low and deliberate, from somewhere in the stacks.

I moved through the front of the shop, breath caught high in my chest. The door was shut tight, just as I'd left it.

The hairs on the back of my neck stood up.

I slid open the door and stuck my head out. The sidewalk bustled like any other late afternoon in Darkly. Old Mrs. Banerjee, draped in a brilliant magenta shawl embroidered with gold thread trudged past with her rolling trolley. Two teenagers stood outside The Magic Cup, deep in a gossipy huddle over large coffees. Across the way, a pair of witches bickered over spell licensure loud enough for the citizens of Cradlerock to hear.

"Mrs. Banerjee!" I called, stepping out onto the stone walkway. "Did you see anyone come out of my shop just now?"

Pyewacket stood in front of me like a hissing ball of attitude, muscles tense, his nose twitching with laser-sharp focus.

She paused and squinted toward the door. "No, sugar. Just you and your little beastie there. Why?"

I scanned up and down the street, then across to the cemetery wall. Just the usual. Neighbors. Locals. All going about their business. A few waved when they saw me looking. One guy with a baguette tipped his hat.

"Never mind. Thank you," I said, forcing a smile.

I backed into the shop. Pye scampered past me.

"How odd," I muttered. My eyes swept the shop. Nothing was out of place. The displays were neat, the shelves still humming faintly with residual travel magic. But the corners of the MET— the places where shadow pooled naturally—had gone wild.

"The shadowmen," Pye whispered.

Their long, twisting limbs reached just beyond their usual perches, stretching hungrily toward the center of the room. They shimmered at the edges like heat mirages. Restless. Agitated. Unhappy.

Someone *had* been in here.

Someone who didn't belong.

And then I saw it.

A single card lay on the counter by the front door. Just sitting there. All casual-like, but I knew better.

I approached slowly.

"Win, I wouldn't," Pye warned from somewhere behind me.

I took another step.

He huffed. "Fine. Don't listen to the cat."

I reached the counter and snatched the card up before I could talk myself out of it. It was heavier than I expected. Textured. Hand-painted.

A skeletal knight in black armor rode a white horse across the cardstock, holding a black banner with a white five-petaled rose. Behind him, the sun lingered between two towers, not quite rising, not quite setting, casting the whole scene in an eerie golden light. People knelt at the horse's feet, some praying, some collapsing. There was no blood. No gore. Just finality.

Like the universe had drawn a line.

"The Death card," I said.

Pye jumped up beside me and peered down at the card. "Oh, fabulous," he muttered. "Because that's exactly the kind of ambiance this place is missing."

"I didn't see them at all. Did you?"

"No," he said, tail snapping behind him. "It's almost like they didn't even come in through the door."

"Then how did they get in?" I said, my voice low.

I turned the card over in my hand, the thick edges cool against my skin. "They knew about the shadowmen."

Pye's ears pricked forward.

"They knew exactly where to leave the card. Just out of the immediate reach of the shadows," I said. "And to get out before the shop pushed back."

I gently prodded a shadowman tendril off the counter. It recoiled into the shelving underneath.

Looking around the MET again, we scanned every inch of polished wood, each glowing lantern and gleaming travel relic.

Then I turned my eyes back to the card. Beautiful, in a terrible kind of way.

"You think it's a threat?" I asked.

Pye scoffed. "What else would it be? A secret admirer sending you murdery artwork?"

I raised an eyebrow.

He shrugged. "I'm just sayin'. If it quacks like a threat…"

"Let's keep this to ourselves, Pye."

"Win—"

"No, Pye. I mean it. No sense rattling everyone over what might be a stupid prank."

He glared at me. "That could have been left by the killer. For all we know, Patch received one too."

"Please. For now."

He gave a slow shake of his head. "Fine. But for the record, I think this is a terrible plan."

"C'mon. Let's head home," I murmured, tucking the card into my bag. "I'll ask Jess to pick me up at Fernwood for our visit to the Sanctuary."

I opened my bag a little wider for Pyewacket to hop in.

"Eh," he said, curling his tail around his feet. "I think I'll pass on the doom-and-gloom express. But thanks."

I hurried to the back to tidy up just a bit and then met Pyewacket by the door.

"How many times since I've known you," Pye muttered, "have I warned you not to do something, you did it anyway, and then you regretted it? We've got to be at...what?...twenty-seven by now. Minimum."

I didn't answer. I just made sure the shadowmen had slithered back into their corners before stepping outside and pushing my bike into the thick, amber glow of late afternoon, viewing each person I passed in a different light.

CHAPTER 11

*J*essamin's sleek black Bentley purred onto a narrow dirt road just north of Darkly, its tires crunching over loose gravel. The rolling fields stretched out before us, a sea of wild purple heather and crimson poppies swaying in the crisp air. Unable to resist, I rolled down the window, closed my eyes, and took in a deep breath, letting the cool breeze tangle through my hair.

The sensation instantly transported me back to yesterday and my first flight with Pyewacket. Just the memory of that exhilarating rush, the endless sky stretching out in all directions, sent a delicious shiver throughout my body. The wind, the freedom, the sheer magic of it—I was hooked.

"So, I did a thing," I announced.

Jessamin side-eyed me, suspicion creeping into her voice. "What kind of thing?"

"Well, that's not the enthusiastic response I was expecting."

"I've learned my lesson. Last time you said something like that we ended up being chased through Greywolf Manor by a lunatic."

I waved a dismissive hand. "That happened *once*." Then, grinning, I dropped the bombshell. "I bought a flying broom."

Jess's expression shifted instantly. "Oh, how cool! I've always thought they looked like so much fun. Like a Vespa in the sky."

"Exactly! Fun, but also freeing. The rush. The wind in your hair. It's like flying is what I was meant to do."

Jess's green eyes sparkled with excitement. "Think you could take me for a ride?"

"I don't see why not."

As we drove past a field bursting with impossibly fuchsia-colored flowers, I imagined myself and Pyewacket gliding over them, the tips of my fingers brushing the petals. It was an intoxicating thought.

Jess steered the Bentley onto another winding road lined with golden pastures. In the meadow beyond the fence, a baby unicorn —a perfectly pearlescent little creature with a spiraled golden horn—hopped and pranced after a swarm of butterflies.

I felt the thunderous pounding of hooves inside the car before a monstrous skeletal horse materialized beside the little unicorn, its hollow, soulless eyes burning like cold embers. It snorted, stamping the ground so hard it sent up a small shower of green clover.

I yelped. "Sweet mother of magic!"

"What's the matter? Never seen an undead mare before?" Jess laughed. "Her name is Whisper."

My pulse steadied as I took in the breathtaking beauty of the horse. Wisps of ghostly mane floated like mist around her head, and her translucent tail drifted as if caught in an unseen current. The most beautiful—and most terrifying—animal I'd ever seen.

A few minutes later, Jess pulled into the Sanctuary's drive, stopping in front of a tumble-down farmhouse draped in ivy and honeysuckle. Bees buzzed lazily while finches burrowed into their nests among the vines.

The second Jess opened her door, a chorus of barks erupted. She ran to a wooden fence where a pack of large dogs barked and hopped, all competing for her attention.

I stepped out more cautiously than Jess, the basket of cozy

croissants in hand, and took in the scene around us. I'd seen a lot since moving to Darkly, but Lila & the Piggles Sanctuary was in a league of its own.

Overhead, a phoenix swooped through the sky, its glowing feathers shedding embers like fiery snowflakes. In a nearby field, a chimera—part lion, part goat, part dragon—lounged in the sun, lazily blowing puffs of smoke into the air. A gryphon, all sleek bronze feathers and piercing intelligence, examined me like they were trying to decide whether I was ally or appetizer.

As we approached Dixie-Deen's farmhouse, I took in the sight of it, an endearingly ramshackle thing like a broken vase a child had glued back together. The fact that it was still standing was either a miracle or magic.

The porch which wrapped around the entire house overflowed with dog beds, rocking chairs, and enough potted greenery to make me feel like I was stepping into a jungle. I glanced up at the sky-blue ceiling.

Dixie-Deen stepped out onto the porch. "Haint blue," she said, catching my gaze. "Keeps out bad spirits."

"Huh." I considered that. *I could definitely use some of that haint blue.*

"What brings y'all out here?" Dixie-Deen said, her head bouncing back and forth between us.

"We wanted to check on you," Jess said.

Dixie-Deen smiled faintly. "Come on in."

We followed her into an eclectic mix of cozy charm and mismatched elegance. A roaring fire crackled in the hearth bathing the room in flickering light. Plush, overstuffed sofas faced what looked like a real Louis XIV mirrored tea table, because why wouldn't that be in a supernatural animal sanctuary?

A crow perched on the twisted branch of a tree growing straight out of the floor, its beady black eyes following me through the room.

I shifted uneasily. "That's interesting."

Dixie-Deen waved a dismissive hand. "You should see my bedroom. Coffee?"

"We don't want to put you out," I said, keeping one wary eye on the bird. Just in case.

"Nonsense." She snapped her fingers, and a tray with steaming mugs and an array of cookies materialized on the table. "It's nice to have company. Since Patch…" Her voice wavered. "Since Patch…well. The only people I've really talked to are Inspector Belleclaire and Matty." She forced a small smile. "If you don't count the animals."

An uncomfortable silence settled over the room.

I reached for a coconut macaroon, unsure what to say, when a sudden wave of warmth spread through the space like a comforting embrace.

If anyone could bring Dixie-Deen even the smallest bit of peace, it was Jess. Hopefully, enough for me to start asking the hard questions about Patch.

Jess finally broke the silence, her voice warm and gentle, and set the basket of pastries on the table. "How are you, hun? I baked some cozy croissants, just for you."

"Oh, Jess, Win. Thank you." Dixie-Deen's red-rimmed eyes flickered to us, brimming with exhaustion and a heavy grief she was trying to hold back. "I'm getting through it. Some bad days. Some good," she said, her voice scratchy with unshed tears.

"Can we help with anything?" I offered. "Meals? The animals?" I gestured vaguely at the entire Sanctuary.

Dixie-Deen let out a watery chuckle. "The animals are my joy right now. When I'm with them, I can forget that I'll never see Patch again."

Dixie-Deen's voice cracked on the last word, and just like that, the tears she'd been fighting won. They rushed down her cheeks in a hot flood. Her hands gripped the fabric of her overalls like she could hold herself together through sheer force of will.

"Why did this happen?" she choked out. "Patch was always so

careful. He'd worked magic for years. He wouldn't have been reckless with those gourds of his. It doesn't make sense."

I leaned forward, placing a steadying hand on her knee. Her fingers immediately clutched mine, like a drowning woman grasping a lifeline.

"Dixie-Deen," I said carefully. "I don't believe it was an accident."

Her head jerked up, eyes wide and startled. "You think someone killed him?"

I glanced at Jess, who gave me a small, reassuring nod.

"I do," I said.

Dixie-Deen sucked in a sharp breath, her trembling fingers flying to her mouth. "Who would do such a thing?" she whispered.

I squeezed her hand, offering what little comfort I could.

Jess spoke up, her voice calm but probing. "Can you think of anyone, hun? Anyone who might've wanted to hurt Patch?"

Dixie-Deen's gaze darted around the room like the answer might be hiding among the knickknacks and stray feathers. "N-no," she stammered. "No one. Everyone liked Patch."

She suddenly let out a sharp, ragged breath and shook her head. "It's because of me," she said, her voice thick with sorrow. "He died because of me."

Jess and I exchanged startled glances.

"Hun," Jess said gently, "what do you mean?"

Dixie-Deen wiped at her cheeks, hands trembling. "When Patch heard Win was coming out to the farm, he wanted me to help him pick out pumpkins for you. He was so excited. He'd liked Miss Minta so much. Wanted Win to have the best of the patch." She smiled at me through the tears. "But instead, I was on the other side of the island. At Devils Hollow."

Jess sucked in a breath. "What were you doing way out there?"

Dixie-Deen bit her lip. "Rescuing abandoned will-o'-wisps," she admitted. "A whole family had been left behind after their haunt was bulldozed for that ridiculous new glamping resort." Her eyes welled up again. "If I hadn't been gone, if I'd been there like Patch asked, I could've stopped it."

I shook my head. "Dixie-Deen, you don't know that."

"But I do!" she insisted. "I would've seen something! Or maybe…maybe Patch wouldn't have been alone. Maybe—if someone did this—they would've thought twice if I were there."

She dropped her face into her hands, shoulders shaking.

Jess smoothed a hand over Dixie-Deen's curls. "Sugar, you couldn't have known. You were doing something good."

Dixie-Deen let out a soft, shuddering sigh but didn't look up.

"I promise you, Dixie-Deen," I said, my voice steady. "If someone did hurt Patch, I'll find out who."

Dixie-Deen opened her mouth to respond, but before she could, a violent banging shattered the moment, rattling the front door in its frame. Her cup jolted in her hands, coffee sloshing over the rim and onto her overalls. "Oh, bother!" she muttered, glaring down at the spreading stain.

"Let me get that," Jess said, flicking her fingers. The mess vanished instantly, leaving Dixie-Deen looking as fresh as if she'd just stepped out of a laundromat.

"I'll get the door," I volunteered, pushing up from my seat before whoever was outside could start battering it down.

"Tell them the Sanctuary is closed to visitors," Dixie-Deen called after me.

I yanked the door open and found myself face-to-face with Borda Wrathfell.

I barely managed to keep my expression neutral. "Borda! Not who I was expecting."

"And I sure wasn't expecting you either," she replied, sweeping one of her infamous head-to-toe inspections over me, her lips pursing slightly at my black Chucks, as if they personally offended her.

I resisted the urge to tuck a stray piece of hair behind my ear.

"Come in, Borda," Dixie-Deen called from the sofa, her voice still thick with grief.

Jess, ever the perfect host, gestured toward the coffee tray as Dixie-Deen dabbed her face with a handkerchief. "Can I get you a cup?"

Borda sailed past me and settled into the chair I'd just vacated. She gave Dixie-Deen a look of studied concern. "Dear, I just wanted to stop in and see how you were holding up."

I pursed my lips and grabbed my cup and a croissant—no doubt I was going to need magic to get through this conversation—and moved to an empty spot on the sofa.

Dixie-Deen exhaled shakily, running a hand over her face. "It's just so shocking. We had such wonderful plans. For the Sanctuary. For the pumpkin farm. For *us*." Her voice faltered, and for a moment, I thought she was going to cry again.

"I know, dear," Borda said, sipping her coffee with a delicately somber air. "Patch was such an important member of the community. Such a shame."

Then she sat up straighter and smiled, all business. "Which is why I believe we should cancel the festival this year."

Jess and I both blinked.

Dixie-Deen gasped, eyes wide. "What?!"

I tilted my head. That was surprisingly compassionate of Borda. I wasn't sure whether to be touched or suspicious.

"No," Dixie-Deen said, her voice firm and absolute. "Patch loved Gumbo Fest. He looked forward to it all year. He would never have wanted that."

Silence.

Even Borda appeared momentarily taken aback.

"Are you sure?" she asked at last.

"Absolutely," Dixie-Deen declared, running her hand down the scaley back of a giant lizard with slitted cat-like eyes curled up on her lap.

Where had it even come from?

"When I think of Gumbo Fest, I think of joy," Dixie-Deen

continued, voice softening. "It's where Patch and I met, you know." A small, nostalgic smile ghosted over her lips. "It would be wrong to cancel it."

Borda's smile returned, broader than before. "Wonderful!" she declared, plucking a macaroon off the tray. "The show must go on, you know."

I rolled my eyes.

While Borda prattled on about the importance of 'decorum' in the wake of Patch's death—her words, not mine—I let my gaze drift back to Dixie-Deen. She sat stiffly, her fingers absently stroking the scales of the lizard. She wasn't really listening anymore. Her grief had settled back in, thick and suffocating.

Jess made polite noises at the right moments, but I could tell by the flicker in her eyes that she was as done with this conversation as I was. When Borda finally drained the last of her coffee and stood with an exaggerated sigh—"I suppose I've taken up enough of your time, dear"—I nearly sagged with relief.

As soon as the door shut behind her, Jess and I exchanged a look.

"Well—" I grimaced and popped the last bite of croissant into my mouth "—that was predictable."

"That was Borda being Borda." Jess murmured, smoothing an invisible wrinkle from her dress.

Dixie-Deen huffed. "I don't know why she even asked. Y'all know she wasn't ever really going to cancel Gumbo Fest."

That was probably true.

Dixie-Deen let out a slow, weary breath. "Thank you for coming. Really."

Jess reached over and squeezed her hand. "Always, hun."

When we stepped outside, the sky was already shifting from warm amber to twilight violet, with low clouds pushing in at the edges. The sounds of the Sanctuary filled the air—chittering, braying, the occasional disgruntled squawk.

Jess shifted in her seat, adjusting the rearview mirror. "I feel so bad for Dixie-Deen."

I sighed. "Me too."

"I mean, she was heartbroken. You saw how she was—she could barely string two words together without breaking down. Her guilt at not being there is tormenting her."

I nodded. "Yeah. But I'm not sure that's the only thing tormenting her. She's holding something back."

"I got the same feeling," Jess said, drumming her fingers against the steering wheel. "When I asked her about anyone who would hurt Patch, she couldn't even look at me."

"But who is she trying to protect? Herself or someone else?"

Jess's fingers tightened on the wheel. "And if someone else—why?"

I watched the moss-draped trees blur past the window. A leaden weight settled in my stomach. "And just how far would she go to keep their secret?"

Jess didn't answer, but the grim set of her jaw said she was wondering the same thing.

I chewed on my bottom lip. "She wouldn't be having an affair or anything like that, would she?"

Jess shot me a quick glance. "I don't know Dixie-Deen well enough to know. But I don't think of her as that kind of person."

"You'd be surprised at what kind of person can cheat," I said, my memory flashing to my jerk of an ex. "But the magic. Boddy said they used a witch's spellveil."

"Boddy specifically said a witch conjured the spell?"

I nodded.

"Like Chase said, anyone can do a spellveil though."

I crooked a smile. "Well, almost anyone."

Jess laughed but I didn't think her heart was really in it.

We fell silent for a beat.

"So," I said, deftly changing the subject as we bumped along the dusty path. "Are you ready for court tomorrow? I still can't believe Elspeth has the nerve to sue over an estate that was never her father's to begin with."

"I just want it over with, you know? Sometimes I feel bad because, after all, Elspeth is part Wilde—"

"And Ebonwood," I added, flashing a grin.

"True. Which technically makes us...second cousins? Third step-cousins once removed?" She quirked an eyebrow at me.

Related to Jess. Wouldn't that be a laugh?

"Every single asset Dorian had was either inherited or bought by you and Brychen," I reminded her. "You've got no reason to feel bad. Not your fault Dorian burned through his inheritance money."

"I know that—I do—but I still feel bad."

That was Jess in a nutshell.

She threw me a sidelong glance. "When I talked to Tzazi, she was champing at the bit. Can't wait to get in the courtroom with her ex."

I snorted. "Pretty sure it's the event of the season. The whole town's waiting on it like it's our very own off-brand Mardi Gras."

All the drama, none of the king cake.

CHAPTER 12

$\mathcal{A}$fter supper and a shower, I padded back into the sitting room to rejoin Hilde and Sibby. I plopped onto the velvet sofa letting the warmth of the fire wrap around me. I'd piled my damp hair atop my head like Pebbles Flintstone, and my fleece pajamas were soft against my skin. The lingering stress of the day melted away like butter on a hot biscuit.

Sibby's bourbon swirled lazily in her glass. "How's Dixie-Deen holding up?" she asked, her tone casual, but her sharp gaze told me she wasn't asking idly.

Hilde, sitting across from me, gave a slow, measured nod. "Poor thing must be in tatters."

I sighed, tucking my feet up beneath me. "To be honest, she's barely holding it together. She blames herself for not being there when it happened."

Pye let out a soft sigh from his perch atop the armrest. "Yes, because grief and misplaced guilt are such rational feelings."

I shot him a look. "Now is not the time for snark."

Sibby chuckled, though the sound was dry. "The cat's got a point. Grief and guilt *are* wasted emotions."

I studied Aunt Sibby for a moment, watching the way she held herself. Solid, steady, unreadable. But every now and then, a crack would show, a flicker of something raw beneath the stoicism.

Finding out your fiancé had moved on was bad enough. I should know. But then finding out he'd been murdered? That was a whole different kind of pain.

And to make matters worse, I, with my big mouth, had practically accused her of being the one who did it. Guilt twisted in my gut.

Hilde sighed and rubbed a hand over her face. "Grief makes folks do damn fool things. That girl's been through enough without blamin' herself for somethin' she couldn't have stopped."

"That's what I told her," I grumbled. "But she's convinced if she'd been at the farm, Patch would still be alive."

Hilde's rocking slowed. "More like she'd be lyin' right next to him."

The room settled into a hush, the fire crackling softly as flames curled around the logs.

Sibby took a slow sip of her bourbon and exhaled. "I reckon she didn't take too kindly to you suggestin' it wasn't just bad luck?"

"She was shocked," I admitted. "But deep down, I think she knew. She just wasn't ready to say it out loud."

"Can't say I blame her," Hilde muttered. "That man was her whole world."

Sibby watched me over the rim of her glass. "And what about the pumpkin that killed him?"

"Bespelled according to Ransom," I confirmed. "Not by Patch, though. Someone tampered with it."

Sibby's eyes darkened. "That's a mighty peculiar thing to do. Guess that means Gumbo Fest's good and gone this year."

I shook my head. "Actually, Dixie-Deen told Borda she wants the festival to continue."

Hilde glanced up from her knitting. "She's not canceling?"

"Nope. Says Patch would've wanted it that way." I sighed,

pulling the blanket tighter around me. "And from what I know of him, she's probably right."

Pye stretched, his tail swinging lazily. "Oh good. Let's all gather in one location so the murderer—who, I must remind you, is still very much at large—can have another go at someone. Brilliant."

I shot him a look. "Not helping."

"I'm not here to help," he said airily. "I'm here to observe and critique. It's what I do best."

Sibby let out a dry chuckle. "The day you stop critiquin' is the day I start drinkin' sweet tea instead of bourbon."

Pye gave a delicate sniff. "Unlikely on both counts."

Hilde's needles resumed their steady clicking. "Well, I sure do wonder if that's the right decision. If Patch's murder is connected to Gumbo Fest, then Darkly's got bigger problems than whether or not the gumbo's got enough kick."

A slow dread spread through my stomach, the weight of her words settling in. I hadn't considered that. "You think Patch's death has something to do with the festival?"

Hilde turned her sharp gaze on me, her needles working faster. "I have to admit I find the timing real suspicious."

"But I don't get it," I said, frowning. "How would Patch's death affect Gumbo Fest?"

"Maybe somebody figured killin' him would put a stop to it," Hilde said thoughtfully. "But why?"

I exhaled slowly, my resolve hardening. "I'm going to find out who did this. And when I do, they'll wish they'd stuck to carving pumpkins instead of using them as murder weapons."

Pye hummed approvingly. "Now, that's the spirit."

Hilde grinned. "Well, you know what folks say. When in Darkly..."

Sibby snorted, knocking back the last of her drink. "Always carry salt, sass, and a second pair of underwear."

We all lost it. Even Pye laughed in that weird wheezy way of his.

"And on that note, I'll be right back." I slipped out of the room and ducked into my bathroom. When I stepped back into my bedroom, the familiar hum of Hilde and Sibby's voices drifted in from the sitting room—then, outside the window, a flicker just at the edge of my vision.

I crossed the room slowly. Beyond the glass, the swamp stretched out in darkness, shifting and breathing with its own ancient rhythm. The moon barely cut through the heavy mist curling between the trees, and for a moment, I saw nothing unusual.

But then—

A shadow moved.

Not a breeze through the trees. Not an animal slipping through the underbrush in the moonlight.

Something else.

Something at the edges of the swamp where the cypress trees took over.

For a long moment, I stood there, staring into the darkness beyond the glass. The way the shadow flickered, forming and unraveling like smoke caught in an unseen current, sent an unease twisting through my gut.

I stepped back into the cozy warmth of the sitting room. Pye uncurled from his impossibly tight ball on the sofa and gave a soft grunt. Hilde and Sibby looked up. Their lively chatter cut off the moment they caught sight of my face.

"What is it?" Hilde asked, her voice low and steady.

I hesitated.

"I just saw something in the swamp."

Sibby stood and reached for her wand. Her gnarled fingers wrapped around the smooth, well-worn wood. Hilde rose too, her movements precise, measured. Her steadiness—no matter the situation—never failed to impress me.

Hilde narrowed her eyes. "What kind of somethin'?"

I swallowed, picturing the way the darkness had moved, the way it had almost felt aware. "A shadow. But not just a shadow. It shifts. One moment it's shapeless, then it seems to take on a human form, only to slink away again."

Sibby flopped back onto the plush chair, popped her unlit pipe into her mouth, and reached for her bourbon. "Sounds like a swamp phantasm," she said around the pipe's stem. "Harmless, although a bit peculiar for one to be this close. They don't like lights—lanterns, candles, fireflies. Makes 'em dissolve."

"But they come right back," Hilde added grimly.

"A phantasm," I said slowly. "That's what Chase saw outside his salon recently. But you said they're harmless, right?"

Sibby gave a nonchalant shrug. "Harmless as in won't murder you in your sleep. But they do feed on fear. If you let 'em, they'll leave you feelin' like you just pulled an all-nighter in a haunted house with a broken coffee pot. Cold, drained, disoriented." She took a slow sip of bourbon. "Had one sneak up on me in the Minoan Mines once. Woke up two hours later spoonin' a stalagmite."

Hilde's lips pressed into a thin line. "With us being right on the edge of the swamp, I suppose we shouldn't be shocked they're curious about the house. But it's awful strange one goin' all the way into town." Her expression darkened. "I think I'll switch on the floodlights out back."

She disappeared into the kitchen, and moments later the area behind the house blazed to life. The sudden glow cut through the murky gloom beyond the tree line, revealing only the usual swaying Spanish moss and the ripple of the lagoon's surface. No slinking shadows. No shifting figures.

Hilde reappeared, looking pleased, brushing her hands off as though that settled it. "That should do it."

"Will that scare off a rougarou?" I asked, hopefully.

"House lights don't bother them cursed things," Sibby muttered, pipe clamped between her teeth. She rocked back in her chair, tapping the bowl in thought. "But you can carry an iron nail to keep 'em away."

The fire popped in the hearth, filling the room with the scent of oak and something faintly herbal, a reminder that magic lived in this house even in its quietest moments.

Hilde disappeared into the foyer. A moment later, the soft glow of a new flame joined the firelight. When she returned, she carried a burning beeswax candle cupped in her hands. Its golden halo flickered across the sharp planes of her face. Without a word, she crossed the room and set it in the window overlooking the courtyard. Its glow pressed weakly against the murk of the swamp beyond.

"We'll keep this burnin' straight through the night," she said, her tone as firm as a nailed-down coffin lid. "Come mornin', I'll set pennies on every sill and doorstep."

I frowned. "Pennies?"

"Thirteen of 'em," Sibby said, shifting her bourbon to one hand while plucking her pipe out of her mouth with the other. "To confuse 'em. Rougarous got no patience for countin' past twelve. They get stuck, go in circles, and by the time they figure out their mistake, the sun's up, and they gotta skulk back to wherever they came from."

Pye, who had been curled up on the armrest of the sofa, twitched his ears and cracked an eye open. "Lackwits."

Then, as if to shake the frightening weight of the conversation from the room, Hilde clapped her hands together. The sharp sound cut through the thick quiet. "Anyone up for an episode of *Midsomer Murders*?"

I went along with the attempt to steer the night back toward something comfortable and routine, something to get my mind off rougarous and phantasms.

I grinned. "As long as there's tea and at least one superficial vicar, I'm in."

Sibby huffed, already reaching for the remote. "I do appreciate the high mortality rate. Keeps things interestin'. I hope it's the one where that jerk gets pinned to the ground and the killer chunks wine bottles at him."

I had recently acquainted both her and Hilde to *Midsomer Murders,* my favorite comfort show, and I'm proud to say I've gotten them both completely hooked.

Sibby topped off her glass, poured generous measures for Hilde and me, then handed them over. With drinks in hand, we settled into our comfy seats just as the episode began—because, of course, it had to be the one with the killer clowns.

I white-knuckled the sofa cushion, cringing at every flash of garish makeup and sinister grin, while the rest of my family seemed wholly unbothered. Hilde chuckled into her drink. Sibby cackled outright. Pye, that traitorous creature, leaped onto the mantel and swatted at the screen every time a clown popped up, apparently finding the whole thing hilarious.

Turns out coulrophobia did not run in the family.

And just like that, the house settled again. The candle burned steadily in the window. The floodlights kept the swamp at bay. And for a while, at least, the shadows stayed where they belonged.

Then—*tap, tap, tap.*

I grabbed the remote and muted the TV.

Sibby threw her hands up. "Hey! What are you—?"

Tap, tap, tap.

Hilde shushed her, tossing aside her needlework. Sibby rolled her eyes but dutifully reached for her wand.

"Here we go again," she muttered.

We all moved toward the foyer.

More insistent now. *TAP, TAP, TAP.*

"Do phantasms knock?" I whispered, following along behind them. The night was too thick with strangeness, and I wasn't about to be left alone in the sitting room with my overactive imagination and a paused frame of a homicidal clown.

"Not unless they need to borrow some sugar," Pye quipped, trotting beside me.

Sibby chuckled but didn't lower her wand.

As we neared the door, Hilde inhaled deeply, then let out a relieved sigh and relaxed her stance. "You bought a broom, didn't you?"

Before I could respond, she swung open the door.

There, hovering just beyond the threshold, was my brand new, absolutely magnificent, flying broom.

It was even more stunning than I remembered. Its cypress twig bristles were interwoven with delicate orchid blooms, while moss and fern leaves curled in intricate spirals down the braided length of the shaft. The moment my fingers brushed against the handle, tiny green ferns sprouted in response. And as if that wasn't enough, Mathilda had added a small lantern hanging from a hook in the front, its witch's fire casting a warm, flickering glow against the porch.

The dragonfly, perched at the tip of the handle, gave a lazy stretch of its iridescent wings before flitting onto my shoulder.

I grinned, unable to help myself. "Yep," I said, running my fingers along the shaft. "I bought a broom."

Beneath the sprawling limbs of the ancient magnolia, Mathilda let out a sharp cackle, balanced effortlessly on her own broom, her skirts billowing like storm clouds. We all startled as she hovered there, a sly grin stretched across her face,

"It's called a *besom*, dear. I hope you enjoy it," she said, her voice magnified by the light, swirling fog.

With another wild peal of laughter, she kicked off, spiraling upward in a blur of dark fabric and moonlit bristles. Within seconds, she vanished into the cold night sky, leaving only the rustle of magnolia leaves in her wake.

Hilde huffed out a laugh and turned back toward the sitting room. "That woman sure loves her job. Now get yourself inside before you let the bog spirits in."

I gave my broom one last admiring stroke before guiding it inside. Pye had already reclaimed his spot on the sofa. Sibby flopped into her chair, swirling her bourbon as she launched into a spirited tirade about how modern witches lacked the natural broom-flying instincts of generations past.

Whatever lurked in the swamp could wait for another night. For now, there was warmth, good company, and a murder mystery to get back to.

CHAPTER 13

t the crack of dawn, Keir and I, along with what felt like half the town of Darkly, gathered outside a modestly-sized, plantation-style building squeezed between the Royal Inspector's office and Butterbean Bakery, smelling unfairly delicious for such a tense morning. This was Darkly's Justice Center, if you could call a too-small building with peeling shutters and a front porch that sagged the 'center' of anything.

A sharp autumn breeze sliced through the crowd and tugged at my coat flaps. Keir slid an arm around my shoulders and pulled me close, his warmth a sharp contrast to the morning chill. "Yeh okay?" he murmured in my ear, guiding me through the heavily guarded doors.

I glanced up at the royal guards stationed at either side of the entrance. Tall, grim-faced, and clad in black, I wouldn't have been surprised to find they moonlighted as highwaymen.

Keir had warned me about the protocol, but it was still unsettling. "I'm not the one testifying," I reminded him, flashing what I hoped was a reassuring smile.

He smirked. "Aye, love. No worries for me. All in a day's."

'All in a day's,' he said, as if Jessamin wasn't about to face my scheming, malicious half-sister in a court battle over an inheritance.

Once inside, Keir led me toward a set of wind-tunnel people conveyors. Apparently, normal staircases were too pedestrian for royal proceedings.

Keir grinned confidently and gestured toward the vortex as the person in front of him was promptly sucked away. "Meet you on the other side."

I nodded and stepped into the swirling tunnel. My body felt yanked in every possible direction at once, like being tumble-dried by magic. An instant later, my feet found solid ground, and I blinked against the dim light of an enormous round chamber.

The Justice Sanctum loomed before me, its dark stone walls adorned with deep blue velvet curtains embroidered with a grand coat-of-arms. A peryton, a unicorn, a phœnix, and a kelpie, each glimmering in silver thread, peered down at the assembled crowd. I found Chase saving our front row seats. He patted the seat next to him in invitation, flashing a wicked grin.

The gallery, lined with ascending rows of stiff wooden seats, overlooked the main floor where two long tables faced a raised dais. Jess and Tzazi occupied the right-hand table. Their heads were bent in a hushed discussion that I prayed involved absolutely annihilating Elspeth's case.

At the opposing table, Mason Beckworth sat with Elspeth. With his slicked-back blond hair and his black pinstriped suit, he resembled a smug mafia don. Beside him, Elspeth appeared perfectly at ease. Her jet-black curls spiraled down her back. Blood-red nails tapped the table as if she were counting down the minutes to her inevitable victory. Dread pooled in my gut.

I turned to look at Keir as he strode into the Justice Sanctum like he owned the place, not in an arrogant way, but with the effortless confidence of a man who knew his power and had no need to flaunt it.

And heavens help me, he looked good.

His three-piece tweed suit fit like it had been conjured by a sorcerer with a flair for dressing dangerously handsome werewolves.

Keir sat in the seat next to mine and leaned in, voice low and teasing. "Like what yeh see, love?"

I cleared my throat, forcing my gaze away from the way his suit pants stretched just right when he crossed his legs.

"You look fine."

His brown eyes danced with amusement. "Aye. Just fine."

At that moment—bless him—the royal bailiff called the court to order. Keir straightened, his expression turning serious, but not before giving my knee a quick, reassuring squeeze.

"I'm glad this will be over soon," I murmured.

"You and me both," Chase muttered, dragging a hand through his hair. "All this stress is thinning my poor hairline, and I am far too young—and far too pretty—for that nonsense."

He wasn't wrong.

I nodded toward Jess. "She's putting on a good show, but I know this trial is tearing her up inside."

Before Chase could reply, something white and leathery clipped him on the back of the head with a resounding thwack. "What in the sweet name of Elvis was that?"

We both turned as Solara Nova slid into the seat beside him, her golden ringlets bouncing like she had just stepped out of a commercial for insufferable confidence.

"Oh, perfect," I muttered.

Chase rubbed his head, shooting her a scowl. "Solara Nova, watch where you're swinging that faux Birkin, sugah. Remember, I'm the one who touches up those roots."

I bit back a nervous laugh when Solara shot him a murderous look.

The soft rustle of courtroom whispers set my nerves jangling. I drew a slow breath and forced myself to stay calm. A gentle nudge from behind signaled the arrival of Conny, Maybelle, Dewey, and Aunt Sibby as they filed into the row behind us. Conny grabbed my hand and gave it a squeeze.

After a moment, a man in a royal uniform stepped from a doorway below and bellowed, "All rise."

I craned my neck, searching for the magickstrate just as a tall, severe-looking woman shimmered into existence on the dais. Her presence snapped the room into silence. With piercing eyes and an expression sharp enough to carve stone, she sank into her throne-like chair. Her fingers skimmed the documents before her with cool precision.

Beside her, a sleek wooden desk appeared, and the woman seated there barely glanced up. A tablet floated effortlessly in front of her. She tapped it a few times, the soft chime of magic humming in the air, then gave a single, deliberate nod to the magickstrate.

"I am Magickstrate Edythe Grouse," she announced in a crisp, unyielding tone. "With me is my court clerk Esmerelda and my bailiff Mortimer. I have been requisitioned to the town of Darkly in the province of Darkly Island to render a binding judgment in the case of Elspeth Wilde versus Jessamin Wilde."

She adjusted her glasses and stared pointedly at Tzazi. "Are the litigants related?"

Tzazi rose gracefully, exuding an air of effortless power in her pristine white suit and killer Manolo Blahniks. "Yes, your honor. The plaintiff is the child of the respondent's former brother-in-law, Dorian Wilde, deceased."

I shifted uncomfortably, praying this wouldn't lead to any unpleasant skeletons being dragged out of my family's closet.

Magickstrate Grouse nodded, then turned back to Tzazi. "Counselor Strangeland, you may proceed."

Tzazi stood tall, exuding a fierce unshakable confidence that made me proud to call her my friend. On that tension-laden podium, she was utterly commanding, holding the room in the palm of her hand. I glanced around searching for Azalea and spotted her a few rows higher. She caught my eye, her grin broad, pride shining through as she gave me a nod.

"To be frank, Your Honor, we are perplexed as to why Ms.

Wilde has brought forth this suit." Tzazi swept a hand toward Elspeth, her tone dry as parchment. "Not only is this an absurd and frivolous case designed purely to harass my client, but it flies in the face of centuries of established case law. Howlton v. Nightclaw. Fanngs v. Lupine. And, of course, the landmark ruling in Fenrirson v. Moon."

A few murmurs rippled through the gallery. Solara huffed beside me.

Tzazi continued, "The World Organization of Lupine Viral & Evolved Shifters, along with the Common Law of the Charming Isles, clearly states that in the event of death, Pack Law supersedes Common Law when the decedent is a member of a pack. Mr. Keir Bane, as Silverfang Alpha had the full right to distribute Dorian Wilde's estate as he saw fit."

She glanced up at Keir, who gave her a small nod of agreement.

Tzazi turned back to the magickstrate, lips curving in a confident, deceptively sweet, smile. "If Mr. Bane had chosen to gift the estate to the Ghoul Scouts cookie fund, that would have been his right. Instead, he did the reasonable thing and deeded the estate to its original and true owner, Jessamin Wilde."

She sank into her seat.

Magickstrate Grouse turned to Mason. "Mr. Beckworth, your response?"

Mason rose smoothly, his smirk widening as he lifted a folder.

"Your Honor, if I may, I would like to enter into the court record the results of a DNA test for Dorian Wilde and Elspeth Wilde."

The room went utterly still.

Oh, hellhound.

Keir squeezed my hand reassuringly as a slow, sickening realization settled in my gut.

This was about to get messy.

A HUSH FELL over the gallery when Mason handed the court clerk a slim, unassuming file folder. My chest constricted under the weight of the moment, each second stretching unbearably as the clerk tapped the folder with a wand. A faint shimmer rippled across its surface. Without a word, she passed it to the bailiff, who received it reverently.

Magickstrate Grouse accepted the folder with a nod. "Thank you, Mortimer." Her voice was quiet but held the kind of authority that made even the walls lean in to listen.

She flipped the folder open, her sharp eyes scanning the document within. Her expression remained impassive. Until it didn't.

Her eyebrows lifted ever so slightly, the only betrayal of surprise. "Why is the mother's name redacted from this document?"

That set off a flurry of motion. Mason and Tzazi both jumped to their feet like someone had set their chairs on fire.

"Your Honor," Tzazi said, smooth as silk, "the identity of the mother of Elspeth Wilde has no bearing in this case—"

"I believe that is something for me to decide, Miss Strangeland."

Oof. Even I winced at that. Tzazi, to her credit, barely flinched, though I saw her inhale deeply through her nose, likely summoning every ounce of her legendary self-control.

Mason, never one to miss an opportunity, cleared his throat in a way that was far too self-satisfied for my liking. "Magickstrate Grouse, I do have another certified DNA test, one that has not been redacted. May I enter it into the record?"

"You may."

The bailiff accepted the new file and passed it to the court clerk, who took an agonizingly deliberate moment to process it. The quiet rustle of parchment and the soft chime of magic filled the air as she verified its contents. Then, with measured precision, she delivered it back to the bailiff. My pulse hammered. That document, without question, held my mother's name within.

Grouse scanned the document, nodded once, and then turned her attention back to Tzazi. "Counselor Strangeland, do you have something to say?"

Tzazi stood, her expression the picture of composed confidence. "Yes, Your Honor. Dorian Wilde was fully aware of Ms. Wilde's paternity and made no exceptions for her in his estate planning. In fact, we all became aware of Ms. Wilde's lineage when officers discovered the DNA results locked in a safe in Dorian Wilde's office at Greywolf Manor."

Which was mostly true. Technically, it was Jess, Tzazi, and me who found the document after breaking into Greywolf under extremely questionable legal circumstances. But I wasn't about to volunteer that information, not when it might earn me an all-expenses-paid night in a jail cell.

Magickstrate Grouse, either satisfied or just tired of the nonsense, nodded once. "We shall proceed. Mr. Beckworth, please enchant your first witness."

I blinked. "Enchant?"

A sudden whoosh of air sent a shiver up my spine as the royal bailiff materialized beside Keir like a ghostly shadow.

Keir gave me a reassuring wink before standing. He adjusted the front of his jacket then, to my absolute shock, placed a hand on the bailiff's shoulder—

And vanished.

I gasped, a little too loudly judging by the way heads turned in my direction. Then, just as suddenly as he had disappeared, Keir reappeared in the witness box next to the judge, looking entirely unbothered by the fact that he had just been magicked across the room.

"Oh, my stars," I whispered, unable to keep the awe out of my voice.

Behind me, Aunt Sibby let out a full-bellied guffaw, while a few other people chuckled more quietly.

I clapped a hand over my mouth. Apparently, sound carried way too well in a round stone room.

Chase leaned in, amusement dancing in his hazel eyes. "Royal bailiffs are sorcerers, hun. Watch. Now, he'll perform a verum enchantment. Forces witnesses to tell the truth."

Below, the bailiff produced a staff adorned with glowing gemstones and slotted it into a sheath attached to the witness chair. He murmured an incantation. The gems began to light up one by one, until only the final stone remained dark. An eerie glow suffused the chamber.

I instinctively reached for Chase's hand. He squeezed mine in reassurance.

The magickstrate, seemingly satisfied, turned to Mason. "Mr. Beckworth."

Mason strode toward the witness stand, hands clasped behind his back, exuding the kind of self-righteous confidence that made me want to throw something at him.

"Thank you, ma'am," he said, standing beside Keir, who looked maddeningly at ease, one leg crossed over the other, his leather loafer bobbing slightly in idle patience.

Mason smiled like a cat who had just found an unattended bowl of cream. "My first witness today is Keir Bane, leader of the Silverfang Clan."

The final jewel on the staff flared to life, a dazzling white light nearly blinding in its brilliance.

"The last part of the enchantment," Chase whispered. "Now it's locked onto Keir specifically. Otherwise, we would not be able to stop ourselves from telling our gallery companions exactly what we think of their ridiculous corkscrew curls."

I slid a glance at Solara. She sat in rapt attention, eyes fixed on the scene below.

Chase followed my gaze and smirked. "Bébé looks like Sideshow Bob."

I choked on my own laughter and had to force myself to look away before I lost all composure.

Below, Mason began pacing, a performance he clearly relished. "Mr. Bane, esteemed Counselor Strangeland cited Pack Law earlier. Do you agree with her assessment that any pack member found in Defiance can be expelled from the pack?"

Keir met his gaze without hesitation. "Aye. I do."

Mason's smile turned sharp. "And yet, Mr. Bane, did you not obstruct Pack Law when you transferred Dorian Wilde's assets to Jessamin Wilde upon his death? By Pack Law, should those assets not have remained with the pack?"

Keir didn't so much as blink. "It was my right as Alpha to do as I saw fit. The property reverted to Silverfang, which means it reverted to me. While Pack Law allows the clan to retain assets, it doesnae require it. The estate was originally Jessamin and Brychen Wilde's. Dorian had already squandered most of what he inherited. The only property left in his name's a cottage out on the outskirts of town."

Mason continued pacing. "Hmm. So, you bend the law when it suits you?"

Keir's lips twitched. "I do what is right."

Mason's grin widened. "Then, by your own logic, wouldn't the right thing be to transfer the cottage to Elspeth Wilde? As that wasn't"—he made air quotes—"'"originally Jessamin and Brychen Wilde's property' but Dorian's?"

Keir nodded, unconcerned. "Elspeth's welcome to it, if it suits her. I've no doubt Mrs. Wilde'd say the same."

Tzazi stood immediately. "My client is willing to relinquish the cottage in Darkly Woods to Elspeth Wilde. And I have no further questions for Mr. Bane."

Mason's eyes gleamed with satisfaction. Only ten minutes in, and he had already peeled away a piece of the estate.

The magickstrate made a note. "Thank you, Mr. Bane."

The bailiff removed the staff, and in the blink of an eye, Keir reappeared beside me.

"Oh!" I yelped, to a smattering of laughter from the gallery.

Keir patted my knee. "Told yeh it'd be fine, love."

He left his hand on my leg, but his attention returned to the proceedings below. Mine remained on my tingling knee.

"Are there any more witnesses to this petition? Either in favor or opposed?" Magickstrate Grouse asked looking over her bifocals at the two attorneys.

"No, Your Hon—" Tzazi began as Mason stood. She narrowed her eyes at him.

"I would like to call one more witness, Madam Magickstrate."

The magickstrate bobbed her head. "Proceed, Mr. Beckworth."

He turned, his smirk wicked.

"I call Windsor Ebonwood."

CHAPTER 14

a sharp gust of wind whispered through the chamber, threading icy fingers through my hair when the Royal Bailiff materialized beside Keir. The man's presence was a force—imposing and immovable. His dark eyes locked onto mine with the weight of a thousand verdicts carved into the lines of his weathered face.

Beside me, Keir bristled, his glare fixed on Mason like a predator sizing up prey.

"Madam." The Bailiff's voice was smooth, steady, and absolute as he extended a gloved hand.

I stood and took his hand.

"Verum dicetur."

The world tilted.

In the blink of an eye, I was no longer standing—I was seated. Keir's warmth lingered on the chair, a phantom comfort I allowed myself to cling to. I exhaled slowly, steadying my nerves.

As before, the Bailiff placed the jeweled staff into its sheath attached to the chair. A whisper of an incantation—words ancient and indecipherable—slid through the air like silk. One by one, the embedded gems illuminated, glowing from the base upward in a slow, hypnotic ascent.

The largest jewel at the top remained dark.

The Bailiff retreated to his position, and I fought the sudden urge to rub my palms on my skirt.

Mason approached, his polished shoes clicking against the stone floor. He smiled—charming to the untrained eye, but I knew better.

"My final witness today is Windsor Ebonwood, half-sister of Elspeth Wilde."

I closed my eyes, shaking my head slightly.

Oh, Mason. Really?

Even without looking, I knew what was coming. The final jewel burst into light, washing me in a warmth so unexpected it almost startled me. It felt as if molten honey was pouring from the top of my head, flowing in gentle waves through every cell of my body, settling deep into my bones.

A spell of truth.

I opened my eyes and locked them onto Mason. Over his shoulder, Tzazi's fingers clenched the tabletop, her expression thunderous. The sight made even me shudder, and I had more immunity to terrifying supernatural beings than most. But a furious vampire? No, thank you.

Mason remained unfazed, his self-assured smile firmly in place. Too confident. My stomach twisted.

"Miss Ebonwood," he said smoothly, gesturing toward the table where Jessamin and Tzazi sat. Jess looked serene, a quiet smile on her lips. Tzazi, however, was all but setting Mason on fire with her gaze alone. I wondered how flammable self-righteous attorneys were. "Are you friendly with Jessamin Wilde?"

"Very," I replied. "One of my best friends, actually."

"At the time of Dorian Wilde's murder were you friends?"

"I wasn't. I had only just moved to Darkly the day before."

Mason nodded, pacing in slow, deliberate strides. "Did you become friends soon after?"

"Yes."

"And did you have many long discussions with Jessamin Wilde?"

I gave a noncommittal shrug. "I suppose so. Most friends do."

He stopped pacing, turning back to me with the precision of someone who had rehearsed this moment far too many times in front of a mirror. "Did any of those discussions pertain to the death of her brother-in-law, Dorian Wilde?"

"They did."

I shifted in my seat, my gaze flicking toward the gallery. I searched the deep shadows for Keir, seeking his steady presence.

Where was Mason going with this? Jess had nothing to do with Dorian's death any more than I did.

"So," Mason pressed, his voice deceptively light, "you were privy to her thoughts concerning Dorian Wilde's murder?"

I tilted my head. "I'm not a mind reader, so...no."

Scattered chuckles rippled through the audience above. Mason's cheeks darkened. He resumed his pacing, though there was a bit more tension in his movements now. I allowed myself a small smirk and caught Tzazi flashing me a quick thumbs-up.

"I'll rephrase," Mason said, pausing directly in front of me. "You stated that you and Jessamin Wilde discussed Dorian Wilde's death, correct?"

"Correct."

"What did Jessamin Wilde say to you about Dorian Wilde's death?"

The words spilled from my mouth before I could stop them. "That Dorian Wilde was a nasty piece of work who made a pass at her, ridiculed her at every opportunity, and—"

Mason's eyes gleamed. "And?"

I bit my tongue, but it was too late.

"She was glad he was dead," I finished, wincing as the gallery erupted in hushed murmurs.

"Just like everyone else in town!" I blurted out, desperate to claw back some of my dignity.

"That's true!" someone yelled, right before a puff of green smoke signaled their abrupt ejection from the gallery.

Mason pounced like a cat on a doomed canary. "And it's true, isn't it, that she was suspected of murdering Dorian Wilde?"

"Yes, but—"

"And didn't she say to him in the Green Gator Tavern that she wished he were dead?"

"Absolutely not," I snapped. "Jess would never say something like that."

Mason leaned forward slightly, his voice dipping lower. "Then what did she say to Dorian Wilde that night at the Green Gator Tavern concerning his death?"

I inhaled sharply. "She said she wished it had been him rather than his brother Brychen who died."

A heavy silence followed.

Mason gave a satisfied nod, bowed before Magickstrate Grouse, then strode back to his table.

I slumped in my seat, barely resisting the urge to bang my head on the desk.

Tzazi, however, was already on her feet, moving toward me with a sureness that sent relief flooding through me. She shot me a reassuring grin before turning to the magickstrate.

"Since neither I nor Miss Ebonwood knew she was going to be called to testify, I'll make this brief, Your Honor," she said warmly.

Tzazi turned back to me and leaned forward slightly. "Since you've known Jessamin Wilde, have you ever known her to make disparaging remarks against anyone—anyone at all—besides Dorian Wilde?"

"Yes. One other person." The words left me before I could stop them.

Tzazi blinked, clearly caught off guard. "Who?"

"Solara Nova."

A beat of silence.

"And she deserved it," I added with a sweet smile.

Laughter exploded through the gallery and someone yelled,

"Ain't that the truth!" Out of the corner of my eye, I saw another puff of green smoke.

Tzazi quickly composed herself. "Ah, I see. Let me clarify. Besides Dorian Wilde and Solara Nova, has Jessamin Wilde ever made disparaging remarks against anyone else?"

I shook my head. "No. In fact, Jessamin is one of the sweetest, most caring persons I've ever met. If she's got something unkind to say, you can bet it's well-earned."

Tzazi nodded approvingly. "Thank you, Miss Ebonwood."

The magickstrate's voice rang out. "I will return with the verdict."

With that, she vanished from the dais along with her clerk.

The Royal Bailiff withdrew the staff from its sheath, and the courtroom shimmered around me.

One blink later, I was back between Keir and Chase. Both threw an arm around me. I squeezed my eyes shut, willing away the burn of tears. I just hoped I hadn't ruined everything for Jess.

THE COURTROOM WAS AS STILL as a graveyard at midnight, the air thick with tension when the magickstrate glimmered back into her seat. The usual low murmur of gossip fizzled out as the spectators took their places, eyes darting from one to another like nervous fireflies.

"Fortunately for all, this was not a difficult case in which to render a decision," the magickstrate announced, her voice crisp and measured. "The precedents and case law are clear."

She inhaled deeply, then turned to the Royal Bailiff, who gave a nearly imperceptible nod. That was when I noticed the royal officers stationed at key exits, their hands resting on weapons both mundane and enchanted. She was expecting trouble. The question was...from whom?

Her sharp gaze swept over the room like a falcon searching for its next meal before landing on Elspeth. A slow, deliberate pause.

"It is the judgment of this Court that an amendment be made to the original distribution of the assets of Dorian S. Wilde."

"Oh, no," I whispered, my fingers tightening around Keir's arm. Below us, Elspeth turned to Mason. Her face split into a gleeful grin, sharp as a knife.

"The original distribution of the assets of Dorian S. Wilde will remain intact with no amendments nor modifications..."

I let out a strangled breath of relief.

"...barring one and one-half acres of property, consisting of a dwelling and outbuildings—"

Chase leaned in. "Did she just say outhouses?"

I elbowed him, biting back a nervous-tinged laugh.

"—located in the Darkly Forest and owned exclusively by Dorian S. Wilde," the magickstrate continued. "Said property shall transfer into the ownership of Elspeth Wilde immediately. So says the Magickstrate."

The Royal Bailiff bellowed, "So says the Magickstrate," and at that exact moment, Elspeth shot to her feet and shrieked loud enough to wake the spirits in the Darkly Cemetery.

"What is wrong with you?! She doesn't even have a speck of Wilde blood in her veins! NOT A SPECK!"

The room lurched with the force of her outburst. Even the magickstrate flinched.

The Royal Bailiff's chin went up as he turned calmly in Elspeth's direction. "This is not a circus, Miss Wilde." He didn't yell, yet his voice reverberated around the walls of the Justice Center. "You will be held in contempt if you continue to defy the Magickstrate's decision."

Elspeth ignored the man completely and flung a furious arm in Edythe Grouse's direction, her long nails curved like claws. The royal officers surged forward, but she twisted and flailed, shrieking at the guards, the spectators, at fate itself.

"You'll pay for this, Grouse! You owe me, Jessamin Wilde!"

With one last, furious struggle, they hauled her toward the

iron door at the back of the chamber. The heavy clang of metal slamming shut echoed in the stunned silence.

For a long moment, no one moved. The crowd seemed collectively stunned into submission. Then, as if someone had released a binding spell, they stirred, murmuring while they filed toward the conveyors.

Tzazi and Jess stepped into the aisle beside us. Jess looked shell-shocked, her eyes rimmed red.

I pushed past Keir and scooped her into a hug. "You okay?" I murmured, brushing her curls back from her damp face.

Jess sniffled. "I can't believe she did that."

"I can," Tzazi muttered.

"Enough Elspeth flipping Wilde talk," Chase said. "Why don't we continue celebrating this evening? Let's all meet at Gumbo Fest."

We'd all accepted the invitation when a heavy presence suddenly loomed behind us. I turned to find Mason Beckworth, his usual complacent expression replaced with something close to regret.

"Tzazi, I am so sorry," he said, shoulders sagging. "I never thought she'd react that way."

Tzazi's expression darkened. "Really? Well, you're the only one. Did you not notice the extra guards the magickstrate brought in for the verdict?" She jerked her chin at him, her tone razor sharp. "And that stunt you pulled with Win? That was low. Even for you."

She jabbed a finger in his chest, making him stumble back a step. "Now move."

Mason had the good sense to obey.

As we stepped outside into the overcast chill of afternoon, the weight in my chest finally lifted. The autumn breeze carried the scent of fallen leaves, hearth smoke, and—somewhere in the distance—the simmering promise of celebratory gumbo.

Jess had won.

But I'd bet my last beignet that Elspeth Wilde wasn't done scheming just yet.

CHAPTER 15

When Keir and I strolled into Oakspider Park, the chilly autumn air greeted us, laced with the warm scent of cinnamon-spiced cider and fried dough. The twisted oaks, usually draped in Spanish moss and their resident magical spiders, now exploded in fiery hues of orange, red, and yellow. The entire park shimmered as if a magical canvas had been thrown over it.

Children shrieked with laughter, flinging handfuls of fallen leaves into the sky. The leaves whirled and danced before vanishing into the breeze. Zydeco music lilted through the air, the accordion spiraling in playful loops while the washboard added its rhythmic rasp.

Keir grabbed my hand and, with a mischievous gleam in his eye, spun me beneath his arm before pulling me close. His deep chuckle tickled my ear. "You're finally learnin' to follow my lead, lass."

"I'm just humoring you," I countered, then sighed.

Keir stopped. "What's wrong?"

"All this." I motioned to the frivolity surrounding us. "It doesn't feel right."

"I knew Patch well," he said, his lips tight. "And this is *exactly* how the man'd want his memory honored." He nodded toward the crowds. "This is Patch."

I nodded and he grabbed my hand, pulling me deeper into the crowd.

The whole festival pulsed with life. Couples swayed to the music, families clinked mugs of cider, and merchants hawked their wares beneath tents bursting with seasonal delights.

Most people were bundled up in scarves and sweaters, since anything below seventy degrees in the South might as well be a blizzard warning. I had opted for a long-sleeved cashmere sweater, wide-leg cords, and my favorite Louboutin boots, a New York holdover I refused to retire.

We wove through the crowd, and I caught sight of Dianthe Petalsigh. I gave her a wave. Her stall overflowed with bursts of autumn color—golden mums, crimson leaves, and sprays of marigold and witch hazel—like the season itself had spilled over her booth in a riot of blooms.

Even from here, the scent reached me, sweet, earthy, and bold. I slowed, breathing it in, when another aroma, rich, heady, and impossibly delicious, crashed into my senses. My breath hitched as the fragrance wrapped itself around me, a siren call of spices and slow-cooked seafood.

I closed my eyes, letting the smell seep into my bones. Cumin. Chili. Simmering onions. And something deeper, darker—roux as rich as sin.

I inhaled again, as if I could drink in the taste of it through the air. "Is that gumbo I smell?" I asked, already moving toward the scent.

Keir chuckled. "Aye, love. Yeh think that's good? Just wait." His fingers brushed the small of my back, a casual touch, but one that sent a shiver dancing up my spine. "Wanna try Phenny's?"

I scoffed. "I think Jess wouldn't speak to us for a full twenty-four hours if we didn't."

"That soon?" Keir grinned. "I'd've expected a full week and a strongly worded hex, at the very least."

With a firm but gentle tug, he pulled me into the thick of the crowd, holding me close as we wound through the jostling festivalgoers. The gumbo tent buzzed with energy—contestants wielding wooden paddles the size of oars, massive iron cauldrons bubbling over open flames, the rich scent of spices thick in the humid air. Gumbo cooks heckled each other across the aisles, throwing down playful challenges and trolling trade secrets in the same breath.

We finally reached the Green Gator's booth, unmistakable by the monstrous, ten-foot gator head looming over it, its enormous jaws forming an entrance. The thing was grotesquely lifelike— scaly skin and rolling yellow eyes that seemed to glare at anyone daring to approach.

Keir gently moved me into one of the long queues. "Best get in line 'fore it's all gone."

We shuffled forward, inch by inch. The smoky bite of sausage and rich, dark broth teased us cruelly. The line surged ahead, and just like that, we stood at the front, staring into the gaping maw of a massive wooden alligator.

Inside the oversized reptilian mouth, pots of gumbo bubbled and steamed as Phenny Guthrie and her team of minions flitted between them like kitchen witches at a cauldron convention. The scent of roux, seafood, and spices curled into the air, making my stomach grumble.

"Win!" Phenny materialized from the chaos, apron flapping, and wrapped me in a warm, damp hug. "I'm so glad you're here!" She beamed, hurrying back behind the counter and grabbing two steaming bowls. "Can you believe this crowd? We have a real shot at winning this year."

"All because of your secret recipe," Clobber quipped as he ladled gumbo into another bowl behind her.

"I'm rooting for you, Phenny," I said, as she handed me a bowl of steaming gumbo and a thick slice of boule. Chunks of shrimp, crawfish (crawdads, as Hilde called them), okra, chicken, and sausage simmered in a mound of hot rice.

Keir wasted no time, tearing off a hunk of boule and dunking it into his gumbo. "Cheers, Phenny," he mumbled, mouth already full, while moving aside to make room for the next customer.

I followed suit, lifting my bowl in a silent toast. "Good luck in the competition."

We wove our way back outside, where the festival crowd had only grown thicker.

"How are we ever going to find anybody in this chaos?" I asked, navigating the crowd while trying to keep my gumbo from sloshing onto an innocent bystander.

Keir tapped his nose. "I know exactly where they are." He took off toward the far end of the park, where the last rows of merchant booths hugged the treeline. "Wolves've got sharp noses, love."

He reached out, gently guiding me in front of him as we pressed into a particularly dense cluster of revelers. "Yeh have a nice scent, Windsor Ebonwood. Did yeh know that?"

I turned around mid-step to catch his expression. "Do I?"

He leaned in, voice husky. "Yeh do. Gardenia and sweet honeysuckle with a whisper of trouble."

I bit back a smile and turned to the front, letting the warmth of his presence settle over me.

Maybe coming out here wasn't such a bad idea after all.

"'Bout time, sugah," Chase drawled from his seat, patting the open space beside him. The autumn breeze spiraled around the table, carrying the scent of caramel apples and bonfire smoke. "Over here."

Keir gave a nod toward his pack, sprawled under a nearby crimson-leafed oak, and wandered off to join them. I veered toward the long table where Ren, Chase, and Tzazi sat, along with a few other townsfolk.

I squeezed in next to Tzazi and reverently placed my bowl in front of me. Finally—my first taste of real Louisiana gumbo! I lifted the spoon to my lips, anticipation buzzing through me. The first bite of Phenny's gumbo hit my tongue, and—Oh. My. Goddess.

Flavors exploded—spice, smoke, the deep, velvety richness of roux—all melting together in a perfect, soul-warming harmony. I let out an involuntary groan, eyes fluttering shut.

Tzazi scooped up a spoonful from her own bowl and smirked. "Phenny's?"

"Mmmmm." I went in for more. "This is so good it has to be laced with magic."

"Not allowed," she said between bites. "To level the playing field. Talent only."

She slid a steaming mug toward me. "But Chase's hard apple cider? Probably a little magic."

Under the influence of Phenny's gumbo-induced euphoria, I'd nearly forgotten all about the cider. I took a deep sip, the spiced apple warmth spreading through my chest, chasing off the crisp evening air.

"Oh, yeah," I sighed. "This is dangerous."

Tzazi lifted her own mug. "Cheers to that."

The festival pulsed around us, and I took in the nearby booths. Right next to our table, Mathilda's stand showcased her besoms with an area cordoned off for test flights. Next to Besoms & Britches stood the booth for Rage, Borda's boutique, and just down the way was Enchanted, a new shop specializing in potions and wands.

"Windsor!"

Jess's voice cut through the noise just as she appeared behind Chase, Jaime in tow and a stack of teetering funnel cake balanced precariously in her hands. Without warning, a sparkling hexdisc zipped through the air and slammed straight into the overloaded plate.

The funnel cake didn't stand a chance. Powdered sugar and crispy dough exploded into the air, a sticky cloud of confection raining down over the nearest festivalgoers. No one seemed to care. Well, except Jess...and a passing golden retriever who set about cleaning up the mess.

"Aww," Jess moaned. "I stood in line for hours."

"No exaggeration there whatsoever," Chase murmured.

"I'll get you another plate," Jaime said.

Jess blinked. "Seriously?"

"Of course." He smiled, easy and open. But the way he looked at her? Like she'd hung the moon and stirred the roux.

"I'll go with you." Jess linked his arm and they headed back into the crowd. "Be right back."

My gaze drift out over the lantern-lit booths and the press of familiar faces. Gumbo Fest shimmered with life—kids darting between tables, music spilling from the main stage, the smell of beignets and fire-roasted sausages mingling in the breeze.

"You think they're talking about it?" I asked, voice low, gazing out at the festivalgoers in front of us. "About the murder?"

Tzazi's gaze didn't shift from the crowd. "No doubt. It's Darkly. Folks are pretending they're here for the gumbo, but you can bet they're sniffing around for gossip."

Chase tore off a piece of boule and dipped it in his gumbo. "Half the people in the gumbo line with Ren and me were whispering about it. Some believe the festival should have been canceled."

"And yet they're here," Tzazi quipped.

I sighed. "I thought the same. But Keir believes Patch would have wanted it to go on."

Nobody spoke after that. Not until Tzazi leaned forward, voice low and sharp. "By any chance, did y'all hear anything useful?"

Ren shook his head. "Just the usual. Wild theories. Shadowy strangers."

"And blamin' anyone who looked sideways at Patch in the last ten years," Chase finished with a roll of his eyes.

I smiled despite myself. For just a moment, the ache in my

chest eased, replaced by the familiar comfort of good friends, hot cider, and gallows humor.

Then Ren stilled, his gaze snapping toward something in the crowd.

"Look. The magickstrate's here."

I followed his line of sight. Sure enough, the Mayórs flanked Magickstrate Grouse as she stepped out of the gumbo tent, an undeniable presence despite the casual cut of her jeans and the warmth of her pumpkin-orange sweater. Some people could wear a tutu and still command authority. Edythe Grouse was one of those people.

My eyes trailed them as they made their way toward the festival's centerpiece, the grand statue of Mayor Mayór examining himself in a mirror. Just as they reached the monument, something strange happened.

Grouse's head lifted slightly, her gaze shifting beyond the statue, straight in my direction.

My breath hitched.

I glanced over my shoulder, expecting to find someone else in her line of sight. But there was no one. Just the soft glow of lantern-lit booths and, beyond them, the vast, dark outline of Darkly Forest, its presence looming just beyond the edge of the festival.

Then, without warning, Grouse went rigid.

Her body tensed, her fingers tightening around the ceramic bowl in her hands. Her eyes widened as if she had seen something—or someone—that unsettled her to the core.

Then—*clatter*.

The bowl slipped from her grasp and crashed to the ground in a splatter of thick, steaming gumbo.

Fernando Mayór, ever the politician, swooped in with the grace of a man well-accustomed to smoothing over awkward moments. He murmured something to Grouse, his hand settling lightly on her elbow as he guided her away. She barely responded, her lips moving in what looked like an automatic apology, but her expression remained shaken.

I swallowed hard.

What in the Sugar Swamp just happened?

An uneasy tension suddenly crawled across my shoulders. Instinctively, I turned toward the Darkly Forest once again. The trees loomed, black and hulking in the flickering festival light.

And then—movement.

A man.

Dark-haired. Standing between two large ferns, partially hidden, watching.

"Tzaz," I whispered, gripping her arm. "Behind us. See that guy near the oak with the hollow trunk? Do you know him?"

She craned her neck. "Win, I don't see anyone."

"What?" I turned back.

No one was there.

Every nerve in my body went rigid. *Had I imagined him?*

Tzazi must've noticed my expression because she patted my arm. "It's been a long day, and I never thanked you for testifying. I'm sorry Mason pulled that stunt."

"It was a rather chickenshit move," Chase declared.

Silence.

Then, the entire table burst into laughter. Chase, of all people, using coarse words?

Tzazi gave Chase a mock-scandalized look. "Language, Prince Charming. You'll melt the pearls clean off some poor widow's Sunday best."

The laughter died down and Mathilda Broomthistle wandered over, looking uncharacteristically serious. "I overheard what you said a few minutes ago, Win," she said. "I just want to tell you, Bane's got that right. Patch would've wanted the festival to go on. And more importantly, Dixie-Deen wanted it to continue. His pumpkins are the stars of the show, ain't they?"

We all turned toward the magnificent pumpkin cart display, surrounded by vines twirling like lazy green serpents through the rich earth. The pumpkins glowed under the lanterns, whispering in their soft voices. Their happiness still unsettled me—especially considering...well.

"I'll be stopping by the Sanctuary tonight after I close up here," Mathilda added.

"Let her know we're thinking of her," I said.

"I sure will," Mathilda said, clapping her hands together in front of her. "Well, who all needs a cider refill?"

Mathilda nod counted the raised hands around the table, then bustled off just as a young girl dragged her father toward the besom booth.

I scanned the crowd again, finally spotting Grouse at Oopsie Daisies, a fresh bowl of gumbo in hand. She looked like she had recovered completely from whatever had thrown her earlier.

Ren set his cider mug on the table, drawing my attention. "Win, please tell me the rumor's true. You bought a broom?"

I perked up. "I did! It's gorgeous. Shimmering crystals, swamp flowers, even a live hood ornament."

Chase raised a brow, one corner of his mouth lifting. "Fancy front-end flair? Sounds like you bought the Cadillac of brooms, sugah. And how does Pye feel about it?"

"He loves it and can't wait to take his first long flight on it." I chuckled and took a drink of my mulled hard cider, emphasis on hard.

"Yeah, I just bet he did." Chase laughed.

I laughed too, and my eyes fell on Keir still standing with his clan. He was leaning against the broad oak, his arms crossed, a look of silent anger marring his features. I sucked in a breath when I saw who had joined them. Elspeth!

He looked at me and smiled softly, raised his chin in acknowledgment.

I wiggled my fingers at him, took another sip of my cider, which was potent enough to peel paint, and willed my cheeks not to flush.

Mathilda soon returned with a tray full of cider, handing out steaming mugs.

"Enjoy! Remember that's award-winning cider there!" Mathilda cackled and scampered back to her booth for another besom customer.

I suddenly felt a familiar heat behind me. I glanced over my shoulder then elbowed Tzaz to move over. She scooted to make room and Keir slid onto the bench beside me. His presence alone shifted the mood.

Tal jostled into the space on my other side, all wind-tousled hair and wolfish charm. A little further down the table, Quinn, Keir's beta, and Laurent Rivier, pack sentinel, squeezed onto the bench with good-natured shoves. Laughter bubbled up as the wolves crammed in around us, bringing their usual mischief along for the ride.

A large shifter, along with a smaller man who looked to be barely out of his teens, squeezed in on the other side of Keir.

Keir extended a hand to the older shifter. "Win, this is Skoll Wrent, one of my most trusted Enforcers. And this little runt," he leaned over and ruffled the young man's hair affectionately, "is Cormac Bane, but everyone calls him Pup."

I must have looked confused because Keir said quietly, "I'll explain later."

Pup smiled. "Hi, Win. I've heard so much about you. It's nice to finally meet."

"Likewise, Pup."

Jess and Jaime finally returned with two stacked plates of funnel cake, placing one at each end of the table.

They squeezed in between me and Tal. Tal straightened up the second Jess sat down, flashing her a slow grin.

The night blurred into laughter, funnel cake, and cider—wolves had a way of turning anything into a party—and I stayed tucked against Keir's side, warm and content.

At a lull in the conversation, Quinn leaned forward, golden bangles clinking as she rested her elbows on the table. "Congratulations on your win, Tzazi! I heard it was quite the spectacle."

Tzazi smirked over the rim of her mug. "That's one way to put it."

"And what about Mortimer the bailiff?" Pup said. He cleared his throat, squared his shoulders, and transformed. Suddenly, he was all stiff-backed and sour-faced, his voice dropping into a humorless, gravelly monotone. "This is a court of law, not a circus, Miss Wilde." He huffed dramatically, pausing just long enough to adjust his imaginary glasses. "If I hear one more outburst, I will hold you in contempt."

The table erupted in laughter and Keir clipped him affectionately on the back of the head. "Yeh better hope yeh never have to be in court with the man."

Mathilda, who had appeared just in time to catch the tail end of our laughter, raised a dark brow as she reached for a few empty plates. "What's so funny?"

"Pup's world-renowned Mortimer impression," I said.

Mathilda smirked. "Always did have a lackluster personality, that one." She wiped her hands on her apron and tilted her head at Jess. "So? I take it you won the lawsuit?"

We filled her in on all the details, from Tzazi's masterful arguments to Elspeth's glorious meltdown at the verdict.

When we got to the part where she had to be physically restrained, Mathilda groaned. "Broomsticks!" She shook her head. "Some people have no respect."

Suddenly, a sharp burst of static crackled through the festival speakers, followed by an overly loud announcement:

"Mrs. Burgundy, please retrieve your husband from the fairy wine tent immediately. He has challenged a sprite to a 'drinking duel' and is currently losing. Badly. He is also insisting he can 'totally take a leprechaun in a fistfight.' This is your last warning before we let the pixies handle him."

"Darkly really is its own brand of chaos," I said between giggles.

Keir smirked. "Yeh've only scratched the surface, love."

CHAPTER 16

"*Well*, well, well. If it isn't Win and the gang," crowed Mayor Fernando Mayór, rocking back on his heels with his thumbs hooked in his polka-dotted suspenders. His bushy red mustache twitched with delight. "Get it? Like Kool and the Gang, except Win and the gang?"

Collectively, we stared at him. Somewhere behind me, a wolf snorted, barely stifling laughter.

Our mayor was unique. A three-foot-tall leprechaun with an ego thrice that size, he was married to Lilith, an axolotl demon in the shape of a devastatingly beautiful Latina woman. If ever there was proof that love saw beyond height, species, and sanity, it was them.

Fernando, undeterred by our lack of response, launched into an impromptu dance routine, wiggling his hips and pointing at the sky before dramatically bringing his finger down. He looked at each of our confused faces and then shrugged.

"Never mind, right?" he said with a cheery grin, clearly unfazed by our collective lack of enthusiasm.

Lilith, ever the vision of effortless elegance, flipped her long black hair over one shoulder and winked at me, completely unfazed by her husband's clowning.

A few feet away, Magickstrate Grouse stopped in front of Mathilda's booth, her keen eyes tracing the trellised walls covered in red blooms. "Now, this is a lovely shop," she said, though her gaze flicked sharply toward Mathilda. "And what is your name?"

Mathilda busied herself with her display. "Mathilda Broomthistle."

"Do I know you, Ms. Broomthistle?" the magickstrate continued.

Mathilda shrugged, absently tugging her ear as she watched a woman test drive a besom. "I wouldn't know. Possibly. I sell a lot of besoms."

"Ah. Maybe that's it," the judge nodded. "You must be very good with brooms."

"They're called besoms, if you don't mind," Mathilda corrected, her voice cool. "And yes, I'm quite good with them."

Overhead, a woman test-flying a besom flipped and twirled with practiced ease.

"Good flyer, that one," Mathilda said. "With a little practice, Windsor, you'll be flying just as good as Hesper up there."

Magickstrate Grouse arched a brow at me. "First broom? You'll find flying is in the blood of every witch. No matter when you start, you'll catch on quickly. Some witches become quite skilled."

"Very true," Mathilda murmured.

"Guess I'll find out," I said, aiming for light, missing by a mile.

Magickstrate Grouse took a step toward our table and squinted. "Is that Counsellor Strangeland I see over there?"

Tzazi raised her head. "Yes, Magickstrate."

"Miss Strangeland, I'd like to take a moment to tell you how extremely impressed I was with your legal prowess and your calm under pressure. Beckworth pulled a fast one bordering on contempt by calling in an unexpected witness as he did. However, you handled it with grace, and I appreciate that. Many don't. If you are ever looking to move to the Isles, I can always use a distinguished law clerk."

Tzazi lifted her chin, clearly pleased. "Thank you. I'll keep that in mind."

Fernando clapped his hands. "Speaking of *distinguished*! Mathilda, my dear, would you share some of your award-winning hard apple cider?"

Mathilda gestured toward the steaming mugs she had already lined up on the counter and with a nod hurried off to speak to another customer examining a besom with Red Hot Chili Peppers hanging from it. And, yes, I do mean little doll-sized figures of Anthony and Flea hanging from its shaft.

"Wonderful! Wonderful!" Fernando drew my attention as he handed mugs to Lilith and the magickstrate before hesitating at the last one. "Would anyone like this one? I mustn't drink while on duty, am I right? Because I'm the mayor, eh."

Jess raised a hand. "I'll take it, Mayor Mayór."

With a bright smile, he handed it over. "Mathilda's cider is always a festival favorite."

Jess took a long sip, smacking her lips in satisfaction. "Ooh, yes. I'd forgotten just how good it is." She cocked her head at Chase. "I dare say, maybe even better than yours, Chase."

He furrowed his brows. "I dare say *not*."

Lilith took a cautious sip and winced. "Ooh. Too potent for me."

"Au contraire!" Magickstrate Grouse exclaimed, already draining her mug. "Absolutely delicious! May I have another?"

"Why, of course, Your Honor," the mayor crowed, ecstatic that the cider at his festival had impressed his distinguished guest. "I myself will do the honors."

"No, no," Lilith said quickly, handing over her own barely touched mug. "You can have mine. If you don't mind my tiny sip."

"Not at all, dear." The magickstrate took it with delight. "I must say, your festival vendors have the best cider and funnel cake I've ever tasted."

Fernando beamed and the trio moved on, the mayor resuming his tour of the festival with exaggerated enthusiasm.

The magickstrate waved a hand at Tzazi one last time. "Keep my offer in mind," she said as she caught up with Lilith and Fernando waiting for her at the Enchanted booth. Its shelves glowed faintly with bottled spells and sleek wands nestled in velvet-lined cases.

A motion caught my attention, and I turned to see Solara and Elspeth, along with Zelda, walking toward our table.

I shook my head, certain the night was about to take a turn, then exhaled in relief as they passed us by without a glance. Instead, they stopped at the Rage booth where Borda's dazzling necklaces were on display along with a few winter sweaters and dresses.

Keir made a low, disapproving sound. "That thir's nothing but trouble."

"Which one?"

He chuckled. "All of 'em."

"Zelda's not too bad," I hedged.

"Aye. But we're only as good as the company we keep."

Suddenly, a loud thump echoed behind us.

Mathilda lay sprawled on the ground, a stunned look on her face as Zelda, Elspeth, and Solara stood around her in a small half circle.

"Oh my!" Zelda rushed to help her up. Solara and Elspeth, meanwhile, shook their heads and laughed.

"Watch where you're going, Mathilda," Solara sneered. "I think you may be getting a little too old for this business."

"Solara, go away," Keir growled and helped Mathilda off the ground, anger rolling off him in waves.

"But she ran into *us*!" Elspeth said, protecting her friend. "We didn't—"

"Now!" Keir's eyes glowed yellow.

Solara and Elspeth hurriedly flounced off, but Zelda hesitated.

She glanced at Solara, then at Mathilda, her expression warring with uncertainty.

"Sorry," she murmured. "I don't know why they act that way." She hesitated, just for a breath, then hurried after them.

Keir walked Mathilda back to her booth. "Yeh okay? Should I call Ileana?"

Mathilda laughed softly. "Thanks, Bane. I'm fine. No need for a healer." She patted his hand gratefully, then wrapped her cardigan tighter around her body and took a seat at her booth, clearly shaken by the fall.

As the tension eased, I turned back to my cider. Beside me Jess uttered a low groan.

"Ugh. I don't feel so good," Jess moaned, her usual porcelain complexion taking on an unsettling greenish tint and she swayed slightly.

I caught her by the arm, steadying her. "Hey, are you okay?"

"Yeah, yeah, I'm fine," she said, waving me off with a faint smile. "Too much funnel cake. Happens every year."

I glanced at the empty funnel cake plate in front of her.

"Your face is pale, Jess," Tal said, his brows knitting together, fists clenching at his sides like he was fighting the urge to scoop her up right then and there. "Would you like me to—"

"You've been here since early this morning setting up the Gator's booth. I'm sure you're just exhausted," Jaime jumped in, pointedly glancing at Tal. "I'm happy to walk you home."

Jess hesitated, just for a beat but long enough for Tal's jaw to tighten. Then she gave Jaime a grateful smile and looped her arm through his. "Why, thank you, Jaime. That's probably a good idea."

We all hugged Jess goodbye. and she assured us, repeatedly, that she'd be fine. I promised to stop by the Manor tomorrow to check on her. They turned to leave, but not before Jess cast a quick, uncertain glance toward Tal, just a flicker, but his face lit with the faintest trace of hope.

Then, with Jaime at her side, she slowly made her way across the festival grounds, disappearing through the gates.

Tal exhaled hard. "She doesn't look well at all. And she goes off with *him*—a guy who wouldn't know what to do if anything were to happen to her."

Keir shot him a warning look. "Tal."

Tal shrugged, arms crossing over his chest. "What? Tell me I'm wrong."

Keir's grip on my hand tightened. "She'll be all right, love," he murmured, lacing his fingers through mine. "But I'm no' so sure about you."

Was this sexy innuendo or…

He frowned down at me. "Did I hear you are now the owner of a flying broom?"

"'Scuse me." Tal leaned his head in between mine and Keir's.

"Say," he said quietly, a frown etched into his usually smiling face. "Is Jess dating Jaime?"

Without warning, a sudden boom rocked the park.

Pink spheres exploded into the sky, pelting people and trees. Festivalgoers screamed and raced for the exit like fire ants fleeing a flood, their feet barely touching the ground as panic pulsed through the air.

And just like that, the Gumbo Festival erupted into chaos.

TZAZI and I hit the ground in a tangle of limbs and urgency and crawled under the table where Chase was already crouched, cradling his cider thermos like a lifeline.

"What in the world is that, *bébé*?" Chase squinted at Tzazi's hair, plucking out a glob of something pink and sticky. He examined it for a second, then popped it into his mouth.

I recoiled. "Chase!"

He grinned wickedly, snatching another blob and chucking it in his mouth. "Cotton candy."

"Seriously?" I hesitated, then plucked a piece from my own hair and sniffed. Sure enough. Spun sugar. The festival grounds were under siege by rogue carnival treats.

Tzazi batted Chase's hand away before he could plunder more from her hair. "I am not a walking dessert table, Abernathy-Wyatt!"

I laughed as a new flurry of chaos erupted outside our wooden refuge. Leaves, once gracefully swirling in the crisp autumn air, now zipped through the crowd with malicious intent, diving into ears, up noses, and glomming onto cotton candy balls clinging to festivalgoers' hair.

"I don't know what's happening, sugah," Chase drawled, leisurely sipping his cider, "but this right here is worth every penny of admission."

We crawled out from under the table, swatting away leaves and cotton candy pellets when Keir, Laurent, Tal, and Quinn joined us. The four shifters looked amused; however, Borda Wrathfell, who suddenly appeared behind them like an ill-tempered storm cloud glowered at the chaos.

"WHO IS DOING THIS?" she shrieked, gesturing wildly at the festival-turned-circus, her face practically vibrating with rage.

Before Borda could launch into another tirade, the band struck up an eerie, off-kilter waltz. The musicians wore identical expressions of dazed horror, their hands moving independently of their wills. As if pulled by invisible strings, the old poppet seller lifted his arms, assumed the posture of an unseen dance partner, and began a box step.

One by one, festivalgoers standing too close to the dance floor were swept into the madness, twirling in an awkward, enchanted choreography.

"Oh, this is too perfect," Chase sighed blissfully, lounging against the table and taking a long draw of his mulled cider.

"Chase Abernathy-Wyatt!" Borda spun on him. "There is nothing perfect about this disaster!"

As she was ranting at Chase, a pig—yes, a flying pig—soared

over her head, greedily snatching cotton candy from the air with delighted squeals.

I was laughing so hard I had to hold onto Keir for dear life. Tzazi doubled over in laughter. I wrapped an arm through hers and turned to Keir. "Are all Darkly festivals this exciting?"

"Not usually," Keir admitted.

We all lounged back on the table, sipping our ciders and enjoying the continuing chaos around us.

No one looked to be injured and as that reality made its way around the grounds, festivalgoers stopped their hasty retreats to watch the pandemonium just as we were.

I choked on my cider as the mayor, his head swollen up like a huge bobblehead balloon, pinballed through the air, Lilith chasing after him, shrieking, "Fernando, you come back down this instant!" Fernando twisted and turned in the air as he screamed, "This is not funny" to everyone he passed who was, indeed, laughing.

"Any idea who or what's responsible for this?" I asked between giggles.

"No idea," Tzazi said, watching as Solara and Elspeth, to their visible horror, waltzed past us in perfectly synchronized steps. "But I'd like to shake their hand."

"Mm-hmm. Same here," Chase agreed. "I'd buy all their drinks for a year." He took a long draw of his mulled cider. "I can't remember the last time I had so much fun at a Darkly festival."

"Aye," Keir said, standing. "But I suppose we should put a stop to the shenanigans."

Chase groaned dramatically. "Keir, *mon ami,* must we be the villains in this grand spectacle? Look at the sheer delight our mystery magician has gifted the town of Darkly."

Keir grinned at Chase's theatrics and nodded toward the dance floor. "Let's ask Mr. Creech."

We followed his gaze to the elderly poppet seller, sweat-drenched and stumbling, still locked in his involuntary waltz.

"So that's his name," I said.

"Abimelech Creech," Tzazi said. "He's a sweet...guy."

Chase sighed. "Fine. But let it be known I'm only doing this for Mr. Creech."

He strode toward the center of the park where the statue of the mayor stood, now defaced with an unsettling amount of clown makeup. Chase clapped his hands together with a resounding boom. The ripple of energy rolled outward like a shockwave.

One by one, the spells unraveled. Leaves drifted harmlessly to the ground. The sticky pink sugar storm abated. Mr. Creech's feet stilled, and he collapsed right into Keir's arms.

For the briefest moment, a golden shimmer passed between them. Keir gently released him, and the old man, looking much healthier, nodded his thanks before shuffling off.

I turned to Tzazi. "Did Keir just heal Mr. Creech?"

She shrugged. "Shifters have minor healing abilities."

I took a final sip of cider and sighed. "Well, I guess the show's over."

Tzazi smirked. "At least for tonight."

I narrowed my eyes at her in question. "What do you mean?"

"Well, you never know in Darkly."

We watched silently as the mayor's bushy red balloon head pushed through the cattails and bobbed out into the dark swamp.

Tzazi smiled. "But I wouldn't live anywhere else."

I BUSTLED into Fernwood as an autumn wind heavy with night, damp leaves, and chimney smoke rattled the porch chimes.

Pyewacket uncurled from the top of a sofa cushion and yawned.

"Winter's not knocking—it's barging in," I said, rubbing my arms against the chill.

"Well, it's about time," Sibby said, lounging in her chair. "I thought I'd never be able to bring out my thermal underwear."

Hilde emerged from the kitchen, wiping her flour-dusted hands on her apron. "How'd the festival go?"

"You'll never believe."

I told them about the spiced cider, the funnel cake, Keir, and Jess's illness, then… "All hell broke loose."

All heads snapped in my direction.

By the time I'd finished describing the chaotic situation, all three were rolling on the floor. Pye literally. Sibby had to set down her carving knife before she did some damage to herself.

Hilde's grin turned downright wicked. "How was Keir? Did y'all have fun?"

I let out a long, dramatic sigh. "Keir's perfect. Absolutely perfect."

Hilde snorted. "That bad, huh?"

I flung an arm over my eyes like some swooning Southern belle. "It's infuriating. He's gorgeous, he smells good, he's maddeningly competent at everything—flirting, tracking, probably folding fitted sheets." I sat up, throwing my hands in the air. "And worst of all, he knows it. He just stands there, all broody and smug, like the universe personally appointed him to drive me out of my mind."

Sibby, lounging in her chair, took a slow sip of bourbon. "Sounds like love to me."

I sat up straighter, eyes narrowing. "No. Don't even say that."

Sibby chuckled, utterly unbothered. "Well, what else would I say? Love's like gumbo, sugar. Starts with a slow simmer, then one day, you realize you'd wrestle a gator for the last bite."

I sighed. "I haven't known him for all that long, Sibby."

My great aunt popped her pipe out of her mouth. "Well, you know what they say?"

I braced myself for this next round of advice.

"Love works in mysterious ways," she said knowingly, popped her pipe back into her mouth, and began carving her latest shrunken applehead project, this one looking a bit like Dixie-Deen.

For once, I didn't need a cipher to understand her.

Sibby's words stuck with me longer than I wanted to admit. I didn't need Keir, not in the desperate, all-consuming way I'd once thought I needed Lucas, my fiancé in New York. But I wanted him in my life, beside me, in a way I'd never desired anyone or anything before. Was that love?

I wasn't ready to answer that question, so I called it a night, swapping my festival-worn clothes for flannel pajamas. Pyewacket had already claimed my pillow, snuggled up into a tight ball. I scooped him up and plopped him onto the other pillow. He didn't so much as twitch.

I lay down, wiggling my feet under the blankets piled at the foot of the bed, but sleep was elusive. My thoughts wandered back to the trial earlier. Jess had won—thank the stars—but Elspeth's behavior nagged at me. The way she'd looked at Jess, like she was already measuring where to slide the knife in. A prickle of unease crawled up my spine.

First thing tomorrow, I'd talk to Chase, Ren, and Tzazi. And Keir. We needed to make sure Jess was protected.

That decision eased my mind enough to drift into sleep, but something pulled me back—a sound. A soft thump.

I bolted upright, peering out the window.

Pyewacket jolted upright beside me. "What is it?"

The courtyard and lagoon beyond shimmered under a lazy veil of fireflies, their golden pulses winking in and out of existence. It could've been nothing. A raccoon, maybe. A falling branch.

Then another sound.

Lighter, more deliberate.

I sucked in a sharp breath.

I sprang from bed, crammed my feet into my Wellies, and snatched up the flashlight I stored in the dresser drawer. Fernwood was prone to power outages, so I had stashed them all over the house.

In the kitchen, I pressed my nose to the window overlooking the dock.

And froze.

A figure loomed by the jon boat, half-shrouded in shadows. It stood at least eight feet tall, its frame a tangle of contorted roots, its black eyes like pits of hunger. It took a slow dragging step toward the house.

My breath hitched.

Then, as if sensing my stare, it turned its gnarled head sharply toward me.

My pulse leaped to my throat. I fumbled with the back door latch and Pye and I charged outside, flashlight beam slicing through the night.

"Who's out here?" I shouted.

The upstairs light in Hilde's apartment snapped on. Seconds later, she burst onto the porch, her footsteps heavy against the planks. Sibby hustled right behind her, barefoot, her silk robe flapping around her like bat wings.

"Win! What in the nine circles of hell are you doing?" Sibby barked.

I kept my eyes on the dock. "I saw someone."

Hilde's sharp gaze scanned the area. But the dock was empty. The water, still.

A lump of doubt formed in my stomach.

Was I losing my mind? First the man in the tree line at the festival and now this?

I turned toward the courtyard, sweeping the flashlight beam across the flagstones. Nothing.

Then, a ripple in the water. Greta Garbo, our ancient guardian alligator, rose silently, her massive bulk breaking the surface. She didn't seem perturbed in the least. Just watching, patient and curious.

"I swear," I murmured, my voice tight. "Something was here."

Hilde crossed her arms. "Describe it."

Beside her, Sibby flicked her wand out of her sleeve, scanning the cypress line on the other side of the lagoon.

"Tall. Black, dull eyes."

Then a new sound shattered the night—footsteps. Fast. Urgent. Racing toward us from the front of the house.

In a blink, Hilde shifted. Her bear form exploded forward, a wall of muscle and fur, standing between me and whatever was coming. Sibby whirled, lifting her wand, ready to blast the threat barreling toward us.

A voice cut through the dark. "Win? What are yeh doing out here?"

My stomach knotted. "Keir?"

Sibby let out a sharp whistle, dropping her arm. "Well, it's a good thing I think before I shoot."

Hilde shifted back to her human form as Keir rounded the corner, his breath ragged, his face grim.

"It's Jess," he said. "She's been rushed to the hospital."

CHAPTER 17

"*W*ait. Start over. Tell me from the beginning." Hard as I tried, I couldn't stop the tears flowing down my cheeks.

Keir nodded, patient as always, and took my hand. I gripped his like a vice.

"By the time Jaime got Jess back to Greywolf Manor, she was so weak she could barely walk. He didn't want to take a chance, so he transported her to Wychwood Hospital."

"Transported? How?"

"Jaime's a warlock," Keir explained. "He can veilshift and take others with him." He squeezed my hand tighter. "Love, I don't know anything else about her condition."

I nodded.

The Range Rover moved deeper into Nocturnelle, the province of the vampires, and the air grew thick and oppressive. The headlights barely cut through the blackened mist curling along the ground. Wind danced through the trees, skeletal and gnarled, standing sentinel, their twisted limbs reaching toward the sky.

Brume, the capital of Nocturnelle, loomed in the distance, a sprawling gothic city where jagged towers lanced the eternal night. Blue witchlights flickered dimly, their glow subdued by the surrounding gloom. The architecture was a study in shadow and grandeur—spires topped with ironwork, slitted obsidian windows, and crumbling bridges that stretched across the city's winding canals.

A deep, bone-rattling bell tolled from Brume's central cathedral, freezing my blood mid-flow. It echoed through the landscape, long and sonorous.

A prickling unease crept along my spine.

"We're being watched," I whispered.

Keir's hand tightened on mine. "Aye. Always in Nocturnelle."

Movement flickered at the edges of my vision. Pale figures stood motionless beneath the trees. Their hollow eyes followed us. As we passed, a murder of jet-black crows lifted in unison from the branches, spiraling upward into the ink-stained sky.

The road narrowed, flanked by crumbling stone walls and wrought iron gates that led to overgrown graveyards. From one, a statue of a woman in mourning robes tilted forward, as though she might step off her pedestal at any moment and join the living.

I exhaled shakily. "How do you ever get used to this place?"

"You dinnae." Keir glanced at me, concern softening the hardness in his expression. "Love, are yeh all right?"

I nodded, though my pulse thudded in my throat. "I just need to get to Jess." My voice broke as I said her name.

He squeezed my hand again, warm, reassuring, and grounding. "Aye. We will."

He drove a few miles further.

"Now listen," he said. "To pass into Wychwood, we have to cross a bridge that is manned by vampires on this side and witches on the other."

"Do they not get along?"

He sighed. "Yes and no. They dinnae trust each other. I just wanted you to be aware."

I gulped. This sounded forbidding.

We passed a black tree, its trunk wider than a small shed,

whose gnarled branches almost touched the ground. It twisted as it followed our passing in Keir's Range Rover.

"What in the world!"

"Yeah, that's a wychwood tree," Keir said. "Indigenous to Wychwood. That's how yeh know we're close. The witches use them as a type of security alarm."

The hostile black trees grew denser along the side of the road until we navigated a curve and came to a stop at a roadblock. A line of men with dark hollow eyes and angular features lined the pavement where it stopped before a sudden drop-off. I craned my neck to see what lay below, but all I saw was a pitch-black void.

A man hidden in the shadows of the wychwoods stepped forward, startling me in his abruptness. His long white hair, ghostly against the dark, fell to his waist and his eyes dark and tinged red, locked onto mine.

I shivered and gave a yelp.

Keir looked at me with a smile. "You're okay."

He turned back to the man and rolled down the window of the Land Rover.

"Draven," he said warmly and stuck out his hand. "How have you been?"

"Keir," the man grasped Keir's hand and pulled it to his chest. "Very well. What are you doing out here? Injured pack member?"

"No," Keir said. "A good friend. She's been veilshifted, and we're here to check on her."

"Quite right," the man said and then peered past Keir at me. "And this is...?"

"Windsor Ebonwood," I said, trusting my voice not to shake.

"An Ebonwood. So nice to meet you, Windsor," he said, giving me a stare, then turning back to Keir. "You may proceed, my friend." Then, with the subtlest of smirks, he added, "Enjoy Wychwood."

The foggy outline of a black bridge rose up through the abyss connecting the two islands, and I steeled myself, preparing to pass into the domain of the witches.

~

THE RANGE ROVER pulled forward seemingly into thin air. I let out a squeak and before I could stop myself, I grabbed the handle. The door cracked open.

Keir grabbed my arm. "Whoa, whoa, there, love. I cannae keep yeh in the Rover *and* stay on this godforsaken bridge at the same time."

I fell back into the seat. "Sorry."

Pulling my coat tighter around my body, I peered cautiously out the window. Nothing but fog and the indistinct shadows of boulders were visible. Black limbs stretched above us while below at the bottom of a deep jagged ravine, waves crashed and roiled as if in a furious boil. Stone blocks flew up from the ravine and formed into a jagged road barely wide enough for the tires to pass over in place of the foggy outline. Behind, the blocks fell off a split second after we passed. After a few minutes, I let myself enjoy the breathtaking experience, much like those rollercoasters that flip upside down and fly off the tracks for a moment.

Immediately after passing over the bridge, a thick ominous fog surrounded the Range Rover blocking any view.

I grabbed his hand. "Keir, what's going on now? I thought we'd already made it through security."

"It's fine, love. This side takes a bit more finessing."

The Ranger rolled to a stop as a tall man dressed head to toe in black leather stepped out of the fog. His black duster almost long enough to drag the ground flapped around him as he strode to the front of the Rover. Two shaggy eyebrows dipped into a scowl above cold eyes and a bushy mustache and beard. I had to look away from the angry red scar running from forehead to cheek along the right side of his face.

As he moved to Keir's side of the Ranger, six more figures stepped from the fog surrounding the vehicle. All in black. All scowling. All with magic coiled at their fingertips.

"Bane." His deep voice resonated through the Ranger.

"Evening, Ruggieri."

"What business do you have here?" His voice was deep, rich with authority—and challenge.

Keir kept his voice even. "A friend of ours is critically ill and has been admitted to Wychwood Hospital."

Ruggieri's dark eyes flickered toward me, and I knew before he even spoke that shifters were not welcome here.

"I cannot permit your entry," he said coldly.

Keir growled. "This is an emergency, Ruggieri. I wouldn't—"

Ruggieri motioned to his guards and yelled, "Turn the vehicle around!"

I felt the fury build up in me.

"What is wrong with you?" I said softly but deeply, my voice reverberating through the fog-filled air.

Ruggieri's head snapped toward me, his dark eyes narrowing, contempt curling his lip. A hush fell over the witches, their magic crackling in the air like a brewing storm.

"Are you speaking to me, shifter?" His voice was quiet, but razor-sharp, slicing through the dense mist around us.

The tension thickened, close and suffocating. Keir went still beside me, his gaze locked on mine—dark, guarded, but filled with something fierce and unwavering.

A steel weight settled under my skin, and I met Ruggieri's gaze head-on. Cold. Unforgiving. Deadly.

"Yes," I said, my voice steady, unyielding. "I *am* speaking to you."

A slow exhale. The barest flicker of unease in the witch's eyes.

"My friend is dying," I continued, my words cutting through the fog like a blade. "And you *will* let me through to see her."

The night held its breath.

The leader of the witch guard laughed, a deeply unfriendly cackle.

"Look at this, Warders," he said, his voice loaded with derision. "Bane's bitch thinks she's going to tell me what to do."

I grabbed Keir's arm when he opened the door to step out.

Ruggieri walked to Keir's side of the Rover and bent to peer through the window. He jerked his head in my direction and one of the figures broke loose from its foggy restraint and strode to my side of the vehicle.

A woman with a furious frown and peroxide blonde hair tapped on the window and motioned for me to lower it.

She cocked her head after I had done so. "And who might you be, little wolf?"

I studied her for a moment and felt, more than saw, her confidence waver.

"Windsor Ebonwood. And I strongly suggest y'all cease with the disrespect."

You could have heard a pin drop.

The peroxide blonde bowed slightly and then moved back into her position against the edge of the forest.

Keir grinned at me and said softly, "Ah. I should have thought of that, *little wolf.*"

To my surprise, each guard backed away from the Rover and turned to Ruggieri for guidance. "What is going on?"

"Ebonwoods are considered witch royalty," Keir said. "Especially here in Wychwood. I guarantee Ruggieri is embarrassed for the arrogance of himself and his guards."

What had our family done to warrant such respect in Wychwood? I wanted to know more but now was not the time.

The commander of the Warders, who had moved a few paces away from the vehicle, strode around to stand next to my window.

He also gave a slight bow. "I am Ercole Ruggieri, Lead Warder of the Wychwood domain under the command of Chantely Crow. Lady Ebonwood, I apologize. In my defense, deadly occurrences have taken place all over Wychwood recently. We had no way of knowing—"

"No harm done," I said quickly, hurrying him along. "Could we pass, please? Like Keir said, our friend is deathly ill, and we need to be there."

"Of course, Lady Ebonwood. Again, I humbly ask for your understanding. Please pass."

He stepped back and made a smooth circling motion with his hand, allowing our admittance, his eyes never leaving mine. The Warders faded back into the fog, and we rolled into the black forests of Wychwood.

THE TREES OF WYCHWOOD, black trunks glossy like wet ink, were by far darker and more frightening than any forest I'd ever seen, even in horror movies. Their branches reached for the road, stark and grasping, and where Nocturnelle had been deathly silent, Wychwood was alive with whispers. The very air hummed with unseen voices, rustling in languages older than time.

A thick fog drifted along the ground, through the tall, black, leafless trees silhouetted against silvery moonbeams. Small creatures flitted about. Some I recognized, like the will-o'-wisps around Fernwood. Other, more sinister beings, slithered along the ground below.

"You were right," I said. "About Wychwood. I'm glad I didn't come here alone."

"I would no' let you travel through here alone. At least no' the first time."

I squeezed his hand gratefully.

"Yeh handled yourself well back there. Reminded me of yer gran."

Having met the force that was Minta Ebonwood when I first moved to Darkly, I was flattered by the compliment.

The Rover wound through the dense fog-covered forest. When we turned a bend, a mesmerizing blue glow rose in the distance ahead of us. Soon, a clearing opened to the quaint town of Tansywick. Floating pointy-roofed cottages, shrouded in mist, their chimneys belching violet-hued smoke hovered above iron-fenced gardens overflowing with wild herbs. Along the cobbled paths, glass globes hovered like fireflies, and from brass cauldrons, tendrils of scented steam twisted into the air.

In the center of the village stood a great mossy Wishing Tree, its gnarled roots wrapped around an ancient stone fountain. Trinkets and charms swung to and fro in its branches.

Beyond, a woven reed boat drifted along a narrow creek glittering under the witchlight. A tiny lantern swung from a crooked pole, casting trembling light while a shadow-cloaked figure glided silently through the water.

Yet, despite its beauty, unease coiled in my gut.

There was magic in Wychwood. A lot of it.

The witch village faded behind us, swallowed by the oppressive tangle of Wychwood's towering trees. The deeper we went, the heavier the air became, thick with the scent of damp earth and something sharper, like burnt herbs and old paper. Shadows stretched unnaturally between the trunks, twisting in the periphery of my vision. I clenched my fists in my lap, willing my heart to slow.

Then, through the swirling mist, it emerged. Wychwood Hospital.

A towering mass of ivy-clad stone, the building pulsed faintly with ancient glowing runes. The windows were dark, deep-set, and ominous. Nothing about it suggested comfort or care.

The moment Keir pulled the Rover to a stop, I moved to fling open the door, but his grip was suddenly firm around my wrist.

"C'm 'ere." His voice was low, soothing.

Before I could protest, his hand cupped my face. His thumb brushed against my cheek as his lips found mine in a kiss both gentle and grounding. For a moment, the dread slipped away, replaced by the warmth of him, the quiet promise in his touch.

When we parted, he held my gaze, his brown eyes serious, unwavering. "Whatever happens in there, I'm here for yeh. I will always be here for yeh."

I swallowed against the lump in my throat, for Jess's life, for

Keir's promise, and brushed my fingers along his jaw. I nodded, holding back tears.

Then we were moving, pushing toward the ivy-covered building. The hospital had no visible entrance, only a looming archway beneath an enormous gargoyle. It perched above the portico, wings spread wide, its stone eyes seeming to follow our every step.

As we reached the arch, the creature let out a low, rumbling growl, deep enough to rattle my bones. Then, as if satisfied, it tilted its massive head and gave a slow, deliberate nod.

Large wooden doors materialized and swung open with a whisper.

The interior of the hospital was both grand and surreal. Warm mosaic tiles of tan and blue shifted subtly, reshaping themselves with each step, leading us forward. The walls were lined with floating sconces, their soft glow illuminating spectral aides that drifted soundlessly from room to room. The doors closed behind us with a finality that startled me.

Keir led the way to the nurse's station, where a quick, hushed conversation sent us down another twisting corridor to a waiting room. At the end of a row of plush chairs, Tzazi and Jaime sat together.

Tzazi looked up the moment we entered. Her eyes—red-rimmed, filled with worry—met mine, and then she was on her feet, throwing her arms around my neck.

"I'm so scared, Win," she whispered against my shoulder. "I don't know if—" Her voice broke.

I tightened my hold on her, willing whatever strength I had into her trembling frame. "What happened?"

Jaime cleared his throat, his freckles standing out, stark against his pale skin. "She mentioned feeling lightheaded, then the nausea hit. When she had trouble breathing—" He swallowed. "I didn't wait. I veilshifted her straight here."

"What have the doctors said?"

"Nothing yet." Tzazi wiped her face, her expression tense and fearful.

Then Chase and Ren arrived, their hands laden with coffee cups, the scent cutting through the sterile air.

Ren silently handed Tzazi and Jaime each a cup before turning to me. His dark eyes were soft and kind, and he pressed a warm cup into my hands, his gentle presence reassuring.

Chai.

"Thank you," I murmured. Ren wrapped me into a brief hug, steady and sure.

Keir leaned down and whispered, "I'll be right back."

He disappeared down a dim hallway.

And then I saw Ransom.

He was standing at the end of the corridor, speaking in hushed tones with an elderly man clad in black leather, one of Wychwood's Warders, no doubt.

Fear tightened around my ribs. Ransom being here could not be good.

Had something happened beyond Jess's illness? Was this more than an accident?

Keir joined them and the three men exchanged grave words before disappearing around a corner. A cold dread settled in my stomach.

Tzazi clasped my hand in hers, her grip almost painful. "She said she felt ill last night," she whispered. "I just...blew it off. I thought it was nothing."

"We all did, Tzazi," I said.

The room fell into heavy silence, the kind of silence that made time stretch into an eternity. Only the rhythmic tick of an ancient grandfather clock in the corner intruded on the solitude.

Then, finally, the door swung open. A witch in emerald robes stepped inside, scanning the room before locking her gaze onto Tzazi. "Are y'all here for Jessamin Wilde?"

Tzazi shot to her feet, pulling me up with her. "Yes," she breathed, her face drawn with fear.

The witch studied her, then me. A flicker of compassion crossed her face before she finally spoke. "We believe she was poisoned."

The room tilted.

I sank back into my seat, the word ringing in my ears.

Poisoned.

Tzazi's mouth opened, then closed, before she finally choked out, "How? What kind of poison?"

The healer sighed, folding her arms. "That we don't know yet. We've flushed her system, and it seems to be helping. But whatever was used, it was potent."

She turned to Jaime, her sharp gaze softening.

"You, young man, saved her life."

Jaime stiffened, his hands flexing at his sides. He looked stunned, maybe even shaken. No matter what he'd done in the past, in that moment, I forgave him everything.

"We're running tests," the witch continued. "She needs to stay here for observation. Her breathing has normalized, and she's stable for now." She offered the smallest of smiles. "It's the best news we could hope for."

Chase, ever the charmer, turned on his deepest, warmest Southern drawl. "Ma'am, I wouldn't dream of being a bother, but if there's any chance you could let us in, I'd be mighty grateful."

The witch sighed, unmoved. "I'm sorry. Family only."

Tzazi's head snapped up. "Have you contacted Faelan and Elysande?"

Jess's parents.

"Yes," the witch said. "They should be here shortly." And with that, she disappeared behind the heavy doors.

Silence fell again, heavier this time. We all sat, the weight of the unknown settling around us like a second skin.

Poison.

Jess had been poisoned.

Which meant someone had wanted her dead.

CHAPTER 18

The rune-covered walls of Wychwood Hospital pulsed faintly, the sigils shifting in a hypnotic rhythm. I stared at them, willing myself not to fall apart. My fingers clutched Tzazi's hand, holding on too tight, I knew. But she didn't pull away. We both needed the anchor.

A rush of violet wings broke the heavy silence and a woman with a wild burst of red hair zipped into the room, her presence like a sun flare in the dim hospital light. Close behind her, a devastatingly handsome man strode forward with the grace of a warrior-prince. His deep plum jacket gleamed under the waiting room's flickering glow. The metal adornments on his coat sent shifting reflections dancing across the walls.

"Tzazi!" The woman's voice was high and musical as she threw herself into my friend's arms.

Tzazi clung to her, fingers gripping the fabric of her shimmering gown.

"Have you seen her?" the woman asked, pulling back just enough to meet Tzazi's gaze, her violet eyes wide with fear.

Tzazi shook her head, her expression tight and worried. "The doctor believes she'll be okay. She was poisoned, Elysande."

The man beside Elysande—tall, aristocratic, exuding a raw

and terrifying presence—turned so sharply his blond-white hair whipped over his shoulder, three small braids falling across his sharp cheekbones. His pointed ears gleamed with multiple piercings, and his light green eyes locked onto mine with such intensity that the breath hitched in my throat.

Power. That was the only way to describe Faelan Darkmoon. His aura radiated old magic, coiled and restrained, potent enough to make the air around him hum.

"How did this happen?" His voice was pure steel and thunder. He turned searching the room, his keen gaze hunting for someone —anyone—who could give him answers.

"They don't know yet," I answered, forcing my voice to remain steady.

His piercing gaze fell back on me. My stomach clenched. This was a man you did *not* want to cross.

Jess's mother turned to me, her delicate hands clasping my arm with surprising strength.

"Are you Windsor?"

I nodded, and without hesitation, she pulled me into an embrace.

Elysande Darkmoon was breathtaking. Her long, curling red hair fell in thick waves to her knees. A single diamond glittered on each delicately pointed ear. Her violet gown, the black lace bodice intricate, elegant, and timeless shimmered with emerald undertones. She was otherworldly, yet the warmth in her touch made her feel wholly real.

"Oh, Win," she murmured. "She talks about you all the time."

A sharp ache bloomed in my chest.

Elysande pushed a stray lock of hair from my face, her expression tender. "Do you have any idea what happened, dear?"

I opened my mouth, but no words came. The weight of everything—the fear, the uncertainty, the crushing guilt—became too much.

Tears welled, then spilled.

Elysande pulled me closer, smoothing my hair as though I

were her own daughter. Her touch radiated comfort and strength. A soothing warmth spread through the room, and I realized Jess got her kindness, her light, *her magic* from this woman.

Faelan's voice shattered the moment. "We'll see our daughter now."

As if summoned, the doctor reappeared, motioning for Jess's parents to follow.

Faelan hesitated at the door, glancing back at us. "I appreciate all of you being here, but you no longer need to stay. We'll contact you the moment anything changes."

Then he was gone, disappearing into the depths of the hospital behind his wife.

The silence settled around us, thick and uneasy. Jess was alive —for now—but none of us felt any less rattled.

Keir and Ransom reentered the room, and Keir dropped into the seat beside me. He reached for my hand, his grip firm, warm, protective.

Keir brushed a kiss against my cheek, and I instantly felt the tension coiled in him like a tightened spring. Something was very, very wrong.

I could barely breathe as I whispered, "What is it?"

Ransom ran a hand through his dark hair, his expression grim.

"I don't know how else to say this."

His voice dropped, rough and final.

"Twelve others were poisoned last night. Including the magickstrate."

A beat.

"She's dead."

A cold wave crashed over me, stealing the air from my lungs.

Thirteen poisonings. One dead.

This wasn't random.

Was there a serial killer in Darkly?

~

THE ROAD HOME stretched out in silence. Tzazi, who had flown to Wychwood when she heard about Jess, decided to ride back with Keir and me, needing the company, though we barely spoke.

Keir dropped us off downtown and kissed me quickly before heading off, his touch warm but brief. Dawn had barely crept over the buildings, but none of us wanted to go home. Not yet. Instead, everyone drifted toward the MET, our feet moving of their own accord.

Inside, the fireplace crackled, casting golden light over the cozy space. We huddled near it like lost animals drawn to warmth.

"It feels strange without Jess here," Ren murmured, his voice barely above a whisper.

Chase shifted closer, slipping an arm around Ren. "I keep listening for her voice. Like she'll walk in any second and roll her eyes at us."

I wrapped my hands around my coffee mug, its heat barely chasing away the chill inside me. Across the room, Tzazi stood by the fire, staring into the flames like they held the answers we didn't.

"Are they connected?" she asked suddenly, her voice edged with something sharp.

"What do you mean, sugah?" Chase asked.

"Jess's poisoning and the magickstrate's death," she said darkly, turning on her heel. "Both happened the same night. The same night as the court ruling." Her eyes flicked to me, narrowed with meaning.

"Elspeth," I whispered.

"And why were none of us poisoned?" Ren asked softly. "All of us had food and drink from vendors all over the festival."

Tzazi's eyes narrowed to dangerous slits. "Because they were targeted attacks."

I sighed. "Elspeth did make threats, not just against the magickstrate but against Jess too."

Chase shook his head, his jaw tight. "But what about Patch? I hate to say it, my darlin's, but Elspeth had no reason to go after him. Far as I know, they'd never even met."

Could there be two killers?

We all slumped back into our seats, deep in thought. Tzazi's question had the gears in my head churning. Were the poisonings and deaths related? If so, what was Patch's part in all this? And the question that scared me the most—Did someone in Darkly want Jess dead?

Tzazi turned away again, slipping into the shadows near the far corner of the shop. Her hands moved subtly, fingers whispering through the air in the quiet, intimate way of someone deep in conversation. A flicker of movement in the darkness made my skin prickle and I realized what she was doing. She wasn't a full shadow person like Mizizi or Azalea, but she did have shadow magic in her blood.

Chase stood and stretched, the tension in his movements evident. "Ren, *mon amour*, we should go." He turned to the rest of us. "The salon is going to be buzzing today about Jess and the magickstrate. Maybe we'll get some of our questions answered." He bent to kiss my cheek. "Let us know if you hear from Elysande."

When the shop door chimed behind them, silence settled back over the room. Tzazi returned to the fireside and flopped into a chair next to me.

"Who could have done this?" she asked.

"I don't know, Tzaz. I was hoping you'd tell me. Grouse wasn't from here. Who in Darkly would've wanted her dead?"

She stared into the fire. The logs shifted with a low groan.

"Only one name comes to mind. Benny the Rat. Grouse sent him to prison for centuries."

Outside, a sudden gust rattled the windowpanes.

When she spoke again, her voice was low and quiet. "Do you think Elspeth or Mason could have hurt Jess?"

"I hope not."

When she met my gaze, the fear in her dark eyes made my

stomach lurch. Normally, Tzazi was unshakable, a force of nature. Seeing her afraid unnerved me more than anything else that had happened in the last twenty-four hours.

"Jess is going to be okay, right?" she asked, her voice barely above a whisper.

"She is, Tzazi. She absolutely is. And you need to hold on to that."

She exhaled, nodding. "I sent one of Papi's shadowmen to watch over her. Until we know what's going on, I need to know she's safe."

"That's a really good idea."

Tzazi nodded absently, rocking slightly in her chair. A long silence settled between us, filled only by the occasional pop from the fireplace and the low hum of the MET's quiet magic.

Before she could respond, the shop door chimed, breaking the moment like a snapped thread. Elspeth Wilde swept in, her dark curls bouncing, her lipstick a perfect blood-red. "There you are!" she exclaimed.

Tzazi's fangs clicked into place with a sharp, deliberate snap. She dabbed at her eyes and stood.

Elspeth, to her credit—or her eternal stupidity—blanched but recovered quickly, pretending Tzazi didn't exist and turned pleading eyes to me.

"Please, Win," she whispered, her voice dipping into something fragile, but calculated. "I need your help."

"Get out!" Tzazi's voice was menacing and deep.

Elspeth glanced at Tzazi and then her eyes returned to mine. "Please, Win."

"Tzazi, I'll be fine. Besides," I pointed to the corners and whispered loudly, "Shadowmen."

Tzazi gave me a hug and left, giving Elspeth one last glare. "If anything happens to her, I promise you'll regret it."

The look on Elspeth's face told me she knew Tzazi meant every word.

I sat down and nodded at the chair Tzazi had just vacated.

Elspeth slid into it as if all the bones in her body had turned to mush. She was visibly shaking.

"What's happened?" My voice probably sounded cold and uncaring, but I'd dealt with Elspeth enough to know that trickery and a play for sympathy are tactics that were right up her sleeve.

"That inspector searched my room this morning and found dried petals in my jacket. But they're not mine! I have no idea how they got there!"

Now, *that* I hadn't expected.

"Dried petals?"

"The poison that killed the magickstrate and made Jess sick came from some kind of flower."

I looked away as she burst into tears.

Crocodile tears, no doubt.

"He says I'm his primary suspect!" she stammered as tears continued to flow down her face.

"Well, yeah, you should be!" I countered incredulously, surprised at the anger that rose up. "You've done nothing but hurt people since you arrived here. Then you lose your case and suddenly the magickstrate's dead and Jess is very ill. The two people you threatened! What would you expect?"

I tried not to shout at her—I did—but the anger and frustration I'd been carrying toward Elspeth surged forward—a tsunami rushing through a village, crushing everything in its path.

"Look. I'm sorry I ambushed you at the MET opening. I was angry. I shouldn't have done it. It was Mason's idea. He said it would create a buzz. Get people on my side. But it did the opposite!"

I canted my head and exhaled deeply.

"You have it all, Win." She looked around the MET. "You're an acknowledged member of the Ebonwood witches. You were raised an Ebonwood." She shook her head. "I just want to belong. I want to be part of a family."

I wasn't falling for her act, but I was curious.

"Where did you grow up?"

"Wentworth Academy. Since as far back as I can remember. Don't look so stunned," she said, a bit of that Elspeth attitude creeping back into her voice. "I'm not an idiot, you know."

"They take children that young?"

Elspeth shrugged. "They accept students at birth."

My heart began to thump out of my chest. "Who paid your tuition?"

Elspeth shrugged. "No idea. When I was about to graduate, I broke into the headmistress's office and found my birth certificate. I figured it was my last chance to find out something about my past. That's how I learned I was an Ebonwood."

"And a Wilde," I added.

"And a Wilde. Although so far, I have yet to show werewolf tendencies." Her face puckered at that admission.

"What kind of witch powers do you have?"

"So far, not a lot in that area either. I can bring objects to myself, but I have to concentrate hard to do it." The smile that flicked across her face gave me pause. "But I did not kill the magickstrate, nor did I kill the pumpkin man, and in no way did I hurt Jessamin. I wouldn't dare, even if I wanted to."

"What does that mean?"

She let out a huge sigh. "I know how much Jessamin Wilde is loved by you and everyone in this town. I'd be a fool to do something like that."

"But it didn't bother you to try to steal her inheritance."

We both sat in awkward silence. I kept my eyes on the fire, watching the flames lick the bricks and spit tiny sparks into the hearth.

"What does any of that have to do with me, Elspeth?" I turned my head and looked into her wide eyes.

"I need your word…"

I pshawed. "Fat chance of that." I began to stand.

"Wait, Win. Please listen." She lightly touched my arm.

Surprised, I eased back into my chair.

"I know the inspector is looking at me. Please prove to everyone that I didn't have anything to do with any of the deaths...or Jess's or anyone else's illness. Please."

I sighed and we sat silently for a few moments. The large grandfather clock ominously ticked down the seconds, while the crackling fire provided warmth and comfort but no resolution.

"If I find out you harmed Jess, you'll regret ever coming to me for help."

"I would expect no less," Elspeth smiled. She brushed her long black curls behind her shoulder and stood. I could see genuine relief in her face. "By the way, do you know if the inspector has a girlfriend?"

I escorted her to the door.

~

MIST DRIFTED through the Fernwood courtyard in swirls that clung to stone and vine, reluctant to lift even as the sun pushed higher. I pulled my robe tighter, my UGGs making soft scuffs against the cobblestones as I padded toward the wrought iron table.

Hilde had taken up her usual perch, swaddled in blankets like a grumpy bear in a den. Pyewacket lay sprawled across her chest emitting a self-satisfied purr while Greta Garbo basked nearby, one massive eye cracked open in lazy observation.

I set my coffee down and stretched. "Won't be long before it's too cold to sit out here."

Hilde grumbled, burrowing deeper. "If I get any colder, I'm shifting just to keep warm."

At that, Sibby meandered out, wearing a flowing silk robe, her white curls a mess atop her head, and her ever-present creepy eye mask dangling from one hand.

"Down, bear," she muttered to Hilde before casually conjuring a small ball of fire in the air. The sphere hovered above us, casting golden light and flickering shadows. The fire snapped and hissed when the mist swirled in too close.

Hilde gave a grudging nod. "Better."

Sibby flopped onto a lounger with all the grace of a cat falling off a windowsill and covered her face with her sleep mask. "Any news on Jess?"

I took a sip of my coffee. "No. Hoping for an update today."

With a flick of my wrist, I snapped open *The Daily Shade*, giving it a good shake to straighten the wrinkles. Nothing quite like the scent of fresh newsprint in the morning—well, maybe the smell of cheese grits, but I wasn't about to be picky.

Predictably, the front page screamed scandal.

MAGICKSTRATE DEAD: CURSES, CRIME BOSSES, AND KILLINGS—OH MY!

"Oh, good," I murmured. "Nothing overly dramatic."

I skimmed the first few paragraphs. "Benny the Rat was a crime boss? I thought he was just a bookie."

Hilde snorted. "Benny *is* a crime boss. He lords over The Graves out on Coastal Road."

"That dismal fog-covered borough outside of town?" I asked. "I drove past it on my way to Patch's farm. Looked like the perfect location for an opening scene of a horror movie."

"That's the one," Hilde confirmed. "Not a place to visit. We leave those people alone; they leave us alone."

Sibby, still in her mask, lifted a hand lazily. "You do not want to go there."

I nodded, making a mental note to add Do Not Visit the Graves to my ever-growing list of Things That Could Get Me Killed in Darkly.

A strip of bacon arced through the air, and Greta Garbo launched from the lagoon in a burst of water, her jaws snapping shut around the prize with a wet, thunderous *clomp*. "Good girl," Hilde cooed, as the massive gator sank back below the surface with a satisfied grunt.

From the lounger, Sibby let out a snort. "Well, honey, one way or the other, that magickstrate's bound to have a suspect list longer than a church potluck line—and twice as juicy, I'd wager."

I snapped the newspaper open and spread it flat across the metal table. "Either of you know who this reporter Beatrice Snarkle is?" I asked, tapping the byline of the article. "Seems like a real troublemaker."

"She's a sneak, that one," Hilde said, her frown deepening. "I don't know that I've ever met her, but she has a reputation for not having much regard for the truth."

Sibby popped up from the lounger again, lifting her eye mask like a woman preparing for battle. "What's the name again?"

"Beatrice Snarkle."

Sibby considered this for all of two seconds before plopping her head back down. "Nope. Never heard of her," she said decisively, mask sliding back into place.

I shook my head at my eccentric great-aunt and folded the paper. "I need to take a shower and get dressed. Keir's coming by, and we're having lunch at Gumbo Fest. They're announcing the winners today, so cross your fingers for the Green Gator's entry. Phenny and Jess worked hard on that recipe."

Sibby sat up so fast her mask went flying. "Well, you stay close to that hunk of a wolfman, Peanut. Don't take any chances—especially with that Elspeth Wilde on the prowl."

"'On the prowl' is an excellent choice of words," I said, thinking of Elspeth hanging on Keir yesterday. I wasn't about to tell these two I had promised her I'd investigate the murders and poisonings.

I gave Hilde a quick peck on the cheek before scampering off toward the house, narrowly avoiding the swat of her hand as she called, "Now you cut that out!"

I could hear the smile in her voice, though, and it made my own grin widen.

eir and I strolled hand in hand into the festival grounds. The golden afternoon light slanted through the autumn air and wispy clouds drifted lazily overhead. The scent of caramel and cinnamon twisted on the breeze.

Keir gave my hand a squeeze, his thumb brushing absently over my knuckles. It was such a simple gesture, but warmth spread through my chest like a well-placed enchantment.

A surprisingly large crowd thronged around the booths and ambled down the grassy walkways. Kids raced past holding cotton candy and caramel apples; parents trailed behind already resigned to the sugar-fueled mayhem. The trees rustled with red, orange, and yellow leaves, adding to the idyllic charm of the day.

"What are you in the mood for?" I asked, pausing as a little boy and his dog sprinted past.

Keir turned to me, eyes hooded, a slow smile curving his lips.

I tugged his hand, pulling him forward before he could catch the blush heating my face. His low laugh trailed behind me.

We ducked into the gumbo tent. "How about The Cloven Hoof?" I pointed to the bright yellow banner. "Tzazi's always raving about their sandwiches."

"Yeh cannae go wrong with the Hoof," he agreed easily, his

fingers brushing over mine before he let our hands swing together again.

We approached a busy booth, where a short, stocky man ladled steaming gumbo while keeping up a lively banter with the customers and passersby around him.

"Keir Bane!" the man's voice boomed with delight. "'Bout time you made it to my booth."

Keir grinned and pulled me forward. "Alvar Vache, have yeh met Windsor Ebonwood?"

Alvar set down his ladle before giving me a respectful nod. "I have not. It's an honor, Windsor. I did hear you had moved to town. How are you liking it so far?"

Any response I had died on my lips when a teenager appeared beside him, bouncing on her toes. Her eyes—one sea-blue, the other dark as midnight—fixed on me with open curiosity.

"Dad," she stage-whispered, "is this Windsor? Miss Minta's granddaughter?"

"Leidy," Alvar sighed, exasperation clear in his voice. "Introduce yourself properly."

She stuck out a hand. "Adelaide. But people call me Leidy."

I shook it, instantly liking her.

"So," she continued, barely containing her enthusiasm. "Were y'all here yesterday for all the craziness? Someone tried to disrupt the festival, then the magickstrate was poisoned along with—oh! Jessamin's one of your best friends, right?"

She clapped a hand over her mouth. "I'm so sorry. I wasn't thinking. Dad always says I let my mouth get ahead of my brain sometimes. Is she okay?"

Her father affectionately rapped her upside the head.

"It's fine, Leidy," I assured the teen. "The doctors believe she'll pull through."

Leidy sighed in relief, then leaned forward conspiratorially, her eyes darting over to her father who had fallen into deep discussion with Keir concerning the special ingredients in his gumbo this year. "That magickstrate, though? Yikes."

My curiosity sharpened. "Did you talk to her?"

"No, but I overheard her telling Mrs. Mayór she'd just seen someone she hoped never to run into again." Leidy's voice dropped to a dramatic whisper. "Called them a *psychopath*."

"Seriously?"

Leidy leaned across the counter, elbows planted. "I know you were the one who figured out Dorian Wilde's killer. Who do you think did in the magickstrate?"

"I really don't know," I said carefully. "Grouse's past opens the door to a whole crowd of suspects."

She hopped down and wiped her hands on her apron. "Name one."

"Well, Benny the Rat comes to mind. And—"

"Nope." She cut me off with a firm shake of her head. "Not Benny."

Her confidence gave me pause. "Why not?"

Leidy leaned in slightly. "Day before the trial, Benny and Grouse showed up at The Cloven Hoof together. They were *laughing*. Totally relaxed around each other. Turns out, they're both obsessed with wine. Grouse even invited him to share a bottle of *Romanée-Conti* next time he's in the Isles."

She shot a glance at her dad, then brushed a crumb off her shirt. "There was *zero* tension. And, believe me, if there'd been friction, I'd have noticed."

Leidy tilted her chin toward a nearby cluster of giggling girls, all throwing not-so-subtle glances at a group of oblivious guys.

I chuckled. "Point taken."

"Got any others you want to run past me?"

"Leidy!" Alvar barked, swatting at her with a dish towel. "Stop that gossiping."

"What?" Leidy shrugged. "It's not gossip if it happens *in public*."

Leidy rolled her eyes and jabbed the wooden spoon back into the gumbo pot.

"You keep rolling those eyes like that, and one day they're

gonna get stuck clean in the back of your head," Alvar said as he turned back to Keir and me. "Sorry about my daughter! She's at that age..."

With a wry grin, he pushed the bowls toward us. "I hope you enjoy the gumbo, Windsor. We're hoping for first place again this year."

"Good luck in the competition," I offered.

As we wandered off in search of a table, I glanced back. Leidy still stood at the counter. When our eyes met, she gave a small nod.

Keir led me to a secluded table tucked beneath the sprawling branches of an oakspider tree. "This is about as private as we're gonna get," he said, nudging me onto the wooden bench.

"It's perfect."

I thought my long-sleeved sweater dress would keep me warm, but the chill still bit at my skin and I visibly shivered. Before I could protest, Keir pulled off his thick jacket and wrapped it around me. The toasty warmth calmed my chills, and I breathed in his spicy aroma of forest leaves and cardamon.

"Us wolf shifters don't feel the cold," he murmured, his voice like melted honey. "But you do, and I'd rather not spend our rare alone time watchin' yeh shiver."

The heat from his jacket seeped through me, slow and steady. I took a spoonful of gumbo, letting the spice bloom across my tongue. "Mmm. This is incredible."

Keir grinned. "Yeh've got a little..." He swiped his thumb across the corner of my mouth, then—without breaking eye contact—licked it off his thumb.

Oh.

I dropped my spoon, scrambling for a topic—any topic—to distract from the fact that my heart was currently trying to beat its way out of my chest. "S-so! How do you like working with Ransom?"

His smirk faltered. "Where's that coming from, then?"

"Well, he's the new inspector, right? And you'll be working

with him on cases now. So, I'm just wondering how you like working with him."

"He's fine." Keir scooped up a bite of gumbo, chewing thoughtfully. "Mmm. Alvar's outdone himself this year."

"Keir Bane. You don't like him, do you?

Keir's eyes suddenly darted behind me, and I felt a hand on my shoulder. A female voice crowed, "Look who I found, guys."

Quinn and Laurent appeared at our table. Silent as wolves. I hated how they did that.

Laurent motioned behind himself at Chase, Tzazi, and Ren who also joined us.

Keir exhaled heavily. "Sorry, love."

I shrugged. "We can't help we're just that dang popular."

He kissed my cheek lightly before turning to greet the newcomers.

Tzazi settled into the seat beside me and Ren and Chase dragged over chairs from a neighboring table. Chase produced his large thermos and began pouring out steaming mugs of hard apple cider. The scent of cinnamon and cloves wafted through the air.

"Any news on Jess?" Ren asked, accepting a mug and watching me closely.

I held my mug to my chest, letting the warmth seep in. "Not yet," I said, shaking my head. "Hopefully soon."

Chase slapped a hand down on the table, making the mugs jump. "You know, the more I sit with it, the madder I get. I mean really. What kind of twisted soul does something like that? The magickstrate? Sure. I get it. Folks like that collect enemies like they collect antique cufflinks. But Jess? And eleven other folks? That's just madness." He let out a frustrated huff, shaking his head.

Quinn flopped into the chair on my other side, eyes immediately zeroing in on my half-finished bowl of gumbo.

"Come on, you all know who's behind this," she declared, grabbing the attention of the entire table. "Elspeth Wilde."

Several heads nodded in agreement, but Chase leaned back in his chair, stretching out one long leg lazily.

"I dunno," he drawled. "She'd have to be real stupid to pull something like this after that embarrassing stunt she pulled in court."

Suddenly, a loud, ear-splitting, buzzing sound ripped through the festival speakers. Several people covered their ears and winced.

"The winner of the Gumbo Fest competition will be announced in ten minutes," the mayor's crackling, distorted voice rang out. "Please join us in the center of the grounds next to the devastatingly handsome statue of your mayor."

I slid my bowl toward Quinn. She accepted it with enthusiasm, her already bright eyes taking on an odd silver sheen.

What was that?

"Ooh. Thanks, Win. Saves me a trip to the gumbo tent," she said, and then proceeded to devour the remaining stew, sopping up the rich roux with a thick slice of French bread.

Keir's fingers reached for mine.

"They're about to announce the winners," he murmured. "Shall we?"

I let him take my hand, his grip sure and solid. "I hope Jess's entry does well," I said, as we stood. "She deserves some good news."

"Aye. I think it will."

We followed the crowd toward the statue. The chill in the air sharpened as the sun dipped lower. I noticed many of the festivalgoers nursed their mugs of cider and mulled wine from personal thermoses, and their chatter seemed quieter than usual.

Keir stepped in behind me, his arms wrapping around my waist, pulling me snug against his chest. Between the warmth of his body, his thick jacket, and Chase's cider, I felt cozy and a little too contented, like I could melt into this moment if I weren't careful.

Chase quirked the thermos at me. "Another round?"

I shook my head. "If I have one more, Keir might have to carry me home."

Keir, without missing a beat, grinned against my ear. "That all it takes? Chase, give her another mugful."

Chase groaned. "Get a room already."

Laughter bubbled up around us, but before I could fire back a retort, Keir turned slightly, his focus shifting as he spoke quietly with Laurent. The moment his attention flickered away, Quinn leaned in, her voice low and brimming with indignation.

"I cannot believe Keir's letting that little wench stay at Wulver Cairns. I tried to tell him—"

"Wait," I said, holding up a hand. "What little wench?"

"Elspeth." Quinn shot me a look. "You didn't know?" She flicked a glance at Keir, who still spoke quietly with Laurent where another pack member, Laird, had joined them. "She's been there for days. Bringing the whole place down with her shifty ways."

I looked over at Keir, heat flaring under my skin. Why hadn't he told me? Every time I started to think I could trust him...I hadn't even been to Wulver Cairns and Elspeth was living there?

I bit back a scowl.

He's here with you, Win. You know he doesn't even like Elspeth.

Tzazi pushed up next to me and wrapped her arm through mine.

"I'm glad to see you out today, Tzazi."

"Yeah, Maman told me it was either grab a dish cloth and help in The Cup or get outside."

I laughed. Tzazi's mom was a dear, but I could see not wanting to cross her. She and Mizizi, her father, were both known for being powerful—and not the kind you wanted to test.

I shot a look at Keir, and Tzazi's eyes narrowed instantly. She always noticed everything. I was starting to believe she was part hawk rather than bat.

"What?" she asked, her voice low, edged with suspicion.

I sighed, rubbing my temple. "Did you know Elspeth is living in the Cairns?"

Tzazi blinked. Then, flatly: "That's got to be a mistake."

I shook my head.

Her expression darkened. "Keir just told you?"

"No." My gaze flicked to the stage where Borda had just stepped up and grabbed a mic, her movements sharp with impatience. "Quinn did."

Tzazi looked like she was about to blow a gasket.

"Quinn?" she hissed, her hands curling into fists. "You need to talk to Keir. Now."

Before I could respond, Keir suddenly slid behind me again, his arms looping around my waist like it was the most natural thing in the world. The warmth of him, the weight of him, the quiet steadiness of him worked against my frustration, cooling it just enough to keep me from stomping onto the stage, grabbing that mic, and demanding answers myself.

Tzazi shot daggers at him, her glare practically boring holes through his skull.

As if sensing the shift, Ransom strode up, dressed in dark jeans and a long-sleeved flannel, his usual sharp edges dulled just slightly by the casual clothes.

I tipped my head toward him, raising a brow. "Well, look at you. You're blending in nicely."

Ransom smirked. "You know what they say. If you can't beat 'em..."

Keir, now practically looming, extended a hand to him. "Any news on Jess?"

Ransom's expression sobered. "Actually, yes."

The crowd around us stilled, conversations cut short as every gaze snapped to him. A weight settled in my stomach, heavy and tight.

Please let it be good news.

Ransom exhaled. "Both the magickstrate, Jess, and eleven other festivalgoers were poisoned by nerium. We found tainted cider in five different vats at the festival that night. All from different vendors."

I saw a few festivalgoers pour out their mugs into the grass.

"Nerium?" I asked, unfamiliar with the term.

Ransom's gaze turned grim. "Oleander."

A collective murmur ran through the group. I frowned, my mind working fast.

"Oleander. That's a flower, right?"

Could that be the poison Elspeth said he found in her jacket pocket?

Quinn draped her arms around Keir's shoulders and leaned in front of him. "It's a flowering bush that grows all over the island," she said to me. "Extremely lethal."

I clenched my jaw. "Yes, I'm aware."

Keir didn't push her away, but he did glance at me, almost as if he felt the storm roiling in my mind.

I gnashed my back teeth together and turned my attention to Ransom, ignoring the way Quinn leaned just a little closer to Keir as she listened.

"That's right. Extremely lethal," Ransom nodded. "Jess was lucky to have Jaime with her when she fell ill."

Chase exhaled hard, running a hand along the rim of his mug. "Tell me something, Ransom. Was this just a case of wrong place, wrong time? What if Jess, or one of the others, was the real target?"

"And what about the festival sabotage?" Tzazi asked, arms crossed stiffly across her chest.

"And Patch? Is it all related?" I added.

Ransom sighed. "We're working on it."

His expression lightened just slightly. "But I do have good news. I spoke to Elysande and Faelan Darkmoon before veilshifting back. Jess is coming home tomorrow."

Relief crashed over me like a wave. The crowd within ten feet of us burst into cheers, applause rippling through the festival like wildfire.

"She'll need a lot of rest still," Ransom said. "But she'll make a full recovery."

I reached for Tzazi's hand, and she squeezed back. Firm, steady, a silent *she made it*.

Ransom cleared his throat and motioned to the stage. "Looks like they'll be announcing the gumbo winners shortly."

Almost in reply, a loud buzzing screeched through the air again drawing everyone's attention to the bandstand where Borda and the mayor stood locked in a silent battle of wills. Borda, tall and storm-eyed, crossed her arms, while the mayor puffed up like an indignant peacock. The festival mic, crackling with leftover static from the last announcement, sat between them like a prized weapon.

Borda reached for the mic. The mayor, predictably, snatched it first.

"Citizens of Darkly!" Fernando bellowed, his voice amplified across the park. "Thank you for coming together once again for our beloved Gumbo Festival, an event that celebrates our town's rich culinary tradition, our sense of unity, and of course your wonderful mayor."

Borda exhaled sharply, pulled the mic over, and spoke over him. "And, of course, the actual gumbo makers who put in the work."

A few cheers and laughs rippled through the crowd. The mayor's left eye twitched.

He cleared his throat loudly, attempting to regain control. "Before we announce the winners, I'd like to acknowledge the unfortunate incident that occurred during our festivities. As you all know, several of our most endearing citizens fell ill due to an isolated food contamination event—"

Borda pulled the mic to her face. "It was poisoning," she cut in flatly.

A murmur ran through the crowd.

The mayor's smile tightened as he yanked the mic back. "Well, yes, but we are handling it."

Borda pulled the mic over again.

"The royal inspector is *investigating* it," Borda corrected. "And we'll be increasing safety measures for the remainder of the festival."

Fernando's jaw clenched, but he forced a smile. "Yes. What she said."

The crowd exchanged wary glances. The tension was still palpable. After all, people had been poisoned in the middle of one of Darkly's biggest festivals. No one liked that kind of disruption, especially when food was involved.

Tzazi leaned toward me. "At least they're acknowledging it."

Borda, clearly done with the mayor's theatrics, yanked the mic out of his hands and walked away a few paces. "Now, let's get to the reason we're all here—the winners of the gumbo competition."

That got a reaction. The crowd perked up, and people adjusted their stances, eagerly awaiting the results.

Borda pulled an envelope from the podium, opened it with a quick flick, and raised her mic.

"Third place in the Gumbo Festival's gumbo competition goes to…Cypress & Sage Glamping Retreat in Devils Hollow."

A mix of cheers and polite applause spread through the audience as a woman in sleek outdoorsy attire stepped forward, clearly thrilled.

Chase leaned into me. "I've always wanted to stay there. Luxury tents in the middle of a lush jungle. There are even wild animals roaming about!"

Ren smiled. "Bucket list, *mon cœur*."

"Not Bucket List. Now List," Chase quipped.

Borda didn't wait for the applause to die down as she pulled out another envelope. "The judges had a hard time deciding between our First and Second place winners."

Fernando pulled up a stool and hopped up so he could read over her shoulder. "Second place—The Cloven Hoof!" Borda shouted.

Louder cheers followed, especially from the shifter-heavy crowd. Alvar and Leidy stepped forward, their movements clipped but composed. Leidy accepted the ribbon, her jaw tight until a quick, stubborn grin broke through. She lifted it high, earning a fresh round of applause. Alvar gave a courteous nod, but his eyes were already scanning the competition like he was taking notes for next year.

Finally, Borda smiled, pulling out the last envelope. "And first place—"

Fernando, now thoroughly irritated by Borda's efficient emceeing, ripped the envelope out of her hand and grabbed the mic. "The Green Gator Tavern!"

The crowd erupted into applause, whistles, and enthusiastic clapping. Jessamin wasn't here to accept the award, but the moment still felt victorious. Quinn and Laurent let out celebratory howls, and Chase beamed, nudging Ren.

"Our girl did it," he said smugly.

"That she did," Ren replied.

I watched as Phenny climbed the steps to accept the award. Alvar and Leidy waited for her at the bottom to give her a big hug and heartfelt congratulations.

Tzazi folded her arms, looking pleased. "Jess is going to be insufferable when she finds out."

"Oh, absolutely," I agreed, already picturing her smug grin. "And I can't wait."

The mayor stepped forward again as Borda scowled next to him. "And, of course, a huge congratulations to all our competitors! Let's give them another round of applause!"

Keir's hand found the small of my back, his touch grounding me as the excitement buzzed around us. "Great night for The Gator."

"Yeah," I murmured, though the victory felt slightly off. Maybe it was the undercurrent of unease that still hung over the festival. Maybe it was the memory of Patch's murder. Maybe it was the fact that someone out there had deliberately poisoned people at the event. Or maybe it was the fact I was beginning to think I didn't trust Keir because he wasn't giving me any reason to do so.

Borda, meanwhile, had zero patience for lingering ceremony. Yanking the mic back, she declared, "All right, folks, enjoy the festival, but keep your wits about you. If you see something suspicious, report it. And for the love of all things holy, stop drinking festival cider until we clear the vendors."

Chase raised his mug in mock salute. "Cheers to that."

The crowd began to break up, some drifting back toward the food stalls, others murmuring about the poisoned festivalgoers.

Keir glanced at me, voice low. "What do yeh say? Ready to head home?"

I nodded. "Sounds good."

"One blink, lass," he said and strode over to his pack.

As I watched Keir leave, my gaze snagged on something—or someone—behind him. In Patch's pumpkin patch, a small man squatted in the vines, polishing a gleaming pumpkin with a small white cloth.

I frowned. "Did Patch have an assistant?"

Chase followed my gaze. "Only the pumpkinheads. Why?"

"Then who's that?"

Tzazi's eyes narrowed. "Oh, that's Mulch, his competitor."

My gut tightened. "I'll be right back."

Tzazi stood. "Not without me, you won't."

THE PUMPKINS GLEAMED in the fading afternoon light, their green, white, and orange hues standing out against the rich, dark soil of Patch's pumpkin patch.

Mulch was a slight man with a ruddy complexion and wiry frame, dressed in overalls and a long-sleeved orange shirt rolled up to his elbows. The official uniform of pumpkin farmers, apparently.

Tzazi drifted through the rows behind me, absently running her fingers over the pumpkins, but her sharp eyes never stopped scanning.

"Excuse me," I said carefully.

The man turned, his weathered face breaking into an easy smile. "Well, hello there. Can I interest y'all in a pumpkin?" His accent was warm, friendly.

"Actually, I had a question," I said. "Aren't these Patch's pumpkins?"

The smile flickered just slightly before he nodded. "They sure are. Shame to hear about his demise. He was a good competitor, that's for sure."

Competitor. Not friend.

"You grow pumpkins too?"

"I do. Mulch is the name. Gordon Mulch." He wiped his hands on his overalls, then gestured around the patch. "Dixie-Deen asked me to take care of the festival pumpkins for her. She's been staying at the Sanctuary since it happened. Can't blame her. Losing Patch like that…"

I hesitated, then met his gaze. "I'm Windsor Ebonwood. I'm the one who found Patch's body."

Gordon Mulch's expression shifted. His brows furrowed, and something flickered across his face. Concern? Fear?

He exhaled slowly. "That must've been awful." He glanced away, his boot scuffing against the dirt. "Thing is, there's something about his death that doesn't sit right with me."

I stilled. "What do you mean?"

He shook his head, lips pressing together. "They're saying it was an accident. But Patch was a professional. He'd never transport his pumpkins over his head. That's pumpkin-rearing 101." He hesitated before adding, "It just doesn't make any sense."

Exactly!

I turned to Tzazi, who had wandered back to my side, a giant golden pumpkin in her arms.

She studied Mulch with sharp, assessing eyes. "So, if it wasn't an accident, what do you think happened?"

Mulch exhaled through his nose. "Oh, I've got a good guess." Then he seemed to catch himself and drew back, patting Tzazi's pumpkin. "Great choice there. One of his best."

Tzazi set her pumpkin on the makeshift counter, pulling out a few coins to pay for it. Mulch rang up the sale, his usual grin back in place, but I couldn't ignore the worry churning off the man.

"Why'd you get a pumpkin?" I asked after we'd thanked the man and started back toward our friends.

"For The Cup," Tzazi said. "It'll look good in the courtyard."

Before I could reply, I heard fast footsteps behind us.

"Wait! Wait!"

Mulch skidded to a stop in front of us, his chest rising and falling as he caught his breath.

"You said you were the one who found Patch's body," he said, eyes locking onto mine.

A strange unease tightened in my stomach. "Yes?"

Mulch swallowed hard. Then in a quiet, urgent voice, he said, "I'm real sorry for that, because, like I said, I don't think it was an accident." His gaze darted around, making sure no one else was too close.

And then he whispered, "I think it was murder. And I hope you didn't stumble into something you shouldn't have."

Tzazi took a sharp step forward, placing herself directly between me and Mulch.

"What exactly are you trying to say?" she said, voice like a blade.

Mulch raised his hands. "Nothing. Just that someone went to a lot of trouble to make Patch's death look like an accident. If Windsor's asking questions…" He hesitated.

Tzazi's entire body went rigid.

I reached for her arm instinctively, feeling the tension rolling off her in waves. "Tzazi—"

But she wasn't having it.

Her voice was low, measured, but dangerous. "If you know anything about someone coming after Win, you'd best say it now."

Mulch took a cautious step back. "I swear. I don't know anything, Miss Strangeland."

He raised himself up and looked over Tzazi's shoulder. "Just be careful, all right? For all you know, the murderer may be closer than you think."

Mulch glanced at Tzazi who towered over him and took another step back. He shook his head. "Just look out for yourself."

With that, he turned and hurried back toward the pumpkins.

"Wasn't that a bit much, Tzaz?"

Tzazi turned to me, her expression dark. "Look, I don't know if he was talking about himself or someone else, but I don't like it."

I swallowed. "Me neither."

"And I'm going to make sure they don't come anywhere near you...or Jess," she said, voice steady as stone.

As we melded back into our group of friends, Keir wrapped an arm around my waist.

"Ready, love?" His voice was low, threaded with the easy confidence that made my heart stutter.

I waved goodbye to my friends as Keir gently guided me toward the exit.

Around us, the festival continued, its joy unbroken, its magic swirling harmlessly around us. A firework burst overhead, momentarily bathing the grounds in silver-blue light. For a fleeting moment, everything felt safe, wrapped in the warmth of revelry and laughter.

But I knew that, somewhere in Darkly, a killer still lurked, perhaps even within the festival tonight, and my fingers tightened around Keir's at the thought.

CHAPTER 20

$\mathcal{T}$he air in Fernwood's courtyard smelled of damp earth and fresh gardenias, their velvety petals still heavy with dew. My brand-new besom hovered in front of me, bristles rustling as though it were breathing, inhaling the earthy scent and exhaling magic.

Pyewacket sat on the iron-scrolled table, watching the broom with deep suspicion. "Been there. Done that. Next please." His tone was edged with feline disdain.

"C'mon. You loved it last time." I patted the little cushion attached to the broom's rear—Pye's "royal seat," as Mathilda had dubbed it. "It's plush, it's fancy, it's everything you demanded."

His whiskers twitched. "A moment please. One does not simply fling oneself into the wild blue yonder without proper mental preparation."

"C'mon. Just a short flight down the coast." I grinned, realization dawning. "You're scared, aren't you?"

Pyewacket narrowed his eye at me.

I cupped my chin between my fingers, pantomiming a person deep in thought. "Hmm. Wouldn't that make you a…'scaredy-cat?'"

He let out an offended hiss. "Do be silent. Cats fear nothing. I am merely exercising due caution in the face of your questionable flying abilities."

"Ah-huh," I said, patting the seat with a challenging glare. He finally leaped onto the cushion nestled among the bristles. Marais swayed and then adjusted as if snuggling him into place, cradling his small frame in a way that made him look absurdly comfortable.

He kneaded the cushion with his claws. "I must admit, it's unexpectedly cozy. Perhaps we could install an in-flight snack dispenser?"

I settled onto the gnarled cypress trunk myself, which adjusted seamlessly to my weight and cradled my rump like a soft and inviting armchair. "Don't push your luck, whiskers."

He huffed theatrically. "Every good airline provides complimentary snacks."

I arched a brow. "Last I checked, you weren't a paying customer."

Pye opened his mouth for a witty (in his mind) retort, but dark clouds gathering on the horizon distracted him. He squinted at the sky. "If you're going to subject me to this, can we do it before we end up drenched? I'd rather not test your lightning-dodging skills."

"All right," I said, gripping the broom handle firmly. "Here goes."

With only a gentle tug, the besom shot skyward like a cat spooked by a cucumber. Greta Garbo's head popped up from the murky water, her eyes following us with curiosity. The courtyard blurred beneath us.

"AHHHHHH!" Pye's yowl rattled the morning air.

I half-laughed, half-gasped at the wild surge. The broom bucked as I tried to steady it, and we whooshed over the rooftop of Hilde's quarters.

"Oh, come on, that was exhilarating!" I tried to mask my own brief moment of terror. "And you're perfectly safe as long as you stay in your bed."

"Seat," Pye growled snappishly. "It is not a bed. It is a *seat*."

This time, I eased the broom forward, focusing on steadying our ascent. We rose smoothly, drifting over Fernwood's rooftop and gardens, and flew through the sky at an unhurried pace, savoring the salt-tinged breeze and the air teased with the promise of rain. The world below stretched vast and green, a rolling landscape of hills and misty woodlands, but my eyes were drawn to something darker in the distance.

Sângele.

I'd only met Veronique a handful of times at the bar in the Green Gator and she'd always been friendly, fascinating, and restrained, all good qualities in a vampire.

I dipped lower, scanning the yard. Veronique herself stood among the leaning tombstones. Her long black dress twisted around her in the restless wind. She lifted a pale hand to shield her eyes and motioned for me to land.

Bringing the broom down in a controlled glide, I touched down beside her. Pye and I both slid off our seats—only for my broom to vanish the second my feet hit the ground.

I spun around in a circle "Where's my broom?" I said, thoroughly perplexed.

Veronique's laughter rippled through the air, rich and ageless. "The newer models disappear when not in use in public. Sleek. Discreet. Perfect for the modern witch."

"Only if 'modern' now means 'reckless with a side of imminent disaster,'" Pye muttered.

"Please, both of you, come. Let's have tea," she said, her crimson lips curving into a smile.

"I would love to," Pyewacket said and scampered ahead of us to a gazebo perched dangerously close to the cliff's edge. The air here smelled faintly of rose petals and salt, a strange mix of the wild and the cultivated, much like her.

The white paint was peeling and sea mist had weathered the

wood, but an ornate iron table had been set with a steaming pot of tea and delicate pastries. Her manservant in tails and spats gave me a polite bow as he arranged a plate of scones.

"Thank you, Ambrose."

Ambrose bowed sharply and returned to the house, giving me one last glance before disappearing through a side door.

The seats surrounding the table were large and comfy. She poured my tea, gave a scone to Pyewacket, and then sat back, watching me with sharp eyes.

I took a sip. It was strange but very good.

"Are they your relatives?" I asked, indicating the tombstones surrounding the house.

"Goodness, no. Most of my relatives are still alive. These people came with the house."

I set my cup down. "You don't find that a little weird?"

She tilted her head. "Whyever would it be weird? The dead deserve respect just as much as the living, do you not agree?"

"Of course, I do," I said, breaking off a piece of scone. "But I don't know how I'd feel about having someone else's dead body in my yard."

She laughed, a coarse dry sound. "Would you rather them be in your house?"

Truth be told, I'd rather they stayed far away from me.

I reached for a moon puff from the tiered silver tray in the middle of the table and took a bite. The silky custard cream melted on my tongue—rich and indulgent. Jess's favorite. Jess!

I set my cup down so abruptly that tea splashed over the rim and pooled in the saucer below. "Oh! You probably don't know. Did you hear about Jess?"

Veronique's expression sharpened, the teasing glint in her crimson eyes vanishing in an instant. Her fangs slipped just past her bottom lip, a small, instinctive reaction. "Whatever do you mean?"

"She was poisoned. At Gumbo Fest. She's in the hospital in Wychwood right now."

Veronique went utterly still. "Poisoned?" she repeated, her voice thin and cold. "Is she—"

"She's stable. The doctor says she'll survive."

I paused then added, "Jess plus twelve others became ill. One person died—the visiting magickstrate."

A sharp *clink* rang out as Veronique set her teacup down, the porcelain rattling against the saucer. The reaction was slight, controlled, but the thorny vines coiling along the gazebo's railing betrayed her, rustling with an agitation that hadn't come from the wind.

"What?" Her voice, usually a measured purr, cut through the stillness. She pushed halfway up from her chair before catching herself, fingers gripping the table's edge.

"So many," she said at last, lowering herself back into her seat. "Was it an accident?"

"The royal inspector believes it was deliberate," I replied cautiously, surprised at Veronique's response to the news.

Veronique's gaze dropped to the table. Her fingers traced the edge of her saucer in silence before she looked up again, the smile returning, but not quite reaching her eyes.

"It's a miracle no more were lost. But Jess will recover." Her voice faltered slightly on Jess's name, just enough to catch my attention.

I hadn't realized they were that close.

"Well," she said, smoothing a wrinkle from the tablecloth. "Thank the goddess for that."

I tried to keep up the conversation as Pye and I finished our scones and tea, but Veronique's gaze kept drifting past me, out to the sea—though she wasn't looking at the waves. She wasn't looking at anything in the present at all. The Veronique who had greeted me with a sharp smile and easy elegance was gone, replaced by someone distant, lost in their thoughts, a dismissal.

"Thank you for your hospitality, Veronique," I said. "I should go before it starts to rain."

A faint *pop* signaled my broom's reappearance beside me.

With a sharp inhale, she shook her head, slipping back into character, adjusting the mask.

"Where are my manners?" She forced a smile, small, sad, but composed. "Come back anytime, dear. Minta used to visit often, and I so miss our chats. You and I should keep up the tradition."

"I'd like that," I said.

As I lifted into the air, I took one last glance back. Veronique hadn't moved. She stood looking out to the ocean, surrounded by headstones that had long since given up their names to time. Her arms hung at her sides, fingers slack.

And then, like raindrops, crimson tears slipped down her cheeks, falling silent and steady onto the headstones below.

AFTER LEAVING SÂNGELE, we soared farther down the coast toward the seaside town of Cradlerock. Beside me, Pyewacket perched with laser focus, scanning the ground below for—

"A bakery!"

The green shutters and sloping red roof of the little building stood out like a witch's candy cottage in a desert. A once-colorful, hand-painted sign boasting an array of pastries and treats swung lazily over a red and white striped awning.

He frantically tapped at my arm with his paw.

"Please, Win. Please, please, please."

He looked up at me with that wide, innocent eye, his most reliable tool for getting exactly what he wanted.

"Okay. A few minutes tops." I cast a wary look at the sky. "We're cutting it close with that storm."

We touched down on the sidewalk, and the moment my feet hit the ground, the broom shimmered and disappeared.

The storm broke a second later, fat raindrops splattering on the pavement.

"Just great," I grumbled to Pye, his face smushed against the bakery window, clearly prioritizing pastries over the weather.

"Look at the sprinkles! And is that caramel glaze? Oh, sweet mother of all baked goods! Let me in there!"

I rolled my eyes. "You are so rude."

Pye gave me a flat look. "Fine. Pleeeeease."

I pushed open the bakery door, bells jingling overhead, and was immediately enveloped by caramel-and-sugar-scented air.

Pye took one sniff and launched himself toward the nearest display case, his paws thumping dramatically against the glass.

"Now this is heaven," he announced, his breath fogging up the glass as he drooled over pastries the size of his head.

The shop was bustling. The din of clinking china and low chatter mixed with a faint, sweet melody that seemed to hum from the floorboards. I waited patiently while a few customers finished their orders. A young woman with bright blue hair and faint webbing between her fingers rang them up. She moved with the gentle grace of someone born from ocean foam. Probably a siren.

Once the crowd thinned, she turned to me with an apologetic smile. "Thanks for waiting. What can I get for y'all?"

Pye nudged my calf with his head, never taking his eyes off the bear claws. "I need three of those," he hissed. "They're bigger than my face, and I will eat them all."

I shot him a warning look.

He flicked an ear dismissively. "Fine. Two and a half."

"We'd like two of those bear claws," I said to the siren, "And two scones with strawberry jam, clotted cream, and a pot of Darjeeling."

"Perfect," she chirped. "Go ahead and have a seat and I'll bring it right out."

We claimed a table by the front window just as a couple left. Pye vaulted into the chair opposite mine and gazed out at the waves lapping the sand. The light filtered through pastel bunting and glass jars of candied sea grapes on the windowsill.

The table next to ours was occupied by three women, all

middle-aged and sharp-eyed, their expressions capable of gutting a fish with words alone.

The first, a blonde with a beehive teased so high it should've had its own zip code leaned forward conspiratorially. Her bangles clinked with every dramatic wrist shake. "Did you hear about that pumpkin farmer in Darkly?"

That caught my attention.

Across from her, a woman with shoulder-length brown hair shot through with elegant streaks of silver raised a well-plucked brow. "Of course I did. Poor man. They say it was grisly."

I casually busied myself with the napkin dispenser, tilting myself ever so slightly in their direction.

"And you say I'm rude…" Pye huffed.

"Hush," I whispered.

"More than grisly," piped up the third, short, freckled, and red-haired with a little fox-shaped brooch pinned to her cardigan. She had a smoker's rasp and the gleam of someone who lived for this kind of thing. "My husband says he was in deep. Gambling debts."

"What?" The blonde clutched her pearls. Literally.

"You don't say."

"I do say. Roderick heard Patch was seen skulking around one of those gambling holes near The Graves. He said someone from his lodge swore it was him. Said he was wearing a path in the floor. Very unbecoming."

The young siren arrived with our order, and I sat up straight, smiling as if I hadn't just been eavesdropping on her customers. She set the tray on our table. "Anything else?"

"We're good," I said, already reaching for the teapot.

Thankfully, she smiled and returned to the counter while I poured a cup of tea and leaned back into the conversation next to me.

The brunette took a slow sip of tea and set the cup down with quiet finality. "Well. That certainly puts a different light on things, doesn't it?"

The redhead nodded, pleased to be the bearer of misfortune. "Roderick said the bookies were sniffing around, real nasty types. Wouldn't surprise me if they got tired of waiting and made an example of him."

I inhaled sharply and took a bite of scone to cover.

"Makes sense," the blonde said with a sharp little nod. "Bookies don't write reminders. They write obituaries."

The three snorted into their teacups.

"Ladies," the brown-haired one said, lifting her cup, "To tasteful friends and tactless town scandals."

They clinked teacups with sinister elegance, then shifted gears into a discussion about hemlines and seasonal lip colors, leaving a cloud of gossip hanging like powdered sugar in the air.

"Did you hear the tittle-tattle next to us?" I asked, magically stirring my tea with a swirl of my wrist while side-eying the women to see if they launched into any more murder-y talk.

"Did you just say 'tittle-tattle?'" He scornfully pronounced each 't' as if it were its own word.

I dabbed my mouth with my napkin and moved a little closer to Pye. "Did you know Patch had a gambling problem?"

"No, but then again, I didn't really know him well," Pye muttered, licking stray flakes of pastry from his whiskers.

"You'd think if Patch was involved with gambling, Dixie-Deen or Sibby would have said something. Or maybe they didn't know."

"Perhaps it was an out-of-character one-time act," Pye said, tearing into the remnants of his first bear claw like it had personally offended him. "He needed money fast and that was the best way to get it."

"Maybe." I sat back in my seat and looked out over the horizon. "Who would the bookie be? Benny the Rat?"

Pye nodded. "That'd be my bet."

I grimaced, both at the bad joke and the thought of Benny the Rat. The name alone made my skin crawl. I'd heard plenty of stories about him since moving to Darkly, most of them unsavory.

He was a kingpin of sorts, a shadow lurking in the corners of the island. When I first arrived in Darkly, he even took bets on how long it would take for Keir and me to get together. Charming guy.

I poured a bit of tea into a saucer for Pye. He lapped at it with contented slurps, and we finished our cream tea in a thoughtful silence.

By the time we stepped outside, the rain had subsided, leaving the cobblestones glistening with moisture. My besom shimmered into view, hovering in the air, alert and ready. It dipped low in front of me, an invitation without words.

"You know," Pye said, hopping into his seat behind me, "if the gossip we just heard's true, solving Patch's murder's about to get a lot more complicated."

"More complicated than you covered in sticky sugar?" I asked, tossing the bag with his second untouched bear claw onto the seat beside him.

"That was strategy, dear. Distraction by deliciousness."

WITH A GENTLE NUDGE, Marais lifted off, carrying us higher until the bakery shrank beneath us, and we left Cradlerock and its sugar-dusted rumors behind.

We flew further along the coastline, soon coming upon Grotto, the sea stretching beyond the waterside restaurant where Keir and I had our first date. The memory still clung to me like sea mist.

Then I saw it.

A sleek black Range Rover parked out front. Keir's Rover.

And he wasn't alone.

A dark-haired woman sat in the passenger seat, head thrown back in laughter.

My stomach lurched.

Pye, sensing my sudden tension, tapped my shoulder with a paw. "What's wrong?"

"Down below," I said, voice tight. "At Grotto."

His gaze flicked to the SUV. "Well, blimey, is that a woman in there?"

I nudged the broom forward, ignoring his hiss of protest. My breath caught somewhere between my ribs, refusing to move.

Then the woman climbed out, tossing glossy black hair over her shoulder like she was stepping onto a stage.

Recognition hit me like a rogue wave.

"Elspeth," I breathed.

The besom wobbled, mirroring the sudden lurch in my gut. I tightened my grip on the handle, a sharp, unwelcome sting flaring in my chest.

"Steady, Win!" Pye screeched, digging his claws into my back. "Unless crash-landing on her head is what you have in mind."

I barely heard him. My thoughts swirled in a tangled mess. Emotions clashed like the brewing storm.

What was she doing there?

Why was he with her?

I forced out a breath, wrestling my voice into something resembling calm. "No big deal," I muttered. "I'm sure there's a perfectly reasonable explanation."

"Oh, sure," Pye said dryly. "Perhaps they're discussing the upcoming storm. Or maybe Keir is just demonstrating the exquisite craftsmanship of his passenger seat warmers."

I shot him a look. "You're not helping."

He twitched his tail. "I can always scratch his eyes out if that would improve your mood."

A breathy, unexpected laugh escaped me—tight and thin, but real. "Thanks, Pye. Tempting. But I'm not going to let them ruin my day."

I turned Marais back toward home, my attention on the sea churning beneath the gray sky, hoping it might calm me. It didn't.

No matter how I tried to distract myself, my thoughts kept ricocheting back to Keir. One moment I was replaying our time together at the festival last night. Then suddenly there was Elspeth again, laughing in his car at Grotto.

I sucked in a breath. And…he was letting her stay at the Cairns.

I turned to my familiar, who had his face deep in his last bear claw.

"Why was Keir with Elspeth?" I said finally, my voice low. "And why is she staying at Wulver Cairns? Does he care for her?"

Pye didn't respond immediately. Just sighed, one of those long, theatrical sighs he reserved for when he knew he couldn't outrun the conversation.

"You need to ask him, not me," he said, voice muffled around pastry. "But I will say this. Keir Bane is undoubtedly the most honorable man in Darkly. He doesn't disrespect women."

"Don't twist it. I'm asking if he has feelings for her not whether he'd throw his coat over a puddle."

"Then ask him that too," Pye said with a swish of his tail. "But don't ask it like it's a trap. You do that thing where you act casual but your eye twitches."

"I most certainly do not."

"You do. In fact, you're doing it right now."

I glared at the sea, then back at him. "So you don't think he's…?"

"I think you're scared. But listen. Elspeth is one of the most manipulative witches I've ever met. And I've met quite a few. That tells you something."

As if sensing my irritation, Marais suddenly veered sharply, and we arced over the coastline. The waves below churned violently, slamming against the jagged rocks. I tried to focus on the scenery, but my mind betrayed me. Keir. Elspeth. The easy way he had of making me feel special only to turn around and make me feel like I meant nothing. He knew all the pain Elspeth had caused to my family and my friends!

We moved inland and crested a green hill. Below us, Patch's pumpkin farm sprawled like an autumn quilt, vines curling up trellises and creeping along the barn's walls. The sight was breathtaking—if not for the shadow of tragedy that clung to it.

I slowed, circling once over the fields. The vibrant colors of the pumpkins seemed too bright in stark contrast to the stormy skies above and violent end that had played out here.

"Such a beautiful place for such a horrible incident," I murmured.

Pye's tail twitched. "Beauty doesn't keep bad things from happening, Win. Sometimes, it just makes them harder to forget."

CHAPTER 21

We circled Patch's homestead in a slow, deliberate arc. Below, Patch's pumpkinheads moved with eerie purpose across the fields, watering fat, bulging gourds, whispering spells to strengthen their enchantments, and, farther out by the crooked fence line, burying seeds into damp earth with careful, clawed hands.

In front of the house, a lone figure knelt in its shadow, his fingers gently lifting the vines winding up the trim beside the door. He stood and peered up at us. His overalls were ragged and his shoulders broad, stuffed too square. The brim of his hat drooped low over one side of his face, hiding all but the glint of one eye.

"How about we go down and take a look," I murmured, tightening my grip on the broom handle.

"Absolutely not." Pyewacket's voice sliced the air. "If Inspector Belleclaire did his job—and I'm willing to assume basic competence—there is zero reason to go poking around a murder house again." He let out a theatrical sigh. "You're being reckless because you're upset."

I dipped the broom downward anyway. The rush of air made the bamboo chimes on the porch clatter like bones. Pye groaned.

"Mark my words, Windsor Ebonwood. You are going to regret this."

"Words marked. Now c'mon." I glanced up at the rolling bruise-colored sky. "I'd like to be home before this storm starts up again."

The moment my feet touched the ground, my broom gave a shimmering shudder, rippled like a silk ribbon caught in the wind and disappeared.

Pye padded beside me, ears twitching, as he regarded the figure before us with reluctant interest.

The man stepped forward to meet us, brushing his straw hands off on his overalls.

"Afternoon, ma'am," he rasped, tipping his hat ever so slightly. His voice was dry and whispery. He stuck out a hand. "Harlan Hayman."

"Windsor Ebonwood." I shook his hand. The knotted straw scratched lightly against my palm.

He gave a slow nod, then turned to a small pumpkin hanging from a vine arching over the front door, humming low under his breath.

"I saw you," I said carefully. "With the other pumpkinheads when—"

He looked at me then. Amber eyes, sentient and still. "Not a pumpkinhead. I'm a golem. Patch's foreman. Built for workin' and watchin'. Don't sleep. Don't stop. Just grow and tend."

A golem. Huh. Shouldn't have been surprising by now, but still.

"Blimey." Pye's golden eye gleamed with interest.

"You were here," I said. "When it happened."

"Aye."

He turned back to the vine, brushing dirt away, careful and reverent.

"Did you see anything?"

"No." His voice cut soft across mine. "Couldn't. Spellveil come down and froze us right up. Couldn't move. Felt like bein' buried alive."

His hand clenched around a vine, I heard his straw fingers tighten with a faint creak.

"Patch was mutterin'," Harlan went on. "Talkin' to hisself, cursin' at the ground like always. Then came a snap. Vine breakin'. Sounded like a neck twistin'."

Harlan finally turned toward me again, amber eyes catching the cloudy light. "It was quiet. Just for a second. But I already knew somethin' was wrong."

I swallowed.

"Then the scream. Weren't a scream like a man makes. Wet. Thick. Like his throat filled with mud. Heard his boots, scuffin' like he was bein' dragged along the dirt."

Pyewacket hopped onto the porch railing and then onto my shoulder.

"Then nothin'," Harlan finished.

I waited for him to continue in his own time.

"Saw y'all come," he said, voice barely a whisper now. "From the house. Hopin' maybe you could help him. Then the bells tolled. And I knew he weren't alive no more."

He reached into his overall pocket and pulled out a small scrap of linen. He unfolded it with surprising care, revealing a few flattened petals, dry, their red hue still apparent.

"Found these," he said, holding them out. "Beside him. I know every growin' thing on this land. No red flowers, Miss Ebonwood. Not a one."

I took a closer look.

I would bet my bottom dollar those were oleander petals.

That cinched the connection.

"They don't belong here," he murmured as he folded the fabric back up and tucked it into his pocket again.

Harlan turned back to his pumpkins, humming again, low and broken.

I hesitated, then gave his back a light pat. He turned, nodded. Sadness flickered in his eyes like the last bit of sun through storm clouds.

With a glance to Pye, I pressed my hand to the door and pushed it open.

INSIDE, Pye scampered through the house and hopped up onto the small table between the chairs, the one that had previously held the whiskey glasses and Patch's will. I followed him over.

The house stood eerily unchanged, as if it were waiting for its owner to walk through the door at any moment. A pair of well-worn slippers sat by the fireplace, a knitted afghan lay draped over the arm of a rocking chair, and the faintest scent of tobacco still hung in the air.

I could almost hear Dixie-Deen's laugh. Almost see Patch setting down a steaming cup of chicory coffee. The patter of feet running through the house and out into the pumpkin patch beyond. I could see what might have been.

But now?

Now, the silence was thick, unnatural.

"I'm not being reckless, Pye," I said, more to myself than anyone else. "Ransom believes Patch's death was an accident. But he had to have missed something."

Silence.

Wait. Pyewacket never passed up a chance to give his opinion, whether it was wanted or not.

"Don't you agree?"

I frowned and turned when I was met by another wall of silence.

"Pye?"

No answer.

Pyewacket was many things—snarky, dramatic, a connoisseur of fine baked goods—but he was not the adventurous type. Not without good reason.

My pulse ticked up a notch.

What is that smell?

It wasn't the sharp coppery tang of death, thank goodness, but something else—something salty, meaty, creeping in from the edges of my awareness. I stepped forward carefully, my Docs barely making a sound against the scuffed wooden floor.

A sliver of movement—just the swish of a tail—caught my eye. Pyewacket.

The skinny, black tip of him vanished behind the kitchen counter.

"Pyewacket," I hissed. My relief at seeing him did little to ease the growing sense of dread pressing at the back of my mind. The feeling of being watched gnawed at me, a familiar, unwelcome presence, just like the last time I had been in this house.

I needed to grab Pye and get the heck out.

I moved quickly, rounding the counter just in time to see Pye slink into the open pantry. The strong scent hit me full force now, the pungent bite of something briny catching in the back of my throat.

This was a trap. I felt it in my bones.

"Pye, don't—!"

Too late.

The little menace was making a beeline for a can of tuna, cracked open and abandoned in the back corner of the large walk-in pantry. His pink tongue flicked out, desperate for a taste.

My heart slammed against my ribs.

"Pyewacket, don't eat that! It's poisoned!"

I grabbed the closest thing to me—a small pumpkin from the counter—and hurled it.

"I can't stop myself!" Pyewacket wailed, his legs moving in an absurd, frantic scramble. "It's tuna!"

The gourd hit its mark, knocking Pyewacket sideways while an unseen force shoved me forward, hard. I stumbled into the pantry, crashing into a shelf of neatly stacked preserves. I snatched up the can of tuna.

The door slammed shut.

I spun and slammed my hand against the thick wood.

Locked.

"Well, hell's bells," I muttered, my voice a sharp whisper in the dark.

Pye sat up, licking his lips, his tail flicking in irritation. He shot me a scowl.

"Indeed."

From somewhere beyond the door, a single floorboard creaked.

THE SLOW CREAK echoed through the kitchen, followed by the deliberate, measured steps of an unseen intruder. Pyewacket's eye locked onto mine, his pupil a thin slit of alarm. I was frozen to the floor.

A whisper of movement brushed against the other side of the pantry door.

I held up a single finger to my lips. *Shhh.*

We stood still, straining to hear beyond the wooden barricade. The footsteps—unhurried—moved through the house. They paused. A long silence, then the faint slide of the glass door leading to the pumpkin patch. Another hesitation. The door clicked closed.

Pyewacket exhaled first, though it sounded suspiciously like a sigh of exasperation.

"Don't worry. I'll get us out of here," I said quietly, not feeling safe enough to speak aloud.

"Hmm," Pyewacket muttered, eyeing the can of tuna still clutched in my hand "But if we're trapped, I suppose there are worse places to be. Like, say, an actual prison. Which is where people who trespass at crime scenes tend to end up."

I glared. "Hush. I'm thinking."

Pyewacket flicked his tail. "Ah yes. Always a promising development."

I ignored him. I'd gotten fairly adept at opening and closing locked doors using magic. How different could it be to pop open a pantry? It was just a door.

Right?

I closed my eyes, reaching inward. As a rule, my magic rose and fell with my emotions, pulled by currents I couldn't fully control. In danger, it was a wild, raw force—stormy and unpredictable. But now, it rose at my bidding, eager to obey.

Power coiled through my veins, sending a cooling rush down my arms, fingertips tingling. I gave the door a push—just a little one.

The pantry door exploded open.

I yelped as I hurled forward, hitting the kitchen floor in an undignified sprawl. A pair of dark brown leather loafers appeared in my field of vision.

"You've summoned Ransom bloody Belleclaire!" Pyewacket shrieked.

I cracked open an eye. And there, looming above me, arms crossed, expression utterly unamused, was indeed Inspector Ransom Belleclaire.

A slow grin spread across my face as I pushed myself upright. "Well, would you look at that, Pye? Not only did I break open the door, but I also conjured the royal inspector."

Pyewacket gasped. "You've gone full sorceress!"

I turned to Ransom, expecting at least a flicker of appreciation for this impressive feat of magic.

Instead, he glared. Hands on hips. Zero whisper of a smile.

Had I pulled him away from a romantic dinner? Had I interrupted an interview with a suspect? Had I—

"You didn't conjure me."

—not conjured Ransom Belleclaire?

He grabbed my arm and, without another word, frog-marched me straight into the kitchen.

"What," he began in that ominously calm tone only detectives and disappointed grandmothers master, "are you doing here, Windsor?"

I yanked my arm free and huffed, slamming the open tuna can onto the counter. "Solving a murder. What are you doing here, Inspector Belleclaire?"

His eyes narrowed. "Trying to keep you out of jail."

Pyewacket let out a dramatic sigh. "See? I told you."

"Quiet!" I jabbed a finger in his direction as he hopped onto the counter and headed toward the tuna.

"Stay away from that!" I grabbed the can from the counter and held it out in front of me. "The killer just tried to poison Pyewacket."

Ransom's sharp expression flickered to surprise. "Poison?"

I nodded. "With this." I nudged the tuna can toward him.

He leaned forward, sniffed, and grimaced. A faint blue glow coated his fingers. Magical latex gloves.

"Someone else was here, Ransom."

Ransom's brow furrowed. "I sensed them too. Sorcerers might not have your innate ability to detect danger, but years as a detective *have* sharpened my hunches."

"Your detective instincts are quite impressive, Inspector, but my supernatural senses are on a whole different level," I said with a smirk.

"Yet you still found yourself locked in the pantry," Ransom deadpanned.

With a sigh, I brushed imaginary dust off my sleeve. "Yes, well, even supernatural brilliance has its off days."

Ransom stared at me for a few moments. "You haven't explained to me yet. What are you and your furry sidekick doing at my crime scene?" he finally asked.

Pyewacket huffed. "It was her idea, not mine."

"Yeah. Thanks for that." I shook my head at my disloyal cat. "I'll remember that next time you're wanting an extra bowl of cream."

Ransom leaned back against the kitchen counter, arms folded, not amused.

"We were looking for evidence that Patch's death wasn't an accident,' I said.

"Speak for yourself, witch." Pye began licking a paw and rubbing it on his face.

Ransom raised an eyebrow at Pye's sudden meow. "Did you find it?"

"Maybe."

"Continue."

I turned to the living room. "When I was here the other day, there were whiskey glasses on the table, along with Patch's will. Why?"

Ransom's arms moved to his waist. His elbows jutted out to the side. "You tell me."

I grinned. "Gladly."

I hurried over to the two chintz chairs and plopped into one, holding up an imaginary document.

"I'm Patch. Dewey just dropped off my newly revised will. I'm double-checking it when, suddenly—" I widened my eyes. "—someone knocks." I rapped three times on the arm of the chair.

I gestured to Pyewacket, who obligingly leaped into the other chair.

"Being a good host, I offer them a drink." I mimed pouring a glass.

Pyewacket flopped against the backrest, legs sprawled. "Give me some whiskey!" he announced in a terrible Southern drawl.

Ransom blinked. "I hate that I understood that."

I continued. "At some point, Patch leaves the room. The killer reads the will, realizes they've been disinherited, and—furious—pours poison into Patch's glass. They leave, and Patch unknowingly drinks his final sip."

Ransom let out a breath. "Not bad. But there are a few holes in your theory."

I narrowed my eyes. "Such as?"

He leveled me with a look—calm, patient, and now vaguely

amused. "Patch didn't disinherit anyone. Just added some codicils that actually benefit his beneficiary."

I blinked. "Okay…and?"

"No nerium was found in his system."

"You're kidding."

He shook his head. "Grim confirmed, however, that the pumpkin *was* magically sealed onto his face. The pumpkinhead workers were powered down by a spell, one that was set to disintegrate after a short time. You just arrived before it could."

I sucked in a breath. "But he wasn't poisoned."

Ransom said. "Patch suffocated."

As I rose from the chair, my hand brushed against something light and cool. "Ransom. What's that?"

I jabbed a finger at the table drawer, where a clear plastic bag stuck out a fraction of an inch.

Ransom followed my stare, then moved across the room to pluck up the bag with a gloved hand and hold it up in the air. Inside: a bit of loose dirt and what looked to be hulls tumbled around.

"I know that wasn't there when we got here today," I said.

Ransom eyed me curiously and examined the contents of the baggie. "I'll have this analyzed." He tucked the plastic bag into his jacket.

A silence stretched between us. Evidence didn't just appear out of nowhere, even in Darkly. Someone had been here. Someone had shoved me into the pantry. And whatever they were up to, they hadn't blinked at killing Pye to do it.

Ransom exhaled, rubbing the bridge of his nose. "Look, Win. I need you to let me do my job."

"So, the dirt must be a clue, right?" I *had* discovered something new at the crime scene.

"Come on. I'll walk you out."

"Wait a minute." I narrowed my eyes, a thought just hitting me. "How did you happen to be here at this time, Inspector?"

We stared at each other.

216

Was I a suspect?

Finally, he turned toward the door. "Let's go. I'd appreciate it if you and Pyewacket—and anyone else you might want to bring out here—stay away from Patch's home until we've caught his killer. Especially if they've also tried to kill Pye. It's best you leave the murder solving to me."

He held open the door and I stomped out, frustrated at his condescending attitude. I grabbed my broom already hovering at the ready. Pyewacket jumped into his bed on the back.

I glanced around. Harlan was nowhere to be seen.

I eased onto the seat and looked up at Ransom. "I really didn't conjure you?" I asked hopefully.

His lips twitched. "Sorry."

Fantastic. I'll be adding that to my ever-growing list of magical humiliations.

THE WIND SLICED around me and Pye as we soared above the twisting ribbon of Coastal Road. I turned my besom sharply, cutting across the bayous toward Darkly. The murky gloom of the Gaslight District loomed ahead. Fog slithered through the stone pillars marking its foreboding entrance.

"Benny the Rat can wait," Pye huffed, clearly irritated with the day's events. "I mean it, Win. We need to get home before the storm hits. Even seasoned witches don't risk flying when there's lightning in the air. One near-death experience per day is more than enough."

As if on cue, thunder grumbled in the distance, rolling through the thickening sky. The storm was closer, heavy and mean. Pye gave me a pointed look.

"Fine," I grumbled.

I'd rather not give this day a chance to get any worse.

I angled Marais toward Darkly where shop and town lights had already flicked on as dusk settled over the town. Townsfolk hurried on the streets and sidewalks, some arm-in-arm, others ducking into restaurants before the storm broke. The scent of rain clung to the wind.

Darkly's cemetery sprawled ahead. I only planned to do a quick spin around the bell tower and then fly on to Fernwood, but as we swooped lower over the cemetery, I spied Bettina and her friends giggling as they skipped rope along one of the winding paths. Then, just beyond them, I saw him.

Keir.

And Elspeth.

They stood next to the stone wall bordering the graveyard, locked in a taut, electric moment. Keir's powerful frame was tense, his hands clenched into fists at his sides. Elspeth, ever the picture of cold amusement, tilted her head at him. Her lips curved into a smirk, her fingers brushing against his arm.

My heart caved in on itself as a sick knot formed in my stomach. Everything I had feared was true.

The besom wobbled.

"Win," Pye snapped, his voice sharp with alarm.

But I couldn't look away. The way she touched him; the way he didn't immediately pull away—

The broom gave a sudden, violent lurch.

I yelped, gripping the handle with both hands as Marais bucked beneath me. A hot rush of panic shot through my veins. The besom wobbled again, harder this time, veering sideways like a startled horse.

"Pull up!" Pye screeched, claws digging into my shoulder as he tried to anchor himself.

I yanked at the handle, but my fingers had gone numb with panic. The broom twisted wildly beneath me, caught in an invisible undertow. My stomach bottomed out as we plummeted, wind screaming past our ears.

The cemetery oak loomed, its thick, knotty trunk rushing toward me at an alarming speed.

A split second later, everything exploded into a blur of snapping branches and slashing leaves.

Pain lanced through my shoulder as I collided with the trunk. The impact spun me, knocking the breath from my lungs. The world turned in a sickening spiral—branches clawing at my face, my besom splintering beneath me, the sky and ground flipping places in rapid succession.

And then—

WHUMP.

I hit the ground hard, the damp earth cushioning the worst of the fall but still rattling my bones. A second later, a furry projectile landed squarely on my chest with an undignified yowl.

Pyewacket.

He staggered off me, his golden eye wide with fury. "I told you—" He cut himself off, swaying slightly, then collapsed in a dramatic heap beside me.

Somewhere above, the storm let loose a distant crack of thunder, as if the universe itself was laughing at me.

Groaning, I tried to sit up, but strong hands caught me first, pulling me upright. Warm, tattooed arms wrapped around me, steadying me as my head spun.

"Easy there, *mo chridhe*," a deep voice murmured against my ear.

Keir.

Of course.

I wanted to glare at him, to demand an explanation, to demand the truth, but the edges of my vision went soft, the world tilting on its axis.

And then darkness swallowed me whole.

WHEN I NEXT OPENED MY eyes, a harsh glare sent a sharp ripple of pain across my forehead.

"Ah, there she is." Keir's voice was quiet, but thick with relief.

Warm fingers brushed my temple, trailing down to my chin. "Had me thinkin' yeh'd gone and met yer maker for a moment, love."

My face burned as memory rushed back. The crash. The reason for the crash. And the absolute mortification of it all.

A wail erupted next to me, piercing and dramatic. "Owwwww!" The room tilted dangerously as I turned toward the pillow beside me.

Pyewacket lay sprawled, exuding the drama of a stage actor in his final scene, his tail swathed in an inch of gauze.

"My tail, Win!" he howled. "You broke my tail!"

I blinked at him. "Are you kidding me?"

"Noooo! It's an outrage! It's a scandal! A cat's tail is his pride and joy!"

I tried to keep my eyes anywhere but on Keir. "Is it actually broken?"

"Aye." A hint of a smile tugged at his lips. "The wee tip's cracked. Ileana offered to sort it for him, but he waved her off."

"My glorious appendage!" Pye wailed from the armchair, cradling his bandaged tail. "The very instrument of my majestic balance! I shall never promenade with dignity again!"

A quiet chuckle came from the foot of the bed. "You scared the stuffing out of me, Peanut," Sibby mumbled, her pipe tipping out of her mouth. "One minute, smooth sailing. Next—BAM. Right into the tree."

"She's lucky she wasn't hurt worse than she was," a male voice said quietly from the corner. Mizizi!

"Luckier than a frog in a hat shop, I'd say." Sibby narrowed her eyes at me. "What in the world happened, Winny? Something in the street distracted you. Something—?"

Her eyes quickly darted to Keir.

I swallowed. "It was dark. And misty."

Sibby canted her head, studying me. "Sure, but Keir and—" Her eyes widened, finally putting two and two together. "I mean —uh—" She coughed. "Totally random flying mishap. Could happen to anyone."

Keir's head snapped toward me, a mixture of concern and warmth in his expression. "Win—"

Pye let out a dramatic sigh. "If this is to be my fate, at least have the decency to fetch me a velvet pillow and a dish of cream."

I groaned, letting my head fall back onto the pillow, which was a mistake. The world tipped again, and a firm but gentle hand caught my wrist.

"Easy, hun. No sudden movements." Ileana pressed cool fingers to my forehead, and the pain and dizziness eased instantly. "You're pretty banged up. Hilde has willowbalm tablets for the pain. Use them sparingly."

"Did I hear Mizizi's voice?" I asked, ready for a change of topic.

"I am here, Windsor." Mizizi's deep, calm voice settled over me like a weighted blanket. The withered but formidable shadowman pulled a chair close as Keir stepped back, gazing at me intently. "How do you feel?"

"Like I went twelve rounds with a particularly churlish oak tree."

Mizizi chuckled, though the sound held no humor. "Just wait until tomorrow. You will feel like an elephant has been dancing on your bones."

"Ah. Something to looking forward to then," I muttered.

His gaze drifted to the window, his expression darkening. "Windsor, I hope you do not resent my intrusion, but I have positioned shadowmen around the perimeter of Fernwood, on top of the ones my granddaughter has already set in place."

I started to object, but he raised a hand. "Something does not feel right. I am not saying you are in danger. However, I also cannot say you are not. I can't make sense of recent events in Darkly or whether they are connected." He glanced at Keir. "Do you know what caused your accident tonight?"

"Inexperienced pilot?" I chuckled quietly.

Mizizi nodded knowingly and changed the subject. "Hilde

mentioned the swamp imp visitation two nights ago. Has anything else happened that I should know about?"

I hesitated.

"Not really," I said carefully. "Just a few nightmares. A phantasm showed up. Oh—" A chill crept up my spine at the memory. "And the night Jess was poisoned…"

Mizizi's gaze sharpened. "Tell me."

I swallowed and described what I had seen by the dock. The towering figure, its body a twisting mass of gnarled roots. The slow, deliberate drag of its steps. But most of all, its eyes. Sharp and intelligent.

Keir took a step forward. "Did—"

Mizizi lifted a hand, cutting him off without looking away from me. "And it looked straight at you?"

I nodded. "And took a step toward me."

"Hmm." Mizizi exhaled slowly and then drifted back to the window.

The mattress dipped softly as Keir sat beside me, his hand warm around mine. "Win, love, I'm sorry if I—"

"Keir—" I cut him off, glancing around the room. This wasn't the place for this conversation.

Before I could say more, Hilde stormed into the room, a steaming mug in her hands. "Enough. Everyone out. Now that she's awake, I need to get her into pajamas and settled for the night."

Keir hesitated. "Are yeh sure she should be alone?"

Hilde gave him a firm shove toward the door. "Honey, she's not alone. I'm here. Sibby's here. We'll take care of her just fine."

"What about me?" Pyewacket wailed. "I'm a bad-ass familiar!"

"And you, Windsor—" She pinned me with a look. "You are not leaving this house for a few days. Need to make sure everything sets right. Mizizi and Ileana's orders. Understand?"

I didn't argue. The ache in my body had settled in like an

unwelcome houseguest. Even if I wanted to leave, I probably wouldn't be able to.

Grand. Just grand.

CHAPTER 22

The next morning, I woke to a blustery, sleet-filled day and a full-blown dramatic performance unfolding on the pillow next to me.

"Oh, my tail. My beautiful tail. My crowning joy," Pyewacket wailed, his voice thick with tragedy.

Even half-asleep, I couldn't stop myself from snorting a laugh. "Your tail is on your rear, not your crown."

Pye shot me a withering look, his ears flattening. "Semantics. My suffering is real."

I groaned and tried to shift upright, but pain shot through me like I'd been trampled by a herd of spectral bog bison. A sharp breath escaped me. Pyewacket, ever the supportive familiar, let out a high-pitched *ohhh* the feline equivalent of a dramatic faint.

And that must have set off some kind of nursing alarm, because within seconds, Hilde was at my bedside, arms crossed, her brow furrowed in Supreme Disapproval.

"And just what do you think you're doing?"

I raised my hands in surrender. "I was just going to the kitchen for a humongous cup of coffee and then straight to the sofa. I promise."

Hilde's eyes narrowed like she was one second away from bear hugging me into submission. "All right then. But let me help."

With her steady grip, I swung my legs off the bed and attempted to stand. Bad decision. The pain was instant, a full-body rebellion, and I nearly crumpled back onto the mattress.

"Ohhh, my tail!" Pyewacket wailed, flopping onto his side like he was moments from death.

"Hush with that yowling!" Hilde snapped, her tone so sharp that I laughed, immediately regretting it as pain shot through me again.

Pye glared at me, affronted. "Oh, sure. Laugh at my pain."

Hilde ignored him, her attention back on me. "Back in bed?"

"No, no. To the sitting room," I said stubbornly, because if I had to lie around feeling like a broken marionette, I'd rather do so near a cozy fire with a blanket, a steaming cup of warmth, and *Midsomer Murders* reruns.

With Hilde's help, I shuffled through the house to the large velvet sofa opposite the fireplace. She eased me onto it as carefully as if she were handling a cursed artifact, gingerly placing my legs onto the cushions.

Pyewacket limped to the side of the sofa and placed his front paws on the cushion generating the saddest, most miserable look he could muster. Hilde huffed in amusement and placed him on the back of the sofa, where he curled up, pitching his tail at a very specific, exaggerated angle to emphasize the *seriousness* of his injury.

Hilde disappeared into the kitchen and returned a few minutes later carrying a steaming mug. The scent hit me first—warm, spicy, and suspiciously not coffee.

I eyed it with deep distrust. "Hilde. Where's my coffee?"

She handed me the mug and sat down in her well-worn rocker by the fire.

"You're having golden milk."

I froze. "Golden what?"

"Golden milk," she said, casually picking up her knitting. "Good for you. Anti-inflammatory, packed with antioxidants. One of Ileana's special blends for healing. And judging by the way you're moving, you could use all the help you can get."

She turned her eyes to me as if challenging me to defy her. "Ileana left instructions for you to drink this for the next few mornings instead of coffee and I have some of her special sweet tea for the rest of the day."

I lifted the mug to my lips, still skeptical. The golden-yellow surface was velvety and speckled with cinnamon. It smelled warm. And slightly sweet. But the moment I took a sip, the spices punched me right in the taste buds.

I coughed. "Hilde! It's spicy!"

She took a sip from her own mug filled with coffee and I stared at her with something close to jealousy. "You'll like it. Just give it a chance."

I wasn't so sure. I took another cautious sip. This time, the heat of the ginger and black pepper settled into something comforting, mingling with the creamy vanilla and the earthy turmeric. It was different. But not bad.

Pyewacket sniffed the air, then gagged dramatically. "Ah, yes. The unmistakable scent of shame and broken brooms."

He leaped out of the way as I swatted at him behind my head. For such a *serious* injury, he was awfully spry.

Hilde kept her gaze trained on me. "So. Want to tell me what happened on that flying branch of yours?"

I glanced at Sibby sprawled in her chair, watching me closely and cradling a large coffee like a trophy.

"Just wasn't concentrating." I took a sip of golden milk, using it as a shield for my pride.

The heat still burned going down, but I had to admit, I was beginning to like the flavor. It knew just how to soothe what needed soothing.

Hilde's sharp gaze made it clear she wasn't buying a word of it but, mercifully, let it go.

Just as I started to settle back into the sofa, a thought jolted me upright. "Hey, wait. Where *is* my broom?"

"Mathilda's got it. She'll repair it, and you can pick it up when you're feeling better."

"Today?" I asked hopefully.

Hilde cocked her head sideways, her expression somewhere between amused and 'are you out of your mind?.'

"I don't think you could ever ask me anything more ridiculous than what you just did."

"Wanna bet?" Pye muttered.

I sighed. "Okay. Not today."

A pang of loss hit me. The broom and I had formed a connection as strong and natural as the one I had felt with the MET, Fernwood, and, over time, even Pyewacket. Maybe even with...Keir.

I groaned and flopped back against the couch. Keir.

Why was I still thinking about him? About the way his presence had always felt like an anchor, steadying me? About how seeing him with Elspeth had made something twist painfully in my chest? I was angry. And confused. And completely unwilling to process any of it right now.

So instead, I popped an orange whip into my mouth from the bowl on the table, welcoming the satisfying snap as it cracked apart. The tangy citrus and rich vanilla reminded me of the Dreamsicles of my youth.

A light tapping at the door connecting the kitchen area and sitting room made me sit up, wincing.

Elysande Darkmoon wiggled her fingers at me through the screen, her iridescent gown flowing behind her like a shimmering river. She opened the door and stepped inside. Hilde glanced up from her chair and smiled at her. "Why, Elysande, good to see you, hun. How's our Jess?"

Elysande's face lit up. "Doing well. I brought her home this morning. She's weak, but she's alive and will make a full recovery."

"Any idea who'd do such a thing?" Sibby asked, narrowing her eyes.

Elysande's lips pressed into a thin line. "None, but believe me, Faelen won't rest until he finds them."

"Ooh," Sibby said, chomping down on her pipe and letting out a low chuckle. "Hate to be them."

"Indeed," Elysande said and turned to me. "I can only stay for a moment. I wanted to see how you are, dear. I heard about your little—ahem—incident with the tree." Her eyes glittered knowingly. "Not your finest landing, I take it?"

I sank deeper into the sofa, pulling the blanket up to my chin. "The tree came out of nowhere."

Sibby snorted from her oversized plush chair. Pye, curled beside me with his tail wrapped delicately in gauze, huffed.

"I've brought something for you, dear," Elysande announced, producing a small glass vial filled with shimmering amethyst liquid. "A treasured elven potion passed down through the women in my family for generations. It will have you right as rain within hours."

Hilde peered over her knitting, eyes sharp with interest. "Well now. Heard tales about them Darkmoon elixirs my whole life. Ain't never seen one in the flesh till now."

Elysande lifted the vial with a pleased smile. "We take great pride in our potions. This one was specially prepared by my niece Aurelia in the Isles just for Windsor."

With a graceful flourish, she uncorked the vial. The moment the seal broke, an acrid scent rolled through the room like an invisible fog.

"Ooh, wee!" Sibby clamped her fingers over her nose. "That'll knock the wind out of you!"

Even Hilde waved a hand in front of her face, wrinkling her nose.

Bracing myself, I took the vial, held my breath, and knocked it back in one gulp. It tasted exactly like it smelled. Like dirty socks steeped in swamp water and rotten eggs.

As I struggled to keep the vile potion down, Elysande clapped her hands together. "Marvelous! Give it a few minutes, and you'll start feeling the effects." She crouched beside the sofa, her expression warm. "I need to get back to Jess, but do rest, dear Windsor. She sends her love."

With one last hug, Elysande vanished in an instant, leaving behind only the lingering stench of that wretched potion hanging in the air.

Sibby shook her head. "Fae-folk. Always flashin' feathers like a strutting rooster."

I turned back to the television for a few minutes, when a ripple of sunshine suddenly unfurled in my chest.

My limbs felt delightfully weightless, pain-free. I giggled.

Hilde glanced over. "You feelin' all right, child?"

I nodded and giggled again. "Hilde, your knitting needles are so pointy. Have they always been that pointy? They could duel. Little sword fights! We should name them!" I clapped my hands together, delighted by my own brilliance.

Sibby, watching with mild curiosity, let out a cackle. "Oh, Elysande, you mischievous faerie!"

Hilde sighed. "Wonder how long this side effect will last."

"Side effect?" I blinked at her, still inexplicably delighted. "Hilde, you look like a wise owl. A *very* wise owl. Oh, and Sibby! You're a—" I gasped. "You're a sparkly hobbit! With fancy boots! Do a dance, Sibby!"

Sibby was wheezing with laughter, sinking deeper into her chair like she was settling in for the main event.

A loud knock sounded at the back door.

"I'll get it." Sibby pulled herself up from her plushy chair. I could hear voices as Sibby and our visitor moved from the kitchen onto the back porch.

Keir.

He strode inside, looking fresh from the outdoors. In his hands, he held a potted plant with velvety red blooms that gleamed and pulsed faintly under the sitting room's soft light.

"Everheart camellia." Hilde nodded approvingly.

He took one look at me and frowned. "How are yeh feeling?"

I gasped. "Keir! You magnificent wolf! You look so—so defined. Like a very serious tree! But a handsome tree. A noble oak! No, a redwood!"

He raised a brow, gaze flicking to Hilde in question. She set her knitting aside and rose with a huff. "Fae elixir."

Keir exhaled, a slow grin breaking across his face. "Ah."

Hilde motioned to Sibby. "Help me in the kitchen."

"I'm good." Sibby settled further into her chair and grinned at me and Keir.

"Sibby." Hilde's voice held a tone Sibby knew better than to argue with.

Sibby huffed and flounced out of the room, well, as much as Sibby can flounce.

Keir crossed to the sofa and set the camellia on the table next to me. Its lovely fragrance floated through the room.

I examined it reverently, eyes wide. "Keir. It's the most perfect plant I've ever seen. A plant of eternal devotion! No, of steadfastness! You are a steadfast wolf!"

Sibby cackled from the kitchen, and I heard the door to the kitchen slam shut and Sibby's muffled voice. "Fun sucker."

Keir settled onto the chair beside me. "Win, I'm glad yeh're all right." He examined the bruises on my arms. "Gave me quite the scare, yeh did." He let out a breath. "But there's something I need to speak with yeh about. It's important."

I beamed. "Is it about the trees?"

His eyes narrowed, puzzled but amused. "Nay, it's about us."

I gasped dramatically. "Us! Keir, are you breaking up with me?" My hands flung dramatically to my chest.

His brows shot up. "What? Naw!"

"Because of Elspeth?" I whispered, voice wobbling.

"Win, listen—"

I threw a hand over his mouth. "Shh. No words. Just hold me one last time."

Keir let out a strangled laugh. "Ah'm no breakin' up with yeh."

Hilde poked her head in from the kitchen. "Keir, you staying for lunch?"

Keir grinned. "Wish I could, but there's an alderman meetin' the day."

Hilde nodded and disappeared back into the kitchen.

I reached for his hand, lacing my fingers through his. "Keir, do you ever think about how fish don't have eyelids? Do they just stare all the time? How do they blink?"

Keir sighed, then laughed. "Win, sweetheart, let's get yeh some water."

"Ooooh, water! That's a great idea. Did you know I'm mostly water? I think. We all are. But does that mean we're just very complicated puddles?"

Having escaped the kitchen, Sibby slid back into the room, giggling, and plopped back down into her chair.

Keir shook his head, chuckling. "I'm never gonna make it through this conversation, am I?"

"Maybe not today, wolfy." I reached up and booped his nose. "Boop."

Hilde appeared in the doorway and sighed. "Heavens help us. Sibby, back in the kitchen."

"Do I have to?"

"Yes."

With a groan, Sibby followed Hilde into the kitchen. Keir turned back to me, still grinning.

"Did yeh honestly think I was breakin' it off with yeh?"

"Yes," I said gravely. Then immediately burst into giggles. "But it's okay! Because I've decided I'm too cute to be sad. And also, Keir, I think I love you. And love conquers all!"

Keir stilled, then let out a quiet laugh. "Let's save that for another day, love. Once yeh're no' high on fae magic."

I gave him a dopey smile and nestled into his side. "Okay. But just so you know… you're my favorite tree."

Keir let out a short laugh, pressing a kiss to my hair. "And you, lass, are my own wee whirlwind."

CHAPTER 23

A few days later, I got the all-clear from Hilde—not that she didn't make it perfectly clear she thought I was pushing it. So that very morning, gray and drizzling, Tzazi and I stood in front of Greywolf Manor, eager to visit Jess and see for ourselves that she was truly on the mend. The sprawling Tudor-style mansion loomed over the expansive green lawn, its dark, baronial charm teetering between stately and spine-chilling.

Before we could even knock, the massive oak doors creaked open.

Miles, Greywolf Manor's longtime butler, stood in the dim entryway, all stiff shoulders and funeral face. I often suspected he had been delivered with the house itself, like a particularly well-preserved relic.

"Greetings, madams," he intoned, his voice smooth and measured, touched with the practiced warmth of old-world refinement. "Miss Jessamin is expecting you."

"I bet you're glad to have her back home," Tzazi said, striding inside without hesitation and heading down the grand hallway.

Miles inclined his head. "A great relief, Miss Tzazi, I can tell you that."

I picked up Pyewacket and followed them, our footsteps

vanishing into the thick, velvet hush of the hallway rug. The chandeliers overhead flickered, not just from the breeze but with a suspiciously haunted sort of quiver. Portraits of Wilde ancestors lined the walls, each oil-painted face tracking our steps with the faintest whiff of disapproval.

"This place smells like ghosts," Pyewacket muttered.

I ruffled the fur between his ears. "Maybe a little."

If Miles heard me, he gave no sign. He simply led us into the parlor, a warm, book-filled haven where the rich scent of coffee drew us in.

The parlor bore the quiet grandeur of a bygone age. The floor-to-ceiling bookshelves groaned with leather-bound tomes, their spines cracked from generations of use. Heavy walnut paneling enclosed the space, making it feel both grand and intimate. The velvet curtains, deep emerald and embroidered with an elaborate floral motif, were drawn back just enough to let in the morning light.

Jess was curled in a corner of one of the four sofas swathed in a steel-blue, faux-fur blanket and an unnecessary mound of pillows. Despite her usual vibrance, her pale complexion and the slight tightness around her mouth told me everything I needed to know. She hadn't yet fully recovered.

Still, she squealed when she saw us.

"I can't tell you how happy I am to see you both," she exclaimed, attempting to rise.

Miles was at her side in an instant, one gloved hand resting lightly on her shoulder. "Madam, please rest," he chided gently. "Unless you wish me to call for your mother."

Jess slumped back into the pillows. "That's all he has to say to keep me off my feet," she grumbled.

Miles permitted himself the smallest, most dignified smirk before retreating from the room.

"Win! How are you? Marm told me about your accident."

I waved it off. "Nothing a little Hilde TLC couldn't fix."

"Good." Jess smiled, her nose wrinkling in that cute way of hers.

"Where *is* Elysande?" Tzazi asked, already claiming a velvet recliner and raising the foot support.

"Upstairs," Jess said. "And let's keep it that way, shall we?"

I leaned down and kissed her cheek, placing a yellow sparkling bag on the table. "You look wonderful."

Jess snorted. "You're a terrible liar."

"She really is," Tzazi agreed, stretching her arms above her head with a luxurious sigh. "But she means well."

Jess chuckled, and then her eyes fell on the bag. "Sugarloaf's!" She clapped her hands delightedly and swept the bag off the table.

"This better be..." She pulled the ribbon and reached inside drawing out a white sparkling puff. "Moon puffs! My favorite! Thank you, Win!" She popped one in her mouth and moaned. "All right. What have I missed? Marm won't tell me anything."

I hesitated, glancing at Tzazi.

Jess arched a brow. "Uh oh. That bad?"

Pyewacket hopped onto my lap, curling into a contented loaf.

"Where do we even begin?"

"Start with the poisonings," Pyewacket declared, stretching out like he was making a formal decree. "Or perhaps you'd prefer to start with that promise you made to Elspeth to prove her innocence." He looked up at me innocently.

I narrowed my eyes at him. "Pye says the poisonings."

Jess sat up straighter. "Poisonings? Plural?"

Tzazi nodded grimly. "You and Edythe Grouse weren't the only ones. Eleven other townspeople were poisoned."

A hush settled over the room. Even the fire seemed to dim, as if the shadows themselves were recoiling at the news.

Jess gripped her coffee cup. "Who else was poisoned?"

I listed the names, watching as her expression shifted from mild surprise to full-fledged horror. When I reached Eryss Umbralace, her mouth parted in disbelief.

"Eryss gave me the spider silk shawl I wore to court," she whispered. "Is everyone okay?"

"They're recovering," I assured her. "Like you. No fatalities."

Jess let out a slow breath. "But that means—" Her gaze sharpened. "Who was the real target?"

"That's the question, isn't it?" Tzazi murmured. "Were all the other poisonings an accident? Was Magickstrate Grouse the real target or did the killer need multiple victims to muddy the waters? Or maybe every person poisoned was targeted by the killer. Considering the identities of the victims, I don't find that a reasonable assumption though."

My stomach twisted at the thought. The sheer callousness of it.

Jess chewed her lip. "And Ransom has no idea who's behind it?"

"There are suspects," I said. "But no solid proof."

"Who are the suspects?"

"Elspeth," Tzazi said darkly before I could even open my mouth.

"She certainly had motive," I admitted.

"But?" Jess tilted her head.

Tzazi sighed. "Win doesn't believe she did it."

Jess frowned and turned to me. "You don't?"

"I agree she's hateful enough, but is she really that stupid?"

Tzazi let out a begrudging grunt of agreement.

Pyewacket cocked his head. "She's clever. And she knows better than to make herself the obvious suspect."

I translated aloud.

Jess exhaled sharply. "He's disturbingly logical."

Pyewacket preened. "Naturally."

I rolled my eyes.

"All right," Jess said, rubbing her temples. "If not Elspeth, then who?"

Silence. The fire sputtered and somewhere in the house, a clock chimed.

I took a slow sip of coffee before listing them. "Mason." Tzazi visibly flinched when I said his name. "Gordon Mulch, Patch's biggest competitor. Benny the Rat."

Jess let out a sharp gasp. "Wait. I just thought of someone else who had an issue with Patch. Mathilda. The day before he died, something happened between them at the Gator. I don't know what was said, but Mathilda slammed hers and Dixie-Deen's coffees down on the table and stormed out."

Tzazi shrugged. "That just sounds like Mathilda on a good day."

"She *is* quite the grump, isn't she?" Jess sank back into the sofa, rolling her mug between her hands.

"Neither of you are going to like this one, but..." Tzazi glanced at me. "...Dixie-Deen."

"Dixie-Deen? Seriously? She was devastated when he died," Jess protested.

Silence. The fire snapped.

"Devastated doesn't rule her out," Tzazi pointed out.

Jess frowned. "Why Benny the Rat?"

"Win found out that Patch owed money to Benny. Gambling debts," Tzazi said.

"Oh no," Jess's hand flew to her mouth. "Do you think there could be two different murderers?"

Tzazi simply shrugged. "If that's true, Ransom's going to have a really hard time finding them."

"I'm almost certain there is only one killer." I told them about my conversation with Harlan and the red petals the killer had dropped.

"Well, then," Jess said. "Who in Darkly would have it in for both the magistrate and Patch?"

We both shrugged.

Pyewacket reached a paw and nudged me. "Oh, get it over with before they find out from someone else."

I cleared my throat but then Tzazi beat me to it. "So what did Elspeth want with you the other day at the MET?"

Is reading minds a vampire skill? Sometimes I thought it was.

"She wants me to prove her innocence."

Tzazi laughed. "I don't know why but her pretentiousness still amazes me."

"How dare her!" Jess exclaimed and then broke into giggles herself.

I opened my mouth to agree when there was a soft but deliberate tap on the parlor door, followed by its signature weighty hush as it glided open.

"Miss Jessamin," Miles intoned, his duty to protect Jess clashing with the understanding that she needed her friends now more than ever. For a moment, his eyes flickered with hesitation. Duty always won. "You have a visitor. Mr. Talmadge Prescott."

Miles stepped aside, revealing Tal in the entryway. He wore his usual easy, lopsided smile, but his eyes betrayed him, brimming with relief and warmth.

His gaze swept the room, landed on Jess, and stayed there. Without hesitation, he strode toward her, barely sparing Tzazi and me a glance.

I exchanged a look with Tzazi.

"Jessamin," he said, his voice quiet, his green eyes bright. "You're okay." The words came out on an exhale, as though he'd been holding his breath since the moment he heard she'd been poisoned.

Jess sat up straighter, her expression fluttering from mild exasperation (for being fussed over) to surprise to something dangerously close to delighted. "Tal."

In his hands, he held a small wooden box, fingers curled slightly around the edges. His usual confidence wavered, just a touch. "I, uh—" He cleared his throat. "I was worried about you."

Jess blinked.

Then beamed.

"That's so sweet." She patted the cushion next to her. "Come sit."

He hesitated just long enough to make me exchange another

glance with Tzazi before stepping closer and lowering himself onto the sofa beside her.

With careful fingers, he handed her the wooden box and leaned back, attempting to recover his usual calm coolness. He almost pulled it off.

Jess opened the box, eyes widening at the sight inside—a delicate silver charm bracelet, covered in tiny, intricate charms. A wolf. A moon. Several small, glittering runes. The craftsmanship was exquisite, full of purpose and care.

She touched one of the charms with trembling fingers. "It's beautiful," she murmured. Her voice was softer than usual, the teasing edge momentarily gone. She turned toward us, holding it up. "Look, Tzazi. Win." The bracelet caught the firelight, sparkling in her hands.

Tzazi let out a low whistle. "Wow, Tal," she said with a wicked grin. "I'm impressed."

Tal shrugged like it was no big deal, but his tan cheeks flushed pink.

"It's for protection," he said gruffly. "My grandmother made it."

Jess pressed her lips together, exhaling softly. "Your grandmother!"

She clasped the bracelet around her wrist, admiring it for a moment before meeting Tal's gaze. "Thank you, Tal. Really."

He cleared his throat again, suddenly looking as though he just noticed he had given Jess an incredibly personal gift in front of Tzazi and me. "I didn't mean to interrupt..." he began, already half-rising.

"You didn't," Jess said quickly. Suspiciously quickly. "Please stay. We were just discussing the murders and poisonings."

Tal nodded and sank back into the sofa, his focus sharpening. "I couldn't help but hear a bit as I was coming down the hallway. It's all strange, isn't it?" His forehead creased. "Even the Cairns is uneasy."

I tapped a finger against the armrest. "There must be a common thread. What do all these people have in common?"

The fire spit and sizzled, throwing restless light against the dark wood. Silence fell as we considered.

"Nothing," Jess said at last. "I would say 'the festival,' but Patch wasn't there."

Tal tapped his chin. "His pumpkins were. Could all of this be connected to the pumpkin farmer in some way?"

I shook my head. "So far I haven't been able to find any connection between Patch and the magickstrate."

"But we know that Patch was using questionable charms on his pumpkins," Tzazi offered. "And we know Mulch didn't like it."

"But why would Mulch kill the magickstrate?" Jess was as perplexed as we were.

Tzazi suddenly sat up straight, her face grave, her voice dropping to an ominous whisper. "I've got it! They had a secret love child, and he didn't want the truth to get out."

The room paused.

And then Tal's warm, rich laughter broke the silence, rolling through the parlor like a sudden gust of summer air.

Jess groaned, rubbing her temples. "Tzazi, stop. This isn't something to joke about." But even as she said it, her eyes slid toward Tal, as though checking to see if he was still laughing.

He was.

And he was looking at her while he did so.

Tzazi, wholly unrepentant, reclined back into the chair and casually flipped on the massage settings. A soft hum buzzed through the room as she wiggled her shoulders into the cushions.

"You say that," she murmured, "but no one here has disproved my theory."

"No one needs to disprove it for us to see it's utter nonsense," Jess quipped. "And I think—"

And then. to Jess's complete dismay, the heavy parlor doors bounced open and in swept Elysande.

ELYSANDE DARKMOON WAS a storm of silk scarves and jangling bracelets. The scent of sandalwood and something vaguely medicinal swirled in behind her, as did the unmistakable energy of a woman who fully intended to take over the room.

She carried a steaming mug of a brew that smelled cloyingly herbal in one hand and an all too familiar vial of purple liquid in the other.

Poor Jess.

"Well!" Elysande exclaimed, her eyes locking onto Tal like a heat-seeking missile. "And who is this?"

Jess closed her eyes briefly, as if summoning patience from another realm. "Mother, meet Talmadge Prescott. He's a Silverfang."

Elysande froze mid-step. It lasted only a fraction of a second, but I saw it—the way her body went completely still, the slightest hesitation in her otherwise effortlessly fluid presence.

Then, her usual warm, bohemian smile spread across her face. "Talmadge. It's so nice to meet you."

She swept forward, setting the steaming mug down on the nearest table and extended a ring-covered hand. "I'm Elysande Darkmoon. Talmadge. What a beautiful name. Are you of the Prescotts from Moon Valley?"

"Why, I am, ma'am," he said, clasping her hand, those bright green eyes working their charm on Jess's mom.

Elysande beamed. "Delightful family. Just delightful." She gave his hand a little squeeze, a calculating glint in her eye. "What a lovely surprise."

Tal grinned as he sat back down. "Well now, Miss Elysande, I'd call that the best welcome I've had in ages."

And then, he winked at Jess.

Jess, who had been watching the exchange with the same kind of weary dread one might reserve for an approaching natural disaster, widened her eyes slightly, her lips twitching in amusement.

Elysande, apparently done investigating Tal's pedigree, whirled toward us and pulled me and then Tzazi into enthusiastic, lilac-scented embraces. "I'm so glad you ladies are here. Our Jessamin desperately needed a mood boost." She stopped to eyeball me up and down, a bright grin spreading across her face. "Win, you have never looked more fantastic. No doubt Aurelia's elixir did the trick."

And then, like an inevitable force of nature, Elysande descended upon her daughter, popping the cork on the vial and pouring the tincture into the abandoned mug.

An immediate rush of rancid air filled the room.

"Jessamin, darling," she cooed, pushing the mug into Jess's hands. "Drink this. It's our family's ancient restorative tonic."

Tzazi leaned forward, sniffed the air—then immediately gagged, waving a hand in front of her face. "That smells like what you'd get if a skunk, a dirty diaper, and the dumpster behind The Cup had a baby."

Elysande turned toward Tal, Tzazi, and me, lifting her chin as if preparing to unveil a great ancestral secret. "It has been passed down through generations of Darkmoon women," she announced dramatically. "A sacred blend of rare herbs and healing elements. It works wonders. Tell them, Win."

"From what I can remember, it does work wonders," I said. Mostly the kind that made you wish you had a rewind spell.

Jess eyed the drink suspiciously. "Mom. Is this the same thing you gave Miles? Because he turned green." She set it on the table in front of her.

Miles, from his usual neutral but all-knowing post at the door, cleared his throat. "A slight exaggeration, madam."

Elysande waved a dismissive hand. "Nonsense! It's full of cleansing properties. Makes sure every bit of poison is flushed out of your system." Her voice hitched at the word "poison."

Jess gingerly lifted the mug, grimaced, and then set it back on the table as Tal and Elysande plunged into a deep conversation about her Darkmoon relatives in the Isles. Apparently, he was friends with two of Jess's cousins, Theodora and Aurelia, the latter being the creator of the fae elixir, if I'm not mistaken.

Out of the corner of my eye, Jess leaned forward, reaching over the mug of elixir for a moon puff. When she pulled back, prize in hand, her elbow smacked into the mug, knocking it clean off the table.

The foul-smelling liquid splattered across the rug.

Jess gasped theatrically. "Oh dear! What a shame!"

Elysande threw her hands up. "Fine, Jessamin! Poison your body with coffee and...and moon puffs instead." And with a grand flourish of scarves, she swept dramatically out of the room.

She popped her head back in, flashing a warm smile, her voice rich with charm. "It was lovely meeting you, Talmadge. Please give your mother my best." Then, she disappeared, the rhythmic click of her heels echoing up the staircase.

Miles, having clearly witnessed this entire charade without comment, stepped forward. With a click of his fingers, the stain vanished in a puff of citrus-scented air, mercifully masking the last traces of fae elixir clinging to the room.

Jess's smile brightened. "Well. What else did I miss?"

We spent the next half hour catching her up on the Gumbo Fest incident—catastrophe if you asked Borda, divine intervention if you asked the rest of us.

By the time we finished, Jess was wiping tears from her eyes. "I can't believe I missed all that."

"We wish you had been there too. You would've loved it. Chase kept the cider flowing while we watched the chaos unfold from under the picnic table."

Jess sighed wistfully, shaking her head. "That's it. I'm never getting poisoned again."

Tal's lips tightened, his gaze lingering on her. "We'll hold you to that."

She flushed slightly, barely hiding it behind a sip of coffee.

I caught Tzazi's eye and tilted my head slightly.

She got the message. "Well, I guess we'll be off."

"It was so good to see you, Jess," I pulled her into a hug. "You have no idea how much better I'm going to sleep tonight."

Jess laughed, a little more lighthearted now. "Well, let's not make a habit of me getting poisoned just so you can catch a good night's sleep."

I waggled a finger at her. "Fair. But I'm not ruling it out entirely." I squeezed her once more before stepping away.

I picked up my bag and turned to leave. "Bye, Tal."

I waved to him, but he wasn't even looking at me. His focus? Entirely on Jess.

She, still weak from the poisoning, cautiously stood.

Tal's brows pulled together immediately. "Jess, you shouldn't—"

"I'm going to walk my friends to the door. I'll be right back," she cut in, ending the conversation instantly. She stopped Miles with a look.

Tzazi finished gathering her things and we headed into the grand entryway alongside Jess.

She opened the door, drew in a long breath of jasmine-laced air, then leaned against the frame, watching us go.

Behind us, the air was light, the laughter still hanging.

For the first time in days, the world felt steady again.

CHAPTER 24

*L*ater that evening, I sat at the island in Fernwood's kitchen, impatiently drumming my fingers on the marble top. My gaze slid to the clock for the third time. "Sibby!" I hollered. "You're the one who wanted to visit the mausoleum! That was two hours ago! How much longer?"

Sibby strode into the kitchen, her ridiculous, red-striped bag clanking with every step. "Hold yer dang kelpies. Don't you know you should never enter a cemetery before dusk?"

I snorted. "Says who?"

"Says me." She hooked her thumb at herself and glared like that settled the matter.

"Fine. Can we go now?"

"'Bout time," she muttered, stepping onto the back porch. I had a sudden, wicked urge to slam the door behind her and lock it. Doubtful that'd stop her from getting back in, but it sure would be satisfying.

Already regretting the missed opportunity, I followed her outside. Sibby grabbed the sleeve of my raincoat, and suddenly, the world lurched. My stomach flipped, and a moment later, I was standing at the entrance to Darkly Cemetery.

I pushed open the gate and we were shrouded in cool, lush darkness.

Night had transformed the cemetery into an entirely different world. The usual riot of brightly colored flowers and creeping vines were swallowed by a black velvet gloom. White clematis blooms in pale clusters glowed along the moss-draped gravestones, while fireflies bobbed through the darkness.

Sibby pushed aside the thick fringe of Spanish moss draped across the path. I stepped through and the air itself seemed to change, thickening with unseen energy. I gasped. By day, the cemetery was a place of stillness, breezy and bright, with birdsong and the occasional scurrying squirrel. Even the dancing statue lent an air of whimsy. Visitors were few, the air peaceful.

But at night? The cemetery pulsed with life.

Ghosts crowded between tombstones, their voices a low, rustling symphony. An elderly woman in full Victorian dress, a frilly parasol balanced on her shoulder, waved at me as though we were on Tataille Street in the middle of the day. I hesitated before weakly waving back.

We were surrounded by ghosts.

Sibby felt me tense and patted my arm. "Nothin' to worry about," she said. "*This* is why you come to the cemetery at night. The Walkers. These are folks who either still have business on this plane or just don't feel like moving on yet."

I swallowed hard.

"Most importantly," Sibby continued, hiking her clanking bag onto her shoulder, "if you ever need information of the dead sort, this is the best place to start. Hear it from the scorpion's mouth, they say."

Nobody *ever* said that. Okay. Except Sibby.

We followed the moon-lit path, threading through the Walkers. Sibby greeted many by name. "Well, hello, Mildred. Namaste to you too."

"Bob!" She swatted at a handsome ghost. "Leave that girl alone. She's half your age."

I sidestepped Bob and hurried after Sibby, keeping my eyes averted as much as possible.

In the cemetery's back corner, the Ebonwood mausoleum, an immense gothic structure loomed, cloaked in ivy and gloom, its once-polished marble façade now cracked and stained with time.

Sibby pushed open the wrought-iron doors, their hinges groaning with age and weather. We stepped inside. Sconces flared to life with a gentle whoosh, casting flickering shadows across the stone walls.

I stayed on the lower level and perched on the edge of the cold bench in the center of the crypt. Sibby moved past me, heading straight to Minta's tomb. She rested her hand on the marble, fingertips tracing the carved name in silence.

Sibby's shoulders shifted, not quite a shrug, not quite a shiver. "Minta and I had a treehouse in the Darkly Woods, did you know that? We'd sneak out there in the middle of the night. Braid each other's hair. Talk about the witches we wanted to be when we grew up. Whispered secrets like the world couldn't touch us." Her voice thinned to a whisper. "Feels like a whole 'nother life."

I studied her profile, the set of her jaw, the way her hand lingered against my grandmother's name.

A giggle echoed above us.

Twitch darted into view, swirling in an erratic loop above our heads. "Hi, little witchy Win."

Sibby let out a squawk, waving a hand at him. "Now who in the blazes are you?"

Twitch ignored her, zipping closer. "Win? Didja miss me?"

Great.

"This is Twitch." I fluttered my hand in Twitch's general direction. "Just ignore him."

I turned back to Sibby. "Sounds like you and Minta were close."

And that's when I remembered Pyewacket's advice, *"Never, ever antagonize a poltergeist."*

But it was too late.

"What's that you say?" Twitch gasped, twirling faster. "Ignore me?"

Leaves whipped into a frenzied whirlwind.

I covered my head. "Twitch, stop it! I'm sorry!"

Instead, the poltergeist zipped back and forth, an impish grin on his face. "Let's see what happens when I am ignored."

He dove toward the statue in the corner, an old effigy of a hooded witch and shoved.

The statue rocked.

Teetered.

Then crashed forward with a resounding boom, shattering against the marble floor and taking a chunk of my mother's tomb with it.

"What the hell, Twitch?!" I shrieked. "You could've hurt someone! And—" I turned, fury blazing, ready to lecture him within an inch of his afterlife—

Only to find Twitch floating in stunned silence, his wide eyes locked on the broken tomb.

Sibby exhaled slowly. "Well, bless my goiter."

"What?" My voice was barely a whisper.

I stepped forward.

The marble lay in shattered pieces at my feet.

And through the gaping break, I saw—

Nothing.

My mother's tomb was empty.

I SAT in the middle of the sofa, a bottle of water in one hand and a glass of brandy in the other, trying to decide which one I needed most. Sibby's veilshift back to Fernwood had left me woozy, and water would help clear my foggy brain.

I went with the brandy.

"It's okay, hun. Tell me what happened."

Hilde sat beside me. Her heavy palm, a warm, grounding

weight against my back as I stared blankly at the flaring fire in the hearth. My body began to shake. The aftershock had finally set in. Thoughts scrambled and fractured, refusing to arrange themselves into anything coherent.

Hilde slipped a fleece blanket over my shoulders. I clutched it to my chest with one hand; the other white-knuckled around the glass.

Sibby, on my other side, drained her brandy in one gulp and padded to the drinks cart for another.

Leaping onto my lap, Pyewacket placed a small paw on my cheek, his presence a soothing pulse against my skin.

Fully topped off, Sibby strode back. She tilted her head, her face pinched—not quite anger, not quite worry. I didn't know her well enough yet to tell.

"Hilde, I'm just gonna blurt it out," she announced, taking a bracing sip. "Gen's tomb is as empty as a church on givin' day."

The room fell into silence, save for the steady tick of the grandfather clock and the wind rattling brittle leaves against the eaves.

Hilde's lips parted slightly. Her eyes darted between me and Sibby, searching for some indication of a prank. When none came, confusion crept across her face. "You sure 'bout that?"

I nodded. "Without a doubt."

Sibby dropped onto the sofa beside me, nearly sloshing brandy onto the cushions. "I knew there was something wonky going on in Darkly. The second I got back into town and heard about everything—Gen and Dorian, Malicent, the trollop trying to steal Jessamin's marriage-right. It never sat square with me. Told Conny and Maybelle the same."

"What does this mean?" My voice was barely above a whisper. "I've already accepted that, for whatever reason, my mother didn't die when I thought she had. But I believed she'd been murdered by the sorceress Malicent. I thought her body was in the Ebonwood mausoleum."

I took another sip of brandy, the warmth settling uneasily in my stomach. Turning to Hilde and Pyewacket, I asked, "You both attended her funeral, right?"

The house settled into another hush, its soft sounds suddenly broken by the chorus of tree frogs outside, their riotous songs rising and falling in eerie harmony.

"Did we?" Hilde finally murmured, drawing out the question like only a Southerner could. "I reckon I done questioned that day more times than I can count. Even then, somethin' about it felt off."

"What do you remember?" Sibby asked, leaning forward, elbows on her knees, brandy glass gripped tight.

Hilde sat back, her brow furrowing in concentration. "I remember...nothin'. Just blurry pictures in my head, bits and pieces of folks talkin'. No service. No casket. No moment I saw her laid in the crypt. It's like knowin' a story but can't rightly say how you heard it."

Pyewacket settled on his haunches next to me, his golden eye narrowing. "Now that I think about it, I only remember *knowing* she died at Malicent's hands. But I don't recall the moment I was told." His ear twitched toward Hilde. "And I don't remember a service either. But my mind insists there was one. Like an echo of a memory, not the memory itself."

I relayed Pyewacket's words to Hilde, who stiffened, realization washing over her face.

"Illusionary imprint," she murmured.

Sibby snorted. "Mind mischief, is what it is. Now why in the blazes would Minta do such a thing?"

"Grandmother?" I exclaimed. "You think Grandmother muddled your memories?"

"More than muddled," Sibby said, pointing her glass at Hilde and Pye. "She implanted a memory in their heads. Made them believe they'd attended a burial that never happened. Wrapped up all their suspicions with a lace ribbon snagged off a widow's bonnet. But to what end? That is the question."

Hilde exhaled, rubbing her temples. "Your grandmama had a

gift for illusion and memory work. And your mama too. Genevieve weren't strong in most kinds of magic, bless her heart —but when it came to illusions? She could spin one so fine, it'd chill you clean through."

She stood, then walked to her favorite rocker by the fire. Her hands trembled as she sat and picked up her knitting, clutching it to still the shakes. "So then what happened to Gen?"

"And what in the world was my sister up to?" Sibby added.

Pyewacket pressed his silky paw against my cheek again, his voice soft. "I'm so sorry, *chère*. I promise. We will uncover the truth."

Sibby lifted her snifter toward Pye. "Dang straight we will."

Hilde stared into the fire. "Law, that was a strange time. You remember it, Pye? Folks swore they saw rougarous near every night. And them swamp imps? Slippin' into town bold as you please."

A shiver crawled up my spine. I thought of the imp that had pressed its grotesque face against my kitchen window just a few nights ago. The strange being out by the dock. The rougarous and swamp phantasms being seen in town and in the Cairns? Was history repeating itself?

"Folks were scared," Hilde went on, her voice low. "And folks died. That much I remember. But Gen's death? Her burial? Nothin'."

"Same," Pyewacket said with a slow nod.

I stood suddenly. "I need to see Ransom."

"No!"

Hilde and Sibby's voices overlapped, their sharp exclamation startling me.

I stared at them. "If danger is escalating the same way it did back then, Ransom needs to know. Plus, he can help us find my mother."

Hilde exhaled through her nose, steady and controlled. "Let's hold on, Win."

Sibby nodded. "It's best we keep this news between ourselves.

At least right now. Like I always say, 'what stays in the swamp usually ends up goin' rotten.'"

Hilde gave Sibby a sidelong glance but nodded. "Sibby's right. So far, we've only seen a few swamp creatures nosin' around the house. No need to panic just yet. Minta always had her reasons, she did. I reckon we just ain't got the full picture yet."

I rubbed my forehead, frustration and fatigue pressing in. "And you agree with this, Pye?"

"Yes, well," he said with impeccable poise, "this does seem the most prudent course for the moment. We've yet to determine whether history is truly repeating itself or what Genevieve's disappearance actually signifies. Far too many unknowns to be ringing up the Royal Investigator just yet. Once that cat's out of the bag, good luck shoving it back in. It'll leave bitemarks and scratches."

Hilde's knitting needles clicked steadily. "So there's a dang fool poltergeist in the Ebonwood mausoleum?"

I sighed. "He's been there a few weeks. Met him the last time I visited."

"And you didn't say nothin'?" Hilde's brows lifted.

I shrugged, used to her gruffness by now. "Is the poltergeist a big deal?"

"Probably not," Sibby said.

"But good to know," Hilde added. "Is he an ancestor?"

"Don't think so. Said his name was Twitch Houlihan."

Sibby snorted. "One of those 'Houligan' boys, I'll bet. Leprechauns. Tricksters, the whole lot."

Sibby wiggled deeper into the sofa, picking up that day's *Daily Shade* from the side table. A lull settled over the room—until Sibby suddenly snapped the newspaper open with a sharp pop. "Well, looky here. That Snarkle woman's got a story about Win's crash in the paper."

Sibby flipped the newspaper around for us to see. Next to the article was an image of me cradled in Keir's arms. The picture captured a moment so private, so tender it made my breath hitch.

Keir was kneeling in the dirt, cradling me against his chest. His face was drawn tight with worry, jaw clenched. There was blood on his shirt—mine, I realized—and his eyes were locked on my face like the world had narrowed to just that one point.

My eyes were half-lidded, dazed, lips parted like I was trying to speak but couldn't. Even then, even bruised and barely conscious, I was reaching for him.

Wait!

I snatched the paper.

"That woman was *right there* taking a photo after my crash? What kind of person does that?!"

My voice had risen to an unhinged pitch. Her action was beyond intrusive. It was vile.

"No one ever knows," Hilde murmured, unfazed. "Most folks pay her no mind." She squinted at the photo. "But I will say, Win, Keir looks so full of concern for you. You can't deny he cares."

I swallowed hard.

Before my heart could respond to her comment, I bolted upright when a sudden clattering at the back of the house sent Pyewacket launching off the sofa.

I ran for the kitchen, magic crackling at my fingertips. Beyond the back door, darkness loomed.

Odd. The porch light was always on.

I opened the door cautiously. A figure lay sprawled on the ground in front of the porch, grumbling and letting loose a few choice expletives.

I lowered my hands and sighed.

"So much for the myth of the stealthy vampire."

"Oh, har-dee-har."

Tzazi glared up at me from the bottom of the steps, surrounded by bits of crushed cake.

She stood, brushing crumbs off her leather jacket. "I tripped over something. And why is the porch light off?"

I scanned the porch boards. "What'd you trip over? I don't see anything."

We both turned, eyes sweeping across the yard.

"There!" Tzazi's eyes flared red as she pointed toward the meadow lining the edge of the Darkly Forest.

A squat, wiry creature with mossy green hair cut an erratic path through the tall grass, shoulders hunched and arms swinging wide. An imp.

Across the lagoon, the familiar swamp light flickered into existence, pale green flames dancing low to the ground.

Tzazi and I exchanged a glance just as the porch light hummed, then flared to life.

"So that's two imp visitations now," I muttered.

"That we *know* of," Sibby countered.

"Bet Jess could turn one of those into a nice stew," Pye said. "Call it *swamp-to-table*. Real artisanal."

I laughed, the tension in my shoulders loosening a bit as I translated for Hilde and Tzazi.

Hilde barked a laugh, hands on her hips, watching the creature scurry through the grass.

We gathered the shattered crockery and the last scraps of cake, our movements brisk, eyes darting toward the swamp.

"Should we be worried?" I asked.

"Naw," Sibby said, shivering as she peered into the darkness. "C'mon. Let's get inside."

Tzazi followed me into the kitchen. "Maman read *The Daily Shade* article about your crash." She placed a heap of porcelain and crushed tart filling on the counter. "She sent you tarts."

"Ooh. Are these what I think they are?" Sibby asked, circling her wand above the broken bits, instantly converting the remaining crumbly mess into a pile of sparkling lavender-colored tarts. She whipped the plate off the counter and sauntered back to the sitting room.

"Your timin' couldn't be better." Hilde squeezed Tzazi's shoulder and followed Sibby into the sitting room.

Tzazi gave me a curious look. "All right. A nosy imp and an

idiotic news article couldn't get your heart pumping this wildly. What's really going on?"

Loved Tzazi. Trusted her with my life. Still didn't like it when she brought up my heartbeat.

I motioned for her to follow me to the sitting room.

Sibby slid the newly re-magicked tarts onto the coffee table and snagged one for herself. "After this night, I could use about a dozen of these," she said, her mouth full of pastry.

I picked up one of the exquisite tarts, so beautiful they looked like works of art. "What are they?"

"Heaven," Sibby said and took a big bite.

Tzazi laughed. "Tranquili-tea tarts. Infused with chamomile and Maman's special touch. Guaranteed to make you feel better after a particularly bad day."

Each tart swirled with soft whorls of lavender and white, creating an effect like the sky at dawn. Dried chamomile flowers, sugared lavender buds, and gold flecks were scattered artfully on top of a small swirl of whipped cream tinged with pale blue, catching the light with a subtle sparkle.

I offered Tzazi the plate but she shook her head, obviously impatient for us to tell her more.

Hilde, Sibby, and I munched on our tarts for a few minutes, basking in the aroma of warm vanilla, chamomile, and lavender. I could feel a definite lightening of my mood.

I turned to Tzazi. "Is this custard I taste in the middle?"

"Enough!" Tzazi exclaimed, startling us all into silence. "I know there's something else going on here besides Snarkle's article and the imp." She looked at each of us in turn.

"Ah." I took another bite. These tarts really were working. "My mom's body is missing."

Tzazi blinked. Then, grabbing a tart, she muttered, "Yeah. Okay. I'm gonna need one of these after all."

∾

THE MOONFLOWERS along the cemetery path glowed like ghostly lanterns, their pale petals luminous against the creeping darkness.

"Can you see the shades?" Tzazi whispered, pushing aside the thick tendrils of a vine.

I nodded and swept my gaze over the wisps of shifting mist that drifted between the trees. Human-shaped and primordial, they moved with a slow, haunting grace. Just like earlier, they talked, played games, generally went about their business as if they were still alive. With Sibby gone, they let us pass without even a glance.

Tzazi had insisted she visit my family's mausoleum immediately, and I wasn't about to let her go alone. So here I was, twice in one night, wandering through a cemetery full of ghosts.

This time with the aim to look inside my mother's empty casket.

A sudden thought chilled me.

Was it possible she was here? A Watcher?

I swallowed hard, scanning the endless parade of shades, hoping—dreading—that I'd see her among them.

Nothing.

I reached into my bag; my fingers brushed against the soft fur of Pyewacket's head.

"You okay in there, Pye?"

His golden eye blinked up at me, and he bobbed his head once.

I knew this was just as hard for him.

As we neared the Ebonwood mausoleum, Tzazi suddenly stopped, gripping my wrist. "You ready?"

Her crimson eyes flickered with an edge of danger—determined, protective, wary, and ready to take on whatever we found inside.

I couldn't trust my voice, so I just nodded.

We crept forward.

The gate groaned as it swung open.

I cringed, my breath catching in my throat.

Most of the shades still paid us no mind. They drifted on, indifferent, lost in their endless murmuring.

Tzazi stepped inside first.

As before, the sconces flared to life, their flickering glow throwing shadows across the marble.

I moved to the far end of the mausoleum. My heart hammered as I pointed. "There."

Tzazi crouched next to the crypt, peering into the rough crack where the fallen sculpture had split the tomb open. Her eyes swept the chamber, taking in the plaque on the casket, the fracture in its side, the numerous family crypts lined up along the walls. Just as she turned toward me, a ghostly head popped through the outer wall.

"Hallooooo."

Tzazi lunged before I could blink.

Twitch yelped, vanishing so fast he left a trail of sparkling mist in his wake.

A moment later, his head cautiously reappeared, followed by the rest of his form as he floated sheepishly back inside.

"Well now, that's no way to treat a man in his own house," Twitch muttered, arms crossed as he squinted warily at Tzazi. "You really ought to visit more often, Winny witch. I get up to all kinds of naughty things when I'm bored."

"Tzazi, meet Twitch," I said, massaging my temples before turning to glare at the poltergeist. "And by *naughty*, he means reckless. Like toppling our mausoleum statue."

"Please." Twitch spun lazily through the air, then draped himself across a tangle of overhead branches like a lounging cat. "That was child's play. You should've seen what I did at Gumbo Fest the other night."

I whipped around. "That was you?"

Tzazi leaned against the wall, eyes glinting. "I have to admit, my respect for you just doubled."

Well, at least we now know The Great Gumbo Fest Sabotage wasn't related to the murders, just a bored poltergeist throwing himself a one-ghost parade.

Twitch tilted his head, his wispy mouth curling into a smirk. "Tzazi? That's an interesting name. You wouldn't happen to be related to the Shadowman, would you?"

Tzazi ignored the question and turned back to my mother's tomb.

"Twitch. Did you see what happened to the body that's supposed to be in this crypt?" she asked

Twitch propped his spectral chin on one ghostly hand, frowning in exaggerated thought. "Hmmm. Can't say as I did. Why do you ask?"

Tzazi shook her head and turned to me.

"When you were here before," she said, her voice measured, "was it dark?"

I frowned. "What does that have to do with—"

Then it hit me.

My stomach flipped.

"You think she could be a vampire," I whispered. "Like you."

I couldn't keep the hopefulness from my voice.

Tzazi didn't answer right away. Instead, she ran her hand along the jagged edge of the break. Her expression darkened.

"No," she said finally. "Not like me."

The weight of those three words made my pulse pound.

"What does that mean?" My voice was barely a whisper.

Tzazi kept her palm against the cold marble, her fingers tracing symbols on the surface.

"Technically," she said, "my brothers and I are dhampir—part vampire. My father, whose parents were both vampire, is a strigoi." She turned to me, her eyes sharp. "Strigoi are the most powerful of our kind."

Silence settled over the crypt, thick and heavy.

"Nosferatu," she murmured, "are the vampires created by black magic."

The way she said it—quiet, reverent, afraid—sent a chill straight through me.

"They are dangerous," she continued, rising to her full height. "And unstable." She turned to face me, her jaw set, her voice like iron.

"Let's hope your mother has not become one."

CHAPTER 25

My thoughts were still in disarray the next morning, looping from my mother's grave to Keir, then to Elspeth—only to start the whole maddening circle again.

There was only one cure for that kind of chaos—work. The MET had books waiting, and with any luck, they'd drown out the noise in my head.

I threw on jeans and a soft sweater, whistled for Pye, and we rode to the MET on my Schwinn with the biting wind tugging at my sleeves and lashing my hair across my face.

"These festivals sure do a number on the portals," I muttered, eyeing the stacks of book carnage on my table. The sheer volume of displaced, battered, and slightly sticky tomes was enough to make me sigh. I set aside the book I'd been working on and plucked a particularly tattered one from the pile, pinching it between my gloved fingertips like it might bite me.

Pyewacket sprawled across my worktable, his limbs draped dramatically over various tools and parchments. He let out a heavy sigh, stretching in an exaggeratedly slow motion. "I dare say Darkly festivals do include a large amount of drinking, and once the books are no longer needed, they tend to wind up in less-than-sanitary places. Like toilets."

I froze mid-examination, the book poised in my hands as I processed the sheer horror of his words.

I wrinkled my nose, gingerly flipping through the pages. "You're joking, right?" I sniffed cautiously. "It doesn't smell bad."

Pye crooked a lazy grin, rolling onto his stomach, his golden eye alight with mischief. "Naturally."

I let out a relieved breath, set the book back on the stack, and re-directed my attention to the one already open, scanning for the imperfection that had triggered its arrival in my lab.

Some books only required minor fixes—mended bindings, unwarping of pages, the removal of an unfortunate smudge of mystery festival food. Others needed a full reconstruction. Once restored, they would zip through the MET, returning themselves to their proper places in the stacks. It wasn't unusual, especially after festivals, to see books flitting through the air like eager birds, weaving between visitors and dodging the occasional outstretched hand of an overzealous visitor.

Pyewacket let out another overly dramatic sigh, this one accompanied by a slow, methodical flick of his tail. The injured tip twitched with painstaking fragility.

I arched a brow, watching as he carefully adjusted his position, shifting just enough to make a show of discomfort. "You're really milking this whole injury thing, aren't you?"

"I have been through quite the ordeal," he intoned. "It is only proper that I am afforded the respect due to a warrior who has suffered."

I snorted. "A warrior? Pye, you fell out of a tree. Onto me!"

He placed a paw over his heart. "And yet the emotional trauma lingers."

"Meanwhile, I got a concussion and my body still feels like a dump truck rolled over it, but do you see me draped across the table in distress?"

His ears flicked forward, his expression turning slightly more serious. "What's a dump truck?"

"Oh, hush."

His whiskers twitched, amused. "Suit yourself. But when I am being showered with sympathy and fine tuna while you're left to suffer in stoic silence, don't come crawling to me."

I tossed a crumpled bit of parchment at his head. He batted it aside with a lazy swipe of his paw.

"After lunch, I'm heading over to White Hart Inn," I said, refocusing on my task.

Pye's ears perked up. "Think the Fricks might have some information?"

"They could. After all, the magickstrate was staying there."

"And Elspeth."

I nodded, fingers carefully smoothing a ragged edge of a page. "And Elspeth."

Pye rolled onto his feet, giving a languid stretch before hopping down from the table with a soft thump. His tail flicked energetically behind him. "I shall accompany you."

I eyed his now-perfectly-functional tail whipping around behind him. "I thought you were on the brink of collapse just moments ago?"

He straightened, all feigned injury forgotten. "Miraculous recovery. Must be the sheer force of my will."

I snorted, shaking my head. "Fine. But if you start dramatically fainting in doorways, I'm leaving you there."

"No need. I reserve my fainting spells for more opportune moments." He flicked his tail—this time careful to keep the broken tip from moving too much—and padded toward the door, pausing just long enough to shoot me a grin over his shoulder. "Like when there's an audience."

I sighed, scooping up another book. "Of course you do."

PYEWACKET and I had just broken for lunch at the front counter when the door chimed, a bright, cheerful jingle completely at odds with the person about to walk in.

Elspeth.

She strode into the MET, all sharp heels and sharper smile, the enchanted lanterns catching the icy chill in her eyes. The scent of her expensive perfume—delicate and insidious, like jasmine laced with arsenic—snaked through the air.

"Win!" she trilled, arms spreading wide like she expected a warm embrace. "There you are."

I sighed. "Unfortunately."

"It's so good to see you, sis," she said with a saccharine smile.

I shot her a flat look. "I asked you not to call me that."

"Oh, come on," she crooned, waving a manicured hand. "We share a mother. Might as well lean in."

I folded my arms. "Some things are better left unleaned."

Elspeth rolled her eyes and draped herself against the counter.

Outside the streetlamps flickered on as another storm crept in, casting jagged shadows through the bay windows. A brittle cold clung to the air, the kind that made bones ache.

"Just checking on your progress," she continued, plucking a tiny brass astrolabe from a nearby shelf and turning it over in her hands. "Any juicy developments?"

Pyewacket let out a low, theatrical groan. "Oh, this ought to be a right spectacle."

"Unbelievable," I said, arms tightening across my chest. "It's always about you, isn't it? Did you not hear I was in an accident, or do you just not care?"

Elspeth gasped, her hand flying to her chest with all the sincerity of a stage actress in the second act of a melodrama. "Win, I'm crushed. Of course, I care! Look at you—so brave, standing there all...upright and everything."

I stared at her, shaking my head. "You *say* you want us to have some kind of relationship."

Her dark eyes widened, lips curving into an innocent smile. "Oh, but I do!"

I let the silence stretch before dropping my voice. "So, then what were you doing in Cradlerock with Keir?"

For a fraction of a second, something real flashed across her face—not just surprise, but something sharper. Guilt, maybe. But it was gone before I could pin it down.

Elspeth exhaled, then recovered with a bright, dismissive laugh. "Oh, that," she said, waving a hand. "Total coincidence. We just happened to be going to the same place at the same time."

Pyewacket snorted. "Yeah, sure. Just like how it's a coincidence glass figurines accidentally fall off counters when I'm nearby."

Elspeth ignored him, but I was pretty sure she understood every word. Her gaze stayed locked on me, dark and expectant.

"Honestly, Win, I don't know why you're so suspicious. What makes you think I even *want* your boyfriend?" She sighed dramatically, toying with the astrolabe again. "I've barely been in town a few months and already people are pointing fingers at me. It's exhausting."

"Maybe if you didn't make it so easy."

She pouted, tracing her fingers over the intricate filigree. "I can't help it if people get the wrong idea," she murmured, voice feather-soft with contrived victimhood.

"Right," I drawled. "I suppose it's another coincidence that two of the people poisoned under suspicious circumstances just happen to be the same two people you had the most open contempt for?"

Her fingers stilled.

Something coiled tight between us.

"That's ridiculous," she said, voice clipped. "And insulting."

"Is it?" I arched a brow. "Because from where I'm standing, the only thing keeping people from outright accusing you is the fact that they don't have solid proof yet."

The lanternlight flickered as Elspeth held my gaze, her lips tightening. Then she tilted her head, slow and deliberate, like she was debating whether to be offended or amused.

"I guess when you shine as brightly as I do, people are bound to squint and make mistakes."

Pye blew a loud raspberry. "Please. You could trip over your own ego and still find a way to blame the carpet," he quipped.

I grinned. "That was actually pretty funny."

He bobbed his head. "Low-hanging fruit."

Outside, the wind picked up, rattling the windowpanes and turning the gaslights beyond into warped, flickering smudges of light. The MET's lanterns cast shifting pools of gold across the shop, making the space feel smaller, more intimate. Just the ambiance I wanted with Elspeth Wilde. Not.

I leaned against the counter, voice light but deliberate. "Tell me, Elspeth. If you didn't do anything wrong, why do you look so guilty right now?"

Her smile faltered, twitching at the edges. "Maybe that's what you see because you're looking for a reason not to trust me."

I tilted my head, watching her. "Maybe. Or maybe you're just really bad at being innocent."

She huffed and straightened, flicking at an invisible speck of dust on her sleeve. "You're impossible. Honestly, I came here to check on you, and this is what I get?"

"Check on me? Elspeth, just go."

"But I—"

"Go!"

She rolled her eyes, but her step was quick as she turned on her heel and strode toward the door. The little brass bell jingled overhead when she pulled it open. A blast of icy air swept in, sharp with the bite of sleet.

I watched her go, a pit settling in my stomach. If she was expecting me to swoop in and save her, she was in for a rude awakening. I wasn't in the habit of rescuing people who made my life harder.

I was doing this for Jess and Jess alone.

∽

THE REST of the afternoon passed more easily once I'd washed the bad taste of Elspeth Wilde out of my mouth. As the festival carried on, a steady stream of visitors drifted in and out of the shop, trailing laughter and the scent of spiced cider behind them.

Pye declined a ride in my bag for our walk to White Hart Inn, claiming his tail was still "too delicate for jostling," but somehow managed to scamper ahead of me along the sidewalk, flicking it in anticipation.

As we passed The Magic Cup, Azalea, busy clearing the empty courtyard of sleet-covered leaves brought in by the storm-stirred winds, caught sight of me and dropped the broom, rushing over for a hug. She wrapped her arms around me carefully, as if she sensed my soreness.

"You all right, *chère*?" she murmured in my ear before pulling away to study me. I nodded, touched by her concern.

"Thank you for the tarts."

"My pleasure."

She lingered for a moment, her gaze sharp despite the warmth in it, as if debating whether to say more. But with a final squeeze of my hand, she let me go, pulling her shawl tightly around her neck as she returned to the patio.

A few steps later, White Hart Inn came into view, standing proudly between Hawthorne & Strangeland Law Firm and Spells & Gels. Its whitewashed facade pristine against the cloudy sky, it was one of the few places in Darkly I had yet to explore. I'd never needed to. But stepping inside now, I was immediately struck by a feeling of deep tranquility. Not just the warmth of a well-run inn, but a deeper warmth—spellwoven and powerful.

The main room was elegant, with clusters of tables and chairs inviting guests to linger. A stunning painting of a white stag with a golden laurel draped around its neck hung on the wall. To the right, a grand wooden bar surrounded by rich green wallpaper bursting with ferns and pineapples stretched across the back wall. On the other side, an elegant dining hall glowed under the soft shimmer of candlelight. A year ago, this kind of place would have been my dream retreat. But these days, I gravitated toward more rustic charm, the kind Green Gator Tavern had in spades. Funny how tastes changed.

We had barely stepped inside when a whirlwind of sequins and auburn curls swept toward us.

"Why, Windsor Ebonwood!" The woman's voice rang out, bright and warm, like we were long-lost friends. "What brings you to the White Hart Inn?"

"Hi, Mrs. Frick. I –"

She suddenly gasped and clutched a hand to her chest. "Mercy me! It's Trixie, dear!" She beamed at me, her eyes crinkling at the corners.

Everything about her glittered, from the sequined swirls on her blouse to the way she spoke, all effervescent energy and effortless charm.

"Trixie. The Inn is beautiful," I said sincerely.

"Thank you, dear. We try." She turned, eyes scanning the room, and with a delighted squeal, tugged over a tall, broad-shouldered man with a bald head and a quiet confidence that suggested he rarely needed to raise his voice to be heard.

"Look who's here, dear! It's Windsor Ebonwood. Minta's granddaughter."

The man expertly extricated himself from his wife's enthusiastic grip and extended a hand. "Boone Frick. What brings you here, Miss Ebonwood?"

"Please, call me Win."

Trixie bounced on her sky-high stiletto heels, clearly thrilled, while Boone simply gave me a nod of acknowledgment. Together, they made a fascinating pair. Her all sparkle and vibrant energy; him a solid, steady presence that balanced the brightness. They were probably a formidable team in both business and marriage.

"Win," Boone repeated with a slight bob of his head. "And? What can we do for you?"

As both fixed their gazes on me, I suddenly felt a little foolish.

What right did I have to march in here, asking questions about their guests?

Pye, sensing my hesitation, lightly ran a claw down my ankle. "Go on then," he urged in a whisper.

"Yes, well." I cleared my throat, meeting their expectant stares. "Elspeth Wilde has asked me to help clear her name. I was wondering if I could ask you a few questions about the night the magickstrate died."

Trixie's face broke into an intrigued grin. She was all in!

Boone, however, immediately frowned. "Absolutely not. How would it look if we gave out private information on our visitors? I'm sorry, Win. I hope you understand."

I did. And I didn't. A person died under his roof, after all. He offered a polite smile before disappearing behind the front desk and into an office beyond, leaving no room for argument.

Trixie, however, was not so easily dismissed. She cocked her head to the side and then looked surreptitiously around the room. I looked around too.

What were we looking for?

Then, with a conspiratorial gleam, she leaned in and whispered, "Meet me around back in..." she glanced at the diamond-encrusted watch on her wrist "...ten minutes. Boone takes a nap every day around that time."

She winked, then turned with a dazzling smile to greet a young couple who were cooing over the stag painting.

Pye let out a low whistle. "Now, that's a woman who knows how to work a room."

"And break a few rules," I murmured, watching as Trixie charmed the new arrivals.

"Our kind of person," Pye said with a grimace, rolling his shoulder as if the act of existing had caused him grievous pain.

I snorted. "Come on, you big baby. Let's get ready for our secret rendezvous."

We slipped out the front, anticipation knotting tight in my stomach.

∼

IN THE ALLEY behind the shops of downtown Darkly, Pye scampered ahead and stopped in front of a rounded wooden door tucked into the brick wall of the White Hart Inn's courtyard. He tapped the doorframe. "I think this is it."

Despite my excitement, the whole cloak-and-dagger scheme made me uneasy. I didn't want to cause Trixie any trouble, and I especially didn't want Boone Frick catching us lurking in his Inn like a bunch of wayward raccoons.

I had nearly decided to abort the mission when the wooden door creaked open an inch. Red ruby lips poked through the gap. "You there, hun?"

"We're here," I whispered.

The door swung open, and Trixie ushered us into the courtyard, shutting the door quickly behind us.

"All right," she whispered, her eyes gleaming with the kind of excitement most people reserved for winning the lottery. "Boone'll wake up in about twenty minutes, so let's do this."

"Trixie, I don't want to drag you into anything," I said hesitantly. Boone seemed like a decent guy, but if he caught Trixie feeding us information, things could get awkward fast.

"No trouble to be caused," she chirped, waving off my concerns. "My son Evon told me you helped solve Dorian Wilde's murder. Bless his heart."

I wasn't sure if she truly meant it as a blessing for her son or if it carried the Southern undertone of suggesting Dorian Wilde could go kick rocks in the afterlife. Probably both.

"Boone is worried the murder will reflect badly on the Inn," Trixie continued. "Anything you can do to help solve it is good for us. Plus—" her grin widened and mischief danced in her eyes "—I find this detective work absolutely thrilling."

She hunched up her shoulders and let out a delighted squeal.

"Oh, I really do like Trixie Frick," Pye said, flashing her his version of a cat smile.

Trixie took a startled step back. Cat smiles weren't for everyone.

"Just a few questions, and we'll be out of your hair."

I glanced at her bouffant and barely held back a laugh. Pye, however, snickered openly. He gets me.

"Questions? Yes, yes, but I can do you one better." Trixie's voice dipped into a conspiratorial whisper. "Let's go take a peek at the magickstrate's room. We haven't touched it since Inspector Belleclaire finished his investigation. Can't get anyone to clean in there."

That was too good an opportunity to pass up.

Pye and I followed Trixie through the back entrance and up a narrow staircase. "The maids are a superstitious bunch," she murmured. "We'll have to get Ileana into town to smudge the room before they'll step foot in it again."

"Understandable," I said, exchanging a look with Pye.

We emerged onto a quiet landing, whitewashed walls and feathery teal carpet giving the hallway an almost eerie calm.

Trixie lowered her voice to a husky whisper. "As you can imagine, Magickstrate Grouse kept to herself while she was here. She was quiet. Polite. Not very friendly but also not unfriendly, if you know what I mean."

Trixie stopped in front of a door in the middle of the hallway. The numbers "1" and "3" were attached to its surface in gold block letters. With a wisp of sound, the "3" suddenly released and swung upside down.

Trixie laughed uneasily. "Lucky 13."

She pushed the door open, revealing a spacious, elegant room. Watercolors of Darkly's landmarks lined the walls. A small desk sat in the corner and a king-sized canopy bed loomed against the far wall, its light blue comforter bunched at the foot.

Trixie wandered the room, absentmindedly picking up knickknacks and setting them down in different places. "Inspector Belleclaire shipped her personal items back to the Isles. But other than that, this is how the room looked that morning."

I stepped to the desk and opened the top drawer. Nothing but a collection of pens rolling around on top of hotel stationery. As I moved to close the drawer, something stopped it.

Reaching in, my fingers brushed against a piece of paper wedged up into the top of the drawer. Carefully, I wrested it loose. A wrinkled, but whole, piece of writing paper covered in handwritten text fell into my hand.

I glanced over my shoulder. Trixie was still fussing with the items on the dresser. I slipped it into my bag.

"Tsk, tsk." Pye gave me a withering look. "Honestly."

"Shh," I hissed, turning to face Trixie.

"Did anyone visit the magickstrate while she was here?" I asked.

She wrinkled up her forehead. "Just the Mayórs. But they met her in the lobby before they all left for Gumbo Fest."

"Elspeth was staying here too, wasn't she?" I asked as I sauntered over to the tallboy and pulled open the top drawer. Empty.

Trixie's expression soured. "Not to be rude, Win, but your sister is a piece of work."

"Half-sister."

"She acted like she was queen of the Isles, expecting us to jump at her every whim. I was thrilled when she lost her case and hightailed it out of the Inn."

And straight to the Cairns.

Bless my little brain for going there uninvited.

Trixie glanced at her fancy watch again. "Ooh. Time for us to go."

As we tiptoed down the service stairs, she said suddenly, "You don't believe Boone and I had anything to do with the tainted cider, do you?"

"Oh, Trixie, no!" I assured her. "Absolutely not, and I don't think anyone else does either."

She exhaled, relieved. "That royal inspector was here. As gorgeous as that man is, I didn't like his tone one bit. I felt like I was being interrogated." She shrugged. "But I guess that's his job."

We arrived back at the courtyard and Trixie prodded us through the gate. "I wish I could help you more," she said.

"You've been more than helpful. Can I ask you one more question?"

"Oh course, dear," she answered happily.

"Did you see anyone else here that night? Perhaps someone who wasn't staying at the Inn?"

"No, dear, can't say I did," She suddenly paused. "Why do you ask?"

I fluttered my hand in the air. "Just covering all bases."

Trixie nodded and flashed me that bright cherry-red smile. "It's been a pleasure sleuthing with you."

With a wink, Trixie disappeared back through the service entrance of the White Hart Inn.

CHAPTER 26

*P*ye and I hurried down the footpath leading to Oakspider Park where Gumbo Fest booths and exhibits still lined the grounds. Kids clustered near the Sanctuary animals and next to the pens, Patch's pumpkins, bursting with color among the green vines, spilled across the grass. But beneath the tall oakspider trees and towering magnolias, the festival noise softened, replaced by a tranquility that felt almost reverent. I made for the nearest bench.

I hadn't even settled in before Pye leaped into my lap and stared me down. "I'm not quite sure you should have taken that scrap of parchment," he said.

I thought for a moment. "I agree. But it might be important. I couldn't take the chance the cleaning crew would dispose of it."

"Plus, you want to know what it says."

"That too."

I smoothed the crumpled page across my lap. The paper felt soft beneath my fingers, its surface mostly clean except for the sharp creases where the drawer had mangled it. Ink flowed in a graceful, old-fashioned script, thin lines swirling in delicate arcs above and below the text. A few faint smudges interrupted the elegance, proof it had been touched, handled, maybe even hesitated over.

We leaned in to read:

My dearest Nick—

As I get older, it becomes harder to lay down old griefs and admit which wounds were truly self-inflicted. I know it was my own bitterness that unraveled what we once held dear. My fault, entirely, that love turned to distance. You followed your heart— as anyone brave enough would. I understand that now. I hold no hatred for either of you. Not anymore.

I had no right to blame you for the path you chose, and I apologize for my boorish dismissal this night. You were right to question my past choices.

It would be dishonest not to confess that my anger once carved out a hollow in me. Something crept in, something I fed without knowing. I mistook it for grief, for the ache of rejection. But it was more than that. It thrived on the shadows I refused to let go of. And still, it stirs when I grow restless. It watches.

I've learned to live alongside it—to quiet it, even charm it. But I fear it has teeth. And should I ever truly come undone, I don't know if I could keep it tethered. It is hungry, Nick. And I fear it has mistaken me for its mother.

If you find yourself awake before noon tomorrow, I'll be at the Green Gator. My portal back to the Isles opens shortly thereafter. I'd like, if nothing else, to share one honest breakfast together. No pretenses. Just truth and peace.

Yours always,
Edythe

I exhaled, staring at the paper. "OMG! Magickstrate Grouse had a lover who lives in Darkly. And it appears the relationship didn't end well."

"Indeed."

I stood, scooping Pye into my bag. "We need to give this to Ransom."

Pye popped his head out, a sticky note plastered to his ear, a pen in his mouth.

"Natwally." He spat the pen onto the ground and glared at me.

THE OFFICE OF THE SHERIFF, now the office of Darkly's royal inspector, was just a short stroll from Oakspider Park. Pye and I hastened along the edge of the swamp where the mayor's ballooned head had recently bobbed, turned a corner, and stood before the town's governmental building.

I had only visited the law enforcement office once before when Tzazi mesmered Boddy so we could sneak out a copy of Dorian Wilde's death certificate. That adventure had involved creeping around like burglars after Delilah Rageheart, the cantankerous dragon-shifter receptionist left for lunch. Apparently, mesmers don't work on dragons, which seemed highly unfair at that moment.

The stone building housing the inspector's office looked brighter and cleaner than my last visit. Although, since the building back then was occupied by a reaper, I guess that's to be expected. Reapers weren't exactly known for their interior decorating skills, unless you counted cobwebs and an omnipresent air of doom.

Now, as I stepped inside, I was taken aback by the abundance of greenery. Flowering plants cascaded from the windowsills, potted trees bore actual fruit in the corners, and vines twined along the walls. The place was bright, fresh, cheerful even.

And then there was Delilah.

She sat like an immovable statue behind her desk, her expression as sour as a dragon-sized lemon. Behind her, a full-scale portrait of Queen Ermione fluttered her lashes at me.

"Hello, Delilah," I said as sweetly as I could manage. "I'm here to see Royal Inspector Belleclaire."

"Do you have an appointment?" Her voice was pure gravel, delivered with the enthusiasm of someone discussing tax codes.

"You know I don't, but I just need to—"

"You can make an appointment and come back."

"Fine," I said, blowing out a huff of breath. "I'd like to make an appointment for..." I glanced at the dragon clock on the wall, flames from its nostrils ticking down the time. "...right now."

"Sorry. He's booked up."

"You didn't even check your appointment book," I snapped.

"I don't need to." She shook her peroxide blonde hair and pointed to her head. "It's all up here."

"Delilah, come on," I said, almost pleading, I'm embarrassed to say.

"Our office maintains the order and discipline of Darkly," she continued in a sing-song voice, as if she'd been reciting this line to inconvenienced citizens for centuries. "If we do not maintain order, how can we expect others to do so as well?"

Ransom appeared in the doorway to the back offices, arms folded, his mouth quirking in amusement. "What's all this?"

Delilah looked triumphant. "Miss Ebonwood believes she can see you without an appointment. I told her—"

"Thank you, Delilah," Ransom said smoothly. "It's fine. Come on back, Win."

Delilah glared at me as if she wanted to char me to bits. I sped past, expecting fire to blaze out of her nose any second.

"You've made some changes, I see," I said as I passed watercolors of delicate landscapes gracing the hallway.

He waved a hand. "I love plants, and I love to paint."

We stepped into his office—formerly Boddy's office—and I stopped dead.

In here, the plants had staged a full takeover. Verdant leaves draped from the ceiling, sprawling vines covered the walls, and bursts of exotic flowers wove through it all. Even his desk had sprouted greenery, sharing space with small sculptures and objects d'art.

"Please, sit," he said, watching my reaction with clear amusement.

Pyewacket leaped onto Ransom's desk and made himself comfortable, clearly anticipating the moment I got verbally roasted.

Ransom's ears turned pink as I continued to stand and look around the office. "I may have gone a little overboard."

I raised a brow. "Just a bit."

"Nature helps me think. It's calming. I *am* elven, after all."

I sat. "Well, I hope your jungle helps you process *this*." I pulled the letter from my bag and slid it across the desk.

Ransom's expression darkened as he read. "Where did you find this?"

I hesitated. "Um. Edythe Grouse's room at the White Hart Inn?"

Ransom suddenly stood and closed the door, his lean frame moving with unsettling grace. He took his seat and fixed me with a steady look. "Why did you remove it from the scene?"

"Well," I began, choosing my words carefully. "The cleaning crew was about to come in, and I was afraid it'd be thrown away."

Ransom's jaw tightened. "You could have asked the Fricks to delay the cleaning."

"Ransom. This is me trying to help. I didn't think of it!" I threw up my hands. "My first thought was to protect it and give it to you. So, sue me."

"Maybe I should." He pursed his lips and leaned back in his chair. "Did you read it?"

"If I say yes, are you going to arrest me?"

Pyewacket let out a snicker. "Rightly so."

I shot him a *traitor* look before pantomiming zipping my lips.

Ransom exhaled heavily, rubbing his temples. "No, Win. I'm not going to arrest you. But for the hundredth time, let me do my job."

"Got it. Next time, don't save evidence."

"You know that's not what I mean." He huffed out a breath and stared at me for a long minute as he played with the folds in the parchment.

"What's your take on the letter?" he finally said, steepling his hands on the desk in front of him and cocking his head to one side, reminding me of a raven.

I leaned forward. "Edythe had an ex-lover here in Darkly. Someone named Nick. And the relationship did not end well."

Ransom's eyes flickered with interest. "Any ideas who he might be?"

"No clue. Although I haven't lived here all that long," I admitted. "Pye?"

Pyewacket flicked an ear. "I know of no Nick. However, are you sure it says Nick? It may say Mick."

I blinked. "Let me see that again."

"What did he say?" Ransom asked expectantly.

I shook my hand at him. "The letter please?"

Ransom hesitated before handing it back. I scanned the messy script, then looked at Pyewacket.

"I see what you mean," I admitted.

"Good grief!" Ransom exploded. "*What* do you see?!"

I smirked and flipped the letter toward him. "The 'N' in 'Nick'? Could be a 'M.' As in Mick."

Ransom studied it with new intensity. "Then who's Mick?"

I shook my head. "I don't know of a Mick either. What about you, Pye?"

"There's a Michey in The Graves. Owns a pawnshop," he said, after a thought. "But I don't know any Micks. Other than Jagger, of course."

I rolled my eyes and interpreted for Ransom.

"If we find this Nick-Mick-Michey person, we may find the killer," Ransom murmured to himself.

I sat up straighter. "And if this person has ties to Patch Priddyholm, we've got something."

Ransom's face went still. "You still believe the murders are connected?"

"Oh, *now* you agree that Patch's death was a murder."

"New evidence supports your theory." He leaned back in his chair and grinned. "Congratulations."

"Thank you," I answered, ignoring his sarcasm. "What's this new evidence?"

Ransom cocked his head and grinned at me.

"Fine," I said. "I know the deaths are related."

"Could simply be coincidence."

"As Agatha Christie supposedly said, 'One coincidence is just a coincidence, two coincidences are a clue, three coincidences are proof.' But you know who you should speak to? Harlan Hayman, Patch's foreman. He's not a scarecrow, by the way. He's a golem. A straw golem. And he was there in the field when the pumpkin smothered Patch."

That wiped the smile off his face.

I'd let Harlan tell him about the petals. He'd probably throw me in jail for suppression of evidence if I let that little tidbit out.

He leaned forward. "Now, how do you know that?"

I tapped the side of my nose. "I keep my nose to the grindstone and my ear to the ground."

He smiled, a lazy self-indulgent grin on his handsome face.

"Well, thank you for bringing in the evidence," he finally said. "Although I really wish you'd let me do my job. Someone in Darkly is a murderer and you need to be careful."

I met his gaze evenly. "Unfortunately, careful's never really been my specialty."

CHAPTER 27

I'd just opened the MET door, shivering in the brittle morning air, when the raspy tone of Mathilda's voice rang out down the sidewalk. "Win! I've got your besom ready!"

I hesitated. Between crashing into a tree and this moment, I'd developed a lack of enthusiasm for flying. At least on a broom. With me in the pilot's seat.

I turned to Pye, perched on my shoulder like a tiny, judgmental gargoyle, and sighed as we headed toward Mathilda's shop. "I don't believe I'm made for flying."

"Oh, c'mon," Pye said, his tail whipping up and poking me in the nose every few seconds. "You were never meant for bicycles either but that didn't stop you."

I snorted and cocked my head at him. "Appreciate that, Pye."

We reached Mathilda's store, and I met her eyes when I spoke. "I'm not so sure about this." I held up my arms so she could see the still evident bruises.

"Nonsense," Mathilda cut in, her tone firm. "Early flying mishaps are practically a rite of passage." She bustled me into her shop with the force of a very determined hen. "Come sit while I grab Marais."

I sank into a cushioned chair near the counter, watching Fara fluff out the flowers on a besom draped in extravagant purple clematis blooms, a broom that screamed *I'm a witch with flair*!

Mathilda returned, setting my besom down on the counter with a flourish. She fussed over the bristles a bit more, adjusting the metal charms and talismans that dangled below.

I eyed the broom skeptically. "It's not going to throw me off midair as punishment for crashing it into a tree, is it?"

"Only if you insult its craftsmanship," Mathilda said, giving me a wink and then patted my arm. "Listen. Every witch has a tough learning curve when starting out on their first besom. Not only is it the flying skill that needs to be developed, but also the relationship with the besom. I dare say, you will be doing loop-de-loops before the month is over."

Rather than thinking about how much damage I could do to the town and myself in the execution of a loop-de-loop, I changed the subject.

"Jess is home now," I said. "Tzazi and I visited her yesterday."

"I heard! That's wonderful news!" Mathilda's face lit up. "How is she?"

"Moving slow, but her sass is back, so I'd say she's on the mend."

"Stars, I was worrying myself sick about that girl."

Relief washed across her face.

"Me too," I admitted, then paused. "But something about the whole thing still isn't sitting right with me."

Mathilda's gaze sharpened. "What do you mean?"

I sighed. "The magickstrate and Jess were both poisoned, but I still can't figure out what links them. What they had in common."

Mathilda frowned. "I wouldn't think they had anything in common."

"Exactly," I said. "So why were both poisoned? And what does Patch have to do with it?"

Mathilda hesitated, then shook her head. "Coincidence, I'm sure. But I thought Patch's death was an accident."

"Ransom thinks it's murder," I said.

Her eyes widened. "Wait—what? No. He can't really think that."

I nodded. "Do you know if Patch knew the magickstrate?"

She pulled gently on her ear. "I wasn't particularly close to the old geezer, but not that I know of."

"What about Dixie-Deen?"

Mathilda immediately shook her head. "Dixie-Deen wouldn't have known Edythe Grouse from Morgaine Blackwell. That I would have known."

I wouldn't have known Magicktrate Grouse from this Morgaine Blackwell either, but anyway...

"I worry about her being way out at the Sanctuary all alone," I said, picking up a golden, walnut-sized ball from the counter that looked suspiciously like a Snitch.

"I'm with her every night," Mathilda said gruffly, as if I'd insulted her. "But anyways, she's at Patch's farm today, cleaning it up and getting it ready to move in. She'll be back at the Sanctuary this afternoon."

I blinked and set the golden ball back down on the counter. "Move in?"

"Well, actually, she's moving the entire Sanctuary." Mathilda grinned. I guess I was forgiven. "Patch left her his estate. She's a very rich woman now!"

My stomach dropped. That was unexpected. And certainly complicated things.

Mathilda's eyes suddenly widened as she must have realized what she said. "I—I need to get back to work," she stammered.

She looked lovingly at my broom and ran a hand down the twisted staff. "One of my very best works I must say. Oh!"

Mathilda grabbed my besom just as I reached for it, closely inspecting it like it held the secrets of the universe. "Hmm. I see a few broken bristles Fara missed.

"Terribly sorry, Win," Mathilda said, dragging her gaze from my broom. "But I'm afraid I'll need to hold onto it a bit longer.

Come back tomorrow. I'll have it ready. You don't want to take any chances, right?"

I agreed—given my recent flying record, I wasn't in a position to argue—and headed out with Pye, his tail looped snugly around my neck as we left Besoms & Britches.

"I hope it doesn't really take a fortnight like it did when Zephy Nightshade had Mathilda repair her broom," I said.

Zephy Nightshade. The name nudged something. Faint. Elusive. But whatever memory it roused refused to fall free.

"Hmm," Pye finally said, "Mathilda really is an odd duck."

"An odd duck who seemed awfully uncomfortable after realizing she'd told us Dixie-Deen inherited Patch's estate," I replied.

"Well," Pye mused. "They are best friends. She has reason to be concerned."

"Maybe." I paused. "I think I'll ask Tzazi to come with me to check on Dixie-Deen later. See if she needs anything."

We walked on in silence for a moment. But the name Zephy Nightshade kept tugging at a thread I hadn't meant to pull. And I had a sinking feeling that when it finally unraveled, I wouldn't like what was at the end of it.

LATER THAT AFTERNOON, I stepped out of Tzazi's Jeep in front of Lila & the Piggles Sanctuary.

The cold bit straight through my sweater, sharp and brittle. Frost still clung to the shadows, and the air carried a thread of something warm and spiced drifting from Dixie-Deen's kitchen, like it was doing its best to fight back the chill.

We met by the headlights and she slipped her sunglasses up into her sleek platinum pixie. "You sure you want to do this?"

"She inherits Patch's estate," I said. "That's relevant. Even if we believe she couldn't have killed him."

Tzazi nodded and we followed the familiar path to her cottage where we found Dixie-Deen on the front steps polishing the golden horn of Timi, the baby unicorn. A soft cloth in one hand, a fond smile on her lips. The little unicorn let out a tiny whinny and nuzzled her.

Dixie-Deen looked up. Her smile was warm, but it didn't reach her eyes. "Hello, ladies. It's nice to see you."

As we stepped closer, the toll of Patch's death became clear. Dark circles clung beneath her eyes, and her complexion had dimmed to a pale, washed-out hue.

Dixie-Deen lifted a hand toward the house, the motion barely more than a flutter. "C'mon in and get out of the cold. I just made some spiced coffee."

"Smells amazing," Tzazi said.

We followed her into the white-frame cottage, a space just as warm and inviting as I remembered, filled with animal beds and the comforting scent of potted herbs.

I passed by the ancient living oak at the center of the room and took a seat while Dixie-Deen moved into the kitchen. Tzazi settled into an armchair, reaching down to pet a large hellhound that trotted over to her. "How've you been, Dixie-Deen?"

Dixie-Deen didn't answer at first. Her gaze drifted to the pasture beyond the window where winged goats and translucent peacocks grazed in the golden afternoon light.

She shook off whatever had taken hold of her thoughts, then carefully strained the spiced coffee into a glass carafe. As the moment stretched, she set four mugs and the carafe on a tray and joined us in the living room.

"Better," she finally said as she sat. "Going through Patch's things is helping. Though I found something I wasn't expecting."

She turned to us, her expression caught between grief and reflection. Slowly, she held up her left hand. A ring glimmered on her finger, the diamond catching the light in a thousand fractured sparks.

My breath hitched. "Dixie-Deen…"

She swallowed. "I found it among his things. He was going to propose."

Silence settled over the room, thick and heavy.

Dixie-Deen let out a shaky laugh, brushing her fingers over the band. "I know it might seem silly, wearing it now. But it makes me feel like he's still here. Like any minute, he'll stomp through that door with some wild new idea and his boots covered in mud." Her smile trembled. "It helps."

A lump formed in my throat. "That's not silly at all."

Tzazi's eyes softened, her usual sharp edges momentarily blunted. "He meant for you to wear it, so you should."

I turned my eyes on Tzazi, surprised by the tenderness in her voice.

"Mathilda told me Patch left you everything," I said, keeping my tone light. "Were you surprised?"

"Oh, dear me, no!" Her eyes lit with a brief flicker of their usual spark. "Patch told me years ago that he wanted me to take over the pumpkin farm when he was gone. I've been helping him run it for years."

She filled our mugs with coffee, then slid them across the table. With a nudge, she sent the sugar bowl our way. Its tower of cubes teetered unsteadily, so I plucked one off the top to prevent disaster.

She dropped a sugar cube into her own mug and stirred absently. "I'm the one who enchanted the pumpkins. I loved hearing them giggle and call out to patrons."

"That's why the magic didn't break," I murmured. Tzazi gave a slight nod.

Dixie-Deen continued. "We had the same agreement for the Sanctuary. Everything here would go to him."

She sipped her coffee. Her fingers tightened around the mug. "I just never thought it would happen so soon. To either of us."

We sat for a while in the quiet, the scent of cinnamon and

nutmeg mingling with the aroma of rosemary from the potted plant next to me.

"He always said he'd whisk me off to the Emerald Isles," Dixie-Deen said eventually. "Said we'd drink mermaid mojitos and watch the sun set over the sea every night." She smiled. "But we both knew we'd never leave here."

She reached for the blanket draped over the arm of the porch sofa and tucked it around her legs. "What did surprise me—truly surprise me—was finding out just how much money he had. Hidden in trusts. Investments I never knew existed."

She let out a breath, eyes wide with lingering disbelief.

"And the craziest part?" She shook her head slowly. "He was the anonymous donor keeping the Sanctuary afloat all these years."

My eyes widened. "And he never told you?"

"No. He knew I wouldn't have let him do it." Her voice caught. "Every time the Sanctuary was short of funds, every time I didn't think we'd make it through another month…it was him, quietly making sure we would. That's the kind of man he was."

She looked out at a pair of griffins basking in the sun. "Honestly, between knowing the farm and the Sanctuary are safe…and Mathilda—" Her voice faltered. "She's barely left my side. Except for work."

Her eyes met mine, damp but steady. "I don't know how I would've made it without her."

"How is she taking Patch's death?" Tzazi asked, taking a sip of coffee.

Dixie-Deen's face fell. "She's crushed. They didn't always get along, but they both knew how much I cared for them." She hesitated. "And the magickstrate being in town didn't help."

I frowned. "What do you mean?"

"Oh!" She waved a hand. "The trial, of course. We were all so relieved Jess won."

"You and me both," I said.

Then I noticed the empty mug on the tray. I raised a brow and pointed at it.

"Mathilda," Dixie-Deen said, waved a hand toward the animal pens. "She's feeding the sky mantas. They love when she flies with them."

"Now that's something I'd love to see," I said.

"It's a sight," Dixie-Deen agreed.

"It sure is," a voice called from the front door.

Mathilda walked into the room, shivering and brushing off her skirt. She joined us in the living room, and Dixie-Deen poured her a mug.

"What brings you two here?" Mathilda asked, eyeing us both.

"Just checking on Dixie-Deen," I said.

Tzazi said nothing, her gaze sharp.

Mathilda took a sip, dunked a cookie. "She's doing just fine, aren't you, dear? We're going to get through this together."

I'd just bitten into a gingered shortbread when the front door creaked open and a voice called, "Miss Dixie-Deen? I brought fresh blankets for the frostlings!"

The woman standing inside the door was young and bright-eyed, with a sunflower tote bag and arms full of folded flannel. She was already talking as she approached.

"I figured the temperature drop might rattle the littlest ones. Tempest phased through her crate yesterday morning and I had the hardest time finding her up in the rafters."

"Brinley's been a godsend since..." Dixie-Deen's voice faded. Her smile didn't quite hold. "Since things got harder. She's sweet with the animals. They trust her."

Brinley beamed under the compliment. "I've got chamomile biscuits for the kelpie colts too. Baked 'em this morning."

Mathilda's mug landed a little too firmly on the table. She glared out the window.

"Well, Brinley, aren't you just a sunbeam," Dixie-Deen said gently, her smile soft but warm. "Come have coffee with us before you get started. It's spiced. Your favorite."

Brinley perched on the sofa beside Dixie-Deen, still practically vibrating with eagerness. "Thank you, Miss Dixie-Deen."

Dixie-Deen patted her arm affectionately.

"I'll fetch her a cup," Mathilda said smoothly, already rising before anyone else could offer. She moved to the kitchen, her skirts rustling like dry leaves.

"Brinley's been helping with the winterlings," Dixie-Deen explained to Tzazi and me. "Knows how to handle all the youngsters—even the ones who scream when they hit a cold spot."

Brinley's smile stretched wide. "I don't mind the shrieking. I like their little fangs."

It definitely took a certain type of person to enjoy working with paranormal animals. I was not that type.

Mathilda returned moments later, mug in hand. She poured Brinley a cup. "Here you are, darling," she said.

Brinley smiled and took a grateful sip.

Then hiccupped. Loudly.

Her hand shot to her mouth. Another hiccup followed. Then another, louder still.

"Oh—hic!—I'm—hic!—so sorry—" she gasped, her whole body jolting with each sound.

Dixie-Deen shot up. "Oh dear, I've got a tincture for that. Brinley, sweetheart, just sit tight. I'll be right back."

She bustled through a side door, floral shawl fluttering behind her.

The second the door closed, Mathilda crossed her legs and adjusted her napkin with meticulous care. Then, without looking up, she said, "Some people get so comfortable in someone else's space, they forget they were never invited to stay."

Brinley blinked, her hiccups stalling for a heartbeat. Her mouth opened slightly, but she didn't speak.

Tzazi went very still beside me.

Mathilda took a leisurely sip of her own drink. "Some people take and take," she said lightly, not looking at Brinley, "and some just don't know when they've overstayed their welcome. But I suppose good intentions can make pests of us all."

Tzazi set her cup down—hard. "You sure it's Brinley who's confused about her role here?"

Mathilda turned slowly. "I've been at Dixie-Deen's side since before most people around here were born. I know what she needs."

Before the air could thin further, Dixie-Deen bustled back into the living room with a tiny cobalt bottle and a honey stick. She knelt beside Brinley with the practiced calm of someone who'd mended everything from bruised wings to broken hearts.

"Here, baby. Sip this and breathe. You'll be fine."

But Brinley was already rising, her face pink and tight.

"I—I just remembered something I've got to do. For my mama," she said quickly. "I'm not going to be able to volunteer right now. I'm sorry, Miss Dixie-Deen."

Dixie-Deen blinked in surprise. "Oh," she said. "That's...all right, sugar. I understand."

Brinley gave a jerky nod, avoided everyone's eyes, and bolted out of the house. We could hear her hiccupping all the way to the gate.

Dixie-Deen stood there for a moment, still holding the little bottle. When she sat down again, she didn't speak right away. Her fingers tightened slightly around the honey stick.

Then, softly, "Well. That's a shame. The little ones liked her."

She didn't look at Mathilda.

And Mathilda—very deliberately—didn't look at her.

Tzazi and I exchanged a glance.

We lingered a while longer, swapping stories over warm, spiced drinks, but Dixie-Deen had already begun to slip back into herself.

Tzazi noticed too. "We should head out."

I stood. "Take care of yourself, Dixie-Deen. We're here if you need anything, Mathilda."

"See you back in the 'hood, Windsor," Mathilda said with a grin.

Dixie-Deen smiled, but there was a distant look in her eyes, like she was already retreating into memories.

Tzazi and I didn't speak on the drive back to Darkly. There wasn't much to say after watching Mathilda gut a girl's spirit with a few well-placed words.

CHAPTER 28

*C*ome morning, the rush of travelers had ebbed to a trickle, probably helped by the storm that crept in last night, bringing icy rain that froze in a glaze across the windowpanes. I leaned against the counter and let the quiet settle in.

"Pye, my broom should be ready. Wanna come with me to pick it up?"

"No," he said yawning and stretching while perched atop the nearest bookcase. "I'm going to go back to dreaming about warm days and birds and—"

"Okay, okay. I'll be back in a few minutes."

I checked my appearance in the antique mirror above the counter and hurried outside. The cold nipped at my cheeks when I stepped onto the icy sidewalk and the sky remained an overcast gray.

When I entered Besoms & Britches, however, the warm, woodsy scent of evergreen branches and cinnamon filled the air. Behind the counter, Fara Boughweaver weaved a string of live holly and pine branches through the bristles of a besom. The greenery glistened as though dusted with morning dew.

"What a work of art, Fara!"

"Thanks, Win. I figured I'd get a head start decorating my

broom for the holidays before all hellhound breaks loose," she said.

"Broom? I thought we were supposed to call them *besoms*."

Fara leaned in conspiratorially. "That's a Mathilda thing. I usually call it a broom. Just not around her."

I laughed. "My lips are sealed. Is she in?"

"Yep. Let me get her."

I browsed the shop and was impressed at the number of charms and decorations displayed. On the far wall hung a line of riding pants in every fabric and color you can imagine. I pulled down a sleek pair of black leather britches. One glance at the price tag and back on the rack they went.

Mathilda's cackle preceded her arrival. "They may be expensive but they're one hundred per cent worth it."

She smirked, arms crossed over her chest. "You think riding's smooth now? Slip into those, and you'll feel like you're floating on a feather bed. Those britches are my best creation yet."

Fara, now back behind the counter, stared at the britches, gave a single slow shake of her head and then turned back to her work.

"Oh! Before I forget," Mathilda suddenly said. "Fara, pop over to Maisie's and grab a few more agate chips. We're nearly out."

Fara frowned. "We've got a full jar in the back."

"Not the smoky ones, the mossy kind. Go on before she sells out. They're on sale today." Mathilda shooed her toward the door and then materialized behind the counter. "You know how fast her shelves clear."

Fara pressed her lips together, then grabbed her coat, and hurried into the frosty street.

Mathilda unwrapped my broom and set it on the counter. The charms and amulets embedded in the bristles sparkled in the afternoon light while the broom itself shined as if dipped in diamonds.

I ran a hand down the polished handle. "It's even more beautiful than before. And you've added more charms."

"I thought you deserved a little something extra," Mathilda

said, pleased with herself. "Felt bad about that spill you took—though, of course, *not* my fault."

"Of course," I echoed dryly.

I raised my eyebrows as she drew in closer. "Say, you asked me the other day if I knew anyone who had it out for the magickstrate. I've been thinking, and there is one person in Darkly who, if you believe any of the gossip, absolutely hated Edythe Grouse." She nodded knowingly holding me in suspense for a few seconds. "Benny the Rat. She sent him to Infernum Rock, you know. I think he was there for a good century or more. Now that's a reason to want someone dead."

Despite Leidy's comments to the contrary, all roads seem to be leading to this mysterious Benny the Rat.

"I'd love to talk to Mr. Rat, but I have no idea how to find him in The Graves."

"Oh, I can help you there," she said, flipping over a pad of paper and sketching me the precise instructions straight to Mr. Rat's house.

Mathilda handed me the directions as two customers walked in. "Let me know if you need anything else, Win. I'm right next door."

THE RAIN that had threatened all day continued to loom, cold and malevolent, pressing low against the serrated skyline of The Graves. I peered down at the streets from above, following the serpentine coils of spectral mist, the witchlights wavering dimly. Ruddy brick buildings rose from twisty cobbled streets, each floor perched precariously on the one below it, like some brick-and-mortar game of Jenga.

I attempted to fly lower over the district, but an unseen force nudged me back—not aggressive, but firm. The Graves apparently had its own rules, and one of them was that no one entered from the skies.

We coasted down to the entrance, and Pyewacket hopped out of his cushy seat, his upright tail twitching madly. On the sign over our heads, *Gaslight District* was spelled out in intricate iron filigree. The metal hummed with latent enchantment, a ward of some kind.

Pyewacket leaped up onto my shoulder, his claws digging into my coat while he took in the eerie surroundings. "Lovely," he muttered.

I consulted the directions Mathilda had given me, inhaled deeply, and stepped forward.

The temperature dropped instantly, a wet chill clinging to my skin. The cobbles beneath my boots were uneven, ancient, like walking across a set of jagged teeth, but at least they weren't iced over. The mist thickened, shifting unnaturally, parting in slow, deliberate movements, as if something vile hovered just beyond my sight.

Blue witchlights sputtered in glass lanterns, their glow too weak to push back the gloom entirely. Shapes moved in the periphery—figures wrapped in long coats, eyes gleaming too brightly beneath the brims of their hats. A few lingered in the doorways of decaying townhouses, watching us as we passed.

We followed the winding street until we reached The Lucky Lounge, a decrepit tavern at the crossroads of Phantasm and Tomb Streets. The sign above the door, its edges splintered and burnt, creaked on rusted chains. Nothing about it looked lucky.

The gaslights on Bacchanal Avenue were marginally brighter, illuminating the slick cobblestones in pools of weak amber. At the midpoint of the street stood a three-story brownstone, its windows lit with the warm, flickering glow of oil lamps. The air around it felt different, calmer, despite the eerie stillness pressing in from all sides.

"This is it."

I climbed the steps, Pyewacket still perched on my shoulder. He didn't say a word, not even a snide one.

Before I could knock, the door swung open.

In the doorway stood a petite, elderly woman with warm dark eyes and delicate hands. Her sleek, gray-streaked hair was twisted into a flawless bun at the nape of her neck, and she wore an elegant yet practical dark dress with a pristine white apron. There was something off about her, but not in a bad way. Just a sense that beneath the grandmotherly exterior lurked something far older and far stranger.

"Ah," she said, her voice rich and warm, her sharp gaze skimming over me, then to Pyewacket with interest. I would guess most witches in The Graves don't carry small black cats on their shoulders. "Miss Windsor Ebonwood, yes?"

I hesitated. "I was told Benny the Rat lives here."

The woman let out a delighted laugh, her teeth just a little too sharp. "Yes, dear. Benicio," she corrected. "You are expected. Come in."

She stepped aside, allowing us entry.

The moment we crossed the threshold, I was enveloped in the scent of rich coffee, tobacco, and something faintly floral—night-blooming jasmine, maybe.

The interior was shockingly elegant. Ornate rugs, gilded mirrors, and deep leather chairs were arranged with a casual opulence that screamed wealth, power, and refined taste. A fireplace flickered in the corner, casting long shadows across the polished floorboards.

As I picked up a book lying casually on a side table and gazed dumbstruck at a very rare first edition *Ars Notoria*, a tall figure strode into the room.

Benicio Kim was nothing like I imagined.

He was lean, dressed in fitted jeans and a well-worn graphic tee that clashed delightfully with his polished Italian loafers. His jet-black hair gleamed under the low light, an errant lock falling forward over one eye. He extended a well-manicured hand. Everything about him was precise, deliberate, effortless.

"I'm Benicio Kim." His voice was smooth, lightly amused. "How can I help you?"

I took his hand, my own feeling small and insignificant against his cool, slender fingers. "Windsor Ebonwood." I hesitated, then before I could stop myself, I blurted, "I saw you."

His dark brows lifted. "Excuse me?" He motioned for me to sit, taking the chair across from me with languid ease.

"At Gumbo Fest," I clarified. "At the edge of the forest."

He looked surprised for a moment, then his face broke into a smile. "You could see me?"

"Well, of course. Why wouldn't I?"

He chuckled, a deep, velvety sound. "It is very unusual for anyone to see or sense me when I cloak myself."

The woman, who I assumed was Benicio's housekeeper, reappeared, setting a tray of coffee and delicate pastries on the table. She moved with a certain weightlessness, as if her feet barely touched the ground.

Pyewacket leaped gracefully onto the armrest of my chair, sniffing the air. "Oh, excellent. Bear claws. Finally, a household with standards."

"Lucasta, could you also bring us a bowl of orange whips? I believe those are a particular favorite of my guest."

"How in the world did you know that?" I asked.

Benicio smirked. "They don't call me Benny the Rat for nothing. Despicable nickname, but highly accurate. Nothing takes place on Darkly Island that I don't know about."

He poured me a cup of coffee and handed it to me before pouring one for himself. I stirred in three sugars.

"So, you saw me cloaked. Interesting," Benicio said softly, leaning in. "You know what that means, don't you?"

I shook my head.

A slow smile spread across his lips. "We're fated mates."

"What!" The word came out sharper than I'd intended.

He laughed, warm and easy, leaning back as he crossed one leg over the other. "Just kidding. It means you have demon eyes. You can see through the veil some of us draw around themselves."

That startled me.

Benicio watched me carefully. "You see ghosts, right?" he asked.

"I have, yes."

He nodded. "Demon eyes. Of course, you don't really have the eyes of a demon." He waved a hand. "An old term. Not sure of its origination."

With a sweet smile, Lucasta returned with a small crystal bowl filled with orange whips. She set it on the table in front of me. I popped one in my mouth.

"Tell Benny these bear claws are delicious," Pyewacket said, crumbs falling from his mouth as he spoke. "Better than the Cradlerock bakery."

I laughed. "Pye loves your bear claws. He's always all about the food."

"Not a bad way to be." Benicio turned to my greedy feline. "Those are homemade by Lucasta. I'll have her send some home with you."

Pyewacket's tail swished so wildly in happiness I thought he was going to fall off the table.

Benicio looked at me kindly for a moment. "What brings you to my doorstep? I doubt it was to eat pastries and orange whips."

"Well, Mr. Kim—"

He shook his head, glossy hair shining in the light. "Benicio."

I met his gaze and got straight to the point. "Benicio. I want to know about you and the magickstrate."

"Ah." He steepled his fingers together. "I heard you were instrumental in the arrest of Dorian Wilde's killer a few months ago, and now it appears you are looking for the person who murdered Edythe Grouse. What do you want to know?"

Lucasta handed him a glass of brandy, giving me a moment to collect my thoughts. Before I could protest, she set a glass of wine on the table in front of me.

"Oh, no. I don't want—"

"Now, now," Benicio interrupted. "You must accept my hospitality, or I will be insulted."

I couldn't help it. I liked Benny. I picked up the glass and took a sip. The rumors were true. The gangster had excellent taste in wines.

"You've been mentioned more than once when conversations about the magickstrate come up."

I took another sip, watching his reaction.

"That's no surprise. In my younger days, I was quite the... scoundrel. Edythe and I got to know each other very well."

He looked at me with a magnetic intensity, like allure was stitched into his very being.

"Only in your younger days?" I teased. "Hard to imagine you ever keep your hands completely clean."

He simply laughed and his amber eyes narrowed as he studied me, making me uncomfortable with their sharpness.

Not answering was answering.

I cleared my throat. "More specifically, she sent you to prison for hundreds of years," I said, steering us back to the conversation at hand.

"Let me guess." He swirled the brandy in its crystal glass, then took a slow sip. "You want to know about my time in Infernum Rock."

"I want to know whether you held a grudge against the magickstrate."

Some of the sparkle left his eyes.

"Now that is an interesting request. If I say I hold no ill will for Edythe, you will say I'm lying. If I tell you that, of course, I held some resentment toward the magickstrate who locked me up, you will assume I killed her." He shrugged." It's a no-win situation for me."

"So did you kill her?"

I took a sip and held his gaze. He didn't even flinch at my question.

"First of all, why would I do something that would put me

back in that abominable place and give up all this?" He gestured to his opulent home. "Second, you didn't ask, but I have an alibi."

"Okay then, where exactly were you when she was poisoned?"

"Poison, huh," he said under his breath, almost a whisper. "Now that *is* interesting."

His gaze sharpened. "Yes. My whereabouts on the night of the magickstrate's death. I spent the entire night at the Lucky Lounge, my club here in The Graves."

Benicio sat back, obviously pleased with his alibi.

Then tilted his head at me, his lips pinched. "Many people saw me."

"But as you are aware, I saw you with my own eyes that night at Gumbo Fest."

"Oh, yes. I popped in for a moment. Cloaked, if you remember, Lady Demon Eyes."

"You know I'm not going to believe what you say just because you say it. How do I get to the Lucky Lounge?"

"You don't," Pye interjected.

"The Lucky is not a place where you will be welcome. I adamantly suggest you stay away," Benicio concurred.

"Well, that figures. You have an alibi that can't be verified."

"I didn't say that," Benicio countered. "I informed you that *you* would not be welcome. Others would begrudgingly be allowed admittance. Like a royal inspector, for example."

"Ransom's been here?"

"I'm sure I was one of the first he questioned, given my long association with the magickstrate."

I nodded slowly, letting that settle. "What about Patch Priddyholm, the pumpkin farmer who was also murdered recently"?

"Ah, yes. The Priddyholms." He steepled his hands in front of him. "I've had many dealings with his ex-wife. Didn't know Patch very well. Only through his pumpkin farm. His jack-o'-lanterns were the absolute best. Even scared the folks around here. And that's saying a lot."

"Wait," I said, holding up a hand clutching another orange whip. "Patch didn't have a gambling problem?"

"Patch? Not as far as I know." He drew in his brows and chuckled. "Is that what you heard?"

"It's not true then?" I asked, side-stepping his question.

"Not true at all. His ex-wife Claira is the one who owes me a bundle of money. Luckily for her, she's paid a good chunk back. Her bet for when you and Keir went on your first date was right on the money."

"Why in the world did people place bets on me and Keir? Or even care?"

He looked at me for a moment in puzzlement.

"You don't know." It was a statement, not a question.

"I don't know what?"

"Keir Bane's full name is Keiren MacIlleBhàin," he said with an exaggerated parody of Keir's accent.

When I stared at him blankly, he continued. "Heir apparent to the Lycan throne?"

Benicio shook his head in surprise when I shrugged and continued to stare.

"Crown Prince of the Werewolf Kinship?"

I narrowed my eyes. "Benicio, what are you saying?"

He leaned back, swirling his brandy lazily. "Keir Bane is the next alpha king of the werewolves."

"What?"

Keir's name rang in my ears, my mind scrambling to make sense of it. The words didn't fit. They didn't belong in the same sentence.

King of the Shifters.

Benicio opened his mouth to repeat himself, but I cut him off with a sharp look.

I shot to my feet, my chair scraping against the floor with a sharp squeal. A rush of heat climbed up my neck, my breath coming in sharp bursts as I paced the length of the room.

King. Keir was to be a king.

I clenched my hands into fists. I had let him in. Trusted him. All those questions I'd pushed aside, all the doubt I had tried to ignore. First Quinn. Then Elspeth. And now this? The depth of his deception cut deeper than I ever could have imagined.

"You're upset," Benicio observed, his voice lined with amusement but not cruelty.

"No, I'm—" My voice faltered. What was I? Shocked? Furious? Hurt? All three twisted together in a sharp, tangled mess beneath my ribs.

"Pye, did you know about this?" My voice came out tight, brittle.

He looked at me with a puzzled expression, his golden eye wide, unblinking. "I'm sorry, Win. I didn't know it was a big deal."

Heat flared behind my eyes, but I refused to let it spill over.

But it changed things for me.

"Well, Mr. Kim—Benicio," I corrected stiffly, my voice forced into something cool and distant. "Thank you for your time, but I should be heading home."

My broom shimmered into existence beside me, its bristles humming with anticipation. I grabbed it, turning sharply toward the door. Pyewacket leaped into my bag when I passed him on the table.

Benicio moved faster than I expected, reaching the door before I could fling it open. His fingers brushed my arm, light, but deliberate.

"You shouldn't leave like this," he said, his voice rich with concern. "Let me help you home."

Yanking my arm back, I stormed out onto the gaslit street, throwing a ball of magic toward the door to slam it shut behind us.

But before I even reached the sidewalk, Benicio appeared in a blink, amusement flickering in his eyes.

He held up a box, grinning cheekily. "Lucasta didn't want you to forget your bear claws."

Pye's head popped up, his eye razor sharp on the box. "Mate, you're my hero."

An enormous shadow suddenly swooped overhead, blotting out the dim moonbeams.

Benicio's expression hardened.

I tracked the figure through the sky as it swirled over the edges of The Graves and turned back. "I thought besoms weren't allowed over The Graves."

"That's not a witch, Win." His voice dropped lower, more urgent now. "You need to leave The Graves. Now."

He stepped back, his smirk returning, though his eyes remained sharp. "And I suggest you straighten things out with Bane."

I stiffened.

"He's a good man to have at your side," Benicio continued. "As am I."

His fingers snapped.

And just like that, he was gone.

CHAPTER 29

After a loud pop, I landed on a stone walkway, the sudden shift leaving my stomach somewhere between where I was and where I now stood. The uneven path threatened my balance, and I barely caught myself before toppling forward.

Pyewacket emerged from my bag, landing lightly on my shoulder before hopping to the ground, stretching luxuriously as if he'd merely disembarked from a luxury carriage rather than being forcibly veilshifted from one end of Darkly to the other. His tail flicked once, then twice, before he glanced around with an expression of profound offense.

"Where are we?" he demanded, his voice laced with irritation. "Because I swear, if this is one of those places where I'll be expected to do something strenuous—"

I reached down, absently scratching between his ears, my attention pulled toward our surroundings. The cold air smelled fresh here, crisp and clean with a bite of pine carried from the forest surrounding us. Overhead, thick clouds muted the sky to soft grays and silvers, and the light filtered through in long, angled beams that gave the landscape a quiet, striking glow.

It took a moment to register what I was seeing, where we had landed. A large stone house loomed before me, perched on the cliffs next to Darkly Falls. It was old and solid, built with a weight that dared the winds and rain to try and tear it down. Below, the landscape sloped downward into a small village nestled at the base of the cliffs. Chalet-style cottages dotted the area, some quaint but others sprawling and grand were surrounded by boulders with rock cairns placed around the commons areas.

Wait!

Cairns?

I sucked in a sharp breath.

No. No, no, no.

Pyewacket, ever attuned to my moods, twisted his head up to look at me, eye narrowing. "Ah. That's a face," he noted, sitting back on his haunches. "And not a happy one. So, I assume we've arrived somewhere dreadful."

I took a step back. We had been dropped into Silverfang territory. The cairns weren't just for decoration, and they weren't there for ambiance.

They were warding stones.

They meant one thing. I was standing in the heart of *his* home. The one person I really didn't want to see right now.

And I wasn't staying.

Before I could turn, the massive wooden doors swung open. Keir stood in the doorway, clad in torn sweats and a Robert Smith tee, surprise flitting across his features. "Win?"

Fury surged inside me. I stepped forward and jabbed a finger into his chest. "The next ruler of the werewolves? Really? Why didn't you tell me who you are?"

Keir recoiled and ran a hand through his unruly hair. "Maybe yeh should come inside," he offered, his voice a tentative olive branch. He reached out for my hand, but I brushed him aside.

"No, right here is fine."

His sigh cut through the tension—a sound heavy with sorrow —and I hated how part of me still wanted to soften toward him, even when every cell in my body screamed that he'd kept something monumental from me.

"'Cause once I told yeh, it wouldn't really have been your choice anymore, would it?" he said, his voice low, steady.

I stared at him, not blinking. "Explain."

His gaze dropped, jaw tightening. "I didnae tell yeh because of what it'd mean for you."

I crossed my arms. "What does that mean? What would it mean for me?"

Keir looked past me, toward the horizon where clouds skimmed low and bruised. "In my world, choosing the heir comes with a bond. A claim. Old magic. It starts off subtle, but once it takes hold, it grows. Even without saying the words out loud. Even if we never agreed to it."

I blinked, the weight of his words beginning to settle.

"I didnae want to tie yeh to me without yeh sayin' aye first," he added. "Didnae want the crown to make your choices for yeh. With every moment we spent together, I knew I was waiting too long. But I had to be sure yeh were choosing *me*, not the heir."

Silence bloomed between us. Even Pyewacket, ever quick with a quip, said nothing.

"You think keeping that from me gave me a real choice?" I asked, my voice tight.

Keir flinched.

"You thought lying was a better alternative to trusting me with the truth?"

"I thought I was protecting yeh," he said quietly.

I shook my head, jaw clenched. "You protected me from nothing. You just made the truth feel like a trap when it finally came out."

His mouth opened, then closed again.

"And now I don't know what else you've kept from me," I added, not trying to hide the crack in my voice. "What other truths you've decided I'm not ready for."

He took a step closer. I held my ground.

"Nothing else," he said. "No other lies. Just this one. And I've hated carrying it since I knew what we were becoming."

I didn't answer. Couldn't.

"Come on in so we can talk," he said, more gently now. "It's freezing out here. I'll put the kettle on."

He reached for my hand. I didn't take it, but I followed him inside.

He patted Pyewacket on the top of his head, deftly jerking his hand away just in time to miss a devious swipe from razor sharp claws.

I stepped inside and instantly stopped in my tracks, awestruck by the sheer beauty of the space. Keir's home was stunning—spacious and modern, with floor-to-ceiling glass walls that framed the rugged cliffs and misty village below. The high ceilings gave the space an open, airy feel, while the furniture—plush leather and soft, earth-toned textiles—spoke of comfort rather than mere design. A massive fireplace crackled in the corner, its warmth flickering over a sleek wooden bar and open kitchen.

"Not bad," Pye murmured, hopping onto the back of a deep-cushioned armchair. "For a wolf."

I wandered through the room, my gaze drawn to the paintings adorning the walls, each one a contrast of wild expression and steady control. Eventually, I found myself next to the glass wall, the world stretched out before me in a breathtaking sweep of nature and quiet civilization.

Sliding the door open, I stepped onto the balcony, letting the cold breeze wrap around me, carrying with it a trace of blossoms, wafting from vines woven thick across wooden lattices. A large crow cawed from a nearby fir tree, the branches creating an oddly beautiful canopy over the deck.

Keir stepped onto the balcony, moving with the effortless grace that always made me hyper aware of his presence. He crossed to the stone wall of the house and flipped a switch. A moment later, warmth began to radiate in steady waves from the floor and the discreet rafters overhead. If not for the icy drizzle falling just beyond the balcony, I could've mistaken it for a warm spring afternoon.

He nodded toward the sofa by the glass railing and set two mugs on the table. I curled up on one end, tucking my legs beneath me, and Keir settled beside me, his long frame stretching comfortably across the plush cushions.

"Built the house for this view," he admitted, his voice low, almost reverent.

I tucked a loose strand of hair behind my ear. "It's incredible."

He chuckled, a quiet, warm sound, before passing me a steaming mug. His fingers brushed mine, just briefly, but the contact sent a tingle skimming over my skin.

I lifted the mug to my face, breathing in the fragrant steam.

"Is this chai?" I asked, peeking at him over the rim.

"Aye," he said, his lips quirking into a grin. "I asked Azalea how it's done."

I took a sip, letting the warmth spread through me. The spiced sweetness grounded me, familiar and steady.

Keir's gaze met mine, deep brown eyes, quiet but stormy. "I dinnae mean to hurt yeh, Win. I just—" he hesitated, exhaling sharply before continuing, "—we have something special. With yeh, I can just be me."

I studied him for a long moment, turning his words over in my mind.

He leaned back against the sofa, his eyes gazing out over Darkly, the silver tarnished light of late afternoon casting a soft glow over his features.

"You think hiding who you are is being yourself?" I asked. "You think I want the edited version of you?"

He looked away. "I didnae want to lose yeh to something I couldnae control."

"Then maybe you should have let me decide what I could handle," I said. "You don't get to protect me from you."

"I didnae think," he said quietly. "I just assumed. And then… once I kept it from yeh, it got harder to find the moment."

I looked back over the magnificent view, letting my thoughts settle in the golden light stretching over Darkly. I had never dared ask Keir about his relationships with other women before. I was too afraid of the answers, but if we were doing this—really doing this—then it was time for the truth.

"There are a few things I've been wanting to talk to you about," I said, my fingers tightening around my mug.

Keir turned to me, his expression curious and attentive. "Such as?"

I inhaled deeply, letting the exhale soothe the ache in my chest.

Was I strong enough to accept the truth?

"Well," I began carefully, "I know you and Solara used to date. But what is your relationship with Quinn Ainsley? And what about my sister, Elspeth?"

The reaction was immediate. He stiffened, not in anger, but something perilously close.

"Now that you've brought that up, lass, why don't yeh start by tellin' me about you and Belleclaire?" he countered, his voice dipping into a low growl and his accent becoming more pronounced.

I blinked. "What are you talking about?" I threw back. "I didn't ask for his attention."

"Oh, didn't yeh now?"

I scoffed. "What is that supposed to mean?"

Keir leaned forward, arms braced against his knees. "What about The Drunken Gull?"

I threw my hands up. "What *about* The Drunken Gull?"

"I don't know. You tell me."

"Good grief, Keir. This is ridiculous. Nothing whatsoever happened. For the record, if I wanted Ransom, I'd be with Ransom."

Keir's expression shifted, some of that taut frustration melting away. His voice was softer when he spoke next. "And if I wanted Solara, or Elspeth, or whoever else yeh've got in your head, I'd be with them."

His words landed like a final note in a song, cutting through all the overthinking, all the unspoken anxieties. It should have ended there. It almost did.

But I was me.

"Or Quinn?" I pressed.

Keir stilled. And then—a slow, teasing grin curved his lips. "Well, I've been meaning to talk to yeh about that, love."

My stomach dropped.

I tossed a pillow aside and shot to my feet, stalking toward the door. Caught by surprise, Pyewacket screeched from the sofa. "Slow down! Wait for the cat! My legs aren't as long as yours!"

Before I could reach the massive front door, Keir caught up, his fingers brushing against my arm, his touch gentle.

"She's my sister, Win."

I stopped dead. "What?"

"My half-sister," he clarified. "I thought yeh knew."

My fingers slipped from the door handle as I turned to stare at him. "How? You told me you were an only child."

He exhaled. "I am. The only child of my parents, the Alpha and Luna of our clan. Quinn and I share a mother but have different fathers. It's common in wolf clans." His voice softened. "After she was older, she came to live with us. I can't imagine being any closer if she were my full biological sister."

A rush of relief flooded through me, swiftly followed by a wave of embarrassment so strong I wanted to sink into the floor.

Keir must have seen it because he reached out and gently tipped my chin up, forcing me to meet his gaze. "Packs are unique, *mo chridhe*. Members are closer than most blood families. You weren't to know that."

The warmth in his eyes chased away my lingering doubts.

He gestured toward the balcony, nudging me back toward the sofa. "Come on. The view this time of day is almost as beautiful as you."

My traitorous heart stumbled all over itself. Damn wolf charm.

We sank back onto the outdoor sofa, the weight of our conversation leaving my emotions stretched thin. The weight of everything—our insecurities, our tangled history, the unspoken fears we both carried—pressed against my ribs, tight and unrelenting.

I picked up my warm chai again, staring out over the landscape as the sky settled into soft grays and silvered lavender. A light drizzle misted the glass partition, and the world felt hushed—suspended in that quiet moment between day and night, caught in transition, much like I felt sitting here with Keir.

"You've never told me about Pup," I said, resting my arm on the back of the seat as I turned toward Keir.

"He's no' my blood brother," Keir said quietly. "Was found in the forest—wee thing, half-starved, abandoned. His family wanted nothin' to do with him. We took him in. Best we can tell, he's half-human."

I swallowed hard. "That's awful. Poor thing."

Keir nodded, the weight of it pulling through his features. "Aye. He always says it was the best thing they ever did for him—leavin' him where we'd find him. But I know it still leaves a mark."

I stared out at the cloud-draped horizon, where the moon was just beginning to rise behind a veil of drizzle and shadowed treetops. The thought of an abandoned child, left to fend for themself because of who—or what—they were, made my stomach turn.

"But...I still don't understand why you've been spending so much time with Elspeth," I said, my voice steady but laced with frustration. "Why take her to lunch in Cradlerock? Why let her move to the Cairns?"

Keir exhaled, shaking his head with something that might have been amusement. "Win, love. Is it no' obvious? For you."

I turned to him sharply. "What do you mean?"

"First off," he said, stretching an arm along the back of the sofa, "I didnae go to lunch with the woman. Maurice interviewed her for a job. She didnae get it, by the way."

I blinked. The pieces clicked together so quickly I nearly dropped my mug. That sneaky—

I knew what she had been doing. She wanted me to find out. Knew how I'd react. And just like always, I fell right into her trap.

Not anymore.

I clenched my jaw and took a slow breath, forcing myself to stay calm.

Keir watched me carefully, as if waiting for me to reach my own conclusions before continuing.

"Second, she's your sister," he said, holding up a hand when I opened my mouth to argue. "I know, I know, you dinnae trust her. But more important than that? I want to protect yeh."

My stomach did a somersault. "Why?"

"She could be the magickstrate's killer, Win," he said, his voice low, careful. "And the one that poisoned Jess."

I let out a slow, measured breath. "I know she's trouble. And I don't trust her, but I also don't think she's the killer. For one thing, why would she ask me to help her?" A bumblebee drifted too close to my head, and I swatted it away absentmindedly. It seemed a little late in the evening for bumblebees, but what did I know. Seemed nothing in Darkly ever played by the rules.

Keir leaned forward, his elbows braced against his knees. "Easy. To send the investigation away from herself."

I froze.

Keir continued, his voice even but edged with suspicion. "After all, there were plenty of townsfolk at the Hexbee game that day. She could've easily heard yeh were headed to the pumpkin farm. Did yeh ever think she might've been trying to set yeh up?"

A breath caught in my throat. Zelda. She'd been at the Hexbee game.

Would Elspeth really go that far?

A cold chill cascaded down my body, raising goosebumps along my skin.

Without a word, he reached for my arms, his fingers warm and steady as they moved in slow, reassuring circles.

"Hey," he murmured, his voice softer now. "I'm no' saying it's true. Just that it's possible."

I swallowed hard and nodded, but the unease remained.

"So you don't care for her?"

Keir reached over and picked up my hand, holding it between his. "Not in the least. Truth be told, love...I'm sorry to say it, but I can hardly stand bein' near her for more than a half minute."

I smiled as we sat quietly, sipping our drinks, the weight of our conversation still pressing on me while the evening sank in around us. I let my thoughts drift, pushing Elspeth from my mind. The sky was low and gray, the drizzle soft but steady, blurring the treetops in the distance. A chill crept in with the damp, and the air smelled faintly of wet leaves and fading magnolia. It was the kind of night that made Darkly feel ancient—unmoved by our troubles, certain to outlast us all.

Keir reached for my hand again, his grip warm and steady. "Yeh've got that look—thinkin' too much again, are yeh?"

I gave him a half-hearted smile. But I couldn't help it. The things we were talking about—the weight of what he was, what he would always be, and, most importantly, the magic involved—wasn't something I could ignore.

The questions lingered, heavy on my mind, but before I could follow them too far, Keir's voice pulled me back to the present.

"Hang on. How did the two of yeh make it all the way up here on yer own?"

My moment of hesitation gave me away and his eyes sharpened instantly.

"We didn't. Benicio sent us here."

Keir drew back, his entire demeanor shifting. "What in the world were yeh doing with Benicio Kim, love?"

I wrinkled my nose, not exactly thrilled to revisit that part of the evening. "Are you sure you want to know?"

Keir sighed, rubbing his temple before muttering, "The murder investigation."

I expected anger, or at least frustration, but instead, he pulled me closer, his arms tightening around me.

We sat in silence for a while, watching as the moon fought to rise behind a veil of mist, its glow soft and blurred against a sky heavy with clouds. The moment still felt right—quiet, expectant—as if we were teetering on the edge of something significant in our relationship.

Keir turned to me, his breath warm against my ear. "I think this is the perfect night to—"

BANG. BANG. BANG.

The loud knocking at the door shattered the moment, making both of us jump.

Keir let out a low growl. "By the saints..."

Pyewacket, who had been dozing at the armrest, snapped upright.

We moved back into the house, Keir striding forward to the door and with one swift motion, flung it open.

I felt the air leave my lungs.

"Elspeth, what are yeh—!" Keir started, his gaze flicking from me to her, his confusion plain.

Elspeth stood on the threshold, adjusting the strap of a dress so tight it looked painted on. An umbrella leaned against the stone wall, its black canopy damp and half-unfurled.

She smiled, slow and deliberate, the kind of smile that made my skin itch. "Is this a bad time, Keir?" she asked, her voice dripping with false innocence. She lifted a bottle, the deep red glass catching the dim light. "I brought your favorite wine."

I didn't need to look at Keir to know what was written all over his face. *What the hellhound is happening right now?*

I didn't know if I was still riled up from our conversation or if I had finally had it with Elspeth. Probably a little of both. In any event, I raised a hand before Keir could say anything and stepped forward. "I'll handle this."

The moment I entered her space, her expression shifted. That smirk—the one that had been daring me to react—faltered.

"No more, Elspeth." My voice was even, steady. "You were upset the other day because no one here respects you? Well, look at how you behave."

Elspeth's eyes darted between me and Keir, her confidence wavering.

"You have the gall to ask me for help when all you've done since you got here is try to hurt people and drive a wedge between Keir and me." My voice rose, my patience snapping like a frayed wire. "Get your act together, Elspeth, because I'm not taking it anymore."

The condescending amusement she'd worn a second ago vanished Her features tightened, her cheeks flushed red. For the first time since I'd known of her existence, she looked rattled.

She turned sharply to Keir, seeking some kind of support. "Are you going to let her—"

"But I *will* take this," I interrupted smoothly, plucking the bottle of Merlot right out of her grasp before stepping back.

And then, without another word, I slammed the door in her face.

Silence.

Keir blinked at me, stunned for half a second, before his lips spread into a wide grin. "Well then."

I exhaled, looking down at the bottle in my hands. At least I got something out of this nonsense.

As I spun around, Keir's arms wrapped around me, pulling me close in a way that left no space between us. His warmth enveloped me, his scent—spice, woodsmoke, pine—flooding my senses.

"Lass," he murmured, his voice low and husky, "d'yeh know how bloody sexy that was?"

I tilted my head up, meeting his gaze, heavy-lidded, dark, and deep enough to lose myself in. I pulled away and lifted the bottle.

"Care for some wine?" I asked.

He smirked. "I'm no' much of a wine drinker, but for you, I'll do anything."

He released me only long enough to retrieve two glasses from the bar. Then, with one easy pull, he took my hand again, guiding me back out onto the balcony.

Setting the glasses and the wine bottle down on the table, he turned to me, his expression playful but his voice thick with suggestion. "Yeh know, no one can see us out here, love."

"Oh yeah?" I breathed.

"Aye." His grin widened, and for a moment, my heart stopped. His mouth found mine, slow and certain.

Then—

"Good thing, 'cause Laurent'd never let me live it down if he caught me with a glass of wine in hand. No matter how much the bloody bottle cost."

I blinked.

He poured the wine with a completely innocent expression, as if he hadn't just stolen the breath right out of my lungs.

Keir settled beside me again, his arm warm around my shoulders. The evening breeze swept his hair into his face. Without thinking, I reached up and gently tucked it back into place, my fingers lingering against his skin.

His hand found mine, pressing it against his chest. "Yeh know I'm crazy about yeh, right?" he murmured, his forehead resting against mine.

The words sent a flutter through my ribs, a quiet, steady happiness I hadn't known I'd been holding out for.

He pulled back slightly, just enough to look into my eyes, those rich, dark brown depths, so open, so honest. "From now on, let's not be afraid to talk to each other. About anything, love."

A slow smile found its way to my lips as I met his gaze, letting the weight of his words settle before offering a soft nod.

He lifted his glass, waiting. "To us."

I smiled and clinked my glass against his. "To honesty."

CHAPTER 30

"*J*ust don't understand why neither of you told me," I said to Tzazi, nodding to Clobber as he set another hot mug of chai in front of me. He gave me a quiet, sympathetic smile, then moved on to the next table.

Okaaay.

"Sorry, Win," Tzazi said with a shrug. "I don't think of him like that so it didn't enter my mind. Keir is just Keir."

"I wish he had told me, but to be honest, I have so much more to worry about right now than Keir's lineage."

Tzazi handed me the folded newspaper. "Does that mean you've seen today's *Daily Shade*?"

I took the newspaper and felt my face blush deep red as I read.

ROYAL WEDDING OR ROYAL TRIANGLE?
An inside scoop
by the romantically-disinclined
Beatrice Snarkle

Rumor has it Darkly's most annoyingly cute couple has hit a teensy snag in the quest for their happily-ever-after. A whisper on the wind reports that the town's most eligible alpha has found himself caught between a storybook romance and a plot twist worthy of a telenovela.

The culprit? A dark horse with a penchant for meddling, manipulation, and moonlit mayhem. Yes, darlings, an unexpected contender has trotted into the race—and if the gossip is true, she's here to Win.

Seems our princely prince, the brooding and oh-so-ruggedly wolfish rake, has been presented with a marry-me-or-else ultimatum by his beloved bookish beauty. Now, now, I know what you're thinking. But don't clutch your pearls just yet— because this scandal comes with a scandal inside the scandal!

The questions on everyone's lips:

Has the dashing wolf fallen prey to the hypnotic wiles of the interloper? Has our brainy belle booked herself a broken heart? Is this a true love triangle or merely a case of a certain somebody reading too many gothic romances?

One thing is certain, dear reader—I won't rest until every single howl, huff, and harrowing heartbreak is laid bare for your reading pleasure. Because as we all know, this beady eye misses nothing.

Stay tuned. The truth, much like love, has a way of coming out under the full moon.

Well, this certainly explains Clobber's strange look.

"Why is this reporter so interested in my life?"

Tzazi dropped her fork and stared at me. "You *are* getting married!"

"No!" I lowered my voice when people at the tables around us turned to stare. "No. We *never* talked about marriage," I said quietly and slowly. "And I *never* gave Keir an ultimatum. This person twisted the conversation and…wrote that!"

"Who is this 'interloper' she talks about?" Tzazi asked.

I breathed in through my nose hoping to tamp down my rising anger. "There's a few things I haven't told you yet."

That got her attention fast.

Jess's absence hit me hard in that moment. I kept thinking how she should've been there, squeezed into the booth beside Tzazi, grinning wide, tossing out some cheeky comment before pulling me into one of her too-tight hugs. That was Jess—always right where you needed her. But not that day. Elysande still had her under lock and key. I couldn't blame her. Nearly losing your child would do that—jolt your heart, rearrange your world, make you hold tight to the people you love and not let go.

I told Tzazi everything. About Elspeth showing up at Keir's house. About finally standing up to her. And, yes, that Keir and I were officially a couple—tentatively, cautiously—trying to rebuild on a foundation of truth this time.

Tzazi leaned back with a slow grin. "Well, it's about time. Let me guess—you flew up to his balcony, all misty-eyed and moonlit, a lovesick witch on a broomstick?"

"Not exactly."

"Don't tell me you climbed those cliff stairs?"

I took a long sip of coffee, putting it off for as long as I could. "Benicio Kim veilshifted us."

Tzazi set her cup down on the table with a smack. "From *The Graves*?"

"It was fine. Honestly. He's a charming man and lives in an elegant townhouse with a sweet elderly housekeeper."

Tzazi folded her arms and looked at me for a second. "You mean Lucasta? Who's not a housekeeper. She's a penanggalan. At night, her head detaches and floats around, trailing viscera and guarding Benicio's house."

I snorted into my cup. "Well, that explains the damp feeling in the foyer."

"I'm not joking, Win. You really need to be more careful. Things in Darkly don't just go bump in the night. They creep up into your bed and holler BOO."

"Which brings me back to the obvious question," Tzazi said, narrowing her eyes. "What possessed you to think going to The Graves was a good idea?"

I stared at her, coffee halfway to my mouth.

Tzazi sighed. Heavily.

I set my mug down before I dropped it. "Okay, so maybe I didn't think it through completely before I made a visit to a paranormal gangster."

Tzazi raised an eyebrow. "Whose house is guarded by a literal floating horror story."

"That too," I said, holding up a hand. "In her defense, Lucasta was perfectly nice."

Tzazi frowned deeper.

"Okay, okay," I said, backing down. "I'll be more careful from now on."

She studied me a moment, then shrugged. "Well, nothing to be done now. What'd you find out?"

"Benicio says he was at the Lucky Lounge in The Graves. And Ransom's already looked into it."

"Supposing Benny's alibi holds. Who is left that would have a reason to kill the magickstrate?"

"Well, there's Veronique," I said.

"Veronique?" Tzazi asked, a puzzled look on her face. "She's not a vampire I would suspect of killing anyone."

"But listen," I said. "You wouldn't believe how twitchy she got when I told her about Jess's poisoning and the magickstrate's death."

"She was probably just upset about Jess." Tzazi tapped her finger on her coffee mug. "What do you think she's hiding?"

"I don't know," I said slowly. "But the more I think about it, the more I'm sure she's holding something back. Tzaz, I think she knew Edythe Grouse. No one reacts like that to the death of a stranger."

We sat in silence, thinking it through, the low hum of voices and clink of silverware wrapping the Green Gator in its usual easy warmth.

"There's always Elspeth," I said, breaking the silence. "She threatened Grouse in front of everyone. Plus, Ransom hasn't hidden the fact he believes she's guilty."

"But with Elspeth, it always comes back to Patch," Tzazi said. "They didn't know each other."

"And the people who did know Patch—Dixie-Deen, Gordon, and Mathilda—don't seem to connect to Grouse."

"Mathilda?" Tzazi's puzzled expression drew my attention.

I shrugged. "Jess said Mathilda got upset with Patch a day or two before his murder. And you and I both saw how badly she treated Dixie-Deen's volunteer. But she has an alibi. Delivering a broom to Zephyra Nightshade at the time Patch was murdered."

There it was again—that sharp little ping in my memory. Teasing, tugging. But the thought stayed buried, just out of reach.

"Ransom is sure there's just one killer," I continued, "but I can't find anyone who had motive for both victims."

I glanced at the newspaper in front of me and a thought struck me, sharp and sudden. "It couldn't have been Elspeth who ran to the reporter with the marriage story. We were on Keir's balcony, the one that juts out over the cliff on the opposite side of his front door. There's no way she could have heard anything we said."

Tzazi's eyes narrowed. "That's true."

"You know, this reporter really could be just about anybody."

"Well, anybody who can become invisible, float below a balcony, or shrink to the size of a bee," she said, slinging her arm along the back of the booth cushion.

The memory of the pesky bee I'd waved away last night surfaced with a horrible jolt. Could Beatrice Snarkle be a bee shifter? That would explain everything—the eavesdropping, the uncanny way she always knew the latest gossip before anyone else. She could go anywhere. Listen to anyone. She didn't need sources. She was the source.

Whoever Beatrice Snarkle was, she had a talent for digging up secrets, twisting them into scandal, and plastering them across the front page. Tracking her down had just gotten a whole lot trickier but I wasn't backing off. I was going to find her.

I glanced around the café, scanning the familiar faces. Could one of them be her? The idea sent a prickle of unease up my spine.

"Know any bee shifters?" I asked, taking a long sip of spiced warmth.

She paused. Sipped her coffee.

"You think the reporter is a bee shifter?"

"There was a bee buzzing around us last night. Persistent little thing."

Tzazi set down her mug with a clink. "Plausible," she finally said. "But there are other explanations just as credible."

I leaned in. "Such as?"

"Pixies," she said flatly. "Nosy, winged opportunists. They'd sell secrets to *The Daily Shade* quicker than they'd steal your earrings. And let's not take Elspeth off the list just yet. She could easily have placed a listening charm somewhere on the balcony."

And just like that, Elspeth was back at the top of the list.

Tzazi's gaze drifted to the window. "You have to admit, it *does* sound like something she'd do."

Any reply died on my tongue when a burst of sequins and hairspray landed beside our table like a glitter bomb from the skies.

"Tzazi! Windsor!" sang Trixie Frick, beaming as if we were the most delightful pair she'd seen all day. Her bouffant was as bright as her outfit, and both sparkled like she'd just stepped off a parade float and into our lives. "How are you both on this marvelous day?"

Then before we could reply, her tone shifted—softer now, more serious.

"Win," she said, leaning in, her voice barely above a whisper. "I came across some information I thought you'd like to know."

Tzazi straightened, her gaze sharpening as Trixie slid onto the bench beside her.

"I was talking to Boone last night…"

"Oh, no!" I groaned. "Please don't tell me he found out."

"I would *not* want to be you," Tzazi murmured. "I heard he used to be a boxer."

"Oh, that was ages ago." Trixie waved that off with a tinkle of bracelets. "But, no, nothing like that. He's still blissfully clueless about our investigation."

This last word she said with a sparkle in her eyes and a sharp, knowing nod. I was surprised she didn't throw in a shoulder shimmy and a giggle for good measure.

"You asked about Veronique della Morte? She *was* at the Inn the night the magickstrate died. At the bar. With Elspeth Wilde."

My breath caught. "What?"

"I know!" Trixie fanned herself with one sparkly hand. "Boone just happened to mention it. Can you believe that man? Honestly. I should've married someone who adores gossip as much as I do."

Then, with a quick air kiss and a toss of her hair, she popped to her feet. "Well, I must be going. Let me know if you need any more help, Windsor. I'll happily be your Watson anytime you need me."

And just like that, she disappeared in a flurry of rhinestones and citrusy perfume.

Tzazi stared after her. "Veronique never said she was at the White Hart the night of the murder, did she?"

"No. She told me she was at a bar in The Graves," I said, rubbing my temples. "Oh, Tzazi, I really don't want her to be guilty."

"It's not looking too good though, is it?" Tzazi glanced in Dewey's direction. "Sorry. I need to head out. Though I fear my exit will not have the same panache as Trixie's. Talk to you later, Win."

Tzaz patted my arm and slid out of the booth, stopping to exchange a few words with Dewey before holding the door open for a group of rowdy teens in coats and gloves piling into the tavern. I watched her go, my mind still turning over what Trixie'd said.

Veronique wasn't at the Lucky Lounge like she'd said. She was at the Inn. The night the murder took place.

I slowly sipped my chai, trying to sort the tangle in my head, and then...I felt him. That calm, steady presence brushing against my rattled nerves. Keir appeared at the table, one brow raised in silent question.

He gestured toward my side of the booth. "Mind if I sit?"

I scooted over, making space.

Clobber arrived with a steaming mug of coffee, setting it in front of Keir with a grunt. Keir gave him a nod of thanks.

"I've been thinking a lot about yesterday." His voice was low, thoughtful. "I'm glad yeh stayed. That yeh let me explain."

I met his gaze. "Me too."

"Just so yeh know," he said, his voice quiet but sure, "I asked Elspeth to leave the Cairns last night. Quinn's making sure she does."

Was that what I wanted? I couldn't expect him to cut ties with every woman he knew. That wasn't fair to him or to me. I wouldn't want a man who was faithful only because he felt obligated to be.

I shook my head. "You don't need to do that. Being kind is a part of who you are, Keir. You shouldn't change that because of me."

He leaned back, studying me. Then, a slow smile spread across his lips. "Yeh're an incredible woman, Windsor Ebonwood." His voice was warm, edged with pride. "Nay, it's better she goes. The pack never did care for her bein' there. Truth be told, I think Quinn's enjoyin' tossin' her out on her arse."

I couldn't help but grin, even though a twinge of sympathy stirred for Elspeth. Keir's second wasn't someone you wanted to cross.

A familiar drawl broke the quiet between us. "Pardon me, Win. Keir."

I looked up. Ransom stood beside our table, one hand resting casually on the booth's backrest.

He gave a small nod to Keir, then focused on me. "Figured you'd want to know, we got the lab results back on the tuna."

Keir's brows narrowed deeply.

"What'd you find?" I asked.

"It wasn't poisonous."

Keir's eyes cut to mine, questioningly.

Um. Yeah. I'd forgotten to tell Keir about the pantry incident.

"Whoever locked you in the pantry didn't want to hurt you. They just wanted you out of the way."

"For what? That bag of dirt?"

Now Keir looked confused and a tad amused.

"Actually," Ransom said, "there was a seed in the bag."

I froze.

"What kind of seed?"

Ransom laughed. "Pumpkin, of course. A very rare one at that."

Confirmation! Aunt Sibby was telling the truth.

I blew out a huff of air. "Why would someone return, rather than steal, a rare pumpkin seed?"

"Return? Why do you say 'return'?" Ransom asked.

Darn it.

"You know what I mean. Why would somebody drop off a rare pumpkin seed to a man who is dead?"

"That is the question, isn't it?" Ransom said slowly. "Well, enjoy your day. Both of you. I've got business to attend to."

He paused, like he was weighing a decision, then turned and strode out the front doors.

Keir glanced at his watch. He let out a soft groan. "Och, I've to be at town hall in a few minutes. Can I walk yeh out?"

I slid on my coat, and we made our way through the tavern. I felt the weight of every single eye on us. Whispers followed in our wake, hushed voices, and not-so-subtle glances. Clearly, everyone had read Beatrice Snarkle's article.

Had Keir?

If he had, funny he hadn't mentioned it.

Outside, a bitter wind tugged at my hair, sending loose strands whipping across my face. Overhead, the sky had cleared to a sharp, autumn blue—crisp and cold. Wisps of cloud drifted by, slow and harmless, a far cry from yesterday's dismal gray. It was the kind of day that fooled you into thinking winter hadn't fully settled in yet, even as the wind bit through your sleeves and rattled the bare trees. The kind of day that made you forget, just for a moment, that the world could be anything but peaceful.

Until—

"No! You've got this wrong! Help me!"

The street chatter died in an instant. Heads turned, eyes locking onto the commotion unfolding before us.

Keir's hand found my arm, fingers firm against my sleeve as he stopped me from stepping into the street.

In the very center of Tataille, in front of the main cemetery gates, Ransom held Elspeth in a steel grip as she thrashed, twisting and kicking, her voice rising in a desperate wail. "It's not me! You've got the wrong person!"

Ransom remained impassive. His grip didn't loosen. "Elspeth Wilde, I'm arresting you for the murders of Edythe Grouse and Phineas Priddyholm and the attempted murder of twelve others."

The words sent a ripple through the street. Gasps. Murmurs. Someone cursed under their breath.

Then, out of the shadows, Boddy appeared—sudden, silent, inevitable. His golden coils slithered from his sleeves, stretching toward Elspeth.

Panic flashed across her face. She turned, wild-eyed, and looked right at me.

"Win! Please!" she shrieked, her voice raw. "I didn't do it! You know I didn't!"

A dense fog of black smoke exploded around them, swallowing her whole. When the haze cleared, Ransom, Boddy, and Elspeth were gone.

For a beat, the street stood still. Then, like the strike of a match, the murmurs reignited. The whispers surged, louder than before.

Now, the town really had something to gossip about.

CHAPTER 31

$\mathcal{T}$he next morning, I threw on a soft, chunky sweater, jeans, and my well-loved, black Doc Martens, the perfect outfit for a prison visit. I looped one of Hilde's handwoven scarves snug around my neck and shrugged into my coat, the weight of it a welcome shield against the damp chill. Outside, the sky had turned a flat pewter, and a heavy dampness clung to everything. The temperature had dropped overnight, not with the crisp sharpness of autumn, but with a slow, seeping cold that hinted snow wasn't far off.

I swept by open-mouthed Delilah and quickly made my way to the royal inspector's office where I found Ransom hunched over his desk, trailing vines covering any spot on the desktop not covered by paper. A half-empty mug of coffee balanced precariously near his elbow.

"Ransom."

He shot to his feet, grinning. "Win!"

Then he caught himself and dropped back into his chair, smoothing the front of his shirt like he hadn't just sprung up like a jack-in-the-box. "What can I do for you?"

I drew in a breath. "I've got a question. Then a request."

He exhaled hard through his nose and waved toward the seat across from him.

"Have you verified Benicio Kim's alibi? Or Veronique's? He told me—"

"Win." His palms smacked the desk. "Enough. I don't need your help doing my job. Got it?"

I nodded. Slow. Measured.

"Fine. Then I'd like to talk to Elspeth."

His jaw tightened as he contemplated my request.

"She's been arrested for murder, Win," he finally said. "Not shoplifting or jaywalking."

"I realize the seriousness, Ransom. I do." I sighed and he indicated the chair in front of his desk.

I sat this time, leveling him with a look. "But I have to know if she did it."

"What makes you think she'd admit anything to you? From what I hear, you have quite often been a victim of her lies and trickery."

"That's truer than you know. But she's my sister, like it or not. I feel like I owe it to her to listen to what she has to say."

Ransom shook his head. "We found the oleander petals in her jacket pocket, Win. The jacket she wore to Gumbo Fest when the poisonings took place."

"Please, Ransom."

He let out a slow breath, rubbing his temple. "Okay. Five minutes. And a guard will be present."

"Thank you."

His chair scraped against the wooden floor as he stood. "This way."

I followed him down a labyrinthine corridor that plunged deep into the ground, which would have been impossible on any other swampy island. Our footsteps echoed on the cold stone walls, finally opening up into a surprisingly cozy room with a desk, a cross-stitched sign declaring "You have the right to remain corporeal," a stoic guard standing to one side, and seven iron doors arranged around the room. A fire flamed in a hearth in the middle. The chair before the desk suddenly twirled around and a little man with a pinched face, a perpetual frown, and skin so white it had probably never seen a ray of sunshine gave me a stare.

"Mumford, Miss Ebonwood has five minutes to visit with Inmate Wilde."

"Yes," Mumford's quiet hiss of a voice sent a chill through me, colder than the jail's stone walls, as he stood and pressed his hand to one of the iron doors.

The door slowly creaked open and the guard moved, strategically placing himself between me and Elspeth, ready to act if necessary.

All of this for Elspeth?

But then I remembered they believed she'd killed two people.

I stepped in and looked around, surprised at the relative comfort of the cell. The room contained a small bed, wood chair, even a side table with a lamp. It looked more like a bad motel than a holding facility.

Elspeth lay sprawled on the bed, flipping through an old copy of *The Wicked Word*, the island's gossip rag. She barely glanced up when we approached, but the second she did, her face lit up with surprise.

"Win?"

"Hi, Elspeth."

The door slammed shut behind the guard, causing us both to flinch. He took his place next to Elspeth's bed, keeping his inmate within easy reach.

We stared at each other for a moment before she extended a hand to the chair. I noticed her broken fingernails and that hit my heart worse than the reality of the prison cell.

"You're the first person to come see me," she said, her voice surprisingly quiet, her clipped, nasally tone that always grated on my nerves, gone.

"Great friend you got there in Solara," I snorted in smug satisfaction.

Shame on me, right?

Elspeth turned back to her magazine and flipped a page. "Solara is very busy."

"Oh sure," I said. "So busy she couldn't even pop in? Bring you a pumpkin spice latte? A sympathy croissant?"

She narrowed her eyes. "Did you come to kick me while I'm down, Windsor? Or is there something else I can do for you?"

I sighed and leaned in closer to her. "Ransom's only given me five minutes. Tell me again everything you did the day the magickstrate was killed. Begin with the trial."

For once, she didn't pout or whine. But instead nodded and sat up straighter on the bed, setting the magazine on the side table.

"After the bailiff released me, Mason took me back to the White Hart Inn. I think he thought I'd calm down, but I was furious."

She rubbed her temples as if trying to massage the regret out of her skull. "I still don't think the ruling is fair."

"Well, you'd be the only one," I mumbled.

"I drank chocolate martinis. Have you ever had one? O.M.G. They are so delicious and the bartender at the White Hart gives them an extra kick," she said, smiling at the memory.

I rolled my hand in the air, gesturing for her to continue.

"I don't remember everything Mason and I said," she continued. "I drank quite a bit that night. Then Mason stomped out and I didn't see him again until the next day. I stayed in the bar, drinking, until Boone announced last call."

Her face suddenly lit up. "Boone! He can tell you I was in the bar all night."

"Yes, but he can't verify what you did after you left the bar."

"I didn't go anywhere near Grouse's room." Elspeth's voice stayed even. Her hand came up to tuck a piece of hair behind her ear. "Believe me, earlier that afternoon, I was angry enough to do something really stupid." She gave a short, humorless laugh, one shoulder rising in a faint shrug. "But by that evening, I'd calmed down."

She looked straight at me then, not blinking. "Oh, I know how this looks. I'm not stupid."

"No, you're not," I said, thinking.

She suddenly looked up. "Oh, there *is* someone who saw me go to my room that night."

I narrowed my eyes at her. "Who?"

"That vampire woman. Veronica something."

My heart skipped a beat. "Veronique della Morte?"

"That's the one. We had a martini in the bar together and then she walked with me up to my room and went on up the stairs to hers."

"To hers?"

"Her room. Why else would she be there?" Elspeth asked, a sincere question in her voice.

Oh, Veronique. Just like Trixie told me.

"What about Patch Priddyholm? Did you know him?"

She tilted her head, considering. "Never met him. But then again, I don't associate with nobodies."

There was the Elspeth I knew and did not like in the least.

"So, why are you hanging around with Solara?"

She frowned and swatted my comment away like a fly.

The guard suddenly shifted as the iron door creaked open and Ransom stood in the doorway. He gave me a pointed look. "Time's up."

I stood and glanced at Ransom, who remained silent but observant. "Do you know who's behind the murders, Elspeth?"

She sighed. "If I knew, I'd have gone to Inspector Belleclaire long before they would have had a chance to frame me for them."

She met my gaze without flinching. No dramatic huffs. No overplayed innocence. I believed her.

I followed Ransom to the door, then paused and turned back. "One last thing, Elspeth. Who is Beatrice Snarkle?"

She blinked at me, genuinely confused.

"Who?"

"*The Daily Shade* reporter who's been writing about me."

"Ohhh, right. Windsor, that is honestly not me. Believe it or not, I would never do that to you."

I studied her a bit longer, but her expression didn't waver. Then I turned without a word.

"Thank you, Ransom," I said, wincing as the heavy door banged shut behind us.

"I hope it helped," he replied, already drifting away from me, back toward his office, still clearly irritated.

I made my way into the front office, swatting aside a curtain of creeping vines that dangled across the corridor, just as Delilah was sliding back into the chair behind her desk.

"I'm sorry, Windsor," Delilah called out, not even looking up from her keyboard, her voice rough and grating.

I kept walking.

"I'm sorry, Windsor," she repeated, louder and more pointed this time when I didn't respond.

I stopped in front of the exit and turned slowly. "Delilah, I didn't say a word to you."

"Like I told you, I'm *sorry*, but you know I can't tell you that certain people were officially seen at The Lucky Lounge at exactly 12:53 a.m. on the thirteenth of October, right?"

My jaw dropped.

"And I definitely can't tell you that *another* someone's death was recorded at 12:50 a.m." She shook her head dramatically. "So quit asking. I'm sorry. But I just can't. You need to leave."

Then she did something that made me question reality more than her cryptic messages.

Delilah Rageheart winked at me.

Without another word, she went back to clacking at her keyboard like the whole exchange had never happened.

Somewhere, Rod Serling was lighting a cigarette.

CHAPTER 32

For the next few days, I was buried in post-festival portal repairs. But the murders hovered, never letting me fully forget. As I worked, I turned everything over in my mind. Most of the puzzle pieces still refused to click into place, but one answer had settled in clear as crystal.

The next morning, Pye and I headed out to face two problems straight on. One, I hoped, would be pleasant. The other? Not likely.

We started at Gumbo Fest, marching straight toward the heart of the park where the mayor's statue rose beside what remained of the pumpkin patch.

As we neared, I spotted Gordon Mulch hunched over a round orange gourd, speckled with pale yellow dots. He gave it a careful wipe with his sleeve, then murmured a few quiet words. The pumpkin lifted off the ground and floated gently to a large flat mat, settling itself among dozens of others lined up in neat, gleaming rows.

He looked up, startled, then straightened with forced cheer.

"Ah, Miss Ebonwood," he said, smoothing his sweater vest like it might help settle his nerves. "How can I help you?"

"Mind if we sit, Mr. Mulch?"

"Of course, of course." He motioned toward a small iron table tucked beneath the twisted limbs of an ancient oakspider tree. Lanterns sat in a loose circle on the ground, their witch fire casting steady heat that chased off the chill. "Just brewed a pot of coffee. Give me a moment."

Pyewacket hopped into the chair beside mine with an exaggerated sigh, tail slicing through the air like he'd been dragged to the Westminster Dog Show.

Mulch returned balancing a carafe, two mismatched mugs, and a plate of custard tarts.

"Hope you like cinnamon," he said, pouring the coffee with a slightly trembling hand. "The tarts are from a recipe my mother used. Well, borrowed from a neighbor and then 'made her own.'" He gave a tight chuckle.

Mulch passed a tart to Pyewacket, who sniffed it suspiciously before devouring it whole.

"You know you're going to spoil him," I grinned, hoping to chip a crack in his anxiety.

"I spoil my pumpkins. Might as well spoil the company too."

I took a sip of the coffee—strong, earthy, with just the right kick of cinnamon—and let the warmth settle before I spoke.

"Mr. Mulch, I need to talk to you. And I hope you'll be honest with me."

His eyes flicked to mine over the rim of his cup. Alert. Wary.

I set my mug down. "I believe you pushed me into Patch's pantry. To return a seed you'd previously stolen."

He froze, mug halfway to his mouth. "What you need to understand about that..." he said finally, setting the cup down with care, "I didn't kill Patch."

I raised a hand. "I know. I've just been trying to make sense of why we were shoved in there at all. When I found out what was in that baggy—a seed—it all clicked. Sibby gave it to Patch the day he died, but it wasn't on his body. And it definitely wasn't hanging out of that drawer before the pantry door slammed shut."

His eyes widened. "Sibby told you she was there?"

My voice softened. "You were trying to warn me about her, weren't you?"

He stared at the ground, shame creeping across his face. "I didn't want to believe she could've been involved. But I *saw* her. And I—I just wanted you to be careful."

"I get it," I said gently. "And I appreciate it. For what it's worth, I don't think she killed him either."

Mulch exhaled, long and slow, like he'd been holding his breath since the day Patch died. His shoulders slumped.

"You're right. I took the seed." His voice cracked. "The day he died, I went to his house to talk about his...methods. He layers enchantments on his gourds. It's not technically illegal, but it *is* unethical."

He glanced toward the patch, expression tight.

"I got there and saw someone entering the house with him. Took me a second, but then I realized it was Sibby. I hadn't seen her in years, but I knew they had been engaged once. So, I left."

I nodded.

"I came back later. Place was quiet. I knocked. Nothing. So, I went in." He swallowed. "I found the baggy with the seed. Cucurbita lunaris occultatum. Do you know what that is?"

I shook my head.

"One of the rarest pumpkin seeds in all the worlds. Also called moonshade seed. Illegal to possess, let alone grow. I was furious. I stormed out to the back field to confront him."

He paused, mug trembling slightly in his grip.

"I saw him lying there. Looked like he'd tripped while levitating a pumpkin, but I knew better."

Silence pressed in, broken only by the rustle of leaves and the squeal of children as they ran past.

"I panicked. Without thinking, I went back in the house, pocketed the seed, and left. But then I got scared it would look like I'd killed him for it. I came back later to put it back. Thought maybe no one would notice."

He looked up, meeting my eyes.

"And that's when you showed up. I hid, hoping you'd leave, but when you didn't, I panicked. Again." He sighed, the way people do when they realize they've done *exactly* what they swore they wouldn't do. "I shoved you in the pantry so I could slip out the back without being seen."

"Why not just wait until we left?" I asked.

He gave a small, sad laugh.

"I didn't know how long you'd stay. Didn't want to be caught snooping around a dead man's house. What would I say? 'Oh, just here returning stolen contraband. Don't mind me.'"

He stared down at his hands. "I wasn't thinking straight. I just wanted to fix my mistake and disappear "

Mulch picked up his mug again, his gaze low. "I'm sorry, Miss Ebonwood. I didn't mean to scare you."

I laughed. "Believe me, Mr. Mulch, I've survived werewolf tag, cemetery brawls, and tree crashes. You're not even top five."

Mulch blinked, then chuckled. "Good to hear," he said with the first real smile I'd seen since we sat down.

IF YOU DIDN'T KNOW it was there, you'd walk right past the offices of *The Daily Shade* without a second glance.

Tucked behind a single whitewashed door, the place looked more like a forgotten curiosity shop than the headquarters of Darkly's only surviving newspaper. Faded lettering curled in the corners of the front window like peeling bark and a tarnished brass bell dangled from the lintel, hanging on by what looked like Superglue and one rusted screw.

I paused outside and peered through the dusty glass.

"Do you see anyone?" I asked Pye, who had made himself comfortable in my tote bag while I prepared to head in.

"Back there," he murmured. "In the shadows. A stork of a man behind a desk."

The door creaked as if it hadn't been opened in twenty years as I stepped inside.

The smell hit me first—ink, old parchment, and something vaguely metallic—a scent reminiscent of my laboratory at the MET.

The man behind the desk pushed himself up. He had long limbs, a narrow beak of a nose, and a slight forward lean that gave the impression he might flap off at any moment.

"Rook. Rook Corvin. Managing editor of *The Daily Shade*," he said, mopping his brow with a handkerchief. "What can I do for you?"

"Windsor Ebonwood. I was hoping to speak with Beatrice Snarkle."

His expression crumpled, and he let out a weary sigh. "Not another one. First, let me apologize. What has she done now?"

"Is she here?"

"Beatrice?" He laughed without humor. "She hasn't set foot in this office since the dust was fresh. Works remote, like most of my staff."

I scanned the dim room—rows of abandoned desks, fossilized coffee cups, and a corkboard filled with pinned clippings, red string connecting disparate stories like a crime board in an old detective film.

"You never see your own employees?"

"They come and go," he said, waving a hand.

"Well, I'd like to speak with her directly. Could you ask her to come see me at the MET next time you see her?"

Relief bloomed across his face. "That I can do."

I started to turn, then paused.

"Actually, while I'm here, can you point me to the newspaper morgue?"

Rook brightened like I'd just asked about his favorite grandchild. "You bet. Right this way, Ms. Ebonwood."

He led us through a narrow doorway into a cavernous room lined floor-to-ceiling with shelves sagging under the weight of bound newspapers and aged files. Loose pages covered nearly every available surface, stacked in precarious towers. The air was thick with the scent of brittle paper and ink.

I eyed the mess. "And I'm supposed to find what I need in this?"

Rook grinned. "Ah. This is what is called controlled chaos, Ms. Ebonwood." He clapped twice. "Bring me all issues published within the last four months."

At once, the room stirred to life. Newspapers rustled, lifting from their piles, fluttering like startled birds before soaring through the air, neatly arranging themselves on the table in front of me.

I couldn't help smiling. "Efficient."

Rook gave a proud nod. "When you're done, just clap again..." clap-clap... "and say, *Revertum*. Everything will return to its proper place."

The newspapers lifted in a gentle flurry, gliding back to their homes on the shelves with the grace of well-trained pigeons.

"I'll leave you be. Let me know if you need any help," he said, rocking back on his heels before disappearing down the hall.

I unwound my scarf and slipped out of my coat, hanging both on a narrow rack by the door. After pulling out a creaky chair, I clapped twice, and said, "I'd like to see any articles you have that include Patch Priddyholm in them."

Newspapers rustled once more, but this time only two slid onto the table. The first one, only a few years old, featured Patch's big win at the Darkly Island Fair. In the accompanying photo, he stood next to a pumpkin nearly the size of a horse. His smile was wide, his eyes warm. There was no mistaking the kindness on his face.

I set it down and picked up the next one. Took me awhile to find the article, a short piece buried near the bottom. Just a short write-up promoting Family Day at Lila & the Piggles Sanctuary. Patch provided a quote on the importance of the sanctuary:

"Lila & the Piggles isn't just an animal farm. It's a place for families to learn and bond. I've never known a place so full of love."

My eyes tearing up, I pushed the papers to the side and clapped twice once more. "Please bring me any articles regarding Edythe Grouse."

The response was immediate. Newspapers rustled from their shelves, twirling through the air with graceful spins before landing in a neat stack on the table.

I flipped open the first one. Nothing groundbreaking, just short write-ups praising her legal wins, awards, and slow-but-steady ascension through the judicial ranks. She'd clearly been impressive long before anyone called her magickstrate.

But then—odd—a piece about Veronique caught my eye. It detailed her time at Wentworth Academy, her involvement in the Spell & Spindle Club, and her upcoming admission to Spectral U.

Interesting. But why was it in this batch?

I frowned, set it aside, and reached for the next.

A wedding announcement.

Okay, Corvin's system might need a tune-up.

I smirked, pushed it aside, and picked up the third.

What's this?

"Spectral University Scholar Vanishes" stretched across the top in faint violet ink, the letter slightly blurred from the damp.

I angled it toward the light, the paper crinkling under my fingertips.

Authorities remain baffled after the sudden disappearance of a third-year student...last seen exiting the east wing library just before midnight... room left undisturbed, belongings untouched...

Curious, but not particularly germane.

The article drifted into quotes—professors murmuring about promise and pressure, students whispering about cold spots and stopped clocks.

Curious. But not obviously connected.

With a sigh, and not expecting much, I slid the next paper free from the pile.

Jackpot.

A feature on influential women of the Charming Isles, with Edythe Grouse front and center. The accompanying photo showed her with arms crossed, lips pursed in disapproval, one brow arched, as if she'd already decided how this was going to go. I skimmed the article, eyes catching on a familiar name.

Known for her unwavering poise and surgically precise rulings, Grouse has presided over some of the most complicated magical trials in modern memory. But none stirred more public horror—or fascination—than the case of Katelyn Blight, a trial that would forever etch both their names into Charming Isles history.

I froze.

Katelyn Blight?

My mind snapped to the jump rope song Bettina and her friends had been singing. Killer Katey.

It was nearly fifty years ago when a wide-eyed girl with a curtain of shiny black hair and a penchant for hexed confectionery took the stand in Royal Court. At just eight years old, Katelyn Blight became the youngest citizen ever sentenced to Infernum Rock, the grim, wind-lashed prison reserved for the Isles' most dangerous magical offenders.

I sank back in my chair.

Magickstrate Grouse had presided over *that* trial?

The one where a little girl killed her nanny because she wouldn't let her have more candy? I kept reading.

According to court records, Blight became enraged after her nanny refused her a second helping of sugared ghostberries. What followed was something out of a cautionary fable. Blight, small enough to still wear

341

spell-stitched socks, levitated her nanny onto the family broom and flew
her high above the estate's thornwood hedges, before letting go. The
nanny, who had no flying abilities of her own, fell to her death on the
ornamental sundial.

I let out a quiet gasp.

It happened exactly how the girls sang it.

Could Killer Katey be living here in Darkly?

That seemed absurd, but then again, so did pumpkin suffocation.

Someone would've noticed if one of the most notorious magical murderers in Isles history had moved to town. Right?

I felt a sudden draft of dread.

I smoothed the edges of the paper and lifted it again, eyes scanning the next column.

Grouse's second most notable case concerned—

The newspaper fell to the table.

This woman *cannot* be involved.

I took a breath, steadying my hands as I picked it back up.

Malicent of the Umbral Vale. The dark sorceress accused of murdering my mother.

My stomach dropped. The magickstrate might have known everything—about Malicent, about my mother, maybe even why she'd left Dad and me all those years ago. But now Grouse was gone, and whatever truths she carried had died with her.

I swallowed hard and read, though the words trembled on the page with each beat of my pulse.

Feared across the Charming Isles and whispered about in coven halls and
council chambers alike, Malicent was not just a dark sorceress, she was a
magical calamity in human form. Her rise was swift, her spells
untraceable, and her enemies short-lived. It's estimated that over one
hundred and thirty-seven deaths were directly linked to her reign of
magical terror.

From magickstrates to marshland monks, broomwrights to

baronesses, Malicent killed without hesitation. Some for opposing her. Some for speaking her name. Some for offering her the wrong tea.

This was the first concrete information I'd ever read about Malicent. Before now, it had all been rumor and legend. But this woman? This woman would have killed a magickstrate without thinking twice. An illusion-casting witch like my mother wouldn't have stood a chance.

The trial was held under full magical lockdown within the Hall of Obsidian Law, its perimeter circled by twelve rune-scribed sentinels and a sealed chamber lined in anti-hex silverleaf. It was the first time in Charming Isles history that the courtroom itself was considered a potential casualty.

I clutched the paper, my stomach twisting. Please let her still be in prison. They couldn't have released her. Not like they did with Katelyn Blight.

I scanned the column, fingers darting down the lines.

And froze.

Twenty-five years ago, Malicent escaped Infernum Rock.

No. No, no.

I searched frantically for more. There had to be more.

Her whereabouts remain unknown, although it is believed the dark sorceress was hunted down and captured by a secret order of knights who destroyed her powers, sealed her soul in an enchanted mirror, and then smashed the mirror on the highest rocky crags of the Aerie Mountains. Rumors of her silhouette appearing in shattered mirrors have surfaced for decades, but nothing has been confirmed.

I sat back, staring blankly at the page as the words rippled and blurred beneath my gaze.

If I had to name one person capable of murdering a magickstrate, it was Malicent of the Umbral Vale.

But no. It didn't add up. Why go out of her way to kill Patch Priddyholm, a pumpkin farmer? Why poison Grouse and twelve other villagers?

That wasn't her style. She was a scorched-earth kind of sorceress. Not a tea-and-toadstools killer.

I leaned forward again, dragging the article closer. There had to be something else. Something I missed.

I flipped back to the beginning of the article, tracing Edythe Grouse's early years. Wychwood. Humble witch parents—potion-makers and charmwrights. Wentworth Academy. Full academic scholarship to Spectral University.

Wentworth. Spectral U.

I reached into the stack and pulled out the article about Veronique, the one I'd dismissed earlier. This time, I read it from start to finish.

Veronique della Morte Set to Attend Spectral University After Standout Years at Wentworth Academy

DARKLY—Veronique della Morte, a standout student at Wentworth Academy for Gifted Children, has set her sights on Spectral University this fall. A member of the esteemed Spell & Spindle Society and an active participant in the Thespian Club, della Morte has made a name for herself among the academy's most accomplished scholars. Her involvement in both academic and artistic circles has solidified her reputation as a dedicated and dynamic student, ready to take the next step in her education.

I clapped twice. "Please bring me articles concerning Edythe Grouse's high school years."

One newspaper shot straight from the bottom of the stack into my hands.

I unfolded it on the table and scanned quickly.

Found it.

344

Edythe Grouse Earns Full Scholarship
to Spectral University

DARKLY—Edythe Grouse, a distinguished scholar at Wentworth Academy for Gifted Children, has been awarded a full scholarship to Spectral University, where she will pursue a degree in Political Sorcery and Bone-Bound Law. Grouse, known for her leadership and academic excellence, serves as President of the Spell & Spindle Club, Senior Class President, and a key member of the Wentworth Debate Team. In addition to her rigorous coursework, she contributes to the school yearbook and mentors incoming freshmen. With an impressive resume and a keen intellect, Grouse is poised to make a significant impact in her future studies and beyond.

I checked the dates.

They had to have known each other. Both were in the Spell & Spindle Club at Wentworth Academy and attended Spectral U at the same time.

I leaned back to stretch, blink the sleep from my gaze—then froze.

In the lower corner of a page poking out from the stack, a photo.

Veronique and Edythe.

Younger. Arms flung around each other's shoulders, hair wild in the wind, laughter suspended mid-frame like a charm gone half-cast.

Wentworth Best Friends Bound for Spectral U
Roommates-to-Be to Study Law and Drama

DARKLY — It's official: Wentworth Academy's own Edythe Grouse and Veronique della Morte are headed to Spectral University this fall—and they'll be doing it together.

The inseparable pair, known across campus for their academic brilliance and unwavering friendship, have been accepted into Spectral's prestigious programs. Grouse will pursue Political Sorcery and Bone-Bound Law, while della Morte has secured a coveted spot in the university's elite School of Drama.

Even more exciting? The two will be rooming together in the historic—and notoriously haunted—Grimthorn Hall, a towering stone residence said to be built atop an ancient burial mound. When asked if the rumors of ghostly moaning and cursed floorboards worried them, della Morte simply laughed and said, "It adds ambiance."

They weren't just classmates. Not distant acquaintances who crossed paths at the occasional club meeting. They were best friends. Roommates. Practically sisters.

So why was she so twitchy when Edythe's name was mentioned? What could have happened between them?

Veronique had lied to me—smoothly, repeatedly—claiming she barely knew Edythe Grouse.

And yet I knew from Elspeth and Trixie she'd most likely visited Edythe the night she died.

My mind jumped to the classics: a man, a betrayal, a rift carved so deep it swallowed a friendship whole. Divorce, envy, power. Darkly had never been short on motives.

I reached for the wedding announcement I'd dismissed at the morgue, suddenly suspicious.

I opened the full spread. There she was, Veronique, in a gown that shimmered like morning frost, regal and untouchable. At her side stood a man so round he looked like he'd been rolled straight from the top tier of a wedding cake. His tuxedo only highlighted the effect, like someone had iced him into place.

But her expression—the way she gazed down at him—was adoring, unguarded. Pure Lucretia and Gomez Addams.

I skimmed the list of bridesmaids: Lorene Charlton. Norma Phillips. Nellie Avera. Annie Marie Grigsby.

No Edythe Grouse.

I picked up all the papers and photos and stuffed them into my bag. No claps, no *Revertum*, just the rustle of evidence with nowhere to go but out the door with me.

Whatever tore Veronique and Edythe apart, it happened before the wedding.

Enough was enough. I wanted to know the truth.

CHAPTER 33

A cold wind knifed past us as we circled the widow's walk of Sângele. Snow flurried in thin spirals, barely clinging to the iron railing running along the edges of the roof. Overhead, the sky churned with low, bristling clouds, rumbling now and then like something ancient turning in its sleep. The resident buzzards hunched along the rooftop, feathers puffed against the cold, their eyes following us with sharp unease.

Far below, the sea crashed against the rocks in a slow, relentless rhythm—less a roar than a warning. The sound rose between thunderclaps, each one splitting the sky open with pale flashes that lit the glassy windows of the mansion in quick, haunted bursts.

"You know, we could still turn back," Pye said.

"I'm not accusing her of anything, Pye. But why wouldn't she tell me she knew Edythe Grouse?"

"Maybe because it isn't any of your business?"

"It is though, isn't it? Because whoever killed Edythe might be the person who poisoned Jess."

"Just tread carefully," Pye advised. "You may like Veronique but don't forget—she's stroiga."

He wasn't wrong. But if I let myself think too long about what

Veronique might be capable of, I'd never walk up those steps, much less knock on her door. Or lair. Depending on how murderous she was feeling today.

I exhaled and guided the broom downward. The cold bit deeper as we coasted toward the cliffside graveyard fronting Veronique's estate. The moment my boots touched the frost-laced path, the broom shimmered and collapsed in on itself.

We threaded through the graveyard, dodging lichen-crusted headstones and rose vines thick with ice. Some of the thorns glittered. Snow drifted between the graves, settling in the worn grooves of the headstones. Wind coiled through the trees, sharp as teeth, lifting my hair and needling my skin.

By the time we reached the cracked front steps, the snow was falling in earnest. Slow, quiet flakes spun through the air, vanishing the moment they touched my coat. I looked up. Sângele rose above us, every crooked turret and arched window outlined in dusky shadow, lit now and then by the silver whip of lightning slicing through the clouds.

A flash tore up the sky, followed by a sharp crack, wood splintering like bone. A massive tree branch, heavy with ice, ripped free from its trunk and plunged off the cliff and was swallowed by the churning waves below.

Without knocking or pausing, I yanked open the heavy door, scooped up Pye, and rushed inside, slamming it shut against the howling wind.

I stepped into the foyer. The hush inside Sângele was thick—muted, as if the storm had swallowed all sound before it could cross the threshold. Only the faintest thrum of thunder rolled behind the walls, distant and dull. Then, under it, I caught a thread of music winding through the halls. Something smooth and old. Perhaps jazz from a bygone era.

A creeping sensation pressed against my ribs, the kind that made you feel small and terribly, terribly mortal. Red velvet walls closed in around me, lined with oil portraits so lifelike they almost breathed. Crimson carpets wound across the floor, their black rose and thorny-vine patterns twisting with every step.

Pye strolled down the hallway, utterly unfazed. His nonchalance should have been a comfort, but instead terror continued to steadily rise in my chest.

What were we walking into?

I followed Pyewacket around a corner and walked straight into a wall of cold bronze feathers.

"Oof," I gasped. The music abruptly cut off.

I staggered back a step and looked up. A massive bronze sculpture—a mythic bird, part crow, part phoenix, its wings half-unfurled and jagged at the tips—loomed before me. One eye cast downward in sorrow; the other missing entirely, a hollow socket staring past me. Embedded in its chest was a small, round mirror. Its surface webbed with fine cracks that caught the dim light and fractured it into ghostly shards along the walls.

Pyewacket halted in front of me when a voice, velvet and deep, threaded through the silence. "Windsor Ebonwood," Veronique purred. "I hear your heartbeat quickening as you step further into my home."

I swallowed hard and pressed forward, following the crimson and gold rug stretching down a dimly lit hallway. The sconces lining the walls cast little light.

The music began again, smooth and unbothered. Count Basie, if I wasn't mistaken.

We stepped into the room.

Veronique reclined on a velvet chaise, one arm draped lazily over the back. An ivory cigarette holder dangled between her fingers, its silver tip glinting in the dim light.

"Veronique," I said, forcing my voice to stay steady. "What's going on?"

"Whatever do you mean, dear?"

I looked around the room, elegant and tasteful, yet a fear and dread I had never experienced around Veronique before set my nerves on edge. It took all my willpower not to bolt from the mansion.

My gaze swept the room, searching for the source of the dread coiling in my chest. The edges of the world tilted slightly. I reached for the back of a sofa, digging my fingers in, anchoring myself before the spin could take me under.

Veronique sat up, concern flashing in her dark eyes. "Ambrose! Please help our guest to the sofa and then bring Windsor some sweet tea and the anaxataria stash in the music room."

She turned to Pyewacket and sighed. "You didn't warn her, did you?"

Pye pawed at a non-existence dust fairy, avoiding my eyes. He finally gave up and dragged his eye to mine. "I have no idea what she's talking about."

Veronique laughed, a deep throated howl at odds with her refinement. "You just couldn't resist your trickster ways, could you?"

She grinned at me, and I couldn't help but smile back, even with fear still ratcheting through my bones.

I stared at the vampiress who was again lounging in the chaise. Half of me wanted to bolt but the other half, the half that felt comfortable with Veronique and wanted to get to know her, begged me to stay.

Ambrose slouched back into the room with a glass of sweet tea and a small dish filled with dark, bat-shaped candies and set them on the table next to me.

He bowed once and quietly left the room.

"Have one." Veronique smiled at me and indicated the bowl.

The uneasiness rose again. "Thanks, Veronique, but I'm not hungry. In fact, we should be going."

I stood, but the instant I moved, a wave of confusion rolled over me, thick and disorienting. My pulse kicked up, panic clawing its way through my chest.

What the hellhound was going on?

"Trust me, Windsor," Veronique murmured. "Have one. You'll feel better."

Her voice wove around me like smoke, laced with something far too persuasive.

"Don't mesmer me," I said weakly.

Pye hopped onto the table, dipped his head into the bowl, and then leaped onto the sofa next to me. His paw brushed my leg, drawing my attention.

Eat this.

I froze. *Are you speaking in my head?*

He nodded, hopped into my lap, and dropped the small dark candy into my hand.

The terror isn't real.

Swallowing hard, I popped the candy into my mouth. Warmth instantly spread through me, rich and golden, chasing the dread from my chest and leaving quiet in its place. The fear, the paranoia, the sharp-edged panic—all of it ebbed away, dissolving like mist in morning sunlight.

Veronique sighed. "I do apologize, dear. I assumed Pyewacket had explained the dangers of entering a vampire's home, invited or not. Without anaxataria, you'll feel confusion, paranoia, terror. It was once a hunting tactic, but now, it serves as a simple defense mechanism."

I took a slow sip of my tea, my head clearing. My gaze wandered the room until it landed on a framed photo of Veronique, laughing as a giant wave crashed over her head. Beside her stood the man I recognized from one of the old newspaper articles—her husband.

I dipped my head in the direction of the image. "What a wonderful photo."

Veronique let out a soft sigh and smiled dreamily. "Dominik and I on our honeymoon. We were so young."

"You both look incredibly happy. Where did you meet?"

Her eyes took on a faraway glint. "Spectral University. In the Isles."

Here was my opening but I wasn't sure how to proceed. Did I have anything to fear from Veronique? She'd always been kind to me, and I knew she and my grandmother had been close.

"You went to Spectral U?" I asked carefully.

"I did," she replied, her gravelly Southern twang drawing out each syllable. "One of the best times of my life."

"The magickstrate attended Spectral U too."

The warmth in her face cooled instantly. Her spine straightened with practiced elegance, expression slipping into a mask of formality.

"I know you lied to me, Veronique." I said quietly. "I know you were good friends with Magickstrate Grouse. I also know you were with her the night she died."

She sighed, picking up a silver-framed photograph from the side table and twirling it in her hands, her dark eyes glinting. "And I'd do it again," she said simply.

My jaw dropped. Pye yelped, "Bloody 'ell!" and scrambled into my bag.

"You admit it?"

"Of course, dear. It's common knowledge." She hugged the photo to her chest with an eerie little smile. "I hate that I hurt Edythe. But what is it they say? Ah, yes. The heart wants what the heart wants, even if that heart beats no longer."

"Hurt? The magistrate is dead, Veronique! You murdered her!"

Her gaze sharpened, the tips of her fangs pressing into her bottom lip. A cold slither of fear coiled in my gut. I popped another bat chew into my mouth.

"Murder?" she whispered. "What in the world are you talking about?"

"What are *you* talking about?" I shot back.

Pye snickered. "Witty as always."

She sighed. "My dear, you could not be more wrong. I did not kill Edythe. I loved her. But I suppose I loved *him* more."

"Him?" My mind raced. "Patch?"

She let out a soft, humorless laugh. "You still don't understand, do you?"

A chime rang through the air as Veronique lifted a delicate silver bell. Moments later, Ambrose appeared. Tall, silent, his dark eyes flickered to mine before bowing to his mistress.

"Scotch for Miss Ebonwood," Veronique instructed. "The Macallan, if you please."

Ambrose inclined his head and disappeared.

Ambrose reappeared, handing me a glass of deep amber liquid. I tossed it back.

"Now," Veronique said, turning her sharp gaze back to me. "What do you need to know, Windsor dear?"

I took a steadying breath. "You and Edythe were best friends once. What happened?"

Her smile faded, eyes clouding with memory. "Have you ever known a love so overwhelming, so absolute, that denying it would be like tearing out your own heart?"

I thought of Keir, of the way he made my pulse stutter, the way I felt pulled toward him by something more than choice.

"Maybe."

Veronique's eyes gleamed. "Then perhaps, dear girl, you understand more than you think."

Veronique's gaze drifted to the photo she held in her hands.

"As I suppose you know, Edythe and I met at a very young age at Wentworth Academy here on Darkly Island. Though we were complete opposites, not only in appearance but in temperament, we were inseparable. Even when we went off to university, we refused to be separated. So we went to university together."

"Spectral University."

"Indeed. Roommates. Spent more time making mischief than good grades." A flicker of amusement crossed her face before vanishing like a shadow in candlelight. "It all changed when Edythe met a boy. Dominic Vair. They met in Advanced Moon Phases and Mysticism."

My brow arched.

"A divination course, dear." She waved a delicate hand. "I was never one for gazing into the void. Dom, however, danced with the spirits like nobles at a midnight masquerade."

Her face grew wistful in remembrance.

Veronique reached for the silver bell at her side and rang it once more. The sound shimmered in the air, strangely harmonious with the old jazz floating from an unseen gramophone.

Veronique's butler materialized as if summoned from the ether, bearing a fresh glass of scotch. "You always read my mind, Ambrose," she purred. "I believe I'll join you, dear."

She drained her glass in one elegant motion, and he refilled it before turning his sharp gaze to me. "A top up, miss?"

"Hey, Lurch! What about the cat?" Pye called from inside my bag.

Ambrose refilled my crystal glass just as Pye popped out of my bag, ready to sling another of his famous quips. Without thinking, I snapped my fingers. His mouth opened, but no sound came out.

He blinked at me in disbelief. *Did you just do that?*

"As I was saying," Veronique continued smoothly, as if my sudden display of magic was an ordinary occurrence, "Edythe fell in love. When she spoke of eternal devotion, I knew it was time to meet this man who had captured her heart."

Her voice softened, a wistful note creeping in. "The moment I met Dominic, I knew. I had never in my life felt such an immediate, undeniable attraction. And when I learned he felt the same..." She sighed, her fingers tracing the edge of the frame. "When we told Edythe, she never spoke to me again. Until the night of her murder."

My stomach lurched. "You did see her the night of her death."

Veronique turned the frame toward me, her thoughts firmly in the past, revealing a faded photo of three young faces. Edythe, Veronique, and Dominic Vair.

Her voice cracked, as blood-red tears streaked down her

cheeks. "Dominic and I had a wonderful life together. But…" She dabbed at her eyes with a silk handkerchief offered by Ambrose. "Unfortunately, my love was mortal. One of the many hazards of being a vampire—often losing those you love sooner than you'd like."

I hesitated. "Veronique, I'm so sorry. I never thought—"

"That I could love so fiercely?" She let out a humorless laugh.

A heavy silence settled between us before I forced myself to ask, "Why did you go see Edythe that night?"

She took a sip of scotch, her voice steadier now. "We weren't speaking when the incident occurred. Edythe blamed me—for Dominic. For him choosing me. For me keeping him." Veronique drew a slow breath.

"But then she found Calendre Drach. A talented student, yes, but unstable. I heard whispers of rituals rooted in magic that didn't belong to this world."

Her gaze went distant, her voice softening to a hush.

"An air of terror hung over the university. Students began withdrawing from classes. Professors avoided certain corridors. Everyone knew something terrible was coming. We just didn't know where it would strike—or who it would take."

Veronique held out her glass for Ambrose to refill and then nodded in my direction.

"I refused to believe Edythe was involved, even when the gossip revolved around her. But then Calendre vanished."

The article!

The one about the missing girl I'd dismissed without a second thought.

Turns out skimming isn't a valid investigative method.

"Not dead. Not missing. Gone. Swallowed up by the dark being she and Edythe tried to control and failed. I learned eventually what kind of magic they were playing with. A creature that could unravel time. Unpick a single moment. The moment Edythe introduced me to Dominic."

A chill ran up my spine. I knew there were all kinds of magic

—gentle, wild, treacherous. But summoning a creature to bend time to your will? That was old magic. Salem-level witchcraft. The kind that always demanded a price.

Her voice tightened, a flicker of genuine anguish slipping through.

"I tried to speak to her once. After Calendre disappeared. She smiled—just smiled—and walked away. As if she didn't care that she'd let an evil entity slip into this world. That's when I knew Dom and I weren't safe. We finished our studies and moved here. As far from the Charming Isles—and that creature—as we could get. And we were happy."

She turned again to the sea, then abruptly to me.

"So no, I didn't lie because I was guilty of murder, Windsor. I lied because I feared the truth. Feared what it would mean to say it aloud. To admit that someone I once loved like a sister was willing to harm another person just to undo Dom and me. And because if I had told you what she did…you would've asked why I didn't stop her. Why I let it happen."

She looked away, voice tightening.

"And the truth is, by the time she found Calendre, I had already walked away. I saw what Edythe was becoming, and I chose to leave her behind. I chose him. And I don't regret that choice. But I hoped she regretted hers."

A pause.

"That night I visited White Hart Inn, I wanted to hear that age had softened her. Or grief. But she wouldn't even open the door."

Veronique clasped her hands, the movement measured, almost ceremonial. "I didn't go for absolution. I've never been foolish enough to expect that. I went because some part of me needed to know she was still Edythe. The Edythe I once loved and trusted more than anyone else in all the worlds. I hoped to see who she was…before everything that followed."

Her gaze flicked toward me, sharp now. "She spoke through the door, of course. Said I was centuries late. Told me to go home."

Veronique gave the faintest smile, bitter and elegant. "I told her I didn't come for forgiveness. I told her I knew I was wrong, but I also needed to know she regretted her own choices. But she didn't want to hear it."

Veronique moved toward the desk and picked up an antique letter opener, studying its shine before setting it down again.

"There are some wounds even immortality won't let heal. And there are things I kept from you, Windsor. Not because I feared your judgment, but because I couldn't bear for you to see me as she did."

Her voice grew quiet.

"She was the most brilliant person I ever knew. And also the most dangerous."

Veronique took another long sip of scotch, her gaze drifting back to the sea. "I did not kill Edythe. But I fear she may have still wished me dead."

I turned the glass in my hands, watching the amber liquid swirl, and thought about the letter I'd found.

"Where did you go after you left the inn?"

"The Lucky Lounge. In The Graves." She smirked. "Benicio can confirm. He never denies me a crimson martini."

I narrowed my eyes. "Are you sure you saw Benicio that night?"

"Most certainly, dear." Her lips curled in amusement. "He was holding court in his booth, as always."

Just as Delilah had cryptically indicated.

I exhaled slowly. "I believe you, Veronique."

Veronique's face fell, sadness pooling in her eyes. "If only I had stayed that night. If I had forced her to open the door, to listen to what I had to say, perhaps she would still be alive."

She turned back to the photo. "And now, I must live with that too."

∼

WE'D MADE it back from Sângele and its thundersnow just as the last flurries fell, leaving behind a heavy, lingering chill. Cold clung to the windows, the glass edged with a lace of frost, but inside Fernwood's sitting room, the fire crackled on, steady and bright. Shadows flickered in the corners, stretching and curling in ways that suggested they might be listening, attentive to any danger that might be lurking. Not that I had time to worry about eavesdropping shadowmen.

I had simply thrown on the same sweats I wore last night and now I sank deeper into the velvet cushions, staring at the documents and photographs spread across the coffee table. The dancing candlelight exaggerated the movements of the people in the photos. Faces shifted slightly, expressions seemed to tighten when I wasn't looking directly at them.

I hated how the pieces of this mystery still weren't quite fitting together. It was like having half a spell and no way to complete it. The coming of winter usually brought a sense of calm, settling around my thoughts like a thick quilt, muffling the noise. But tonight, everything inside my head was sharp and loud and frayed at the seams.

Pye sprawled across one side of the sofa, belly up and paws thrown dramatically in the air like he'd just fainted from boredom.

I stretched my legs, pressing my fingertips to my eyes before leaning forward, determined to make sense of the documents I had organized into careful piles.

I picked up my mug of chai, savoring the rich, warming scent. The photos fanned out before me felt accusatory in their stillness. An angry Benicio Kim growling behind electrified columns. A seemingly sweet child pulling on her ear. Veronique and Dominic gazing lovingly into each other's eyes. And Patch Priddyholm, proudly standing next to his prize pumpkin.

I pulled out the article concerning the disappearance of Calendre Drach and a shiver crept down my spine. Shadows stretched long in the corner, and for a brief irrational moment, I wondered if the creature might have followed the magickstrate to Darkly. I shook out my arms to rid myself of the creeping feeling, then refreshed my mug.

Somewhere in here was the key. It felt like the prickle of magic against my skin just before a spell wove itself into being. But was it one of these photos? All of them? None of them?

"There are a number of people who may have wanted to get rid of Grouse," I murmured, tapping my fingers against the edge of a document. "But Patch? He has to be the key."

Pye sighed dramatically and pawed at my knee without bothering to lift his head. "Not so much the key," he said, voice thick with sleep. "But perhaps the catalyst."

I blinked at him. "What do you mean?"

He rolled upright and gave himself a half-hearted shake. "Whatever set the killer off, it happened before Grouse even arrived. Maybe if Patch hadn't been murdered, the magickstrate would still be alive."

I straightened, staring at the photos again. "Hmm. You don't think the murders were planned?"

"Not in a grand, scheming sort of way," Pye said. "More like something personal. Something snapped. Patch died first for a reason. And once that line got crossed…"

He flicked his tail and drew a paw across his neck. "Everything else followed."

I traced a finger over the photograph of Patch Priddyholm. He was smiling widely. A happy smile. A happy man. I pressed my lips together. "Who in all of Darkly did you anger enough to kill you?"

I took a sip of chai, relishing the comfort it brought. Where's a tranquili-tea tart when you need one?

"There must be someone else. Someone we haven't even suspected."

Pye's face twisted with theatrical thoughtfulness. "Well, if you want my opinion—and why wouldn't you—I think we should look a bit closer at Bettina. She always looked a bit shifty to me."

"Bettina? Pye!"

He bounded onto the coffee table, peering down at the spread I had arranged in front of me. "She could be a little criminal mastermind." He patted the photo of the little girl. "Just like her."

I narrowed my eyes at him, but the half-smirk on his face ruined any attempt at solemnity. "Be serious, Pye. You're ruining my concentration."

"I *am* serious. Bettina. Or Sibby. My mum always said, 'Never trust an old witch who does tai chi in a cemetery.'"

"Your mother never said that."

"She could have. You didn't know her."

I groaned, dragging a hand down my face. And then stopped.

I quickly rearranged the photos, sliding them across the table like puzzle pieces instead of frozen moments. The child in the picture, tugging at her ear—such a tiny, throwaway gesture. Unless it wasn't.

Bettina.

My heart gave a sharp kick.

"Oh no," I breathed.

I tapped the photograph, my voice barely a whisper. "The ear. Red petals around the body."

"Huh?" Pye leaned forward, squinting at the image. "Speak louder, you're mumbling like a swamp hag."

I ignored him, eyes still on the child in the photo. "Think about it like this. What if we've been looking at it all wrong? What if the question we should have been asking ourselves isn't 'who *hated* Patch and the magistrate enough to kill them' but 'who *loved* someone else enough to kill them?'"

His face went slack for a beat, then lit up with mischief. "Ah, yes. I see now. Love. The most dangerous magic of all." He paused. "And, as I already said, Bettina's got—"

I swatted at him, and he leaped theatrically into the air to avoid my hand. "Fine! Fine! You're ruining my digestive process."

"You haven't even eaten.

"Digesting the information, Win. Keep up."

Sometimes he was impossible. I take that back. *Usually* he was impossible.

"Pye," I said, quietly now. "What if a murderer has been here in Darkly the whole time and we never knew?"

He went still. Eyes narrowed. Voice lower. "You believe Malicent is here? And you're just telling me this now? Before I've had time to prepare a dramatic reaction?"

"No time for dramatics," I said, grabbing my bag. "You coming?"

Pye groaned. "This better not end with me running. These legs are only decorative."

I opened my bag, and he hopped in with a grumble. "Better?"

"Much!"

I shoved my feet into my boots and grabbed my coat from its hook, pulling it tight as I stepped toward the door. A thick scarf followed, then gloves, and finally a knit hat tugged low over my ears.

We almost made it out the door when—

"Now where y'all think you're runnin' off to? I was just fixin' to make some eggs, bacon, and cheese grits for a proper late breakfast," Hilde called from the sitting room, hands on her hips, a take-no-prisoners look on her face.

"I'm sorry, Hilde," I said, nonchalant and casual. "But there's something I need to do."

"Oh lawd. This ain't gonna be good if cheese grits don't stop her," I heard Hilde mumble as I opened the door.

The snow was now falling in slow, deliberate drifts, already nesting in the corners of porches and muffling the world beneath its weight. The kind of snow that didn't plan to leave anytime soon. I braced myself and stepped out into it.

I didn't know what we were about to walk into, but I knew one thing for sure.

It was time to confront a killer.

CHAPTER 34

The brisk walk from the royal inspector's office helped clear my head. Snow spun around me in soft flurries, and each step pressed a clean print into the blanket of white settling over the sidewalk. I'd promised Ransom I wouldn't do anything rash before he arrived. And I meant it when I said it. I really did.

"Just observe. Like Ransom said. That's all we're doing, right?" Pye scampered along next to me, pausing now and then to bat at a few snowflakes.

"That's it."

Mathilda stepped out of her shop, broom in hand. We exchanged a wave through the falling snow before I slipped into the MET. Inside, a handful of shoppers wandered the aisles, shaking off the cold.

I stopped as the heavy door shut behind me.

"Wait. Was she getting on her broom?"

I turned back to the door.

"Win, don't." Pye's paw brushed my ankle, drawing my attention.

I burst back out the door so suddenly one of my customers gasped behind me.

"Mathilda!"

She hovered on her broom just above the cobblestones, speaking to her assistant, Fara, who waved at me.

Mathilda's eyes narrowed as she rose in the air, her hand frantically tugging at her ear.

"Mathilda! I need to talk to you!"

"About what?" she called down, her broom rising steadily through the snow, flakes gathering on the handle and bristles,

A small crowd began to gather, and I saw Jess and Tzazi hurrying over from the courtyard of The Magic Cup.

"I think you know, *Katelyn*."

A figure stepped out of the MET. I hadn't noticed her on my brief entry.

Dixie-Deen's eyes traveled from me to Mathilda, who now hovered well above the centuries-old oaks in the cemetery. "Matty! What's going on?"

The terror in Dixie-Deen's voice sent a chill through me. She yanked a wand from inside her wool coat and turned in my direction. I drew in a breath. No, not Dixie-Deen too.

My broom appeared next to me, and I slid onto the seat.

Mathilda hovered above, eyes gleaming with triumph. She knew exactly what I'd just realized—on a broom, she had the upper hand.

As she rose higher, Tzazi sprang into the air, moving faster than I could track, her hands clamping around the broom's staff. It jerked wildly under the sudden weight.

"Tzazi! No!"

Mathilda snarled, one hand crackling with light. A bolt of magic shot from her fingertip.

Tzazi screamed, releasing the broom and tumbling back toward the ground.

The crowd screamed as she plummeted. My pulse hammered in my ears.

I shot into the sky without thinking, icy wind tearing at my eyes.

With a thump, her body landed in Pye's bed, its overstuffed cushions barely containing the force of her fall. Her limbs sprawled at sharp angles, too still, too slack. Wrong in a way that made my stomach twist.

I reached for her hand. "Hold on, Tzaz. Please."

Then—light. A shimmer of magic flared around her, lifting her from the bed, weightless in a glowing orb.

In a panic, my eyes searched the skies until I found Mathilda hovering over The Magic Cup courtyard. But she wasn't looking at us. Her hand wasn't even spelling us. She was staring below, her face twisted with disbelief and hurt.

I followed her gaze. Below, face fierce with focus, Dixie-Deen stood in front of the MET, wand raised, gently lowering Tzazi to the ground. Azalea broke through the crowd, already chanting spells under her breath.

Tzazi was safe.

Mathilda's head whipped between me and Dixie-Deen, her eyes wide, glassy with unshed tears. "Why couldn't you just leave it alone, Windsor Ebonwood?!" she shrieked, her voice jagged with grief and fury, as the wind whipped around her.

A blast of magic shot up from the crowd, slamming into the bristles of Mathilda's broom. The jolt rippled through the air. My own broom pitched hard, nearly knocking me sideways. Wind tore at my clothes, and my hair whipped across my eyes as I fought to stay upright.

Below, Dixie-Deen stood frozen in the street, wand still raised, her face streaked with tears.

Mathilda hovered midair, her eyes wide, her breath hitching in shock. "I did it for you, Dixie-Deen!" she shouted, voice cracking. "I was happy for the first time in my life. Patch. The magickstrate. They were going to take it all away!"

A shiver traveled up my spine as a low murmuring slithered through the air, a deep eerie echo that prickled against my skin.

Mathilda turned back to me, a wicked grin stretching her face. "*Mors malediction!*" she shrieked, voice splintered with rage.

"Mathilda! No!" Dixie-Deen screamed from below.

Green mist burst from the medallions dangling beneath my broom, wrapping around my limbs, whispering, hissing. The air around me shimmered, raw and sickening.

Terror flared sharp and hot inside me, but my magic rose to meet it, threading through my veins, steadying my breath. My right hand shot forward, fingers outstretched, while my left gripped Marais like a lifeline.

The broom yanked hard, throwing off my balance.

I bit down against panic and glanced below. The crowd was thicker, their upturned faces frozen in horror. I had to end this. Now.

I raised my hand again. This time the broom jerked violently left.

She'd cursed it! Mathilda had cursed my broom! The medallions swayed and chimed beneath me, their silver sheen gone murky, corrupted by whatever foul spell she'd woven.

I reached down, desperate to tear them free. The second my fingers touched one, searing pain lanced through me. I yanked my hand back, blisters already rising across my fingertips.

My broom bucked beneath me, wild and mean, and I threw every bit of strength and magic I had into staying upright.

Gasps rippled through the crowd as dark shadows slipped through the walls of the MET, whispering up into the air. They twisted around me. Their susurrous moaning drowned out the shouts from below.

Mathilda hurled another bolt of magic screaming toward me. I braced for impact and—

—it vanished.

The shadows thickened, their tendrilled arms wrapping around my broom, forming a shifting wall between me and her magic. My breath caught. I could see them now. Faces, blurry and indistinct. Guardian spirits, summoned by the old magics buried deep in Darkly's bones.

I didn't hesitate.

I raised both arms toward Mathilda.

She threw back her head and laughed, wild and unafraid, her wand limp at her side.

The blast I sent struck her square in the chest.

The laugh cut short.

She froze in midair.

Then, I turned my hands, pressing the air like I could cup her between them. Gently, I lowered her down.

As her boots touched the ground, Boddy's golden coils slithered from the shadows of his cloak, silent and quick, wrapping tight around her limbs.

I drifted down on my own broom, breath ragged, heart still thudding in my ears. The moment I hit solid ground, Jess barreled into me, throwing her arms around me, holding me tight.

"You saved her," Jess whispered fiercely, anticipating my question. "Tzazi's okay. You saved her life."

"And I didn't even fall off my broom," I muttered, still clutching the handle with a death grip.

A low hiss snapped our attention back. Mathilda writhed in the golden coils, her body nearly swallowed by them. Only her head remained free, her face twisted with rage as she turned toward me.

"Besom!" she snarled. "It's called a besom, you ignorant child."

Dixie-Deen broke through the crowd, breathless, and ran to Mathilda's side, her wand still trembling in her hand. I moved beside her, one arm instinctively wrapping around her waist.

"Why, Mathilda?" Her voice cracked under the weight of it. "You knew how much I loved him."

For a moment, the fury drained from Mathilda's face. Her expression flickered—remorse, longing, regret—and her voice wavered. "He said he was going to take you away from me, Dixie-Deen," she said quietly. "I couldn't let that happen. I couldn't lose you."

"Oh, Mathilda." Dixie-Deen shook her head, the words barely

holding together. "He wouldn't have. *I* wouldn't have. He knew what you meant me...what you *mean* to me."

Dixie-Deen sagged in my arms, her balance giving way to the crush of grief and betrayal. I tried to guide her toward the nearest bench, but she stiffened, gathering herself with quiet resolve.

"But you—" she whispered to Mathilda. "—*you* have taken me away from you."

Mathilda's face lost all color as she dropped her head, refusing to meet our eyes.

"Mathilda," I said softly.

She turned her gaze on me, the coils cinched tight around her, binding her magic and rage alike.

"The cursed medallions. The Death card. Did you *really* want me dead?"

My voice had dropped to a whisper when her eyes met mine, hollow now. Her bluster and nerve gone, replaced by sadness and defeat.

"Death card? I don't know what you're talking about, Win. I..."

And then she was gone.

In one final surge of energy, the golden coils pulled tight, and Boddy vanished with her in a dark swirl that left behind only silence, and a broomstick clattering to the stones with a hollow, final thud.

I SHOVED PAST STUNNED ONLOOKERS, slipping through smoke and shivering light until I spotted Azalea, down on her knees, Tzazi's limp body cradled in her lap like a broken wing. Her gold bangles jangled as she tried to hold still, her fingers trembling against Tzazi's brow.

I dropped beside them, breath ragged, throat tight. My palm skimmed Tzazi's cheek, brushing aside the sweat-damp strands of blonde hair clinging to her skin.

"Oh, Tzazi..." My voice caught in my chest. "I'm so sorry."

Azalea's hand found mine and squeezed hard, steadying me in the way only she could. I turned to her, my heart beating too loud in my ears.

"Azalea, I didn't think—I should've—"

Then Tzazi groaned softly. One eye cracked open, unfocused but unmistakably annoyed.

"Yeh eejit," she rasped. "I'm fine. Vampire, remember?"

Azalea let out a strangled laugh of relief and helped her sit up with surprising strength. Tzazi swayed but grinned, her fangs peeking just enough to make her point.

Before I could exhale, Elysande appeared in a swirl of glitter and confidence, bounding over with a suspiciously shimmering vial of violet liquid.

"No one panic. I've got just what she needs!" she declared, holding up the ampoule like it was a magic wand.

"No!" we all shouted in unison—Azalea, Tzazi, and me.

Elysande stopped mid-step, blinking. Tzazi and I looked at each other, then laughed, deep and shaking, the kind that bubbles up when the danger has passed but your nerves haven't caught on yet.

She was okay.

I was okay.

And that fae elixir wasn't going anywhere near our lips tonight.

I sat with Dixie-Deen on an iron bench nestled against the old stone wall as snow drifted steadily from the sky, gathering in the crooks of bare tree limbs overhead.

"I knew about her past," Dixie-Deen said, her voice so low I could barely hear her. "But she wasn't that girl anymore. She'd changed."

She turned to me, eyes glassy with unshed tears. "She had a

life here. One she loved. People she loved. People who loved her back. Why would she throw that away?"

I softly cradled her hand in mine. "Because she believed it could all vanish in an instant. If the magickstrate exposed who she used to be, she thought Darkly would turn its back. Forcing you to do the same."

Dixie-Deen's fingers trembled in mine.

"And with Patch, she believed he was taking you away."

Dixie-Deen lifted her head and nodded sadly. "He was joking. That was just Patch."

"I believe Mathilda was afraid he meant it. Or perhaps she knew he was going to propose. Either way, she thought she was about to lose you."

Dixie-Deen burst into tears as Jess and Tzazi joined us. Jess knelt beside her, wrapping her arms around Dixie-Deen's trembling frame. A subtle pulse of magic rippled from her, gentle and steady, the kind of magic that made your shoulders drop and your breath come easier. Tzazi settled beside me with a grunt, her knee bumping mine.

"You good?" I asked, clasping Tzazi's hand in mine.

"Oh, peachy," she deadpanned. "Just got hurled out of the sky by a psychotic broom jockey. But thanks for asking."

"Whew. I was afraid you'd lost your sense of sarcasm. Guess we're good on that front."

I pulled her into a quick hug, my eyes sweeping the crowd beyond her shoulder. I found Ransom in quiet conversation with Azalea. Their faces tense, voices low.

I wanted to know what came next for Mathilda. As horrible as her deeds were, some part of me felt sorry for her—even if she did call me an 'ignorant child.' Her heart was right; her actions were not.

Chase appeared next to me, cradling Pye in his arms. "You know," he drawled, "you nearly gave us all simultaneous cardiac arrest."

Pye huffed. "Nearly? I'm convinced I flatlined." His paw

flailed in the air. "Do you have any idea what it was like watching you go full broom rodeo while hanging on by sheer dumb luck and shadowmen?!"

Ren, standing behind them with arms crossed, nodded. "You should've seen Keir's expression. That man was ready to rip the heavens apart to get to you."

I swallowed. I *had* seen his face. Just a glimpse before the broom almost bucked me into open air. It had been fear, pure and unfiltered, grief-before-the-fact.

"I wasn't exactly having fun either," I said, attempting to inject some levity. "But, hey, I didn't die. Let's call it a win."

Jess gave me a withering look. "Not funny, Win."

"Not remotely," Chase added, still pale.

Pye let out a deep breath and shook his head. "Next time, just —just don't do that, okay?" His voice wavered slightly, but he recovered. "I can't afford to be stress-eating my way through Darkly's entire pastry supply because you decide to try airborne heroics again."

I smiled faintly. "I'll do my best."

Movement in the crowd caught my eye—Ransom, cutting through the chaos with his hands shoved in the pockets of a woolen coat and a look that didn't bode well. I rose from the bench and met him halfway, dodging a cluster of whispering townsfolk.

He stopped a few feet from me, head cocked. "I've got half a mind to arrest you."

"Well," I said, arching a brow, "that's better than a full mind. What's the other half thinking?"

"That I should thank you. Maybe offer you a job."

A laugh escaped before I could stop it. "Pretty sure that's against your department's hiring policy."

He didn't smile, but his voice softened. "You were right. Mathilda Broomthistle was indeed Katelyn Blight. I spoke with Dixie-Deen and Fara. Turns out, Mathilda hexed your broom with cursed medallions and fetish charms. Fara's unbinding the last of it now."

I thought back to when I picked up my broom—how Mathilda had sent Fara off to fetch agate. She knew Fara would recognize the curses. That's why she got her out of the way. The chill sank deeper into my bones.

"She planned to come for me from the start?"

Ransom shook his head. "Mizizi examined your broom. The curses were passive until triggered—voice-locked. Only she could activate them. She made the choice to do so."

"*Mors malediction.* Latin for *death curse.* I should have realized." *If not for Mizizi's shadowmen...*

I looked up. "What happens to her now?"

Ransom sighed, shoulders sagging slightly beneath his coat. "She's under containment until a magickstrate from the Isles issues judgment. Given the charges—murder, magical assault, identity fraud—she's likely headed to Infernum Rock."

I winced. "That's a horrible place."

"It is," he said quietly. "But so were her choices."

I swallowed the lump in my throat. "I know she did awful things, but—"

"She wasn't always a monster," he finished for me. "No. But she let fear turn her into one."

I nodded, a quiet sadness settling in my chest.

"I'll stop in tomorrow to take your full statement," he added.

He turned to leave but then paused when he spotted Keir pushing through the crowd toward us.

"Thank you, Ransom," I said, reaching out to touch his sleeve.

He nodded once. "Good job, Windsor."

Ransom spun on his heel and headed back toward the crowd of townspeople, magical notebook at the ready, giving Keir a nod as they passed.

Keir's arms closed around me before I could speak, pulling me in so tight it stole my breath. His grip was fierce—like he didn't trust the world not to steal me away again.

"What am I ever gonna do with yeh?" he whispered, voice ragged, frayed at the edges.

I pressed my face to his chest, drawing in the warm, familiar scent of earth and pine. Beneath my cheek, his heartbeat thudded hard and fast. His arms tightened around me, his breath catching as if he didn't trust it to stay steady.

"Oh, I have some ideas," I murmured against him, trying to keep my voice light.

He let out a breathy almost-laugh, but his arms didn't loosen. Instead, he dipped his head, his lips brushing my temple, lingering there like he needed to prove to himself I was still real. One hand moved slowly across my back in calming circles, steady and sure.

"I thought I'd lose yeh," he said, barely above a whisper.

I tilted my head to look up at him, his eyes—stormy, wild, raw. I reached up, brushing my fingers along his jaw.

"You didn't," I said softly.

He swallowed hard, something shifting in his gaze, something deeper than words. Then he leaned in, resting his forehead against mine, our breath mingling in the space between us.

The crowd faded. The noise dimmed.

We were here. Alive. Together.

And no spell, no curse, no darkness could touch that.

CHAPTER 35

$\mathcal{S}$now fell thicker now, layering Fernwood's courtyard in a quiet, growing blanket. The glow from the sitting room windows spilled across the accumulating white, softening the edges of the darkness. Inside, the fire burned low and steady —the kind of heat that burned deep—warming the room and soothing your bones.

Keir slid an arm around my shoulders and drew me in. He pressed a kiss to my temple, slow and steady. I leaned against him, spent. The last of the adrenaline drained out of me, leaving nothing but bone-deep exhaustion and the quiet strength of him holding steady at my side.

Jess appeared with a tray full of coffee mugs, shaking her head. "I still can't believe Mathilda is Katelyn Blight. Feels like we've been dropped into the middle of some cozy mystery novel."

She ruffled Chase's hair on her way past, then wedged herself onto the love seat beside him and Ren.

The scent of cinnamon and peppermint bloomed through the room. Jess's hearth magic curled into the air, sweet and spicy and perfect for the moment.

"Aye," Keir said, taking a long sip. His shoulders eased down an inch as the strain in his body unspooled. "And livin' in Darkly all this time. Right under our bloody noses. I dinnae think even Ransom saw through her."

"Dixie-Deen knew who she was," I said quietly, staring at the blazing fire. "I think she even knew Mathilda was behind the murders but didn't want to believe it."

"I think it's sad," Ren said softly. His deep capacity for empathy warmed my heart.

I reached for Keir's hand and squeezed. "Mathilda brought on herself the one thing she feared most," I said. "Losing everything."

"But, sugah," Chase said, giving his coffee a lazy swirl, "how'd you put it all together?"

"I didn't see anything that pointed straight at Mathilda," Tzazi added, lifting a brow.

"It wasn't just one thing," I said, voice low, tired. "It started with the way she snapped at Patch the day he died, something Jess mentioned. At the time, it seemed unimportant. But it stuck with me.

"And do you remember at Gumbo Fest when we were telling her about the trial? She made a comment that made me think she knew Bailiff Mortimer."

"Did she?" Jess scrunched up her face, attempting to remember.

"She did. And how would she have known unless she had dealt with him through the court system?"

I paused, bracing myself.

"I borrowed—"

"Stole," Pyewacket muttered from his curled position by my hip, not bothering to open his eyes.

"—a few articles and photos from *The Darkly Shade*'s newspaper morgue," I finished, ignoring him.

"Oooh, yay! You met Beatrice Snarkle," Jess said, grinning.

Keir's eyes flicked toward me, the question unspoken.

"No, she works remotely," I said. "But those articles were the first clue that Grouse and Veronique weren't as distant as she'd claimed. For the longest time, I thought Veronique had killed the magickstrate. She lied to me over and over. But then I remembered my conversation with Harlan Hayman. He'd told me about some petals he'd found and everything shifted. That's when I knew the murders had to be connected."

I held my mug tighter. "But no one person had a clear motive against both victims.

"It was Bettina's jump rope song that lit something up," I said. "Made me wonder if someone in Darkly wasn't who they claimed to be."

I glanced at Keir. His mouth twitched into a half-smile, equal parts amused and impressed at my little dig.

"Every time I was around Mathilda, something tugged at me. Like walking into a place you've never been and somehow knowing where everything is."

"Déjà vu," Ren said with an understanding nod.

"Exactly. But stronger. I'd never met her before moving here, so why did she feel so familiar?

"This morning, I was looking through the images again and the one of young Katelyn Blight caught my eye. And it hit me. Her ear. Katelyn had a habit of tugging on her ear. Just like the song says. Just like Mathilda."

Chase sat up straighter. "Mathilda does do that. Especially when she's upset or frustrated."

"Right," I said. "Not a common habit. Then there's Zephyra Nightshade."

"The Eldritch councilwoman?" Keir asked.

I nodded. "Mathilda said she was delivering a broom to Zephyra at the time of Patch's murder. But Zephyra was in town days earlier picking it up herself. Which means Mathilda lied."

Tzazi leaned forward. "So how'd Mathilda manage to slip the petals into Elspeth's jacket?"

"The collision at Gumbo Fest," I said. "Elspeth swore Mathilda ran into *them*. Not the other way around. And, for once, she wasn't lying."

Understanding flickered.

"Ahhhh," they all said at once

A hush fell over the room, softened by the crackle of the fire and the whisper of snow against the windows.

"So why did that witch try to kill Jess?" Chase asked, his voice still sharp with anger.

"She didn't," I said. "Not directly. Remember when the mayor, Lilith, and the magickstrate stopped by her booth for cider? Mathilda poured three mugs, set them down, then hurried off to help a broom customer. She had no idea Jess drank the cider."

"But she put poison in all three mugs," Jess said quietly, a tremor in her voice. "She knew Lilith and the mayor would drink them."

I nodded.

"That's not just cold," Jess murmured, grabbing onto Ren's arm. "That's evil."

He pulled her in closer, jaw tight.

"And the magickstrate ended up with a double dose after drinking Lilith's too," I added with a shrug. "Maybe Mathilda only meant to make Grouse sick. Who knows?"

After a beat, Tzazi stirred. "One thing though. I thought the murders were connected to all the strange behaviors of the swamp creatures."

"Hmm. Me too," Chase said. "So what is causing their restlessness?"

All eyes swung to Keir. He raised his hands in surrender.

"We don't know, yet" he admitted. "But I'm certain it's not rogue werewolves again."

A collective sigh moved through the room as everyone took that in.

"I'll be reaching out to some of the swamp guardians," Keir added. "See if they've noticed anything."

"There are swamp guardians?" I asked.

Keir blinked, then gave a slow nod. "Aye. Deep in the wetlands. Part of the agreement we made long ago with the Blue Elves."

I turned to the window. Snow still fell, steady and thick, blanketing the trees that edged the swamp.

"Are there lots of guardians?" I asked.

"Quite a few," Keir said. "But I've only dealt with Ghoulmar and Roi Marais."

"Marais," I repeated under my breath.

"Ghoulmar leads the swamp lads," Jess explained. "Little gnomes that live in the swamp. Roi Marais, he's the king of the swamp."

My eyes widened.

Chase chuckled. "Not as glamorous as it sounds."

"Don't forget," Tzazi cut in, "there are also vile creatures out there. Not everyone in the swamp plays nice."

I stared out at the snow-covered marsh, the scene still and lovely.

Guardians in the swamps. Would I ever truly know everything about Darkly?

Probably not.

But I liked the idea of a protector watching from the shadows. Maybe that was the light I sometimes saw during the night. Maybe someone was watching over us after all.

I looked around the room, this odd little constellation of people who'd somehow become my home. Best friends. Family. Confidants. The ones who'd seen me at my worst and never flinched.

How terrifying it must've been for Mathilda, thinking she was about to lose the only person who had ever truly accepted her. Loved her, imp warts and all.

Tzazi with her head tipped back, one arm slung lazily over the chair, looked more at ease than I'd seen her in days.

Across the room, Chase and Ren leaned in close, their heads

nearly touching as they spoke in soft tones meant only for each other.

Then there was Jess. Squished up on the love seat next to Ren and Chase, cradling her coffee, contented and happy. The fairy with a sugar-sweet smile and steel in her spine, our group's quiet anchor.

And Keir. My Keir. The one who looked at me like I was magic, even when I felt like a mess. He never tried to cage me or fix me. Just stood by ready to guard the gate if the world came clawing.

From the kitchen, Hilde and Sibby's voices floated through, half laughter, half arguing, all affection. The clatter of porcelain plates, a faint thwap of a wooden spoon, and Sibby's unmistakable cackle made my heart swell.

Murder wasn't the answer. It never was. But I understood the ache Mathilda must have carried. That bone-deep fear of being left behind.

The room buzzed with easy conversation—plans for the holidays, lingering questions, and stories already shifting into legend. Laughter warmed the corners, chasing off the worst of the gloom. But even in the light, a quiet weight pressed behind my ribs, reminding me that not everything could be so easily shaken off.

Oh, yes. I understood.

Understood what the thought of that kind of loss could stir up in someone. Understood what it would do to me, if I ever lost this ragtag, maddening, precious family of mine.

To the bone, I understood.

EPILOGUE

$\mathcal{V}$eronique took a slow sip of her champagne, her ice-blue eyes watching me over the rim of her glass. "Though I imagine you did not come here merely to toast my innocence."

I exhaled through my nose. "No, I didn't."

She gave a knowing smile, more amused than offended. "And yet, you once thought me capable of murder."

I shifted in my seat, suddenly very aware of the gothic weight of the house pressing in around me. The air smelled faintly of salt and roses, the undertone of something richer, older. I glanced at the chandelier overhead, its candles burning with an eerie, wavering flame, though I felt no draft.

"You're a powerful vampire with a mansion full of secrets," I said plainly. "Forgive me for being thorough."

Veronique chuckled, but it was a sad sound, thin and strangled. "You would not be the first to suspect me of murder," she murmured. "And I fear you will not be the last."

She let the moment settle, then tilted her head in silent question.

I swallowed, the parchment suddenly a heavy weight in my

pocket. I pulled it free, smoothing it between my fingers before holding it out.

She accepted it without hurry, her fingers brushing mine, cool as the grave. As she read, the sun caught the fine etching of blood-red veins in her irises, deepening their glacial hue.

Then, she stilled.

Veronique's fingers clenched the letter, but her face betrayed nothing. Not at first. But then, like a crack in marble, the façade started to break.

Her lips parted slightly, as though she might speak, but no words came. Instead, she let out the softest of laughs. An aching sound, brittle and sharp. She lifted her gaze to mine.

"She wanted to mend things," Veronique whispered. Her voice was velvet-thin, a thread of something almost human breaking through the centuries. "And she never had the chance."

I said nothing.

She stared down at the letter again, fingers drifting absently over Edythe's words, as if she could conjure her from the ink. "I waited too long," she murmured. "And so did she."

A draft slipped through the cracks around the terrace doors, enough to stir the edge of the heavy curtains and carry in a whisper of cold. Outside, everything lay hushed under white—the gazebo, the roses, even the gravestones, nearly lost beneath the drifts.

Veronique exhaled sharply, composing herself with a subtle wave of her hand.

"Well," she said, setting the letter down with great care, as though it might crumble. "That is a cruel thing to learn on a day of supposed celebration."

Her gaze flicked to the champagne in her hand, then back to me, and for once, the ever-poised Lady Veronique looked tired.

I hesitated, then lifted my own flute. "Veronique? I'd like to make a toast, if you don't mind. To Edythe," I said quietly.

Veronique met my gaze. After a long pause, she nodded and clinked her glass softly against mine.

"To Edythe."

We drank in silence, the sea breaking violently below, the house swaying with each crash.

Then, with the letter tucked safely in her grasp, Veronique smiled, slow and sad.

"First of all," she finally said. "It's Nick. All my dear friends call me Nick...only...please don't accuse me of murder again. We vampires have bad enough reputations as it is."

I couldn't help but quirk a smile.

"Second," she said, setting her glass aside and leaning in my direction. "Tell me everything."

IF YOU AREN'T QUITE ready to leave the world of Win and Pyewacket yet, turn the page and check out Chapter 1 of *Christmas Carols & Yuletide Perils*, the next book in **A Darkly Southern Mystery series**.

CHRISTMAS CAROLS & YULETIDE PERILS

CHAPTER 1

$\mathcal{T}$he shiny red sleigh brushed past a snow-covered bough, and there it was—Greywolf Manor, every gable and turret glittering like a castle in a fairytale. The sleigh bells fell silent as Whisper, the magnificent undead mare from Lila & the Piggles sanctuary, came to a graceful stop beneath the porte-cochère of the manor, steam curling from her nostrils in ghostly spirals. Frost clung to her hollow eye sockets, and when she stomped a bone-white hoof, it echoed like a warning from the grave.

A stable boy hurried over, taking Whisper's reins with the careful deference of someone who wasn't entirely sure she wouldn't hex him simply because it tickled her fancy.

"Easy girl," I murmured as Whisper huffed cold fog from her nostrils and gave the poor boy a baleful stare and a subtle skeletal clink.

I turned toward the mansion—and paused, stunned into silence by the sheer spectacle.

Greywolf Manor had dressed to dazzle, every inch dripping in Christmas magic. Frosted garlands twisted up the wrought iron railings, lanterns dangled from the bare trees like stars caught mid-fall, and the enormous front door wore a wreath so large it could've comfortably housed a family of Christmas elves. A cluster of Wentworth students in lopsided elf hats belted out carols beside the carriage porch, their voices wobbly with enthusiasm and just enough magic to keep the snowflakes dancing.

Another young man, lanky with a shock of blond hair and a bowtie half undone, hurried around to open our door.

"Welcome to Greywolf," he said, when Keir stepped from the sleigh.

As Keir's black dress shoes touched the frosted ground, the boy's head snapped up. "Wait. Y'all hear that?"

"What?" his friend called from the other side of the sleigh. "The out-of-tune singing?"

"Ding, ding, ding. We have a winner, folks." The head of Pyewacket, my black cat familiar, popped out from under the faux fur blanket covering my legs, his green and gold bowtie shimmering under the lanterns.

The young man's friend, holding the next sleigh door, snorted. "It's just the singing, Colby. Don't go spookin' the guests."

"I'm serious," Colby said, glancing toward the woods. "It sounded like... I dunno. A howl? Or maybe weird singing?"

I tucked Pye in my arm and accepted the boy's hand, stepping down onto the snow-cleared path, the air crisp and fresh with the scent of pine. Around us, the forest shimmered under a veil of snow.

Keir Bane—renowned alpha of the Silverfang Clan, all quiet strength, sharp warmth, and my boyfriend (a word that still felt strange and sparkly every time I thought it)—stepped beside me, took my hand, and pressed a kiss to my knuckles. Snowflakes clung to his dark waves and the shoulders of his black tuxedo, which fit him with maddening precision.

"You look absolutely gorgeous," he said in a low voice meant only for me.

I gave his hand a light squeeze.

I had my close friend Chase Abernathy-Wyatt to thank for that.

Chase had worked his magic, sweeping my hair into an elegant bun with soft tendrils framing my face. I wore a crimson Zuhair Murad ballgown from my New York days—low-cut, shimmering, and impossible to ignore—and twinkling Christian Louboutin sandals, also relics from the Big Apple, now spelled to handle snow like a dream.

The jingle of sleigh bells filled the air, and I turned as Tzazi Strangeland's sleigh pulled up behind ours. Tzazi—another of my best friends and a platinum-blonde vampire lawyer with a bravado that would make Dracula seem like a wallflower—stepped down in a dazzling winter coat lined with silvery fur that shimmered like moonlight on water. Behind her was a young man I didn't recognize.

"Win, this is my brother," Tzazi said as she approached. "Zavier."

Zavier Strangeland. Even I had heard of him. A professional Hexbee player—Midflame for the Charming Stormshards. Think fast-paced frisbee, then add in spells and strategy—that's Hexbee, and Zavier wasn't just good—he was a star. Powerful, precise, and almost impossible to avoid once he melted into the shadows. Hexbee was fun for amateurs—dangerous at the pro level.

With tawny skin and corkscrew curls that bounced with each step, Zavier stood tall and confident. His grin was easy, his presence magnetic, and his eyes sparkled with the kind of mischief that meant he and Pyewacket would either become fast friends—or try to hex each other before the night was over.

"A pleasure," he said, offering his hand, dimples flashing in his cheeks.

Suddenly, Colby, the blond valet, twitched again and turned toward the woods. "There it is again. I swear I heard something."

Everyone paused.

For a breath, all was still.

Then, just beyond the tree line, a sound drifted through the snow — low and strange.

"Did y'all hear that?" one of the valets asked, glancing toward the woods. "Was that... growling?"

I adjusted the holly-red velvet ribbon around my neck and brushed my fingers over the protection charm, a gift from my great-aunt Sibby, tucked beneath. Just feeling it there helped steady my nerves.

That's what solving two murders in a town full of magical weirdos will do to a girl.

Between being nearly unalived in the Darkly Cemetery and almost taking a flight to my death, I'd learned to pay attention when things felt off. Add in the emotional hurricane of discovering I had a half-sister I'd never known about — thanks, Mother — and I had every right to scan the tree line like a paranoid Christmas elf.

"Sounds more like singing," the other muttered, squinting. "Weird singing. But yeah—definitely singing...I think."

"I bet it's Cassia," another boy said, nudging his friend. "She swore she'd sabotage this thing somehow. Said galas were a tool of the elite."

"Why does she even come if she hates it so much?" his friend asked.

He shrugged. "Moral outrage and free dessert?"

Just then, a second sleigh pulled up in a shimmer of enchanted frost, its runners barely whispering across the snow.

Lorenzo de Zavala stepped down first, serene and steady as always. He wore a tailored charcoal suit with a subtle pine-branch motif stitched along the collar, his dark hair neatly swept back, the image of mountain-born refinement. Everything about him said quiet strength with excellent tailoring.

Then came Chase—who did not step so much as descend. His cream jacket shimmered with golden stars that caught every flicker of lanternlight. A burgundy velvet scarf trailed behind him like a comet's tail, and his smile sparkled with the knowledge that he was the best-dressed man at the gala—and maybe in all of southern Louisiana.

I couldn't help but grin. Just seeing them—especially Chase, full of extra (and himself)—made the night feel brighter, like the party had officially begun. Since moving to Darkly to take over my grandmother's enchanted travel shop, the MET, these people had become my found family. Chase and Ren. Tzazi. Pyewacket. And, of course, Jessamin Wilde—a sweet hearth fairy, who owned both Greywolf Manor and the Green Gator Tavern. They were all strange, magical, and completely over-the-top in all the best ways.

"Evening, darlings," Chase called, all tousled blond waves and golden surfer-boy charm. "Y'all throwing a woodland rave or just forgot to tell me where the party moved??"

"Y'all heard that too," I asked as we made our way up the steps toward the mansion.

"Couldn't help it, cher," Chase said, tugging dramatically at the scarf around his neck. "Gave me chills—and not in the good, Ren-running-his-hands-through-my-hair way."

Ren blushed, and we all laughed as the doors swung open in a rush of warm vanilla and candlelight. Big band music drifted from the grand hall, mingling with the hum of voices and the soft clink of champagne glasses.

A whisper of unease brushed my thoughts as I reached the doorway. I turned.

Beyond the glowing lanterns and garland-strung archways, at the edge of the woods, a figure stood half in shadow beneath a snow-laden tree. Too tall for a child. Too still for comfort. The figure raised one hand, as if in greeting.

I blinked.

Gone.

Just trees. Just snow.

I shook it off and stepped inside, where warmth and light and the hum of celebration wrapped around me like a spell.

∾

THE BALLROOM of Greywolf Manor shimmered with enchanted elegance. Tall arched windows framed in evergreen garlands and silver ribbon lined the curved walls, while chandeliers dripped with mistletoe and glowing icicles, casting a soft, icy glow over the room. Couples whirled across the marble floor, their gowns and tuxedos catching the light in glints of crimson, emerald, and deep midnight blue. Miles Everhart and Moonlight & Brass's silver-toned rendition of Moonlight Serenade floated beneath the soaring ceiling, dreamy and romantic.

Keir slid the velvet wrap from my shoulders, handing it to the coat check attendant with a polite nod. Pyewacket, done with being held, launched from my arms and landed squarely on a silver side table. He knocked over a crystal bowl of sugared cranberries with deliberate flair, scattering them across the polished surface.

The woman behind the coat check gasped, obviously a Pyewacket neophyte. He batted a cranberry toward himself, swiped it into his mouth, and looked absolutely unrepentant.

"I know that face," I warned, leaning in. "Remember. The gala is important to Jess and benefits Wentworth Academy. So behave."

He blinked at me, ears twitching innocently. "I would do nothing to disrupt Jess's gala."

I narrowed my eyes at his tiny feet. "Are your toes crossed?"

He glanced down. "Hmm. You have better eyes than I thought."

I sighed. "Pye."

"Fine. I will celebrate quietly," he said, lifting his chin.

"Make sure you do."

I looped my arm through Keir's and nudged him toward the massive Christmas tree anchoring the far end of the ballroom. Pyewacket strutted along next to us. The tree sparkled from base to tip with enchanted pearls and old-world ornaments—glass birds, nutcrackers with jointed jaws, hand-painted baubles gleaming with tiny scenes of Darkly winters past. At the base, gift boxes in rich velvets and embossed gold foil encircled the tree in a burst of holiday splendor, catching the light with every turn.

I waved to Gertie Briar, an elderly good-natured witch who lived downtown over Maisie's jewelry store[TS1] and had a habit of yelling at passersby from the windows of her apartment. What she said was based on whether she like you or not that day.

Tucked in beside the tree, a string quartet played a graceful jazz waltz. The bows of their instruments shimmered faintly, charmed for extra resonance. The notes danced just above the sound of laughter and the soft clinking of glasses.

I took it all in, my voice hushed. "I don't think I've ever seen anything so gorgeous. How in the world did Jess pull this off?"

"She didn't," Chase said as he and Ren drifted up to us. Chase's cream-colored dinner jacket sparkled faintly under the lights, the pocket square folded with surgical precision. "Our Jess is many things. A party planner, she is not."

"She did pick out the theme," Ren offered mildly.

Chase waved a hand. "Picking a theme and executing the vision are two very different skill sets, darling. Jess gave her blessing. Dulcinea Puckman conjured the magic."

"Mmm, was that my name I heard?" came a sweet southern drawl just over my shoulder.

I turned to find a woman in a gown of deep green tulle that shimmered like spun sugar, her auburn curls piled high and pinned with tiny gold bells that jingled softly when she moved. Her smile was all charm and teeth—bright, practiced, and just a touch dangerous.

"Dulcinea Puckman," she said, extending a hand gloved in sheer black lace. "But everyone calls me Dulcie. You must be Windsor. I've been dying to meet you."

"Should I be flattered or concerned?" I asked, taking her hand. Her grip was light, but charged—like shaking hands with a sparkler.

"Why not be both, sugar?" she said with a wink. "Let's meet next week for a drink. The Gator?"

I agreed and she turned to greet someone else, her skirts sweeping dramatically behind her, leaving a faint trail of vanilla, candle wax, and mischief in her wake.

"Dulcie's a trickster," Chase said in a low voice, swirling the last of his champagne.

"A trickster?" I echoed. Each week in Darkly added another entry to my mental field guide of things-that-look-human-but-aren't.

"A mischief demon," Ren said. "Technically called a jestling."

Keir leaned against the wall, arms crossed. "The kind that finds humor in completely disrupting your life."

I raised a brow. "Sounds like half the people I dated in college."

Pyewacket stretched luxuriously across the back of the nearest chair. "Frankly, from what I hear, I'd trust the demon before I'd trust your exes."

Luckily for Pyewacket, a waiter appeared with a tray of champagne flutes, each glass rimmed with sugared herbs. I took one. Keir declined. Chase took two.

Zelda Merryman swept toward us, a tray in one hand and a tumbler of scotch in the other.

"Windsor! Hi!" she chirped, handing the glass to Keir with practiced ease.

He accepted it with a nod and a quiet thank-you, already lifting it to his lips.

Neat, of course. No ice, no water, no nonsense—just the way he liked everything.

Zelda wore her blonde hair up in a sleek bun, pearls wrapped like a crown. Her smile was bright and sincere. On the tray, bite-sized pastries sat in precise spirals, each tied with a sprig of rosemary.

"Would anyone like a caramelized fig and goat cheese roulade?" she offered.

Chase plucked one off the tray. "Honey, I've been counting down the hours to this moment."

Keir raised an eyebrow, his mouth quirked sideways in a "you don't expect me to eat this" grin.

"Don't worry," Zelda laughed. "Uncle Jove is on his way out with crawfish beignets."

"Your uncle made these?" I asked, popping a roulade in my mouth. One bite delivered everything—golden warmth, sticky fig, and a sharp tang that made me go back for another.

"Yep! SpellSpoon Cookin'. One of the best on the island."

A voice behind us chimed in. "The best."

Jove Merryman swept into the group like a magician unveiling his next trick. He was tall, his white chef's coat crisp, a red scarf tucked jauntily into the collar. A blond goatee curled at his chin. He held a silver tray stacked high with golden beignets dusted in cayenne and paprika.

"Bane," he greeted, nodding to Keir. "These are straight out of the fryer."

Keir took one, bit in, and closed his eyes, bringing a hand to his heart.

"Jove. Unparalleled," he declared solemnly.

He wrapped an arm around me.

"Jovial, I don't believe you've met Windsor Ebonwood," Keir added. "Win, this is Jove Merryman."

"Charmed," Jove said, passing me the tray. "Please try one."

I took a beignet. "They smell amazing. Did you make the beignets too?"

"I did. One of my most requested appetizers. Ah—Zelda, before I forget, champagne's running low. Already."

Zelda rolled her eyes. "Chase."

Chase lifted his empty glass in salute. "You're welcome."

Keir's mouth quirked up in a smirk and I stifled a giggle.

"Nice to meet you, Win," Jove said and then turned to the next group of chatting attendees.

Zelda vanished with a wink, leaving behind the scent of rosemary, sugar, and buttered pastry.

Before I could comment on the likelihood of her actually being the weak link in anything, a silver-haired gentleman paused beside us with a polite smile. Keir clasped his hand with practiced ease.

"Evening, Selvin," he said.

The man gave me a brief nod before continuing on.

I leaned in. "Is he one of the town elders?"

"Selvin Trout," Keir confirmed, voice low. "He's one of the longest-standing elders after Minta."

Minta Ebonwood—my grandmother. The lineage ran through her: the power, the responsibility, and the Magically Enchanted Travel shop. I barely knew her growing up. My dad had made sure of that, keeping me at arm's length from anything Ebonwood-related. My mother, Genevieve, left us when I was still small, slipping back to Darkly and into a world I'm only now beginning to understand. Since arriving on the island, I'd been piecing together her story—shards of truth buried under layers of rumor and grief. And the deeper I dug, the darker it got.

With a bang, the side doors leading to the sculpted gardens burst open. A blast of icy air swept through the ballroom, curling around ankles and lifting hems, chased by a tangle of teenagers half-screaming, half-scrambling over one another. They spilled inside in a whirlwind of shouting, laughter, and breathless panic.

"The Christmas witch! We saw her!"

Guests nearest the door let out startled gasps, clutching their pearls or drinks with wide eyes. One woman yelped as her champagne sloshed onto her satin dress. A waiter dropped a tray of macarons with a tragic crash.

Chase clutched his chest and staggered a half-step backward, eyes wide with mock horror. "Well butter my biscuits and hang the stockings—we've got ourselves a holiday haunting!"

A few heads turned at the outburst. One woman fanned herself with a napkin. Another crossed herself behind a champagne flute.

I looked around for Pyewacket and found him beneath the Christmas tree, where he'd appointed himself gift critic—pawing open random presents and loudly assigning them scores from one to ten.

Whatever was going on wasn't his doing. For once.

Reaching out instinctively, I caught the arm of the one familiar face in the group of teens—Evon Frick, the son of Trixie and Boone Frick, owners of the White Stag Inn. His cheeks were flushed red from the cold, curls wild, and his coat was half-buttoned over his gala clothes like he'd thrown it on mid-sprint. His bow tie hung askew, one shoe missing.

"Evon, what's going on?" I asked, steadying him as he swayed slightly in place.

I heard the crisp click of heels across the marble just before Tzazi stepped up beside me, eyes already scanning the chaos. Zavier followed a step behind, eyes sharp and shoulders squared, his usual easy confidence edged with caution as he took in the panicked teens.

"What in the world did y'all get into?" Tzazi asked, inspecting the breathless teen with one arched brow, clearly slipping into lawyer-mode.

Zavier glanced toward the open garden doors, his eyes narrowing as he positioned himself between the cold air and his sister.

Evon shook his head, dragging in a shaky breath as his chest rose and fell like he couldn't get enough air.

Keir stepped forward and rested a calming hand on Evon's shoulder. "Breathe, aye? Yer no' out there anymore. What'd yeh see, lad?"

Evon's eyes turned to Keir, wide and darting.

"The Christmas witch," he gasped. "I swear. She was in the garden—near the Mab sculpture."

Chase stopped mid-sip and lowered his glass. "Perchta?"

He glanced at Keir, who didn't speak, but the grim shift in his expression said enough.

Evon nodded, voice shaky. "Perchta," he whispered, like saying her name might summon her all over again.

I turned to Keir, keeping my voice low. "There's a Christmas witch?"

He took a slow sip of his scotch, eyes meeting mine over the rim, sharp and steady. "Aye. But probably not the kind you're imagining."

"No, she's not exactly known for her generosity," Ren added dryly.

Tzazi leaned in slightly, her earrings catching the ballroom light as she spoke. "But she is known for punishing the wicked by ripping them open and stuffing their bodies with straw and rocks. Super merry."

I shivered, thinking of the figure I had seen at the forest line. "And here I thought the Brothers Grimm were terrifying."

Tzazi's hand brushed my arm. "I'm going to go find Jess."

I nodded as a gust of wind moaned through the cracked doors behind us, and for a beat, the scent of pine and cold earth curled through the warmth of champagne and vanilla. I didn't say anything else—but Evon's wide-eyed panic didn't feel so theatrical.

A sudden hurricane of perfume and sequins swept into our circle as Trixie Frick descended upon us, her towering red bouffant miraculously untouched by the chaos. Her diamond-studded gown twinkled with such aggressive sparkle it looked like it might combust if she turned too quickly under the chandelier.

"Evon! What in glittered heaven is the matter with you?" she demanded, her hand smoothing his jacket while checking him for injury and _ in one go.

"I'm fine, Mama," he panted. "But it was her—I saw her with my own eyes."

Trixie's eyes narrowed. "Her who?"

"Perchta," he said, barely above a whisper.

Trixie's gaze flicked to me, then Keir.

"Perchta," she hissed, dragging out every syllable. "Absolutely not. Don't be ridiculous."

Evon opened his mouth to reply, but Trixie threw out an arm like she was fending off a dramatic monologue. "No, sir. That's enough excitement for one evening. You've had too many fig thingies, not enough protein, and way too much imagination.

"We're going to sit with your father, and you're going to drink a glass of water, and we are not—I repeat, not—going to tell people you saw a feather-covered Christmas witch creeping around the gardens."

As she steered her son through the crowd, she paused beside us and murmured, "Thank you, Keir. Win." Then she whisked him away, the train of her gown flashing silver stars in every direction.

Keir reached for my hand. "Belleclaire's here somewhere. I'm sure it's just one of the kids pulling a fast one, but...I'll be right back."

He kissed my cheek and I watched as he disappeared into the glittering crowd, swallowed by tuxedos, champagne flutes, and the low hum of polite laughter.

But my thoughts lingered on Evon's face—that wide-eyed fear, the way his voice had caught on her name. That wasn't sugar panic or a teenager trying to stir up drama. That was real. And whether the figure in the garden had been cloaked in tattered skirts ruffling like feathers or a gala attendee wrapped in shadows and bad timing, something had scared those kids enough to burst into a ballroom full of donors, ice sculptures, and rosemary-tied pastries. Was it the same person I saw when we arrived?

I turned back to the doors, still cracked open to the night. The music carried on, the string quartet weaving a light, festive melody through the air. Chandeliers glinted like frost. Guests danced, laughed, and clinked their glasses. The whole room shimmered with holiday cheer.

But outside, beyond the trimmed hedges and glowing paths, the snow held a strange stillness—unnerving and sharp-edged.

Pyewacket leapt up onto a table beside me, ears angled toward the open doors. "Someone's idea of festive mischief got out of hand."

"Or," I murmured, eyes trained on the dark stretch beyond the glass, "someone's out there."

I stepped away from the warmth and hum of the ballroom, toward the doors still bumping gently on their hinges in the wind —the cold slipping in like a warning.

Chase raised his champagne glass. "Darling, if you're about to go chasing witches, do take a beignet for the road. And if you disappear, just know I'm keeping the cat."